The Truth About the Savolta Case

ALSO BY EDUARDO MENDOZA

The City of Marvels

The Truth About the Savolta Case

A Novel

Eduardo Mendoza

Translated from the Spanish by Alfred Mac Adam

■

Pantheon Books New York

 Published in the United States by Pantheon Books, a division of Random House, Inc., New York, and simultaneously in Canada by Random House of Canada Limited, Toronto. Originally published in Spain as *La Verdad Sobre El Caso Savolta* by Editorial Seix Barral, Barcelona in 1985.

Library of Congress Cataloging-in-Publication Data

Mendoza, Eduardo, 1943–
[Verdad sobre el caso Savolta. English]
The truth about the Savolta case : a novel/by Eduardo Mendoza;
translated from the Spanish by Alfred Mac Adam.
p. cm.
Translation of: La verdad sobre el caso Savolta.
ISBN 0-679-40949-1
I. Title.
PQ6663.E54V413 1992 91–53086
863′.64—dc20

Book design by Adriane Stark

Manufactured in the United States of America

First American Edition

NOTE

In writing some parts of this book (especially those that simulate newspaper articles, letters, or documents) I used, modifying them for my own purposes, passages from:

P. Foix, *Los archivos del terrorismo blanco.*
I. Bo y Singla, *Montjuich, notas y recuerdos históricos.*
M. Casal, *Origen y actuación de los pistoleros.*
G. Núñez de Prado, *Los dramas del anarquismo.*
F. de P. Calderón, *La verdad sobre del terrorismo.*

All other characters, events, and situations are imaginary.

To Diego Medina

The class whose vices
he pilloried was his own,
now extinct, except
for long survivors like him
who remember its virtues

W. H. Auden, "Marginalia," V.

You need not be afraid; for what you feel, without seeing, are, doubtless, the feet and legs of some robbers and banditti, who are hanged upon these trees; for here the officers of justice hang them, when they can catch them, by twenties and thirties at a time, in clusters; whence I guess I am not far from Barcelona.

Miguel de Cervantes, *The Life and Exploits of Don Quixote de la Mancha,* Volume II, Book the Fourth, Chapter VIII, translated by Charles Jarvis (London, 1831), p. 322.

Part One

Chapter 1

Photostat of Article from Barcelona Newspaper *The Voice of Justice*, October 6, 1917, by Domingo Pajarito de Soto

Entered into Evidence: Document No. 1

▪

English translation by court interpreter Guzmán Hernández de Fenwick

THE AUTHOR of this article and those that follow in this series has taken on the task of clarifying in a concise form accessible to the simple minds of workers, even the most ignorant among them, those events which, because they were presented to the public in diffuse, obscure fashion, camouflaged in rhetoric and a glut of figures more appropriate for experts than for readers eager to learn clear truths and not mathematical puzzles, still remain unknown to the working masses, who are, nevertheless, their principal victims. Because only when truth shines forth and the most ignorant have access to it will we in Spain have attained the position proper to us in the family of civilized nations, to whose progress and peaceful level we have been elevated by constitutional guarantees, freedom of the press, and universal suffrage. And it is in these moments when our beloved country is emerging from obscure, medieval darkness and is scaling the arduous peaks of modern development when obscurantist, abusive, and criminal methods that plunge citizens in despair, terror, and shame become intolerable to those of good conscience. For that reason, I will not forgo this opportunity to denounce, objectively and dispassionately, firmly and accurately, the unspeakable and base behavior of a certain sector of our industry; concretely, of a certain company of international renown, which, far from being the seedbed of a new era and a hive where the future is forged in work, order, and justice, is a breeding ground for pimps and gangsters, who, not content to exploit workers using inhuman and unheard-of means, destroy their dignity and transform them into frightened puppets with the exercise of their tyrannical and feudal egoism. I refer, if there is anyone who still doesn't know, to the recent events that took place in the Savolta factory, a company whose activities . . .

Typescript of Notes Taken During the First Statement Made by Javier Miranda Lugarte on January 10, 1927, to F. W. Davidson, Supreme Court Judge for the State of New York.

(Folios 21 and following)

▪

English translation by court interpreter Guzmán Hernández de Fenwick

JUDGE DAVIDSON: State your name and profession.
MR. MIRANDA: Javier Miranda, stock and bond salesman.
JUDGE: Nationality.
MIRANDA: United States citizen.
JUDGE: When did you become a citizen of the United States?
MIRANDA: On March 8, 1922.
JUDGE: What nationality were you before?
MIRANDA: I was Spanish, born in Spain.
JUDGE: Where and when were you born?
MIRANDA: In Valladolid, Spain, May 9, 1891.
JUDGE: Where did you reside between 1917 and 1919?
MIRANDA: In Barcelona, Spain.
JUDGE: Do you mean you lived in Valladolid and commuted daily to Barcelona, where you worked?
MIRANDA: No.
JUDGE: Why not?
MIRANDA: Valladolid is more than seven hundred kilometers from Barcelona . . .
JUDGE: Could you clarify that?

MIRANDA: . . . approximately four hundred miles away. A two-day trip, almost.
JUDGE: Do you mean you moved to Barcelona?
MIRANDA: Yes.
JUDGE: Why?
MIRANDA: I couldn't find work in Valladolid.
JUDGE: Why couldn't you find work? Was it because no one wanted to hire you?
MIRANDA: No. There were few jobs to be had.
JUDGE: And in Barcelona?
MIRANDA: There were more opportunities.
JUDGE: What kind?
MIRANDA: Higher salaries and a greater chance for promotion.
JUDGE: Did you already have a job when you reached Barcelona?
MIRANDA: No.
JUDGE: Then how can you say there were more opportunities?
MIRANDA: Everyone knew that to be the case.
JUDGE: Explain.
MIRANDA: Barcelona was a city with a fully developed industrial and commercial base. Every day, people came there from other places looking for work. The same thing that happens in New York.
JUDGE: What happens in New York?
MIRANDA: No one would be surprised, for example, if someone moved from Vermont to New York to look for work.
JUDGE: Why from Vermont?
MIRANDA: I just used it as an example.
JUDGE: Should I assume that things are the same in Vermont as they are in Valladolid?
MIRANDA: I don't know. I'm not familiar with Vermont. Maybe it's a bad example.
JUDGE: Why did you choose Vermont?
MIRANDA: It's the first name that came into my head. Perhaps I read it in the newspaper this morning . . .
JUDGE: In a newspaper?
MIRANDA: Without noticing . . .
JUDGE: I still don't see the relationship.

MIRANDA: I said it probably wasn't a good example.
JUDGE: Should Vermont be stricken from your statement?
MIRANDA: No, no, it doesn't matter.

.....

"AND WE'D BEGUN to think you weren't coming," said Mrs. Savolta, squeezing the hand of her newly arrived guest and kissing his wife on both cheeks.

"Neus's manias," answered Mr. Claudedeu, pointing to his wife. "Actually, we could have been here an hour ago, but she insisted on waiting so we wouldn't be the first. It just didn't seem correct to her, see?"

"Well, to tell you the truth," said Mrs. Savolta, "we really had begun to think you weren't coming."

"You don't mean," said Mrs. Claudedeu, "you'd already sat down to dinner?"

"Sat down?" exclaimed Mrs. Savolta. "We finished quite a while ago. You've missed your meal."

"That's a good one!" laughed Mr. Claudedeu. "If we'd known, we'd have packed some sandwiches."

"Sandwiches!" squealed Mrs. Savolta. "What an idea, Mother of God!"

"Nicolás thinks like a fireman," declared Mrs. Claudedeu, lowering her eyes.

"But seriously now, it isn't really true that you've already eaten, is it?" inquired Mr. Claudedeu.

"Of course I'm serious, what did you think? We were hungry, and since we didn't think you were coming . . ." said Mrs. Savolta, pretending to be upset. But her laughter gave her away, and her final words dissolved in a choke.

"No, so after all that we're still the first to arrive," added Mrs. Claudedeu.

"Don't be afraid, Neus," Mrs. Savolta calmed her. "There are at least two hundred people coming. There won't even be room for everyone, believe me. Can't you hear the racket they're making?"

In effect, violin music and voices poured through the door that connected the vestibule to the main drawing room. The vestibule, on the other hand, was deserted, silent, rather dark. Only one liveried servant stood guard at the door that led into the house from the garden: serious, stiff, and expressionless, as if he didn't notice the presence of the three people who chatted next to him and were paying attention to some invisible master floating over his head. His gaze wandered over the carved ceiling panels, and he thought about his own affairs, or listened, pretending not to, to their conversation. A highly flustered maid arrived to take the guests' hats and coats and the gentleman's stick, even as she avoided his impudent, joking eyes. She was more attentive to her mistress's alert eyes as they followed her movements with feigned indifference.

"I hope you haven't held up dinner because of us," said Mrs. Claudedeu.

"Oh, Neus," Mrs. Savolta chided her, "you're so considerate."

The door to the drawing room door opened, and Mr. Savolta appeared, surrounded by a halo of light and bringing with him the clamor from the next room.

"Well, well, look who's here!" he shouted. Then, in a tone of reproach, "We thought you weren't coming."

"Just what your wife's been saying to us," noted Mr. Claudedeu, "and she gave us a good scare besides, didn't she?"

"Everyone's been asking where you are. A party without Claudedeu is like a dinner without wine." He turned to Mrs. Claudedeu, "How are you, Neus?" and respectfully kissed the lady's hand.

"Now I see that what you missed was my husband's foolishness," said Mrs. Claudedeu.

"Don't inhibit poor Nicolás now," Mr. Savolta reproached the lady. Turning to Mr. Claudedeu, "I've got some firsthand information. You'll split your sides laughing—excuse me." Then to the ladies, "With your permission, I'll just take him with me."

"Tell me how our María Rosa's been behaving," asked Mrs. Claudedeu.

"Oh, she's been behaving well enough, but she doesn't seem very lively. A bit upset by all this confusion, as you might say."

"Only natural, my dear, only natural. You've got to deal with them as they are."

"You may be right, Neus, but it's high time she started to change her ways. Next year she finishes her studies, and we've got to begin thinking about her future."

"Not so fast, my dear, let's not rush things! María Rosa has nothing to worry about. Now or ever. An only child and with your position . . . come, come. Let her be as she pleases. If she has to change, she'll change."

"Don't you believe it. Her personality doesn't annoy me: she's sweet and calm. A bit insipid, that's what it is. A bit . . . how should I put it? . . . a bit like a nun . . . you understand what I mean."

"And that bothers you? My dear, I see what you're getting at."

"Let's just see, what do you mean?"

"You're hiding an idea that's going around and around inside your head, and don't deny it."

"An idea?"

"Rosa, cross your heart and tell me the truth: you're thinking about marrying your daughter."

"Marrying María Rosa? Where do you get such ideas, Neus?"

"Not only that. You've already decided on a candidate. Come on now, tell me it isn't true. I dare you."

Mrs. Savolta blushed and concealed her confusion behind a quiet, prolonged giggle.

"Heavens, Neus, a candidate. You don't know what you're saying. A candidate! Jesus, Mary, and Joseph . . ."

JUDGE DAVIDSON: Did you find work in Barcelona?

MIRANDA: Yes.

JUDGE: How?

MIRANDA: I had letters of recommendation.

JUDGE: From whom?

MIRANDA: Friends of my father. He was dead.

JUDGE: To whom were they addressed?
MIRANDA: Businessmen, lawyers, and a doctor.
JUDGE: And one of them hired you?
MIRANDA: Yes, that's right.
JUDGE: What was his name?
MIRANDA: Mr. Cortabanyes, a lawyer.
JUDGE: Would you spell his name?
MIRANDA: C-O-R-T-A-B-A-N-Y-E-S, Cortabanyes.
JUDGE: Why did this lawyer hire you?
MIRANDA: I'd taken two law courses in Valladolid. That allowed me to . . .
JUDGE: What kind of work did you do for Mr. Cortabanyes?
MIRANDA: I was his assistant.
JUDGE: Explain.
MIRANDA: I carried messages to the Hall of Justice and the city jails, accompanied clients when they made statements, brought documents to notaries, took care of unimportant formalities at the Tax Office, put the agenda in order, and looked up things in books.
JUDGE: What things?
MIRANDA: Decisions, precedents, expert opinions on juridical or economic matters. Sometimes, newspaper or magazine articles.
JUDGE: Did you find them?
MIRANDA: Often.
JUDGE: And were you paid for all that?
MIRANDA: Of course.
JUDGE: Were you paid according to what you did or according to whether you were successful or not?
MIRANDA: He paid me a regular monthly salary.
JUDGE: No incentive pay?
MIRANDA: A bonus at Christmas.
JUDGE: Always the same amount?
MIRANDA: No, it varied.
JUDGE: How?
MIRANDA: It was higher if business had been good that year.
JUDGE: Was business usually good?
MIRANDA: No.

.....

CORTABANYES PANTED incessantly. He was very fat, and as bald as a mountain peak. He had purple bags under his eyes, a button nose, and a thick, hanging, damp lower lip he used to moisten stamps. A taut double chin ran down to meet the top of his vest; his hands were delicate, as if they were stuffed with cotton, and each of his fingers consisted of three rosy spheres; his nails were very narrow, always shiny, stuck in the center of the finger. He would hold his pen or pencil with all five little fingers, the way a child holds his pacifier. When he spoke, he would blow tiny bubbles of saliva. He was lazy, sloppy, and slow.

Cortabanyes's office was on the ground floor of a house on Caspe street. It consisted of a vestibule, a waiting room, an office, a storeroom, and a lavatory. Cortabanyes had sold the other rooms in the house to his neighbor. The reduced size of his offices saved him money in cleaning costs and furniture. In the vestibule there were some chairs covered in dark red velvet and a little black table covered with dusty magazines. The waiting room walls were lined with bookcases, only interrupted by a window on the street covered in the same velvet covering the chairs, and three doors, the entry, a wired glass door that led to the rear stairs, and a third that led to Cortabanyes's private office. In it was his desk made of dark wood, on which were carved helmets, harquebuses, and two-handed swords. There was a chair similar to a throne behind the table and two leather armchairs. The storeroom was filled with file cabinets and small cupboards with sliding doors that opened up and down and which slammed shut whenever they pleased with a crack. The storeroom also contained a table made of white wood and a chair on casters: Cortabanyes's assistant, Serramadriles, worked there. In the library–waiting room, there was a long table surrounded by upholstered chairs used for group meetings, although they rarely occurred. That was where Doloretas and I worked.

.....

A NICE SUN was shining, and there were people taking advantage of the warmth in the outdoor cafés. The Ramblas boulevard looked grand: passing by were silk-hatted bankers, serious military men, and starched nannies who pushed their way through the crowds behind the patent leather hoods of prams; there were screeching flower women, students skipping class and pretending to fight with each other as they dodged among the passersby, one or another undefinable individual, recently disembarked sailors. Teresa was skipping along and smiling, but soon she became serious.

"This noise dazes me. But I don't think I could stand to see the streets empty: cities are made for crowds, don't you think?"

"What I see is that you don't like the city," I said.

"I hate it. Don't you?"

"Just the opposite, I wouldn't know how to live anywhere else. You'll get used to it, and you'll feel the same way. It's all a matter of keeping an open mind and letting yourself be carried along without fighting back."

In the Plaza de Cataluña, opposite the Maison Dorée, there was a portable speaker's platform draped in front with the Catalan flag. At the lectern, a speaker was haranguing a sizable crowd that listened in silence.

"Let's go somewhere else," I said.

But Teresa didn't want to.

"I've never seen a political rally. Let's get closer."

"And what if there's a fight?" I said.

"Nothing's going to happen."

We went closer. It was barely possible to hear the speaker's words from that distance, but because he was well positioned on the platform, we could all follow his vehement gestures. I thought I could make out something about the Catalan language and *la tradició cultural i democràtica* and also about *la desídia voluntària i organitzada des del centre* or *pel centre,* sentence fragments and applause, and then sentences that mixed with the buzz of the comments made by the public, shouts of *molt bé!* and the disjointed, unsynchronized beginning of the anthem "Els segadors." Along

Fontanella street came a detachment of the *Guardia Civil,* marching two by two, each one carrying a carbine. They lined up on the sidewalk, their backs to the row of buildings, and stood at ease.

"This is starting to look bad."

"Don't be such a coward," said Teresa.

The songs went on, interspersed with subversive slogans. A young man stepped away from the ring of listeners, picked up a stone, and threw it furiously against the windows of the Equestrian Circle. As he did so, his hat fell off.

"Fora els castellans!" they were shouting now.

A figure dressed in black, with a gray beard and a birdlike face, appeared in one of the windows. He stretched out his arms and shouted, *"Cataluña!"* But he stepped back when he saw that his presence evoked a flood of stones and a chorus of whistles.

"Who was that?" asked Teresa.

"I couldn't see him clearly. I think it was Cambó."

Meanwhile, the *Guardia Civil* stood their ground unperturbed, waiting for orders from an officer holding a pistol. Small groups ran along the Rambla de Cataluña waving clubs and shouting, "Republican Spain!" which led me to believe they must be Lerroux's "young barbarians." The separatists threw stones at them, the officer holding the pistol made a sign, and there was a bugle call: the carbines were cocked. The "young barbarians" pummeled the separatists, who retaliated against the clubs with stones, fists, and kicks: there were more of them, but their ranks contained women and old men, useless in a fight. A few bloody bodies fell to the ground. The *Guardia Civil,* stoically standing at ease, suffering the occasional tossed stone, took aim at the combatants.

Then the cavalry came down Pelayo street. They regrouped in front of the Salón Cataluña with their sabers bared. Then they advanced in fan formation, first at the trot, then at the gallop, and finally at full speed, like a cyclone. They passed between the palm trees, jumped over benches and planters, raised clouds of dust, and made the earth shake with their sharp hoofbeats. Except for those entangled in hand-to-hand combat, the crowd scattered. They took the nearest exits: Rambla de Cataluña, Ronda de San

Pedro, and Puerta del Angel. The speaker disappeared, giving the "young barbarians" the opportunity to rip the Catalan flag to shreds. The horsemen beat the fugitives over the head with the flat of their sabers. Those who fell stayed on the ground so they wouldn't be trampled: they covered their heads with their hands and waited for all the horses to pass. Meanwhile, the *Guardia Civil* on foot had formed a circle, closing off any escape through Puerta del Angel. They fired occasional shots in the air. A few individuals, caught between the cavalry and the foot patrol, raised their hands in surrender.

At first, we ran toward the Ramblas and mixed in with the passersby. Very soon, a group of policemen appeared, leading three men in handcuffs. The prisoners spoke to the people on the street: "As usual, it's people like us who pay the piper."

The passersby pretended not to hear. We went on running, hand in hand. Those were days of irresponsible plenitude, of imperceptible happiness.

CONTINUATION OF THE ARTICLE FROM *THE VOICE OF JUSTICE,* BARCELONA, OCTOBER 6, 1917, BY DOMINGO PAJARITO DE SOTO

Entered into Evidence: Document No. 1

▪

English translation by court interpreter Guzmán Hernández de Fenwick

. . . THE SAVOLTA FACTORY, a company whose activities have developed in a colossal and incredible way during the past few years aided by and at the expense of the bloody war devastating Europe, just as flies fatten and feed on repugnant carrion. Everyone knows how the aforementioned company went in a few months from being a small industry that supplied a limited national or local market to supplying all nations under arms with its products, capturing in this way, thanks to its extortion and its abuse of the compromised situation of those nations, considerable benefits and fabulous profits for itself at the expense of those nations. All of that is known; over the course of years, nothing escapes sensitive, alert minds: many of us are aware of the nature and character of this business, and of the pressures and abuses to which the company has resorted, which are such that if they were known by all would at the very least produce a shock and a firm reproach. Also well known are the names of those who have dedicated and continue to dedicate their intelligence and their brave efforts to the aforementioned desire for wealth: they are Mr. Savolta, founder of the company, its principal stockholder and chief executive; Mr. Claudedeu, the sinister head of personnel, in whose presence the workers tremble and whose name arouses such indignation and fear in all proletarian homes that he is known by the nickname the Man with the Iron Hand, and last, but certainly not least, the slippery and perfidious Lepprince, of whom . . .

.....

I REMEMBER that cold November afternoon, just as I remember Pajarito de Soto, stiff, on the edge of his chair, lost at the far end of the meeting table in the library–waiting room, his checked cap on his knees, just about to step on his scarf, which had slid down and submissively coiled at his feet, while Doloretas hastily picked up his overcoat, his oversleeves, and his umbrella with its imitation silver handle encrusted with imitation green and red stones. I remember that Serramadriles never stopped making noise in the little room with the rebellious file cabinets and the typewriter and the chair on casters, and that Cortabanyes did not leave his office, even though he was the only one who could have moderated the violence of the meeting and probably for that very reason remained silent and invisible, doubtless listening through the door and looking through the keyhole, both things which now seem to me quite unlikely. I remember that Pajarito de Soto closed his eyes as if the meeting had affected him like flashpowder set off by surprise, which made it hard for him to see what he already suspected, what he already knew because I had insinuated it to him first and revealed it later, that the man who was smiling at him and scrutinizing him was Lepprince, always so elegant, so measured, so fresh in appearance, and so jovial.

JUDGE DAVIDSON: Had you met Mr. Lepprince through your work, or were there other reasons why you came into contact with him?
MIRANDA: It was through my work.
JUDGE: Was Mr. Lepprince a client of Mr. Cortabanyes?
MIRANDA: No.
JUDGE: I seem to detect a contradiction here.
MIRANDA: There is none.
JUDGE: Why?
MIRANDA: Lepprince was not Cortabanyes's client, but he came to the office once to use his services.
JUDGE: I call that being a client.
MIRANDA: I don't.
JUDGE: Why not?
MIRANDA: A client is someone who habitually and exclusively uses a lawyer's services.
JUDGE: Wasn't that the case of Mr. Lepprince?
MIRANDA: No.
JUDGE: Explain.

.....

LEPPRINCE OPENED a small case attached to the car's running board and took out a pair of pistols.

"You do know how to fire a gun, don't you?"

"Will it be necessary?"

"It's impossible to predict."

"Well, I don't know how."

"It's easy, see? They're loaded, but they won't shoot. This catch is the safety; you push it up and then you can squeeze the trigger. I won't do it now, of course, because it would be dangerous. Just so you see how to do it in case something comes up. In any case, it's always better to keep the safety on so the gun won't go off when you carry it in your belt and shoot a bullet down your pants leg. Understand? It's easy, see? You pull back the hammer and the cylinder turns, placing the new cartridge in the chamber. Then all you have to do is turn the cylinder to get the used cartridge out of the way, which you would have to do beforehand in any case. Anyway, the important thing is not to squeeze the trigger before you pull the hammer back . . . into firing position, see? Just the way I'm doing it. Then all you have to do is fire, but more carefully. And you should never do it if there isn't real, certain, danger at hand, understand?"

.....

LEPPRINCE!

.....

"CIVILIZATION DEMANDS OF MAN a faith similar to that which medieval man had in providence. Today we have to believe that the social rules imposed on us have a meaning similar to what the seasons of the year, the clouds, and the sun had for the farmer. Those demands made by the workers remind me of religious processions begging for rain . . . What did you say? . . . More cognac? . . . Oh, revolution . . ."

.....

THE SLIPPERY AND PERFIDIOUS Lepprince, of whom little or nothing is known, except that he is a young Frenchman who came to Spain in 1914, at the outset of the terrible conflagration which has caused and continues to cause so many tears and deaths to the homeland of the aforementioned and unknown Mr. Lepprince, who quickly became known in the aristocratic and financial circles of our city, being an object of respect and admiration in all of them, not only because of his intelligence and outstanding social status, but also because of his arrogant figure, his distinguished manners, and his ostentatious prodigality. Soon this new arrival, who appeared on the scene haughty and satisfied with life, who seemed to have all the money of the neighboring Republic in his account, and who took up residence in one of the best hotels under the name Paul-

André Lepprince, was the object of lavish attentions that turned into tempting proposals made by people in high economic circles. We shall never know what those proposals were, but it is certain that barely after having been here for a year, we find him carrying out executive duties in the most flourishing and renowned company of the moment and the city: Savolta . . .

. . . . .

IN THE DRAWING ROOM, an orchestra perched on a velvet-covered platform played waltzes and mazurkas. A few couples danced in what little space was left open by the crowds. Dinner was over, and the guests were impatiently waiting for midnight and the arrival of the new year. The young Lepprince was chatting with an elderly lady.

"People have told me so much about you, young man, but can you believe that until now I've never met you in person? The isolation we old people live in, son, it's just terrible, terrible . . ."

"Don't say that, madam," answered the young Lepprince with a smile. "Say instead that you have chosen a tranquil modus vivendi."

"Nonsense, son. Before, when my poor husband, may he rest in peace, was alive, things were different. We never stopped going out and visiting. . . . But now, it's impossible. These gatherings annoy me. They tire me out enormously, and as soon as the sun goes down, all I want is to go to bed and sleep. We old people live on our memories, son. Parties and amusement aren't made for us."

The young Lepprince stifled a yawn.

"So you're French, eh?" insisted the lady.

"Yes. I'm from Paris."

"No one would think so listening to you talk. Your Spanish is perfect. Where did you learn it?"

"My mother was Spanish. She always spoke to me in Spanish, so one might say I learned Spanish in the cradle. Even before French."

"How wonderful! I like foreigners. They're very interesting and tell new things, different from those we hear every day. We're always talking about the same things. And it's only natural, I say, right? We live in the same place, see the same people, and read the same newspapers. That must be why we're always arguing: because we don't have anything to talk about. On the other hand, it's unnecessary to argue with foreigners: they tell their stories and we tell ours. I get along better with foreigners than I do with people from here."

"I'm sure you get along well with everyone."

"Don't you believe it, son. I'm a grumbler. As you get older, your character also deteriorates. Everything declines. But, talking about foreigners, tell me something: do you know the engineer Pearson?"

"Fred Stark Pearson? No, I never met him, although I've often heard people talk about him."

"A great person, believe me! A great friend of my deceased husband, may he rest in peace. When poor Juan—my husband, you know?—when poor Juan passed away, Pearson was the first to visit me at home. Just imagine, him, such an important man, the one who illuminated all of Barcelona with his inventions. That's right, he was the first to visit, and he was so upset that the only language he could speak was English. I don't understand English, do you know, son? But listening to him speak in that voice of his which was so smooth and deep, I understood that he was telling me how much he admired my deceased husband, and that made me weep more than all the sympathy cards I received later. Barely a year later, poor Pearson died."

"Yes, I know."

JUDGE DAVIDSON: What kind of relationship did you have with Lepprince?

MIRANDA: I did work for him.

JUDGE: What kind?

MIRANDA: Different kinds, always related to my profession.

JUDGE: Which profession?
MIRANDA: Legal.
JUDGE: Before you said you weren't a lawyer.
MIRANDA: Well . . . I worked with a lawyer, on legal matters.
JUDGE: Did you work for Lepprince because Cortabanyes ordered you to do so?
MIRANDA: Yes . . . no.
JUDGE: Yes or no?
MIRANDA: At the beginning, yes.

.....

I'VE FORGOTTEN the exact date of our meeting. I know it was at the beginning of the autumn of 1917. The turbulent days of August had passed: congress had been dissolved; the noncommissioned officers jailed and set free; Saborit, Anguiano, Besteiro, and Largo Caballero were still in prison, Lerroux and Macià in exile; the streets were calm. There were political caricatures hanging from the walls, dissolving in the rain. Lepprince appeared just before closing time, asked to see Cortabanyes, was led into the office; both conferred for half an hour. Then Cortabanyes called me in, introduced me to Lepprince, and asked me if I were engaged for the evening. I told him the truth, that I wasn't. He asked me to accompany the Frenchman and to assist him, to become, for one night, "something like his private secretary." While Cortabanyes spoke, Lepprince put his fingertips together and stared fixedly at the floor, smiling and distractedly corroborating the lawyer's words with slight nods of his head. Then we went out to the street, and he showed me his automobile, a Fiat *conduite cabriolet,* a two-seater with a red body, black roof, and gold trim. He asked if automobiles frightened me, and I said they didn't. We dined at a luxurious restaurant where they knew him. When we left, Lepprince opened a small box attached to the running board of the car and took out a pair of pistols.

"Know how to use a gun?" he asked.

"Will it be necessary?" I asked.

JUDGE DAVIDSON: Did you meet at that same time Domingo Pajarito de Soto?
MIRANDA: Yes.
JUDGE: Do you recognize as his, that is, as being by Domingo Pajarito de Soto, the articles deposited with the court which are entered as evidence, document number 1?
MIRANDA: Yes.
JUDGE: Did you personally deal with Domingo Pajarito de Soto?
MIRANDA: Yes.
JUDGE: Assiduously?
MIRANDA: Yes.
JUDGE: Did this gentleman, in your opinion of course, belong to the anarchist party or to one of its splinter groups?
MIRANDA: No.
JUDGE: Are you sure?
MIRANDA: Yes.
JUDGE: Did he explicitly tell you he did not belong?
MIRANDA: No.
JUDGE: Then how can you be so sure?

.....

PEPÍN MATACRÍOS'S TAVERN was on an alley off Aviñó street. I never learned the name of the alley, but I could get there blindfolded if it still exists. Infrequently, conspirators and artists would visit the tavern. On most nights, there were immigrants from Galicia settled in Barcelona, wearing the uniforms of their various jobs: watchmen, trolley ticket-takers, night patrolmen, park and garden guards, firemen, sanitation men, doorkeepers, servants, porters, ushers in theaters and movies, policemen, among others. There was always someone playing the accordion, and occasionally, a blind woman singing strident songs from whose verses all the consonants had been deleted, so that "I will always love you" became I—I—AA—Y—O—OU. Pepín Matacríos was a feeble, gray-haired little man, with an emaciated body and a huge head on which there was no other hair than his thick handlebar mustache. He was in a kind of local mafia that in those days would meet in his tavern and which he controlled from behind the bar.

"I'm not openly opposed to the idea of morality," Pajarito de Soto told me as we finished off the second bottle. "And, by the same token, I respect both traditional morality and the new revolutionary ideas that today seem to be springing from every thinking mind. If you think about it seriously, both tend to the same end: to channel and give meaning to human behavior within society; and they share a common element—the will to unanimity. The new morality takes the place of traditional morality, but neither adopts the position of coexistence, and both deny the individual freedom of choice. This, in a certain sense, justifies the autocrats' well-known rebuke of the democrats: 'They want to impose democracy even on those who reject it.' You've probably heard that expression a thousand times, haven't you? Well, then, with that paradox, and setting aside their caustic intention, they reveal a great truth, that is, that political, moral, and religious ideas are authoritarian in themselves, because any idea, in order to exist in the world of logic, which must be as savage and miserable as the world of living beings, has to carry on a continuous battle with its opponents for supremacy. This is the great dilemma: if a single member of the community does not respect the idea or doesn't live the morality, both the community and the morality disintegrate, become useless, and morality, instead of strengthening its advocates, weakens them and delivers them into the hands of their enemy."

And on another occasion, strolling in the port, almost at daybreak:

"I'll confess that I'm much more concerned with the individual than with society and lament the dehumanization of the worker more than his living conditions."

"I don't know how to respond. Aren't both things closely linked?"

"Not at all. The peasant lives in direct contact with nature. The industrial worker has lost sight of the sun, the stars, the mountains, and vegetation. Although their lives are identical in their material poverty, the spiritual indigence of the industrial worker is greater than that of the peasant."

"What you're saying seems to me a simplification. If it were that way, the peasants wouldn't be migrating to the cities as they are."

One day, when I was talking to him in laudatory terms about the automobile, he shook his head with sorrow.

"Soon horses will disappear, overwhelmed by machines. They will only be used in circuses, military parades, and at bullfights."

"And that worries you? The disappearance of horses wiped out by progress?"

"Sometimes I think that progress takes away with one hand what it gives with the other. Today it's horses, tomorrow it will be all of us."

Statement made under oath to the Consul of the United States of America in Barcelona by the ex-inspector of police Don Alejandro Vázquez Ríos on November 21, 1926

Entered as Evidence: Document No. 2

▪

English translation by court interpreter Guzmán Hernández de Fenwick

I, Alejandro Vázquez Ríos, do solemnly swear:

That I was born in Antequera (Málaga) on February 1, 1872, that I entered the Police Force in April of 1891, and that I carried out my duties in Valladolid, being promoted in 1907 and transferred to Zaragoza, being promoted again in 1910 and transferred to Barcelona, where I currently reside. That I left the Police Force in 1920 to take a position in the commercial section of a business in the food industry. That over the course of my tenure with the police I had occasion to follow the events known today as "the

Savolta affair" closely. That prior to my being assigned to investigate those events, I knew of the existence of Domingo Pajarito de Soto and his articles in the labor newspaper *The Voice of Justice,* which is of a decidedly infamous, rabble-rousing, and subversive character. That the details of the life of the aforementioned individual were not known: it was known that he came from Galicia, that he had neither employment nor a fixed abode, that he lived with a woman by whom he had a child, that it was not known if their union had taken place in conformity with the Catholic Church; that among his readings were found the following authors: Roberto Owen, Miguel Bakunín, Enrique Malatesta, Anselmo Lorenzo, Carlos Marx, Emilio Zola, Fermín Salvoches, Francisco Ferrer y Guardia, Federico Urrales, and Francisco Giner de los Ríos (among the most prominent) as well as pamphlets by Ángel Pestaña, Juan García Oliver, Salvador Seguí (a.k.a.) *el Noi del Sucre,* and Andrés Nin, among others, as well as antigovernment publications such as *The White Review, The Voice of Labor, The Condemned,* among others, and the aforementioned *The Voice of Justice,* where he published. That he apparently had contact with the aforementioned Andrés Nin (see attached card) and perhaps with other leaders of the same or similar tendency, without it being known to what degree. . . .

JUDGE DAVIDSON: When did you meet Lepprince?

MIRANDA: I've forgotten the exact date. I know it was at the beginning of autumn in 1917. The turbulent days of August were over.

JUDGE: Briefly describe the meeting.

MIRANDA: Lepprince came to Cortabanyes's office, who, after speaking with Lepprince, ordered me to place myself at his disposal. Lepprince took me to his car, we went out to eat, and then to a cabaret.

JUDGE: Where did you say you went?

MIRANDA: To a cabaret. A nightclub where . . .

JUDGE: I know perfectly well what a cabaret is. I was expressing my surprise, not my ignorance. Continue.

.....

It consisted of a room, not a very large room, where a dozen tables were grouped around an empty, rectangular space, at one end of which there was a piano and two chairs. On the chairs were a saxophone and a violoncello. A highly made-up woman wearing a tight dress that reached her ankles but which was split up the side sat down at the piano. The woman played a polka but slowed it down to a nocturne, which she interrupted when we came in.

"I was sure you wouldn't fail me," she said enigmatically. She got up and walked toward us, smiling, and moving her foot forward as if she were testing the temperature of the water from the shore. As she moved, her leg, sheathed in a stocking that shimmered like glass, emerged from the opening in the dress. Lepprince kissed her on both cheeks, and I gave her my hand, which she held, saying, "I'll give you the best table—near the orchestra?"

"Far, if possible, madame."

The conversation was slightly absurd, because only one of the tables was occupied—by a bearded, powerful-looking sailor who buried his face in a huge goblet of gin and barely ever came up to take a breath of the club's musty air. Then a refined old man arrived, his face smeared with creams and his hair dyed a coppery blond. He ordered a liqueur which he daintily tasted as he watched the show. Then came a standoffish type wearing thick glasses who could only have been an office worker: he asked the price of everything before ordering a drink and made cheap, unsuccessful propositions to all the women. Four half-dressed women, all overweight and partially tweezed, wandered through the crowd, going from table to table, getting in each other's way, striking ecstatic poses for a few brief seconds, as if fulminated by paralyzing rays. The one who came most assiduously to our table was named Remedios, "the She-Wolf of Murcia." We asked Remedios to bring us the same huge glass of gin that had been served to the sailor. Then we waited.

.....

"THE GERMANS SHELLED THE SHIP I was traveling on. And it was only a passenger ship, imagine that. Until then I'd sympathized with the Germans—see, son?—because they seemed a noble, warlike people to me, but from then on, I hoped, with all my heart, they'd lose the war."

"Only natural," said Lepprince, who bowed and walked away. A servant placed a tray before him from which he took a glass of champagne. He drank some so he could walk without spilling it, and in doing so he caught the surprised eyes of Mrs. Savolta and her friend Mrs. Claudedeu who were staring at him. He smiled at the ladies and bowed again. Then he noticed the presence of a young woman next to them, who, he concluded, was María Rosa Savolta. She was little more than a girl with long blond hair. She was wearing a silk knit cocktail dress covered by a pleated crepe tunic, a bodice decorated with strands of peau de soie that ended in garlands. Lepprince took careful note of Miss Savolta's large, shining eyes, which stood out against her pale skin. He favored her with a wider smile than those he'd hitherto granted, and the young lady averted her eyes. A short, thick man with a glistening bald head approached him.

"Good evening, Monsieur Lepprince. Are you enjoying yourself?"

"Yes, of course, what about you?" Lepprince had not recognized the man.

"I am as well, but it was not that I wanted to talk to you about."

"It wasn't?"

"No. I wanted to apologize for our unfortunate encounter."

Lepprince scrutinized the man: he was dressed with a certain provincial lack of elegance and was perspiring. He was surprised by the man's gray, cold eyes, hidden under thick brows that resembled the mustaches of a Prussian officer. Lepprince told himself that he would never manage to remember those features, but that tonight he felt an uncommon perspicacity for capturing people's spirits through their eyes. An omen of events to come.

"I'm terribly sorry . . . but I can't recall where we've met before, Mr. . . ."

"Turull. Josep Turull, real estate agent, at your service. We met a short time ago in . . ."

"Oh yes, now I remember, of course . . . Turrull, you said?"

"Turull, just one *r*."

He shook the unknown man's hand and then went on strolling through the room, walking through groups of bejeweled, silky, aromatic ladies who made the gentlemen slightly dizzy. In the library next to the drawing room, he breathed an acrid smoke of cigars while titters and noisy guffaws mixed with the whisper of the latest joke or the latest anecdote about some well-known personage.

"Did they really throw tomatoes and rotten eggs at him?"

"Stones, a rain of stones. Of course they couldn't catch him, but it's the gesture that counts."

"You just can't shout, 'Hurrah for Cataluña!' from the windows of the Equestrian Circle, don't you think?"

"We were talking about our friend . . ."

Lepprince smiled.

"I know who you were talking about. I heard that story."

"In any case," he added, "you'd have to have that man's devilish mind to play with Madrid, with the Catalans, and, as if that were nothing, with all those unhappy officers."

"Who almost dragged him off to Montjuïc."

"He would have been out in twenty-four hours, in a cloud of popular fervor: a Maura with Ferrer's halo."

"Don't be such a cynic."

"I'm not defending him as a person, but I do recognize that a half dozen politicians like him would change the nation."

"I'd like to see what kind of change that would mean. As far as I'm concerned there's not much difference between him and Lerroux."

"Balls, Claudedeu, let's not exaggerate," said Savolta.

Claudedeu turned red.

"They're all the same: they would betray Cataluña for Spain

and Spain for Cataluña—if it would bring them some kind of personal profit."

"And who wouldn't do the same?" observed Lepprince.

"Quiet now," interrupted Savolta, "here he comes."

They turned toward the drawing room and saw him walking toward the library, greeting people left and right, with a black smile and a creased brow.

.....

WE'D BEEN IN THE CABARET for quite a while, and then the show began. First a man came on stage only to be greeted by the sailor's belches. He turned out to be the instrumentalist, the man who played the saxophone and the violoncello. He took up his violoncello and sawed a few lugubrious notes out of it accompanied by the piano. Then the woman playing the piano got up and spoke a few words of greeting. The sailor took a foul-smelling sandwich out of his oilskin bag and began to gnaw it, spilling crumbs and saliva out of his mouth onto the table. The lugubrious office worker with the thick glasses took off his shoes. The old man made eyes at us. The woman announced the Chinese, Li Wong, about whom she said, "He'll lead you by the hand to the kingdom of fantasy."

I was wriggling around, made uncomfortable by the pistol that was digging into my thigh.

"I hope his magic won't allow him to find out we're armed," I whispered.

"It would create a terrible impression," agreed the Frenchman.

The Chinese whirled some pennants around and made a dove appear. The dove flew over the dance floor and landed on the sailor's table to peck at the crumbs. The sailor broke its neck with a blackjack and began to pluck it.

"Oh, hol-lol," said the Chinese, "the cluerty of man."

The vice-ridden office worker went over to the sailor's table with his shoes in his hand and insulted him.

"Be so kind as to return that poor little animal to its rightful owner, you shameless beast."

The sailor picked up the dove by the head and waved it in the office worker's face.

"It's lucky for you you're wearing glasses, because if you weren't I'd hit you . . ."

The office worker took off his glasses, and the sailor slapped both his cheeks with the dove. The shoes slid across the floor, and the office worker clutched the edge of the table in order not to fall.

"I'm an educated man," he shouted, "and just look where my evil ways have led me."

"What's your problem, sonny?" asked the old man, who had picked up the shoes and was tenderly hugging the office worker.

"I've got a wife and two children, and look where I am, what a pit!"

We were all watching the office worker while the abandoned Chinese performed acrobatic feats with colored ribbons. Remedios, "the She-Wolf of Murcia," whispered, "Last week a customer committed suicide here."

"In brothels, many truths spring forth," declared Lepprince.

.....

WAS IT THE ARRIVAL of the fatuous, pomaded Lepprince or was it the ill-fated events that proved the old adage, "It's an ill wind turns none to good," that is, some people always seem to benefit from the disasters of others. I have no intention of clarifying that enigma. The truth is this: shortly after we "acquired" the brand-new little Frenchman, business doubled, tripled, and redoubled its benefits. Someone might say, how wonderful, how the humble, self-sacrificing workers must have benefited, especially because in order for those profits to be made possible, they had to increase production in an extraordinary way, adding two or three hours to the workday, suspending even the most basic security measures as well as rest to speed the manufacture of the products. How wonderful, readers who don't have a prayer of knowing the facts might say; and may the ecclesiastical authorities forgive me for bringing up prayer in the context of that hell which is the world of labor . . .

.....

"OURS IS NOT A SIMPLE TASK," said Inspector Vázquez.

Lepprince offered him a cigar, which the inspector took.

"Now that's a nice cigar," he commented. He was perspiring: "It seems to be hot here, am I right?"

"Take off your jacket, make yourself at home."

The inspector took off his jacket and hung it on the back of the chair. He lit the cigar with noisy puffs and exhaled a mouthful of smoke followed by a smack of his lips.

"Just what I said: a nice cigar. Yessir."

Lepprince pointed to an ashtray where Vázquez could throw the cellophane wrapper which had once enfolded the cigar and which, conscientiously twisted up, served to light it.

"If it's all right with you," said Lepprince, "we might touch on the subject that concerns us."

"But of course, Monsieur Lepprince, of course."

I remember that at first I didn't like Inspector Vázquez, with his supercilious eyes and his ironic half smile and the professional slowness of his words and movements, intended no doubt to exasperate and disturb and to provoke the listener into a quick and unstoppable confession of guilt. His premeditated pomposity reminded me of a serpent hypnotizing a small rodent. The first time I saw him, I judged him to be childishly, almost pathetically pedantic. Then he attacked my nerves. Finally, I understood that beneath that official pose there was a tenacious method and a vocational decision to discover the truth no matter what. He was indefatigable, patient, and perspicacious to the highest degree. I know he left the police force in 1920, that is, according to my calculations, when his investigations must have been coming to an end. There's something mysterious in all that. But we'll never know all the details because a few months ago he was murdered by someone connected to the case. It doesn't surprise me: many died during those bellicose years, and Vázquez was just one more, although perhaps not the last.

.....

"Moral codes are nothing more than the justification for a need, taking need to be the maximum exponent of reality, because reality manifests itself to mankind when it transcends the frontiers of lucubration and becomes a pressing need; the need, therefore, of a unanimous conduct has made the idea of morality spring from the human mind."

That's what Domingo Pajarito de Soto said to me late one afternoon as we walked along Caspe street and the Gran Vía after getting out of work. We were sitting on a stone bench in the Queen Victoria Eugenia gardens, totally empty because of the cold wind that was blowing. When Pajarito de Soto stopped talking, we both sat there a while, stupefied, contemplating the fountain.

"Freedom," he went on, "is the possibility to live in accordance with the morality imposed by the concrete realities of each individual in each era and circumstance. Which is why its character varies, why it is relative and impossible to delimit. In this, as you see, I am an anarchist. I differ, however, in believing that freedom, insofar as it is a means of subsistence, is linked to submission to the norm and to the rigorous adherence to obligation. The anarchists, in this sense, are correct, since their idea derives from real need, but they betray it in that they do not take reality into account as a basis for their thesis."

"I don't know enough about anarchism either to agree with them or to refute your arguments," I replied.

"Does the subject interest you?"

"Yes, of course," I said, more to be agreeable than out of sincerity.

"Then come with me. I'll take you to an interesting place."

"Hold on: it won't be dangerous, will it?"

"Don't be afraid, come on."

.....

THAT AFTERNOON Teresa and I had gone to a dance hall in the upper part of the city, where Barcelona blends with the town of Gracià. The place was called Queen of Springtime. It was vast, but even so it overflowed with people. No matter, it was agreeable and happy. There were gas lamps hidden behind colored glass that scattered feeble beams of light on the couples, the overflowing tables of perspiring families, the raucous band, the harried waitresses, and the bouncers clutching billy clubs who stalked the dance floor peering into corners. Balloons rose through the layers of smoke until they reached the peeling paint of the ceiling, from which hung wreaths and streamers against which the balloons bounced as they began their languid descent toward the glistening heads of the dancers. We were having a good time, until Teresa suddenly said, "I'm a cut flower without dirt under my feet. I'm burning alive—let's leave."

I studied the face of the woman swaying in my arms and noticed in her smooth skin a tinge of bad color, an irregular network of grayish veins, and the beginnings of wrinkles in the corners of her eyes and mouth. Behind her raised eyelids, I guessed I might find the riverbanks to which the fresh pastures descend, the cloying breeze of the forests, and the noise of water and leaves and things in movement that constitute a secret childhood language. I shall never forget Teresa.

JUDGE DAVIDSON: Did Mr. Lepprince frequent cabarets?
MIRANDA: No.
JUDGE: Did he drink?
MIRANDA: Moderately.
JUDGE: Do you ever recall seeing him drunk?
MIRANDA: I would say tipsy, not drunk.
JUDGE: But you did see him in such a state?
MIRANDA: A few times. Everyone . . .
JUDGE: Did he lose control of himself?
MIRANDA: No.
JUDGE: Did he sober up if the circumstances required it?
MIRANDA: Yes.

JUDGE: Do you think he used toxic substances?
MIRANDA: No.
JUDGE: Did he ever seem mad or out of his head to you?
MIRANDA: No.
JUDGE: Summing things up, then, do you consider Lepprince a perfectly normal man?
MIRANDA: Yes.

.....

. . . ONLY THE PHARISAICAL and boorish hypocrisy of the spirits of order who subordinate the march of the world to the preservation of their bastard privileges at the cost of any injustice and of the suffering of all others could be shocked or surprised by the facts. What happened, then, except that the undeserved prosperity of the profiteers, traffickers, hoarders, falsifiers of merchandise, in sum, the plutocrats, caused a foreseeable and always badly received rise in prices which was not compensated for by a just and necessary rise in salaries? And thus took place what has been happening since time immemorial: the rich became richer and the poor poorer and more miserable. Is it blameworthy, as some say it is, for the disinherited, the weak, the poor relations of the inhuman and insensible social family to have recourse to the only road, the only measure that their condition left them? No, only a fool, an oaf, a blind man could see something censurable in such an attitude. In the Savolta company, I must say this, gentlemen, and thus enter into one of the darkest and most painful passages in my article and in our social reality, was thought, planned, and attempted the only thing that could be thought, planned, and attempted. Yes, gentlemen, a strike. But the forsaken workers did not take into account (shall I dare to state his name?) that guardian of capital, that fearful shadow before whose memory all proletarian households tremble . . .

.....

"THE MAN WITH THE IRON HAND sent me," said Lepprince. "Ever heard of him?"

"Who hasn't, sir? All Barcelona . . ."

"Let's get to the point," said Lepprince.

The room where the contract was arranged was not large, but large enough so that five persons could speak in it at their ease. The walls were papered with rags, and there was a worm-eaten table, two chairs, and a sofa. From the ceiling hung an oil lamp that sputtered, and there were neither windows nor any other source of ventilation. The two men sat in the chairs; Lepprince and I were on the sofa, and she, wrapped in her sequin-covered cape, curled up on the table with her legs crossed.

I vividly remember the profound impression María Coral made on me the first time I saw her. She had thick black hair that fell in calm waves down her back, her eyes too were black and very big, her mouth small, with thick lips, her nose straight, her face round. She was overly made up and still wore the velvet cape and costume jewelry she decked herself out in after her act. My heart in my mouth, I had followed her leaps through the air, tossed and caught by those muscular, awkward, bestial idiots who touched her everywhere and ordered her around with the authoritarian gestures of breeding bulls. Every time I saw her whirl and tumble in the void, always about to fall and smash against the filthy floor of the ill-fated cabaret, a cry stuck in my throat, and I cursed the dubious paths that had led her to the dangerous and marginal profession of acrobat in such an obscene place, befouled by everything low and evil in this world. Perhaps I sensed future sufferings. I remember that without even knowing him I hated the Man with the Iron Hand. I hated everything in his poisonous spider's web that conspired to shape the future of that girl, sentenced to the underworld and a dramatic labyrinth of crime. I hated poverty, I hated myself, I hated Cortabanyes, who had made me into a participant in the complot, I hated the Savolta company, especially the Savolta company.

Continuation of the statement made under oath to the Consul of the United States of America in Barcelona by the ex-police inspector Don Alejandro Vázquez Ríos on November 21, 1926

Entered as Evidence: Document No. 2

▪

English translation by court interpreter Guzmán Hernández de Fenwick

. . . That later I learned of the existence of a woman named María Coral, a young woman, apparently pretty, an artist by profession, involved in matters relevant to my statement. That the aforementioned María Coral, whose name and origins were unknown, a gypsy (as I could deduce from her physical features and complexion), came to Barcelona in September or October of 1917, in the company of two unidentified strongmen with whom she executed acrobatic tricks in a cabaret of the lowest sort in this city. That the two strongmen, following reports received from other cities where they'd exercised, under the mantle of their artistic activities, the even more lucrative profession of professional killer, a profession favored on the one hand by their physical strength and training and on the other by the fact that they continuously moved from one place to another, even to foreign countries. That, in accordance with my conjectures, which lack proof, the aforementioned María Coral abandoned the company of the two strongmen in Barcelona, she remaining, they leaving. That the breakup of the act was due (always in the realm of supposition) to the intervention of some powerful figure (Lepprince? Savolta? the Man with the Iron Hand?) who made her his lover. That after a certain period of time she disappeared again without leaving a trace. That she reappeared under strange circumstances in 1919 . . .

.....

"Ah, Rosa," said Mrs. Claudedeu, "I have a strong suspicion who your candidate is."

"Neus, will you stop saying foolish things?" argued Mrs. Svolta. "I tell you the child is still too young even to think about that."

María Rosa Savolta had left her mother for a few minutes to have a soft drink and returned just in time to hear the last sentence.

"What were you two talking about?"

"Nothing, my dear, nothing. Neus's silly ideas."

"We were talking about you, sweetheart," clarified Mrs. Claudedeu.

"About me . . . ?"

"Of course, you're the most important person at this party. I was just saying to your mother, with the assurance of a person who saw you born confers on me, that you've become quite a young woman, and quite pretty into the bargain. And I'm not just saying it to butter you up, because that would be like feeling good for telling the truth when you're under oath . . ."

The young María Rosa Savolta blushed and stared into her glass.

"I was just saying to your mother that it's time you were thinking about your future. About what you're going to do, I mean, when you finish your studies at boarding school. You understand what I mean."

"Not really, no, ma'am."

"Look here, child, stop calling me 'ma'am' and call me by my name. Don't think that by playing the goody-goody you're going to stifle my curiosity."

"Oh no, Neus. I wasn't trying . . ."

"I know very well you were. Don't you realize I was young once and tried the same tricks? Come on now, silly, let's be friends and tell me the truth. Are you in love?"

"Me? What a mad idea, Neus . . . how could I fall in love with anyone stuck in school all day?"

"How do I know? It's in the blood. If girls don't see men, they invent them, they dream them up. . . . That's how we women are! At your age, of course."

The fortunate appearance of Mrs. Parells plucked young María Rosa from these dire straits.

"Can you guess what I've just been told?"

"Of course not. Is it worth hearing?"

"You tell me once you've heard it. Child, go take a little walk."

"Be discreet," warned Mrs. Claudedeu.

"Go see the ladies in the library, María Rosa," said Mrs. Savolta. "I'm sure you haven't said hello to anyone yet."

"Please, Mama, not the library," begged María Rosa.

"Do what I tell you and don't answer back. You've got to get over that ridiculous timidity. Get going."

.....

As THE OFFICE WORKER felt around for his glasses, the old man covered his face with kisses. The sailor finished plucking the dove and put it in his pocket.

"For breakfast," he said hoarsely.

"What a brute," squealed the old man.

The office worker quieted down and sat there silent and half asleep in his remorse, lulled in the old man's arms. The Chinese had disappeared.

"And just how did that customer kill himself?" I asked Remedios.

"He shot himself. The fool ruined us just to pull a theatrical trick. Now we're waiting to see if the police decide to close us down."

"What would you do if that happened?"

"Walk the streets. Got any better ideas, young man? No one would hire us, we're not spring chickens anymore. How old do you think I am?"

An obese woman, about fifty years old, dressed up like Manon Lescaut, had taken the Chinese's place. In a contralto voice, she began to sing a little song with a double meaning.

"No more than thirty," said Lepprince, making an ironic face.

"Forty-seven, big boy, and no jokes now."

"Well, you're as hard as a rock."

"Touch, touch, don't be afraid."

The sailor threw the rest of his sandwich at the singer, and the office worker burst into tears in the old man's arms. The singer peeled the bread off her dress, red with anger.

"Bastards! Sons of bitches!" she shouted in a powerful, deep voice.

"Singing? I can do it myself," said the sailor, who launched into a ballad about rum and pirates in a harsh voice.

"Sons of bitches!" bellowed the singer. "I'd like to see you pull these tricks in the Lyceum."

"And I'd like to see you singing there," said the old man, who had disentangled himself from the office worker and was waving his arms around.

"I've got more than enough to sing in the Lyceum, you old turd!"

"Especially good manners, you old slut!" howled the old man.

"A lot of women wish they had what I have more than enough of," shouted the singer. Then she reached into her décolleté and pulled out a pair of breasts as big as washbasins. The old man unbuttoned his fly and began to urinate mockingly. The singer spun on her heel and staggered offstage in a dignified way, without waiting for any applause. When she reached the curtains behind the piano, she turned around and said, in solemn tones, "You were born in a spittoon, faggot!"

The old man turned to the office worker and whispered, "Don't pay any attention to her, sweetheart."

Remedios sat down on my chair. I would have fallen right on my face if she hadn't clasped me in her titanic arms.

"This is nothing but a dump now," she commented, "but once upon a time there were lots of good things happening here."

I was half asphyxiated and begging Lepprince with my eyes for help, but he had drunk the entire jar of gin and answered my look with the glassy eyes and gaping mouth of a fish.

"It was a secret spot," said Remedios. "That's right, what you see now turned into a festival of obscenity. And it was only a few years ago, you wouldn't believe it, barely three or four, when the war wasn't this big hoax it's turned into now."

The woman at the piano, the one wearing the tight dress with the slit, begged the rowdies to respect the artists, who were only trying to earn an honest living, and the audience who only wanted to see the show in peace. The office worker walked to the center of the floor, his eyes filled with tears.

"It's all my fault, ma'am. I'm responsible for all the uproar and ask to be punished severely."

"Don't take it so hard, young fellow," said the pianist. "Go sit down and enjoy yourself with the others."

"Spies and arms traffickers from every country would come here," said Remedios. "They came to have a good time and forget the war. Their governments would send them to carry out God knows what job, but they have only thought about this."

The office worker had gone down on his knees, his arms crossed over his chest.

"I won't leave until I've publicly confessed my sins."

The pianist was nervous, no doubt frightened that this would be one more, perhaps final, tragedy for the business.

"They'd arrive together, in a group, and they'd forget all about the war, their countries, their very mothers. The moment the madam figured out who they were, she would say, 'Girls, get ready, the spies are coming.' We already knew what they liked. They were from different countries—some were even enemies—but they were all alike, and I mean alike. And what strange fancies they had!"

"There's no harm in having a little fun," the pianist was saying. "We're all nice people here, right? A little fooling around from time to time, what harm can it do?"

"It isn't from time to time, ma'am," said the office worker. "It's almost once a week."

"A lot of them buggered each other behind that curtain," Remedios told me. "The spies, I mean."

Suddenly everything turned upside down.

"No more clowning around! Let's get on with the party!"

It was Lepprince who shouted. I was startled and would have fallen over if Remedios's arms weren't still holding me fast. The Frenchman had stood up, his face bright red, his hair a mess, his shirt half open, his eyes flashing fire.

"Can't you hear me? I said let's get on with the party. You!" he said to the office worker. "Get back to your chair and stop annoying everyone with your whining! And you," to the pianist, "play the piano, which is what you're being paid for. What's wrong? Can't you hear me?"

He grabbed the office worker by the lapels of his threadbare suit and carried him bodily across the dance floor, depositing him in the old man's lap. Then, without stopping to take a breath, he kicked the sailor's chair. The sailor woke up furious.

"What the hell's going on?" he bellowed.

"Your noises bother me, most especially your snores. Understand?"

"What I understand is that I'm going to crack you one in the nose," said the sailor, pulling out his blackjack. But he dropped it when he saw that Lepprince had his pistol pointed at him.

"If you want trouble, I'll put one between your eyes."

The sailor smiled sullenly.

"This reminds me of an adventure I had in Hong Kong," he said, pulling up his trouser leg and showing a wooden leg. "It ended badly."

The pianist went back to work, and the man playing the violoncello, who had followed the development of the incidents unperturbed, picked up the saxophone and played a little song. The curtains parted, and two extremely muscular men and a little gypsy girl wearing a black cape and costume jewelry made their entrance.

.....

. . . THE MISERABLE WORKERS reached an accord, they pooled their courage, their hearts beat as one, and their brutalized brains were imbued with a single idea: The Strike! In a few days, perhaps in a few hours, they said in their exhilaration, our misfortune will turn into victory, our troubles will cease just as an anguishing nightmare vanishes, retreats, and flows back into the night world whence it came. Their nervousness made them perspire, and not because of toil—those hard and experienced workers no longer perspired or felt tiredness or fatigue, even in the hottest summer days. But, alas, they did not take into account the firmness and apparent ubiquity of the Man with the Iron Hand or the cold, calculating brain of the enigmatic Lepprince . . .

.....

"I'M LEPPRINCE. The Man with the Iron Hand sent me."

I saw Pajarito de Soto turn pale. He looked at me in the same way the victim must look at the executioner as he raises his ax. I smiled at him and gestured that he should be calm.

"I've read your articles in *The Voice of Justice*. I think they're brilliant, but a bit—how shall I put it?—a bit impassioned. Passion's a fine thing in a young man, I don't deny it. But don't you think your assertions are exaggerated? Could you prove what you describe in such vivid colors? No, of course not. You, my friend, have gathered only rumors, one-sided versions, innocently but exaggeratedly skewed and deformed by the perspective of those taking part, those who have, to put it this way, their own interests at stake. Tell me, Don Pajarito, would you be satisfied with my version of the facts? You wouldn't, would you? Of course not, of course not."

JUDGE DAVIDSON: The two of you went to the cabaret looking for relaxation?
MIRANDA: Oh no.
JUDGE: Why do you say "Oh no"?
MIRANDA: It wasn't really a cabaret.
JUDGE: What do you mean?
MIRANDA: It was a disgusting pit. A dump.
JUDGE: Then why did you go there?
MIRANDA: Lepprince wanted to speak to someone.

JUDGE: There, in that pit?
MIRANDA: Yes.
JUDGE: Why?
MIRANDA: The people he wanted to talk to worked there.
JUDGE: Doing what?
MIRANDA: They were acrobats, they did circus tricks. They were part of the show.
JUDGE: And why did Lepprince want to see them?
MIRANDA: To hire them.
JUDGE: Did Lepprince have interests in any circus?
MIRANDA: No.
JUDGE: Explain.
MIRANDA: The acrobats, during their free time, were paid assassins.
JUDGE: So Lepprince and you went to hire murderers?
MIRANDA: Yes.

.....

"I SUPPOSE," LEPPRINCE BEGAN by saying, "I shouldn't reveal how I came to know of your existence."

The muscle men exchanged glances.

"It's only natural," said one of them, "we're well known."

"Nor should I mention the nature of the proposition I've come to make you."

"A proposition?" said one of them. "What proposition?"

The Frenchman seemed disconcerted, but he reacted.

"A job you should do for me . . . for us, I mean. I've heard you do this kind of work . . . aside from your artistic activities."

"Artistic?" asked the other. "Oh yes, artistic activities, our routines. Do you like them?"

"A lot," answered Lepprince. "They're good."

"We have more, believe me. Quite a few more you'd like just as much. My partner thinks them up, and so do I, sometimes. That way there's more variety, because we think them up between us. Understand?"

"I see," Lepprince cut him short. "But I'd like to take care of the other subject first: the job I'd like to propose to you."

"It's natural for you to be interested in these things," said one of them.

"My partner and I," said the other, "always think up new routines so we won't bore the audience. The ones you saw are old, because we've only been performing in this city for a short time. When we get to a place, we do our old routines because no one knows us yet unless they've seen us do them before, somewhere else. But when we change cities . . . Well, when we change cities we do the old ones, understand? Because no one knows them."

The Frenchman turned toward me, taking advantage of the fact that the two strongmen had become involved in the discussion of a new routine.

"Do something," he whispered.

"I'd like you to tell me about those new acts," I said to the muscle men. "Why don't we take care of this gentleman's matter, and then we can talk them over in peace?"

The two of them looked at me in surprise.

"But we're already talking about the new ones!"

In the silence that followed, María Coral's voice rang out.

"We understand, gentlemen. Who do you want taken care of?"

Lepprince blushed.

"Well now . . . that is . . . ," he muttered.

"We have to be clear in these matters. Is it someone important?"

"No," said the Frenchman, "people of no importance whatsoever."

"Do they carry weapons?"

"None."

"Risk raises the fee."

"There is no risk in this case, but I'm not going to discuss fees."

"Give us the facts, if you please," interrupted the gypsy.

"I represent the people who run a large business," said Lepprince. "I suppose I can keep the names of my superiors secret."

"Of course."

"Recently, among the workers, there have appeared elements that disrupt the . . . smooth working of the business. We know who they are because of loyal workers—you know what I mean."

"I suppose so," said María Coral.

"Our intention . . . that of my superiors, of course, is to dissuade those disruptive elements. At this point in time, they do not constitute a serious danger within the company, but the crisis is growing, and the seeds of their ideas may take root in the soul of the working element. We've decided to nip things in the bud, for the good of one and all, although in principle we oppose the dissuasive system."

"Does the job include finding and following these individuals, or will you give us all the information?"

"We . . . my secretary here, specifically"—he pointed to me—"will give you a list of the individuals in question, as well as the place and time when, in our opinion, you should carry out your task. I don't have to tell you that any initiatives on your part that might exceed our exact instructions could create considerable ill will and that . . ."

"We know what our obligations are, Mister . . ."

"Please allow me to keep my name a secret, María Coral."

The gypsy began to laugh.

"As to the method of payment," she said.

"My secretary," said Lepprince, "will come to you in a few days with the list I mentioned and a part of the price we agree upon. When the first job is taken care of, you will be given the rest of the money and can then begin the second job. Agreed?"

María Coral thought for a moment and finally nodded agreement.

"There's no need for your . . . secretary to come to this pigsty again. We usually eat dinner in a tavern near here called Casa Alfonso. You'll see it as you leave. Between nine and nine-thirty you can find us there. When can we expect your first visit?"

"Quite soon," said Lepprince. "Keep mum about all this. Anything else?"

The gypsy posed provocatively.

"Well, as far as I'm concerned . . ."

"Insofar as it's possible, I would like," said Lepprince, clearly flustered, "our relations to be reduced to a mere exchange of services for fees. Any and all contact between us should be effected through my secretary and, of course, should there be complications with the authorities, you should leave my name as well as that of my superiors out of things, even if the authorities should know about them."

"Anything else?" asked María Coral.

"Yes, a warning: don't try to play any tricks on us."

The gypsy laughed again. When we left, it was dawn, and an icy breeze was blowing. We turned up the collars of our jackets and walked rapidly toward the automobile, which was slow to start because all its liquids had frozen. We drove through the deserted city until we reached my place. Lepprince stopped the car without turning off the motor and commented, "Fascinating woman, don't you think?"

"That gypsy? She certainly is."

"I'd even dare to say mysterious: like the undiscovered tomb of some pharaoh. Inside, there might be an infinite beauty, an occult mystery, but also death, ruin, the curse of the ages. Do I seem a bit literary to you? Pay no attention to me. I lead a life of routine, like every executive who takes himself seriously. These little adventures drive me insane. It's been years since I've seen the sun come up after a night on the town. What a night! What a good time we had. Listen, you're not asleep, are you?"

"No, of course not. I wasn't sleeping. I just closed my eyes because I feel tired, but I wasn't asleep."

"Good. Go to bed now. It's late, and you probably have to get up early. Get a good night's rest."

"How will we arrange this business of the lists and the payments?"

"Don't worry about a thing. You'll be hearing from me. Now go and rest."

"Good night."

"Good night."

I got out of the car and realized, half asleep as I was, that Lepprince did not leave until I'd locked my door from the inside.

.....

WHEN MARÍA ROSA SAVOLTA LEFT, the three ladies put their heads together. Dry, freckled, her neck a mass of wrinkles, her nose long and bony, Mrs. Parells began to whisper.

"Don't you know? A week ago, the police found the Rocagrossa woman in a third-class hotel with an English sailor."

"What are you saying?" exclaimed Mrs. Claudedeu.

"I don't believe it," added Mrs. Savolta.

"But it's true. They were looking for some thug or an anarchist and they searched all the rooms. When they brought them all to the police station, the Rocagrossa woman identified herself and asked permission to telephone her husband."

"Shameless! Impossible!" said Mrs. Claudedeu. "And what did he say?"

"Nothing—you'll see. Mrs. Rocagrossa was very astute. Instead of calling her husband, she called Cortabanyes, and he got her out."

"And how do you know that?" asked Mrs. Savolta. "Did Cortabanyes tell you?"

"No. He would never reveal a thing like that—a professional secret. I found out from another source, but that's a secret," declared Mrs. Parells.

"An outrageous scandal," said Mrs. Claudedeu.

"What about the sailor?" asked Mrs. Savolta.

"No one knows a thing. They let him go too, so he ran back to his ship as fast as a scalded cat, apparently not in the mood for any more trouble. He was of no importance, a stoker or something like that."

"Why would she ever do something like that?" reflected Mrs. Savolta.

"That's life, my dear," said Mrs. Claudedeu. "She's young and half foreign. They have different ideas."

"Besides," added Mrs. Parells, "there's that business about her husband—I don't know if you've heard."

"About Rocagrossa? Lluis Rocagrossa? What's happened to him?"

"What? Haven't you heard? They say . . . well, they say he likes men . . ."

"You said it first!" said Mrs. Claudedeu. "Every day another one joins your list."

"What can I do? I can spot them a mile away."

"But, girls," said Mrs. Savolta, "I can't understand why you like to talk about these dirty things. They disgust me. I just can't help it."

"I don't like them either, Rosa," protested Mrs. Parells. "I'm telling you because someone just told me, but I don't get pleasure from this filth."

"Things get worse and worse," said Mrs. Claudedeu.

.....

. . . AND NOW I MUST RESTRAIN my trembling fingers and hold back the indignation and shame I feel within me to describe in the plainest, most objective, and dispassionate style possible the events, the bare events which took place that fateful night, a few days before the prearranged and anxiously awaited date to carry out the long-expected, necessary, and just strike.

Over the course of the conflict I have just described, a man named Vicente Puentegarcía García had stood out among the workers, a man of noble, austere character, balanced and energetic, of honest intentions and clear intelligence, and of absolute probity. At about one o'clock in the morning on September 27 of this year, Vicente Puentegarcía was returning to his domicile, on Independence street, in the San Martín district. He was completely at peace and unaware of the hideous assault to which he would be subjected a few minutes later. It was a beautiful, peaceful night. In the pure, limpid, serene, bluish sky a few stars timidly shone, and democratic Independence street was solitary, silent, tranquil. The placid tranquility and the silent repose of that neighborhood were only interrupted from time to time by the powerful footsteps of the modest night watchman, Angel Peceira, as he made his rounds. Neither he nor anyone else could suspect the tragic drama being prepared in the mysterious solitude and which in a short time would take place with the greatest impunity.

Soon a young, hardy, strong, robust worker appears, a man with sharp features, a man filled with life and illusions. This young worker is Vicente Puentegarcía, who, after attending a strike meeting, was going home to rest, happy and confident. When he reached the intersection of Independencia and Mallorca, Puentegarcía stopped to talk awhile and smoke a cigarette with the watchman, to whom he said an affectionate good night soon after.

A few yards from the door of his house, two powerful men with menacing eyes stepped out of the shadows and walked toward him. Puentegarcía, unarmed, continues to walk straight toward the two men, slowly and calmly.

"Stop where you are!" shouts the one who seems to have most authority and the coarsest, the rottenest, the most thievish face.

The worker stops. One of the men consults a list, supplied no doubt by the cowardly instigators of that vile act.

"Are you Vicente Puentegarcía García?"

"I am."

"Then follow us," the inquisitorial hoodlums command him. And seizing him by the wrists with their iron hands, they lead him to a dark, isolated corner.

"Don't treat me this way," Puentegarcía cries out. "I'm not a criminal, just a poor worker!"

But one of the thugs had already landed a hard punch on the poor victim's face. Puentegarcía doubled over, on his face a grimace of intense pain.

"Hit him hard!" exclaims the one who seems to be the leader. "That way he'll learn his lesson once and for all."

The unfortunate man begs with his tear-filled eyes, but the brutal torture does not cease. Punches rain down on him, and Puentegarcía staggers, a martyr to the terrible pain of the beating, then falls to the ground, bloody and almost unconscious. Even when he's down, the two assassins continue to kick and beat him. The miserable Puentegarcía, seeing himself at the feet of those villains, felt a convulsive tremor, saw flashes of light, luminous circles, and fiery swords.

His wretched wife, who had gone out on the balcony, nervous because of how late her spouse was and alarmed by the noise, ran out to the street like a madwoman, weeping her eyes out, piercing the air with shrill, cutting cries of grief, of tremendous consternation. The cowardly murderers run when they see her coming. Aroused by the shouting, the honorable watchman comes. He and the wife carry the worker's battered body to his bed, and he, writhing in a pool of thick, smoking blood, can still mumble out, "Wretches, scum!"

The next day Vicente Puentegarcía García, who had always been so punctual, so hardworking, so irreproachable, does not appear at his job. His serious condition keeps him from warning his comrades about the danger lying in wait for them. So, on successive nights, the following workers fall: Segismundo Dalmau Martí, Miguel Gallifa Rius, Mariano López Ortega, José Simó Rovira, José Olivares Castro, Agustín García Guardia, Patricio Rives Escuder, J. Monfort, and Saturnino Monje Hogaza. Informed about the assaults, the police carry out investigations, but the criminals disappear as if by magic, and none of the details given by the victims allows their identification. Although the names of those who pulled the strings in this bloody and infamous puppet show were in the thoughts of the people, there was nothing that could be proved against them. The strike never took place, and thus ended one of the most shameful and repugnant chapters in the history of our beloved city.

.....

DURING THAT MONOTONOUS AND MISTY SEPTEMBER, I strolled through the fog of the port district carrying the envelopes. The first night I had difficulty finding the tavern because the previous time I'd gone by car and barely taken any notice of the route. I found the strongmen and the gypsy finishing their supper. The men greeted me joyfully. I noticed that María Coral, without makeup, wearing a simple seamstress's dress, away from the lewd world of the cabaret, no longer had the dominating effect on me she'd had on more than one night. Even so, I could see that the gypsy's smile and way of speaking kept the same ease that flustered me.

"I liked you the other night, understand?" said María Coral.

I'd gone to carry out a mission and placed the envelope in the gypsy's hands.

"Your boss isn't coming this time?" she asked mockingly.

"No. That was our agreement, if I remember correctly."

"That was our agreement, but I would have wanted to see him. Tell him that tomorrow—will you remember?"

"As you wish."

The second time I went to Casa Alfonso I brought two envelopes instead of one. María Coral laughed, but said nothing about it.

"Tell your boss," she said as I left, "that we won't cheat him in any way whatsoever."

And she threw me a kiss from the door, which started the other people in the tavern talking. The third time, I found the strongmen stuffing themselves, but María Coral wasn't with them.

"She's gone, the ingrate," said one of the strongmen. "She walked out on us a couple of days ago."

"Too bad for her," his partner consoled him. "Tell me how she'll do her act without us."

"It's all the same to us, understand?" they said to me. "Because we can go on doing the same thing. The audience comes to see us. Except that it really makes me mad that she ran off after all we did for her."

"After all the help we gave her."

"We found her dying of hunger in one of those towns where we used to put on shows before, see? And we brought her with us because we were so sorry for her."

"But when she comes back, she'll find out who she was dealing with."

"We won't let her back into the show."

"You bet we won't."

"Was she . . . ?" I asked. "What kind of relationship did she have with you two?"

"A relationship of ingratitude."

"A relationship of running out on us after all we did for her."

I gave up trying to learn more about the gypsy from them and asked them about their work, not their cabaret act, but the work they were doing for Lepprince.

"Oh, it's going fine. We look for the guy on the list and we beat him up a little. When he's on the ground, we tell him, 'So you learn not to meddle in other people's business!' That's what she told us we had to say, 'in other people's business.' And then we run for it, in case the police are on the way."

"The last time, they almost caught us. We ran until we couldn't run anymore and had to go into a bar and drink a couple of beers we were so out of breath. And here's a coincidence for you: there in the tavern is the guy we beat up the last time. As soon as he saw us, his mouth fell open in shock: he was also missing two teeth my brother here knocked out. We shouted, 'So you don't meddle in other people's business!' and the guy ran out. So did we, just to be on the safe side."

That was the last time I brought envelopes to Casa Alfonso.

.....

"CAREFULLY CONSIDERING IT," I said, "your theory leads inevitably to fatalism, and your idea of freedom is nothing more than a combination of boundaries set up as a result of the consequences of events which are, in turn, the consequence of other events."

"I see what you're getting at," replied Pajarito de Soto, "even though I think you're wrong. If freedom doesn't exist outside the framework of realities (like the freedom to fly, which transcends man's physical limitations), it is no less certain that within those limits freedom is complete. According to the use we make of it, the following conditions will take shape. Let's take as an example the workers' protest taking place now. Are you going to tell me that such a movement is not conditioned by circumstances? No. Nothing could be more self-evident: the wages, the imbalance between prices and salaries, the working conditions, in sum, could only produce this reaction. Now, what will be the result? We don't know. Will the working class see its demands satisfied? No one can say. Why? Because defeat or triumph depends on the *selection* of means. Therefore, my conclusion, the mission of each and every one of us is not to fight for freedom or progress in the abstract—they're only empty words anyway—but to contribute to the creation of future conditions which will give humanity a better life in a world of wide, clear horizons."

CONTINUATION OF THE STATEMENT MADE UNDER OATH TO THE CONSUL OF THE UNITED STATES OF AMERICA IN BARCELONA BY THE EX-INSPECTOR OF POLICE DON ALEJANDRO VÁZQUEZ RÍOS ON NOVEMBER 21, 1926

Entered as Evidence: Document No. 2

▪

English translation by court interpreter Guzmán Hernández de Fenwick

. . . THAT EVEN BEFORE participating directly and personally in what is known today as the "Savolta affair" I was aware of the supposed assaults perpetrated against ten workers from the aforementioned company. That it is said that the assaults (none of which went beyond a simple beating without complications) were perpetrated at the express order of company executives by thugs in order to stop a supposed strike before it took place. That after the investigations carried out (and in which I had no part whatsoever) it was concluded that there was no proof, not even circumstantial evidence, of the company's guilt. That it was suspected the assaults came from within the workers' group itself and were caused by internal dissension or a supposed struggle for power or control within the workers' group carried on between two well-known agitators, a certain Vicente Puentegarcía García and a certain J. Monfort, the first being a well-known Andalusian anarchist and the second a dangerous Catalan communist and friend of Joaquín Maurín (see enclosed file). That as a result of charges filed by one of the supposed victims (I think it was a certain Simó) and the aforementioned investigation, there were some arrests made later, among which were the aforementioned Vicente Puentegarcía and J. Monfort, that of a certain Saturnino Monje Hogaza (communist), a certain José Oliveros Castro (anarcho-syndicalist), and a certain José Simó Rovira (socialist). That all or almost all of the above were immediately set free and that none was imprisoned when I took charge of the case.

Chapter 2

Typescript of Notes Taken During the Second Statement Made by Javier Miranda Lugarte on January 11, 1927, to F. W. Davidson, Supreme Court Judge for the State of New York

(Folios 70 and following)

▪

English translation by court interpreter Guzmán Hernández de Fenwick

Judge Davidson: Explain in a concise, orderly way how you came to meet Domingo Pajarito de Soto.

Miranda: I was in Cortabanyes's office when, one day, Lepprince walked in . . .

Judge: When was that?

Miranda: I don't remember the exact date. It must have been in mid-October of 1917.

Judge: Was that the first time Lepprince came to the office?

Miranda: No, the second—as far as I know.

Judge: When was the first time?

Miranda: A month or so earlier.

Judge: Tell us about that first visit.

Miranda: I told you about it yesterday. In his first visit, Lepprince requested my services, and I accompanied him to a cabaret.

Judge: Fine. Go on with the second visit.

Miranda: Lepprince was carrying a briefcase. He went into Cortabanyes's office, and they conferred. Then I was called into the office.

Judge: Aside from you, who was present?

Miranda: Lepprince and Cortabanyes.

Judge: Proceed.

Miranda: Lepprince had spread the contents of the briefcase on the desk.

Judge: Describe them.

Miranda: There were three copies of *The Voice of Justice,* a newspaper

I was unfamiliar with—it was a low-circulation tabloid that only appeared sporadically. A copy was opened to one of the middle pages. An article had been outlined in red pencil; the author's name was also circled in red.

JUDGE: Who was the author?

MIRANDA: Domingo Pajarito de Soto.

JUDGE: Was it one of the articles entered as evidence as items 1a, 1b, and 1c in this file?

MIRANDA: Yes.

JUDGE: Proceed.

MIRANDA: Cortabanyes ordered me to find the author of the articles.

JUDGE: Why?

MIRANDA: At the time I didn't know.

JUDGE: Did you agree to carry out that order?

MIRANDA: Not at the beginning.

JUDGE: Why?

MIRANDA: I had heard rumors about attacks on workers and was afraid of being implicated . . .

JUDGE: Did you explain your reasons to Lepprince?

MIRANDA: Yes.

JUDGE: In those same words?

MIRANDA: No.

JUDGE: What were your exact words?

MIRANDA: I don't remember.

JUDGE: Make an effort.

MIRANDA: I asked him if this was to be a job similar to the one we'd arranged the previous time.

JUDGE: Did Lepprince understand what you meant?

MIRANDA: Yes.

JUDGE: How do you know?

MIRANDA: He began to laugh and told me to stop worrying, that I could be present during every phase of the operation he was planning and intervene any time I saw fit—if things seemed to be getting out of hand.

JUDGE: And is that what you did?

MIRANDA: Yes.

JUDGE: You found Pajarito de Soto with no difficulty?
MIRANDA: I found him, but it was difficult.
JUDGE: Tell me how you found him.

.....

WHY? THERE WERE LONG DAYS of tiring walks, tedious conversations, wasted bribes, aimless, sterile shadowing of suspects, until I found the right trail. I wanted success at any cost, not so much to impress Cortabanyes as to please Lepprince, whose interest in me was opening the doors to unforeseen expectations, the wildest hopes. I saw in him a possible escape from the morass of Cortabanyes's office, from those long, monotonous, unproductive afternoons and from a poor, uncertain future. Serramadriles was my conscience, a warning voice if my spirits flagged or if I allowed myself to be dominated by apathy or discouragement. He said Lepprince was "our lottery," the client we should fuss over and gratify, the one to whom we should at all costs be helpful and useful to the point of being obsequious, to whom we should appear efficient, to whom, out of self-interest, we should be loyal. He painted a sordid, odious future for me if I remained at the orders of Cortabanyes, who was getting older and older, more and more irritable, more and more careless. By contrast, he painted a glorious panorama for me with Lepprince—the highest circles of finance and commerce in Barcelona, the highest society, with its automobiles, its parties, its travel, its clothes, its sylphlike women, and a flood of money in shining, tinkling coins that would flow from the pores of that rampant beast, the Catalan oligarchy. Going around in circles, bored after wasted, useless hours but keeping at it out of sheer desire, I found Pajarito de Soto one night, in mid- or late October, in a ruinous mansion on Unión street, where he had rented an apartment. I'd knocked on lots of doors and received lots of disappointments, so my voice must have sounded weary when I asked if the journalist lived there. A young woman with a pretty smile answered my knock. I didn't know it then, but her name was Teresa; she was to be the first great love in my life. The image of that instant comes back to my mind like a piece of wreckage from a shipwreck tossed onto the shore by the waves. The apartment was a rectangular room, very large and filled with a labyrinth of miscellaneous furniture that turned it into a complete living space without there being any need for partitions. The furniture was grouped according to necessity (that theory of necessity again!): in one corner, there was an unmade double bed, two night tables, a floor lamp, and a little cradle where a child was sleeping; in the opposite corner, there was a table surrounded by different-sized chairs; elsewhere, two ragged armchairs whose springs were poking out, a bookcase with warped shelves, a half-open wardrobe, a corner cabinet that leaned to one side, and a bombé sideboard. Books and piles of magazines were scattered over the floor, invading to one degree or another the surfaces of several other pieces of furniture. The room was dominated by a potbellied stove from which radiated a blazing heat, "so the child doesn't catch cold." In one of the armchairs, Domingo Pajarito de Soto was dozing. He looked short (which he was), large-headed, and sallow, with black, shiny hair like freshly poured India ink. His hands were small and his arms excessively short, even for a person his size; his eyes bulged, his mouth was wide and fleshy, his nose was flat, and his neck was short: a frog. He was surprised to see me and even more surprised when I told him I'd read his article in *The Voice of Justice* and that important people, whose names I was not authorized to mention, had taken an interest in him. At first he supposed those people to be magazine editors or the leaders of some political party. When I saw he was so naive and full of illusions, I practically revealed the secret. He didn't understand, his romantic ambitions blinded him. I remember that cold November afternoon and Pajarito de Soto sitting stiffly on the edge of his chair, lost at the far end of the meeting table in the library–waiting room. Lepprince appeared cordial and respectful, praising his "incisive style" and his courage; he rejected the version of the events Pajarito had depicted and made him a surprising proposition: Pajarito could make a complete study of the Savolta company from the worker's point of view, including working conditions, production, the current crisis, and the strike. He offered Pajarito complete access to all the administrative and manufacturing facilities, all necessary information and assistance—"as much as Savolta himself received." He guaranteed Pajarito impunity and freedom to publish as much as he might want to write. In exchange, he asked him not to reveal his conclusions to the public until he'd given the company's officers "the chance to correct any errors." He announced that when his work was done there would be a meeting or mixed assembly of capital and labor in which the various groups would discuss—"in your presence"—the problems brought about by the change of circumstances. In exchange for his services, Lepprince promised Pajarito "the sum of forty *duros*." The total package was more than Pajarito could ever have hoped for, and he accepted in a state of exaltation. I confess that at the beginning I was afraid for him. But Lepprince repeated his promise not to use coercion of any kind against the journalist. He gave his word as a gentleman, and I believed him, so I did not oppose the transaction. Of course, I don't think Pajarito de Soto would have paid any attention to warnings at that moment. When our friendship was stronger, after frequent chats and walks, I reminded him of how unstable his position was, between two lines of fire. I did it in part out of affection and in part because I'd absorbed the fears that Teresa confided to me when we were alone. He paid no attention: he wanted to carry out a positive and truthful piece of work; he was simple, both in his soul and in his intentions, he wanted a clear future for his son, a horizon aglow with work, prosperity, and plenty. Together we made and unmade large-scale plans, not only individual projects. We argued over details until dawn, explored every corner of the sleeping city, which was filled with magical vibrations. If we found an open doorway, we would enter the ominous courtyard, lighting our way with a match, and climb the stairs to the roof, from which we would contemplate Barcelona. Domingo Pajarito de Soto felt, and his impression was not far from the truth, that he was like a modern version of the devil on two sticks, that he could fly over Barcelona and spy on life by looking through roofs. With his finger extended over the railings at the edge of the roof, he would point out the various residential zones, the proletarian conglomerations, the peaceful and virtuous neighborhoods of the middle class, of the merchants, the shopkeepers, and the artisans. Together we emptied many bottles of wine, wine that animates at night and takes its revenge in the morning; we attended political meetings, we defended the ideologies each of us believed, always different ones, more out of friendship than conviction. I never knew before and I never knew later what having a friend meant. As for Teresa, I've already said she was my great love. We saw each other every day, and I used any flimsy pretext that would let me run out of the office and keep me out for a couple of hours. The first time she called me, she did so as a friend, and she maintained that tone throughout the conversation. An obliging neighbor took care of the child. She met me in a dairy store near her house, a long narrow place divided into two halves by a wooden shutter. The first half contained a chipped marble counter where a fat woman wearing a yellowish oilcloth apron sold milk, cheese, butter, and other dairy products. Behind the shutter, there were four little tables close to the wall, along which ran a bench. Young couples would sit at the tables: students, artisans, and youthful apprentices, accompanied by waitresses, maids, shopgirls, secretaries, nurses, and working women. They would speak in whispers, hugging, or they would kiss and fondle each other, protected from mutual curiosity by the back room's weak light and by the complicity of a commonly shared risqué activity. Teresa received me with discreet affability, asked me to forgive her choice of place, alleging that she'd promised her helpful neighbor she wouldn't go far, which justified the choice of the dairy bar, the closest place to her house. In the chat, which must have lasted longer than an hour, she revealed her fears about her husband's work and Domingo's obstinacy in not listening to reason. I told her I didn't see any danger unless Pajarito de Soto were to do something seriously imprudent. She seemed relieved by what I said, and the conversation took a more general turn: we talked about the hard life of cities, about the thankless effort necessary if one was to make his way, about the responsibility of having a child, and about our society's gloomy future. When we'd finished talking, she asked me not to bother to accompany her, that I should leave the dairy bar first without waiting for her or following her. I signaled that I would do exactly that and offered her my hand, but she came close to my face and gave me a kiss on the lips of the kind that those who live alone without love give and receive in dreams. Thus began a long series of dates and walks, aided and abetted by the helpful neighbor, Cortabanyes's disciplinary negligence, and Pajarito de Soto's prolonged absences—drowned as he was in work, in his factory, and in his mad theories. Teresa loved her husband with all her heart, but living with him was arduous: he was a good man but inconstant, nervous, and irresponsible, blind to everything unrelated to his reformist ideals, completely absorbed in thinking up and elaborating slogans, denunciations, and demands; he swung back and forth between violent states of overbearing creative energy and sudden depressions that sank him in ill humor and silence. Teresa silently suffered his neglect and, insecure and unprotected, put up with her husband's brusque, despotic reactions out of fear. I also suffered. My prior experiences in matters of love were nil: a few nocturnal incursions and long hours of febrile imagination. Once, trying to understand her husband's incapacity, I spoke to her of the difficulty of loving, of love's impossible language, of indecisive gestures, of words that want to express but do not express, and of glances that want to say something yet cannot. Actually, I was talking about myself, about my bewilderment at life and about my desperate indecision as I stood at the crossroads of life. And so, while I was divided and tortured, unforgettable weeks went by: by day I strolled around with Teresa, or we went dancing, or to the dairy bar which witnessed the beginning of our talks, and at night I argued and got drunk with Pajarito de Soto in Pepín Matacríos's tavern. I should make clear that my relations with Teresa during those weeks were not adulterous, neither in form nor in content. If there was conscious love, it did not manifest itself. Our souls united out of a mutual need for company, and if we acted out the kisses and gestures of lovers, we did it to create a fictitious world of tenderness that would make our dreams real, like a child in search of adventure who sits astride the arm of a chair wearing a paper hat and waving a broomstick. The few times the three of us were together, Teresa and I were not afflicted with guilt. I blushed because of my sudden fear that our secret would be revealed and was sullen and distant with Teresa, which, paradoxically, worried Pajarito de Soto. He was sorry his wife and I didn't get along well, and on several occasions he made me swear that if anything happened to him that I would protect Teresa and the child. She would laugh at us and make fun of us with a fearlessness not free of malice. But our consciences were clear. Until the end came with the crushing force of an earthquake and the precise steps of a chess match. It happened a few days before Christmas. I was working and fighting against the lethargy the previous night had left me in when the call came. Serramadriles handed me the telephone, which I took with a nervousness charged with foreboding. It was Teresa. She urgently needed me to come to her house. She gave me no reason, just a desperate plea. I ran out. Even then I knew the streetlights, the buildings, and the very pavement of Unión street as well as I knew my own house. I knocked, and her voice told me to come in. The big room was dark, the only light coming from the weak glow of the coal in the stove. Before my eyes were used to the tenuous light, Teresa threw herself into my arms and covered me with kisses and caresses, whispering fiery, maddened words, pulling off my clothes, unbuttoning her own until our chests touched, tremulous and shocked. Without saying a word we moved to the bed. In the little crib, the child slept. For an instant, we penetrated the darkness, torturing and suffering at the same time, blending victim with executioner, like the fiery whirlwind the universe must have been in its beginning, until a gigantic, invisible hand separated us with the same strength that will split the earth at the Last Judgment. We stayed there, stretched out on the bedspread, our legs still intertwined, swimming toward the edge of consciousness, searching for the breath we'd lost along with our senses. I vaguely heard a voice in which I recognized Teresa, a new Teresa who told me she loved me, who told me to take her away with me, far from that house, far from Barcelona, that for me she would abandon her husband and her child, that she would be my slave. I felt a pain that began within and spread outward. For the first time, I was afraid of being discovered, a fear that made me stop perspiring and made my skin dry and raspy. She assured me that Pajarito de Soto wouldn't be back for hours. It was late, and I asked why he was late. She told me that the company he was working for, that is, the Savolta company, or rather Lepprince, had scheduled the famous meeting or assembly for 7:00. When I heard that, I understood the extent of my betrayal and imagined my friend doubly abandoned. I got dressed, I walked out without listening to Teresa's shouts and pleas, and took a taxi. Before leaving the house, I heard the child crying. It was dark, and a clock said 8:30. The taxi left me at the station. There I had to wait twenty minutes for the train to leave. Soon it picked up speed, and shortly after leaving the station, it entered the suburbs, going toward the industrial zone of Hospitalet. I contemplated the landscape nervously, hunched over in the back of the half-deserted car in order to protect myself from the cold drafts of air piercing my body. It must have been quite cold outside: I found I had to wipe the window clean with my hand because my condensed breath, mixed with the soot, formed a swampy, slimy film. I unsuccessfully tried to put some order in my thoughts. The suburbs we were passing through, unfamiliar to me, were seriously depressing. Alongside the tracks, as far as the eye could see, were shacks without light, squeezed together on a grayish, dusty earth devoid of vegetation. Among the shacks wound lines of immigrants who had come to Barcelona from all corners of the country. They hadn't succeeded in entering the city: they worked in the factory belt and lived in the outskirts, the anterooms of the prosperity that attracted them. Brutalized and hungry, they waited and kept silent, clinging to the city the way ivy clings to the wall. That's what I remember of the trip, that and, when I reached my destination, a frozen platform swept by the wind. I hired a broken-down carriage that took me to the Savolta factory. I remember that the sad old cab from beyond the grave traced its way at an unalterably slow pace wading through pestilential quagmires and secret avenues. I remember that the air, corrupt from foul smoke, made my throat sore. I don't know what conclusions I drew or how much time passed. I only knew we reached an enormous building that looked like a metal circus, that the carriage left and I walked around trying to find the entrance. I saw Lepprince's red car next to a door and entered: it was a corridor illuminated by gas lamps. A night watchman stopped me, and I told him who I was and what I wanted. He had me cross a silent bay where there were some canvas cones scattered around, tarpaulins that covered, I supposed, the machines. When I passed through another little door, I felt the thickness of a rug under my feet. The guard said good-bye and disappeared. I walked along the carpeted corridor until I reached another, larger door made of wood. I pushed open the door and was instantly blinded by the light. I was in a brightly illuminated hall hung with pictures. In the center of the hall was a long table, much longer than the meeting table where Doloretas and I worked, and around the table were sitting some thirty people, half of whom looked like workers and the other half management. Among the executives, I recognized Lepprince; among the workers, Pajarito de Soto. The meeting was just ending when I arrived; spirits were running high. A thickset man sitting in the seat next to that of the man presiding over the meeting slapped the table, producing a dry sound, as if his hand were made of iron. Which is how I found out who he was. Savolta had to be the one presiding over the meeting. All of them were shouting, but above all the other voices Pajarito de Soto's rang out: he was insulting, accusing, threatening the executives and society in general. I understood what I already knew, what I had understood when Teresa told me where her husband was: that it had all been a fraud, that Lepprince had been playing with Pajarito de Soto for unknown reasons, and that Pajarito, at last, had seen through the trick and reacted with one of those violent fits that frightened Teresa so much. I also understood that if I had been there from the start nothing would have happened and that my betrayal therefore had been complete and irreversible. I understood nothing of what they were arguing about. I think the discussion phase had passed before I came. Confusion reigned until one of the workers begged Pajarito de Soto to be quiet and not to worsen the situation, that "he'd caused enough trouble for one day," that he let them resolve their problems on their own. Workers and executives booed Pajarito de Soto, who walked out of the room. Only Lepprince stayed calm and smiling. I followed my friend along corridors and through bays without catching up to him. I shouted, but it was useless, and all I managed to do was get lost. I sat down next to one of the canvas cones and began to cry. Lepprince's hand on my shoulder brought me back to reality. It was late, time to go, the assembly had been postponed. He drove me home. The next day, I didn't go to work; the following day was Sunday, and I stayed locked in, not even going out to eat. On Monday, I decided to face facts again. Pajarito de Soto had died on Saturday, as he was entering his house at dawn, half drunk. There was talk of an accident, of a crime, of two men cloaked in overcoats seen at midnight by someone who happened to mention it to a night watchman, of a mysterious letter that Pajarito de Soto was on his way to mail, that his wife and child had fled precipitously without leaving a forwarding address or any messages. The police questioned me. I told them I knew nothing, that I couldn't imagine what happened. I realized in my confusion that it would be useless to offer theories not based on facts. Nor was I certain that Lepprince was responsible for the death. Before saying anything, I had to make inquiries of my own. Of course, I made no effort to find Teresa. There was nothing more logical than her desire to lose sight of me forever. Besides, even supposing I did find her, that she forgave me and that we managed to erase those dramatic events from our memory, what could I offer her? I was just an underling whose only hope of subsistence rested with Lepprince.

Chapter 3

MARÍA ROSA SAVOLTA HESITATED at the door of the library and stared straight ahead as if the room were empty. Next to her, a shiny man and an old gentleman with a white beard were arguing.

"What I always say, Turull my friend," said the man with the white beard, "is that prices go up, consumption goes down; consumption goes down, sales go down; sales go down, prices go up. What do you call a situation like that?"

"A slaughter," said Turull.

"Before a year goes by," went on the old gentleman, "we'll all be in the poorhouse; and if not . . . time will tell. Do you know what they're saying in Madrid?"

"Tell me. You've got me on tenterhooks, as the expression goes."

The old man lowered his voice.

"That before spring García Prieto's cabinet will fall."

"Oh, yes . . . I see. So García Prieto has already formed a new government?"

"He formed it two months ago."

"Imagine that. But tell me, who is this García Prieto?"

"But my dear fellow, don't you read the newspapers?"

Two titanic hands seized María Rosa Savolta under her arms and lifted her bodily over everyone's head. The young woman was horrified.

"Just look who's come to see us, I'll be damned!" bellowed the author of the mischief. By his voice, María Rosa recognized Don Nicolás Claudedeu.

"Don't you remember me, you little rascal?"

"Of course I do, Uncle."

"You little sausage!" exclaimed Don Nicolás, depositing her once again on the floor. "Just a few years ago, you'd sit on my knees, and I'd have to play horsey for a whole hour. And now, just look: to hell with Uncle Nicolás!"

"Don't say that, Uncle Nicolás. I often think about you tenderly."

"Kick the old folks into the trash, go on confess. I know what you think about tenderly, hussy. With that face. My God, and those cute little titties."

"For the love of God, Uncle . . . ," begged the young woman.

Everyone looked on with a smile. Everyone except the elegant young man whose glance a few minutes earlier had surprised her and made her lower her eyes in a blush. With a glass in his hand, the elegant young man fell silent and meditated, leaning against the library doorway, dominating that room and the salon.

.....

THE OFFICE DOOR OPENED, and Doloretas and I pretended to be hard at work. Cortabanyes had to call us several times because we made believe we didn't notice his presence, as absorbed as we were in our work. He asked us to call in Serramadriles, who took a while to answer even though he must have been listening through the door of the storeroom. Standing before him, the three of us awaited the chief's words.

"Tomorrow is Christmas," said Cortabanyes, stopping to pant.

"Tomorrow is Christmas," he went on, "and I don't want to let the day pass without . . . uhhh . . . communicating my affection to you and . . . my appreciation. You have been loyal and . . . uhhh . . . efficient collaborators, without whom the smooth working of the . . . the office would not have been . . . umm . . . possible."

He paused and looked at us one at a time with his ironic little eyes.

"Nevertheless, it hasn't been a good year. . . . But we're not going to be discouraged, of course. We've survived, and so long as we stand firm in the . . . uhhh . . . breach, opportunity may walk through the door at any moment."

He pointed to the door, and we all turned to look at it.

"Let's think there's no doubt that . . . umm . . . next year will be better. The most important thing is . . . is . . . is work and interest. You're lucky . . . but only when you . . . Enough. Know something? I'm tired of talking. Take your envelopes."

He took three sealed envelopes with our names on them out of his pocket and handed one to Serramadriles, another to Doloretas, and another to me. We put them away without opening them, then smiled and said thank you. As he was leaving, I ran for his office.

"Mr. Cortabanyes, I'd like to speak to you. It's urgent."

He stared at me in surprise and then shrugged.

"All right, come in."

We walked into his office. He sat down and looked me up and down. I was standing in front of him. I put my hands on the desk and leaned forward.

"Mr. Cortabanyes, who killed Pajarito de Soto?"

Typescript of Notes Taken During the Third Statement Made by Javier Miranda Lugarte on January 12, 1927, to F. W. Davidson, Supreme Court Judge for the State of New York

(Folios 92 and following)

▪

English translation by court interpreter Guzmán Hernández de Fenwick

JUDGE DAVIDSON: In the reports concerning the death of Pajarito de Soto reference is made to the existence of a letter. Did you know that?

MIRANDA: Yes.
JUDGE: Did you know at the time about the letter?
MIRANDA: Yes.
JUDGE: Did Pajarito de Soto mention the existence of the letter to you before he died?
MIRANDA: No.
JUDGE: Then how did you come to know of its existence?
MIRANDA: Inspector Vázquez spoke to me about it.
JUDGE: I understand Inspector Vázquez is also dead.
MIRANDA: Yes.
JUDGE: Murdered?
MIRANDA: I think so.
JUDGE: Just think so?
MIRANDA: He died after I left Spain. I can only tell you what I was told and what I can conjecture.
JUDGE: According to your . . . conjectures, did the death of Inspector Vázquez have anything to do with the case under investigation, which is the object of this interrogation?
MIRANDA: I don't know.
JUDGE: Are you sure?
MIRANDA: I know nothing about Vázquez's death. Only what came out in the newspapers.
JUDGE: I think you do know something . . .
MIRANDA: No.
JUDGE: . . . that you're concealing evidence of interest to this court.
MIRANDA: I'm not.
JUDGE: Let me remind you, Mr. Miranda, that you can refuse to answer questions but that if you do answer, you are under oath, so your answers must be the truth and nothing but the truth.
MIRANDA: No one is more interested in clearing up this case than I am.
JUDGE: So you still say you know nothing of the circumstances surrounding Inspector Vázquez's death?
MIRANDA: That is correct.

.....

That I knew about the death of Domingo Pajarito de Soto immediately after it took place even if I took no direct part in clarifying the events. That the inspector in charge of the case closed the investigation, alleging that Pajarito died a natural death when his head struck the curb. That while the body showed signs of other contusions, they resulted from Pajarito's being struck down by an unidentified vehicle. That there was no evidence to support the conclusion that the acts leading to the deceased's death were intentional. That nothing is known with regard to the letter which is supposed to have disappeared. That after questioning the persons closest to the deceased, nothing could be deduced from their statements, there being no contradictions to support a change in the opinion of the agent who carried out the investigation. That the woman with whom Pajarito de Soto lived disappeared, her whereabouts remaining unknown. That later on I had the opportunity to review the case myself . . .

.....

"I think wanting to . . . investigate the case on your own is an insane idea," said Cortabanyes. "The police did . . . all they could. Or don't you think so? It's your affair, . . . my boy, your affair. I only . . . I'm telling you this for your own good. You're just wasting your time. And that's not . . . the worst of it: you young people don't have to be miserly . . . with time. The worst thing is that you'll get involved in . . . a mess and you won't . . . learn anything. People don't . . . like anyone sticking their nose into their . . . business, and they are perfectly right. Everyone . . . is jealous of his own tranquility . . . as he sees it. No one likes to have someone sniffing around between . . . his legs. I know perfectly well . . . I won't convince you. I haven't convinced anyone . . . for many years. . . . Just try to think that I'm not speaking in the name of . . . wisdom but in the name of the affection . . . I feel for you, my boy."

He spoke in short, quick phrases, as if he were afraid he'd use up all his breath and suffocate before finishing.

"I was young and hard-headed once. . . . I didn't like the

world, just as you don't . . . but I did nothing to change it, no . . . and I did nothing to conform to it, just as you don't . . . like everyone else. I started out as a secretary . . . to an old lawyer, who gave me . . . little work and little money and . . . no experience. Then . . . I met Lluïsa, who . . . who was to become my wife, and we . . . we got married. Poor Lluïsa . . . admired me and in . . . infused in me, out of love, a confidence . . . a confidence that a farseeing Providence had . . . denied me, rightly. Because of her, I set up on my own; it was an exciting . . . ad . . . adventure. The only adventure . . . We bought the furniture secondhand . . . and we hung a sign . . . a sign . . . on the door. . . . No one came . . . no one came and Lluïsa told me . . . not to get impatient, that soon a . . . a client would come and then the rest in . . . in a chain, but the first came . . . and I lost . . . lost the case, and he didn't pay me . . . and the rest didn't come. . . . That's how it went with everyone. . . . The first always . . . came, but . . . he didn't open the way . . . for a flood after him. We had no children, and Lluïsa died."

"Cortabanyes is a great man," Lepprince said on a certain occasion, "but he has one serious defect: he's sorry for himself, and that engenders in him a heroic modesty that makes him mock everything, beginning with himself. His sense of humor is blunt: it frightens people away instead of attracting them. He will never inspire confidence and only rarely affection. In life, be anything but a crybaby."

I asked him how he came to know Cortabanyes so well.

"I don't know him, but I do know his mask. Nature creates infinite human types, but man, from his origins, has only invented half a dozen."

.....

FROM THE LINDEN TREES on Rambla de Cataluña, there hung strings of lights that formed bows, crowns, stars, and other Christmas motifs. People discreetly left work in order to celebrate Christmas Eve at home. There were few cars on the streets, all leaving town. If Cortabanyes hadn't given me Lepprince's address, if something had interfered with my plans, I probably would have abandoned them. I didn't stop to think that, given what day it was, Lepprince would be eating in company or would have gone out, invited somewhere. In the courtyard of his building, a uniformed doorman with white muttonchop whiskers stopped me. I told him where I was going, and he asked me why.

"A friend of Lepprince," I answered.

He opened the doors of the elevator and pulled on the cable. As we went up, I saw him blow into a metal tube and talk to someone. He must have announced my visit, because a servant was waiting for me outside the gate of the elevator when it stopped on the fifth floor. He showed me into a sober foyer. There was a diffuse, balanced heat throughout the house, and the air was impregnated with Lepprince's cologne. The servant asked if I would be so kind as to wait for an instant or two. Alone in the warm, austere foyer, my spirits began to flag. I heard footsteps, and then Lepprince appeared. He was wearing an elegant dark suit, but he wasn't in evening clothes. Perhaps he wasn't intending to go out. He greeted me affably, unsurprised, and asked the reason for my unexpected presence.

"I should apologize for choosing such an inopportune moment and such an inappropriate date."

"To the contrary," he answered. "I'm always happy to be visited by friends. Don't just stand there: come in, or are you in a hurry? At least you'll have a drink with me, I hope."

He led me down a short corridor to a small sitting room in one corner of which some logs were burning in a fireplace. Over the mantle hung a picture. Lepprince informed me it was a genuine copy of a Monet. It represented a little wooden bridge covered with ivy over a brook covered with water lilies. The bridge linked two sides of a leafy forest, the brook curled through a tunnel of green. Lepprince pointed to a metal and glass cart on which there were various bottles and glasses. I accepted a cognac and a cigarette. Smoking and drinking and in a reverie brought on by the glowing coals in the fireplace, I felt sleepy and tired.

"Lepprince," I heard myself say, "who killed Pajarito de Soto?"

JUDGE DAVIDSON: I have here before me the statements you made to the police concerning the death of Domingo Pajarito de Soto. Do you recognize them?
MIRANDA: Yes.
JUDGE: Nothing has been added or taken away?
MIRANDA: I don't think so.
JUDGE: Aren't you sure?
MIRANDA: Yes, I'm sure.
JUDGE: I want to read you a passage. It says: "Asked if he suspected that the death of Pajarito de Soto could be the result of a criminal attack, the witness answered that he had no suspicions whatsoever. . . ." Is that paragraph correct?
MIRANDA: Yes.
JUDGE: And yet, you began investigating on your own to clear up the matter of your friend's death.
MIRANDA: Yes.
JUDGE: Did you lie to the police when you said you had "no suspicions whatsoever"?
MIRANDA: No, I didn't lie.
JUDGE: Explain yourself.
MIRANDA: I had no evidence that would have allowed me to affirm that the death of Pajarito de Soto was a deliberate act. That's why I told the police what you've read in the report.
JUDGE: Nevertheless, you did investigate. Why?
MIRANDA: I wanted to learn more about the circumstances surrounding his death.
JUDGE: I ask you again. Why?
MIRANDA: Suspicion is one thing and doubt is another.
JUDGE: Did you doubt that the death of Pajarito de Soto was accidental?
MIRANDA: Yes.

.....

"PEOPLE TOLD ME TO . . . appear important. . . . I didn't want to, I . . . the only thing I had . . . was to fail and to trick . . . poor Lluïsa. . . . But I did it. . . . I tried to look important but . . . nothing happened; it was a . . . comedy show . . . a grotesque . . . I made clients . . . wait for hours . . . as if I were very busy. . . . They left without even waiting a few minutes. . . . I don't know . . . don't know why they didn't fall . . . into the importance trap. Other lawyers . . . do the same thing and it works. . . . I tried other tricks . . . with the same results . . . but I had no reason to go on . . . after poor Lluïsa . . . passed away. I did it to . . . prove that her confidence . . . her confidence in me was justified and that . . . if she had lived, I . . . would have given her everything . . . she deserved. But life . . . life is a merry-go-round that goes round and round . . . and round until you get dizzy and then . . . and then . . . it stops at the same spot where you . . . got on. . . . In all these years, I never . . ."

.....

HE TOOK A FEW PUFFS on his cigar before he spoke, and when he did, he adopted a reiterative, didactic tone. He gestured little, underlining a phrase or important fact or the end of a particularly tragic paragraph with his index finger. But he revealed a profound knowledge of the matter and a more than ordinary memory for dates, names, and statistics: Inspector Vázquez.

"During the second half of the last century," he said, "the anarchist theories that proliferated all over Europe entered Spain. And they caught on like fire in a leaf pile; let's see why. There are two centers of contamination to be mentioned: rural Andalusia and Barcelona. In rural Andalusia, the theories were transmitted in a primitive way: pseudo-holy men, more or less insane, wandered the region, from large estates to towns and from towns to large estates, preaching these terrible ideas. The ignorant peasants took these preachers in, gave them food and clothing. Many of them were seduced by the chatter of those peddlers of holiness. That's what it was: a new religion. Or to be more accurate, since we're educated men, a new superstition. In Barcelona, it was just the opposite. The preaching took on a political and openly subversive tone from the beginning."

"But we know all that, Inspector," interrupted Lepprince.

"Possibly," said Inspector Vázquez, "but for the purposes of my explanation, we have to have certain information in common, without ambiguities."

He coughed, rested his cigar on the edge of the ashtray, and concentrated again, rolling up his eyes.

"Now then," he went on, "it is essential to make a basic distinction. Which is that in Cataluña there is a clear mixture which should not fool us. On the one hand, we have the theoretical anarchist, even the fanatic, who functions for subversive motives of obvious origin who, we could say, is autochthonous."

He looked at us through his half-closed eyelids, as if asking us and himself if we had assimilated his terminological contribution.

"These are the famous Paulino Pallás, Santiago Salvador, Ramón Sempau, Francisco Ferrer Guardia, among others, and, in our own times, Angel Pestaña, Salvador Seguí, Andrés Nin . . . as many as you'd care to imagine."

"Then come the others, the rank and file . . . do you understand what I mean? The rank and file. It's made up in the main of immigrants from other regions who've recently arrived. You know how these people get here: one day they throw away their farm implements, hang onto the top of a train, and get off here in Barcelona. They come without money, without guaranteed jobs, without knowing anyone. Easy prey for any confidence man. In a few days, they're dying of hunger, disillusioned. They thought that as soon as they got here their problems would be solved by magic, and when they understand that reality is not what they dreamed, they blame everything and everybody except themselves. They see people who have managed to make their way in the world by their own efforts and view their success as an injustice directed expressly against them. For a few reals, for a piece of bread, or for nothing they would do anything. Those that have wives and children or have reached a certain age are more compliant, reconsider what's happened, and take things calmly, but the young ones, if you follow me, usually adopt violent, antisocial attitudes. They group together with others of the same ilk and circumstances, hold meetings in dives or in the open air, then harangue and excite each other. The criminal element takes advantage of them for its own ends: tricks them, confuses them, and plants false hopes in their hearts. One fine day, they commit a crime. They have no relationship with the victim; in many cases they don't even know the person. They obey orders given by those who stay in the shadows. Then, if they fall into our hands, no one speaks for them, we don't know where they come from, they don't work anywhere, and, if they can speak, they don't know what they've done, nor to whom, nor why. They don't even know the name of the person who pushed them into it. You can understand, Mr. Lepprince, that with things as they are . . ."

"Your job is not easy," said Lepprince. "I understand perfectly well, but what news is there of the case that concerns us?"

.....

I REMEMBER THAT AFTERNOON. Pajarito de Soto met me as I left the office. Doloretas and Serramadriles waved to us from a distance and then went to take the trolley. Pajarito de Soto was shivering with cold, his hands in his pockets, wearing his checkered cap and his gray scarf with the threadbare fringe. He wore no overcoat because he had none. Not two hours before, I dropped Teresa off at her house. Life was a mad merry-go-round, as Cortabanyes was fond of saying. We walked along Gran Vía chatting and sat down in the Queen Victoria Eugenia gardens. Pajarito de Soto spoke to me about the anarchists, and I answered by saying I knew nothing about them.

"Does the subject interest you?"

"Yes, of course," I said, more to please him than because I meant it.

"In that case, come with me. I'll bring you to an interesting place."

"Listen, it won't be dangerous, will it?" I exclaimed in alarm.

"Don't be afraid, come on."

We got up and walked down Gran Vía and across Aribau street. Pajarito led me into a bookstore. It was empty except for a young salesgirl reading a book behind the counter. We walked by her without saying hello and passed through a space between two bookcases. The storeroom contained more cases filled with old, unbound, yellowed books. In the middle of the room, there was a semicircle of chairs around an armchair. An old man with a long gray beard was sitting in the armchair and speaking. He was wearing a well-worn black suit covered with stains and shiny at the elbows and knees. On the semicircle of chairs were seated men of all ages, of modest means (judging by their appearance), and a mature woman with reddish hair and pale skin covered with freckles. Pajarito de Soto and I stood behind the chairs and listened to the old man's talk.

"I didn't think," he was saying, "and I must confess my mistake in this, that the subject of my lecture the day before yesterday would inspire so many polemics and so many counterstatements here and elsewhere. It was a subject I wanted to develop, but almost as a family matter, something intimate, something internal, not a matter of Party policy but something that involves all of us who have closely followed our position and who could, at any given moment, share the concerns and orientations of the Party. Perhaps you might say, or someone might say, elsewhere, that the interest aroused by my talk, quite deficient in itself, proves my mistake in an irrefutable manner. I don't see it that way, although I declare I am ready to recognize my mistakes, which, no doubt, were innumerable, and if I do speak in a tone that someone might term pretentious, it's only out of the conviction that bringing into the light the essential themes of anarchism is much more beneficial than the mistakes that I might make in the process of my assertions which are daring—I don't deny it—but charged with honest intentions."

.....

LEPPRINCE, WITH A GLASS IN HIS HAND, fell silent and stared, his back against the jamb of the library door, dominating it and the main salon. The guests had overflowed the salon, and voices and laughter resounded in the vestibule. Servants pushed open the wooden panels that separated the two rooms, thus forming one huge space. Lights were brought into the vestibule.

"There must be at least two hundred people here, don't you think?" said Lepprince.

"Yes, at least that."

"There exists an art," he continued, "although it may actually be a science, which is called 'selective perception.' Ever heard of it?"

"No."

"It consists in seeing, among myriad things, those that interest you. Understand?"

"By an act of will?"

"Consciously and instinctively, in equal doses. I would call it an ambiguous perceptive sense. For example, take a quick look over there and tell me who you've seen: the first you can think of."

"Claudedeu."

"Now you see: all things being equal, he was the first. Why? Because of his size, which indicates the participation of the visual sense. But only because of it? No, there's something more. You've been behind him for a long time, isn't that so?"

"There's something in what you say," I answered.

"Perhaps you don't believe the legend."

"Of the Man with the Iron Hand?"

"The nickname is part of the legend."

"Perhaps the facts are also part, and in that case . . ."

"Let's go on with the perception experiment," said Lepprince.

JUDGE DAVIDSON: During yesterday's session, you admitted you carried out an investigation of your own. Will you confirm that?

MIRANDA: Yes.

JUDGE: Describe the nature of that investigation.

MIRANDA: I went to see Lepprince . . .

JUDGE: At his home?

MIRANDA: Yes.

JUDGE: Where did Lepprince live?
MIRANDA: On Rambla de Cataluña, number two, fifth floor.
JUDGE: What was the date, approximately, on which you went to see him?
MIRANDA: It was December 24, 1917.
JUDGE: How can you remember the date so precisely?
MIRANDA: It was Christmas Eve.
JUDGE: Did Lepprince receive you?
MIRANDA: Yes.
JUDGE: What did you do then?
MIRANDA: I asked him who killed Pajarito de Soto.
JUDGE: Did he tell you?
MIRANDA: No.
JUDGE: Did you find out anything?
MIRANDA: Nothing concrete.
JUDGE: Did Lepprince reveal anything you didn't know and which you deem relevant to these proceedings?
MIRANDA: No . . . that is, yes.
JUDGE: Which is it?
MIRANDA: There was one marginal bit of information.
JUDGE: What was it?
MIRANDA: I didn't know that Lepprince was María Coral's lover.

.....

"SHE WAS SOFT, FRAGILE, and as sensual as a cat; and just as capricious, egoistic, and disconcerting. I don't know why I did it, what impelled me to commit such a folly. I felt dominated by her from the first moment I saw her in that cabaret, remember? She absorbed my will. I watched her move, sit, and walk, and I lost control of myself. When she caressed me, I'd have given her everything I owned if she'd asked me for it. She knew it and abused her power; she waited before giving herself to me . . . do you understand what I mean? And when she did, it was worse. I told you just now, she was like a cat playing with a mouse. She never gave herself completely. She always seemed on the verge of interrupting . . . anything and disappearing once and for all."

"Which is what she did, right?"

"No. I told her to go away. I threw her out. I was afraid of her. . . . I don't know if I'm being clear. A man like me, in my position . . ."

"Did she live in this house?"

"Practically. I made her leave the two bullies she performed with and installed her in a little hotel. But she wanted to come here. I don't know how she found out my address. She would appear at the most unexpected moments: when I was busy with a visitor, when I had very important guests. A scandal, you can just imagine. She would spend the whole day . . . No, what am I saying? Days at a time! There in that armchair where you are right now. She would smoke, sleep, read picture magazines, and eat continuously. Then, suddenly, even if I needed her, she would go out, on the pretext that she needed exercise. She wouldn't be back for two, three, or four days at a time. I was afraid for her and wanted her never to come back, both things at the same time. I suffered a lot. Until one day, last week, I got up my courage and returned her to where I found her: the street."

"Do you regret your decision?"

"No, but I'm sad and alone since she's gone. That's why you found me here at home, because I didn't want to accept any invitations or see anyone I knew tonight."

"In that case, it would be better if I left."

"No, for God's sake, you're a different matter. I'm happy you've come. In a way, for me you belong to her world. Your image and hers are united in my memory. You dealt with her, were an intermediary. One night you brought two envelopes instead of one, remember? In the second there was a letter in which I told her I had to see her and that she should come to a certain place at a certain time."

"Right. I noticed that there was an illogical redundancy. And that the other letter had a strange effect on her."

Lepprince remained silent, his eyes fixed on the smoke from his cigarette, which swirled up thickly in the warm air of the little salon.

"Won't you stay to dinner? I need to have a friend around," he said, almost in a whisper.

JUDGE DAVIDSON: Isn't it strange that a man investigating the death of his friend would accept a dinner invitation from the man he suspects of being the murderer?
MIRANDA: It isn't always easy to explain the things that happen in life.
JUDGE: I'd like you to make an effort.
MIRANDA: Pajarito de Soto inspired feelings of affection in me, and Lepprince . . . I don't know how to put it . . .
JUDGE: Admiration?
MIRANDA: I don't know . . . I don't know.
JUDGE: Envy perhaps?
MIRANDA: I would call it . . . fascination.
JUDGE: You were fascinated by Lepprince's wealth?
MIRANDA: Not only that.
JUDGE: His social position?
MIRANDA: Yes, that too.
JUDGE: His elegance? His polite manners?
MIRANDA: His personality in general. His culture, his taste, his language, his conversation.
JUDGE: And yet, you've depicted him in earlier sessions as a frivolous, ambitious man insensible to everything unrelated to the progress of his business, and egocentric to the highest degree.
MIRANDA: I believed that at first.
JUDGE: When did you change your opinion?
MIRANDA: That night, over the course of our conversation.
JUDGE: What did you talk about?
MIRANDA: Lots of things.
JUDGE: Try to remember them. Be specific.

.....

IS THERE ANYONE WHO MIGHT CARE to listen to me with other ears than those of cold reason? I know, I know. For the sake of my own dignity, I should have rejected the flattery of those who directly or indirectly provoked the death of Pajarito de Soto. But I couldn't pay the price of that dignity. When you live in a crowded, hostile city, when you've got no friends and no means to make them, when you're poor and live terrified and insecure, sick and tired of talking with your own shadow, when you eat your dinner in five minutes, in silence, rolling the bread into little pellets, when you leave the restaurant right after you've swallowed the last mouthful, when you wish Sunday would just be over and done with so the workweek would return along with known faces, when you smile at your co-workers and amuse them for a few seconds with an improvised, futile commentary of no importance, when you're in that kind of a situation, you'd sell yourself for a dish of lentils seasoned with half an hour's worth of conversation. The Catalans are very clannish, Barcelona is a closed community, Lepprince and I were foreigners, to one degree or another, and both of us were young. Besides, with him I felt protected: by his intelligence, by his experience, by his money, and by his privileged situation. There was nothing like camaraderie between us. It was years before I could deal informally with him, and when I began speaking familiarly to him it was because he ordered me to and because events, as we shall see, required it. And our talks never turned into impassioned polemics, as they had with Pajarito de Soto almost as soon as we met: those heated discussions that now in my memory grow in importance and become the nostalgic symbol of my life in Barcelona. With Lepprince, conversation was slow and intimate, a soothing exchange, not a constructive fight. Lepprince listened and understood, and I appreciated that quality above all. It isn't easy to find someone who knows how to listen and understand. Even Serramadriles, who could have been a perfect companion for me, was too simple, too empty: a good pal for a night on the town, but a terrible conversationalist. Once I heard him say, apropos of the labor problem:

"The workers only know how to have strikes and plant bombs, and they still want us to think they're right!"

From that moment on, I never expressed my opinions in his

presence. On the other hand, Lepprince, despite being more compromised than Serramadriles, was more thoughtful in reaching conclusions. Once, chatting about the same subject, he said to me:

"A strike is an assault on work, man's fundamental function on earth, as well as a damage to society. Nevertheless, many people think it a means to struggle for progress."

And he added:

"What strange elements interfere in the relationship between men and things?"

Naturally, he did not sympathize with the proletarian movements or with any other subversive workers' theories, but, as far as the revolutionary point of view was concerned, he had a wider, more comprehensive vision than others of his class.

"In this modern world in which it has fallen to us to live, where human acts have become those of the mob, as have work, art, living, even war, and where each individual is a small part in a gigantic mechanism whose meaning and functioning we do not understand, what reason can there be for codes of conduct?"

He was an individualist, 100 percent, and allowed that others also were and that they should try to achieve it by all the means available to them and to the maximum degree. He made no concessions to anyone who got in his way, but he did not despise the enemy or see in him the personification of evil. Nor did he invoke sacred rights or immovable principles to justify his actions.

With regard to Pajarito de Soto, he recognized that he'd falsified the memorandum. He admitted it with the greatest naturalness.

"Why did you hire him if you intended to trick him later?" I asked.

"It's a common occurrence. I had no a priori intention to trick Pajarito de Soto. No one pays for a job in order to falsify it and anger its author. I thought that perhaps it would be useful to us. Then I saw it wasn't and I changed it. Once I'd paid for it, the memorandum was mine, and I could use it for whatever purpose I saw fit, isn't that so? That's how it's always been. Your friend thought he was an artist, but he was nothing more than an employee. Despite all that, I confess that I feel a certain sympathy for these novelistic characters: they aren't bright, but they're filled with fancy. Sometimes I envy them: they squeeze more juice out of life."

And with regard to the death of my friend:

"I of course did not do it. And I don't think the idea came either from Savolta or Claudedeu. Savolta's too old for that sort of thing and doesn't want complications—he practically takes no part in administering . . . business. He's a figurehead. As for Claudedeu, despite his legend, he's a good man, a bit crude in his way of doing things and in his thinking, but he doesn't lack common sense. Pajarito's death brought us no benefits. Actually it's causing us myriad problems. And that's not even taking into account the bad atmosphere it's created for us among the workers. In any case, if we'd wanted to ruin his reputation, we could have done it through a lawsuit, given the libels in his articles. He couldn't have afforded a lawyer and would have ended up in jail."

One day we were gossiping, and it occurred to me to ask:

"How did Claudedeu lose his hand?"

Lepprince burst into laughter.

"He was in the Lyceum the day Santiago Salvador threw the bombs. The shrapnel sliced his hand off as if he were a clay doll. You can understand that he isn't fond of anarchists. Ask him to tell you about it. It'll be his pleasure. No, he'll do it even if you don't ask him. He'll tell you that his wife hasn't wanted to set foot inside the Lyceum since that tragic night, and how that more than makes up for his lost hand. He says he would have given up his entire arm not to have to put up with more operas."

About the current state of Spanish politics he also had clear ideas:

"There's no way out for this country, even if it isn't right for me to say so, being a foreigner. There are two major parties, in the classic sense of the word, conservatives and liberals, both of which support the monarchy and both of which take turns at being in power with skillful regularity. Neither party seems to have a well-defined program, just some vague general concepts. And even that handful of ambiguities, which constitutes their ideological skeleton, changes as conditions and opportunities change. I would say that both limit themselves to supplying concrete solutions to problems they raise, problems they suffocate, once they're in power, without really solving them. After a few years or months, the old problem breaks through the improvised solution they've provided and causes a crisis. Then the party out of power takes the place of the party that took its place. And for the same reason. I don't know of a single government that has solved a serious problem: they always fall, but it doesn't worry them because their successors will also fall.

"As for politicians: Cánovas del Castillo and Sagasta are gone, and no one's come to take their place. Among the conservatives, Maura is the only one with enough intelligence and personal charisma to discipline his party and drag public opinion along behind him, at least in sentimental terms. But his pride knows no limits, and his pigheadedness blinds him. Over time, he creates internal dissension and angers the people. As for Dato, the party's replacement, he lacks the necessary energy and deserves the nickname Maura's most indignant followers have given him, the Vaseline Man.

"The liberals have no one. Canalejas burned himself out making solemn promises that fooled everyone until an anarchist blew his brains out while he was looking in the window of a bookstore. The liberals, in sum, maintain themselves with their only trump card, anticlericalism, which wins them popular support, which is easy, useless, and short-lived. The conservatives, on the other hand, try to look like devout churchgoers. Both parties play on the lowest instincts of the people: the conservatives, Catholic sentimentality, the liberals, anarchic libertinism.

"Within the parties, there is no discipline whatsoever. Party members fight among themselves, they trip each other up and try to defame each other in an insane struggle for power that ruins all of them and benefits none of them.

"These two parties, which lack both the support of the people and the moderate middle classes, are doomed to failure and will lead the nation to ruin."

I told Lepprince about my solitary life, my projects, and my illusions.

.....

I NUDGED PAJARITO DE SOTO and we stepped back into a corner of the bookstore.

"Who's that?" I whispered.

"Master Rocca, a schoolmaster. He teaches geography, history, and French. He lives alone and dedicates his existence to the propagation of the Idea. When he finishes his work at school, he comes to this store and lectures about anarchism and the anarchists. At nine on the dot, he leaves, prepares his dinner himself, and goes to bed."

"What a sad life!" I said, without being able to avoid a shudder.

"He's an apostle. There are many like him. Let's get closer."

Master Rocca was one of the few anarchists I managed to see before the violent eruption of 1919. Anarchism was one thing, and the anarchists something quite different. We lived immersed in anarchism, but we had no contact with anarchists. In those days, and for quite a few years after, I had a very picturesque vision of the anarchists: bearded men, frowning and serious, wearing a sash, a worker's blouse and cap, born for silent waiting behind a barricade of broken furniture, behind the bars of a cell in Montjuïc jail, on the dark corners of twisted streets, in the slums, waiting for their time to come, for good or ill, when the bony wing of a gigantic, cold bat would brush the city; men who hid, exploded with fury, and were executed at dawn.

POLICE SHEET ON ANDRÉS NIN PÉREZ, SPANISH REVOLUTIONARY SUSPECTED OF HAVING DIRECT OR INDIRECT RELATION TO THE CASE CONTAINED IN THIS DOSSIER

Entered as Evidence: Document No. 3i

▪

English translation by court interpreter Guzmán Hernández de Fenwick

ON THE UPPER LEFT- AND RIGHT-HAND CORNERS of the sheet are photographs of the individual described in the sheet. The two photographs are almost identical. In both, the individual faces front. The photo on the left shows him bareheaded, the one on the right shows him wearing a wide-brimmed hat. His tie and shirt are identical, and the expression and shading are so alike they make the viewer think that in fact they are the same photo, the hat merely being the retouching of a skillful photographer. A more detailed examination reveals that in the second photo (the one on the right), the individual wears an overcoat, difficult to distinguish from the jacket he wears in the first photograph (on the left) because both the color and the lapels (the only visible part of both items of clothing) are very similar. Possibly these are two photographs taken on the same day in the same place (almost certainly a police station). In which case, they would have had the individual put on his hat and coat in order to identify him more easily on the street. The individual is a young man, thin, with a longish face, angular, prominent chin, aquiline nose, dark, squinting eyes (probably myopic), black, straight hair. He wears oval, rimless glasses, with flexible arms.

(Facts supplied by the Department of Photographic Analysis of the Federal Bureau of Investigation, Washington, D.C.)

The attached sheet says:

Andrés NIN Pérez
Dangerous Propagandist

Schoolmaster

Born in Tarragona in 1890

He was a member of the Socialist Youth of Barcelona, which he left to join the Syndicalists, being, with Antonio Amador Obón and others, founding members of the First Syndicate of the Liberal Professions.

He was a delegate to the Second Syndicalist Congress held in Madrid, December, 1919.

He was arrested on January 12, 1920, in the Catalan Republican Center on Peu de la Creu street during a clandestine meeting of delegates of the Executive Committee, whose purpose it was to foment a general, revolutionary strike. He was held in the castle of Montjuïc.

Released on June 29, 1920.

In March of 1921, Evelio Boal López was arrested and Nin became secretary general of the National Confederation of Labor. However, because of being pursued by the Barcelona police, he fled to Berlin, where he was arrested by the German police in October of the same year.

.....

"Let's go on with the perception experiment," said Lepprince.

He had invited me to the New Year's Eve party held, as was customary, in the Savolta mansion in Sarriá.

I met Lepprince at his house. He had just finished dressing, and when I saw him I understood what Cortabanyes meant when he declared that the rich belonged to a different world, and that we would never look like them, never understand them, and never be able to imitate them.

Lepprince warned me that the entire board of directors of the Savolta company would be at the party:

"So don't annoy them with the story about Pajarito de Soto's death," he teasingly chided me.

I promised to behave properly. Lepprince drove us to Savolta's house in his car. He then introduced me to Savolta, whom I already knew by sight, having seen him at the factory when I went looking for Pajarito de Soto. He was a man of a certain age, but not old. Nevertheless, he had a wan look, bad color, and trembling voice and gestures. I imagined some disease was eating away at him. Claudedeu, on the other hand, overflowed with vitality; his deep voice echoed everywhere, and his body, like that of the giant in children's stories, was ubiquitous. He had the gift of a contagious laugh. I took careful note of his gloved hand and of the metallic noise it made when it struck objects. Then the image of an angry Claudedeu insulting Pajarito de Soto and pounding the table came back to me. I also recognized Parells, who on that fateful night was sitting near Savolta. I was struck by the expression of intelligence that emanated not only from his eyes but from every detail of his old lady's face. Lepprince had told me that he was the company's chief accountant and financial manager. His father had been shot by the reactionary Carlists in Lérida during the civil wars, and Pere Parells had inherited from him a deep devotion to liberalism. He bragged of being a freethinker and an atheist, but every Sunday he accompanied his wife to Mass because "by marrying me, she acquired the social right to be accompanied." I would add that the wives of these gentlemen, and of others to whom I was introduced, all seemed cut from the same pattern, and that no sooner had I given their hands a perfunctory kiss than I mixed up their names and faces.

The first half of the party took place under the sign of tranquil gossip. The men smoked in the library; their remarks were short, biting, and they laughed at hidden meanings and malicious allusions. In the salon, the women commented on events with a grave and pessimistic air; they barely ever laughed, and their conversation was composed of alternating monologues to which the listeners assented with affirmative gestures and other monologues that corroborated or repeated what had already been said. Some young men attended the chorus of women. They too adopted a circumspect air and limited themselves to showing conformity or agreement without speaking.

In a corner, I spied a pretty girl, the only young woman at the party, talking with Cortabanyes. Later we were introduced, and I found out she was Savolta's daughter, that she was at boarding school, and that she had come to Barcelona to spend the Christmas holidays with her parents. She seemed timid and confessed her fervent desire to return to the nuns, whom she loved so much. She asked just what I was, and Cortabanyes said:

"A young and valuable lawyer."

"Do you work with him?" she asked, pointing to my boss.

"I am at his orders, to be precise," I answered.

"You're lucky. There's no one better than Mr. Cortabanyes, isn't that so?"

"That is so," I answered with a note of sarcasm.

"And that gentleman who was speaking with you, who was he?"

"Lepprince? Haven't you been introduced? Come with me, he's one of your father's partners."

"He's already a partner, and so young?" She blushed intensely.

I introduced Lepprince to María Rosa Savolta because I intuited her desire to meet him. When they'd exchanged formalities, I excused myself, a bit annoyed at the obvious preferences of the tycoon's daughter and a bit fed up at playing the marionette.

JUDGE DAVIDSON: Give us a general description of Mr. Savolta's house.

MIRANDA: It was in the neighborhood called Sarriá. On a hill that dominated Barcelona and the sea. The houses were of the kind we call a "tower," that is, a structure of one or two stories surrounded by a garden.

JUDGE: Where was the party held?

MIRANDA: On the ground floor.

JUDGE: Did all the rooms on the ground floor have windows or doors which opened to the outside?

MIRANDA: All the rooms I saw did.

JUDGE: Did they open to the garden or the street?

MIRANDA: To the garden. The house was right in the center of the garden. To get to the door, it was necessary to cross a piece of the garden.

JUDGE: The door led directly to the salon?

MIRANDA: Yes and no. When you entered, you were in a foyer in which there was a stairway that led to the second floor. Sliding open some wooden panels made the salon and this foyer into one room.

JUDGE: Had those panels been opened?

MIRANDA: Yes. They were opened shortly before midnight in order to make space for the growing number of guests.

JUDGE: Now describe the layout of the library.

MIRANDA: The library was a separate room. It could be entered from the salon but not from the foyer.

JUDGE: What was the distance between the library and the stairs in the foyer?

MIRANDA: I would say twelve meters . . . approximately forty feet.

JUDGE: Where were you when the shots were fired?

MIRANDA: Next to the library door.

JUDGE: In the library?

MIRANDA: No, outside, that is, in the salon.

JUDGE: Was Lepprince with you?

MIRANDA: No.

JUDGE: But you could see him from where you stood?

MIRANDA: No. He was right behind me.

JUDGE: Inside the library?

MIRANDA: Yes.

.....

LEPPRINCE AND THE TYCOON'S DAUGHTER had been chatting for half an hour. I was getting impatient because I wanted him to leave her once and for all so we could resume our conversation. But Lepprince wouldn't stop saying things to her and smiling like a robot. And she listened in a rapture, smiling. The two of them made me nervous, looking at each other and smiling as if they were posing for a photograph, each one holding a little bag of grapes and a glass of champagne.

.....

THAT I DID NOT PERSONALLY ATTEND the party. That I became aware of the events a few moments after they took place, and that a half hour later, I was present at the residence of Mr. Savolta. That according to what I was told, no one had left the house after the events, except the person or persons who had fired the shots. That they were fired from the garden, rifle shots. That the shots broke the salon windows, at the angle where the salon meets the door to the library . . .

JUDGE DAVIDSON: Are you sure the shots came from the garden and not from the library?
MIRANDA: Yes.
JUDGE: Nevertheless, you were equidistant between those two points.
MIRANDA: Yes.
JUDGE: With your back turned to the place the shots came from.
MIRANDA: Yes.
JUDGE: Would you repeat your description of the house?
MIRANDA: I just described it. You can read it in the typescript.
JUDGE: I know that. What I want you to do is repeat the description to see if you contradict yourself.
MIRANDA: The house was located in the residential area of Sarriá, surrounded by a garden. To enter, it was necessary to cross a piece . . .

.....

AT MIDNIGHT, Savolta walked up the foyer steps and called for silence. The servants lowered the lights, except the ones focused directly on the tycoon. With no other place to look, the guests concentrated their attention on Savolta.

"Dear friends, once again I have the pleasure of seeing all of you gathered in our house. Within a few minutes, the year 1917 will cease to exist, and a new year will begin. The pleasure of being with you in these memorable instants . . ."

Then, or perhaps just after, the shots began. When he was saying something or other about the change of the year and how we would all be crossing the bridge together.

AT FIRST, THERE WAS ONLY A SINGLE GUNSHOT

At first there was only a gun shot and a noise of broken glass. Then shouts and another shot. I heard the bullets whistle over my head, but I didn't move, paralyzed as I was by shock. Some of the guests crouched down, flattened out on the floor, or hid behind anyone nearby. Everything happened so quickly, I don't remember how many shots came after. I think I saw Lepprince and María Rosa Savolta facedown on the floor, and I thought they'd been killed. And I saw Claudedeu shouting that the lights be put out and for everyone to seek cover. There were people shouting, "Light! Light!" and others screaming as if they'd been wounded. The shooting stopped instantly.

IT HAD ONLY GONE ON FOR AN INSTANT

It had only gone on for an instant. On the other hand, the shouting did go on and the darkness as well. Finally, seeing that there were no more shots, a servant threw the master switch and the lights went on, blinding everyone. Around me there was weeping and hysteria: some were saying that the police had to be called, others were saying that the doors and windows should be closed, but no one moved. The majority of the guests remained on the floor, but they didn't seem wounded because they were looking around with their eyes wide open. Then a heartbreaking shriek rang out behind me, and it was María Savolta who called to her father in this way: "Papa!" And we all saw the dead tycoon. The banisters of the stairway were broken into pieces, the rug was turned to dust, and the marble stairs, pocked with bullet holes, looked as though they were made of sand.

.....

MASTER ROCA COUGHED and said in a tremulous, deliberate voice:

"And so I settled, as you may recall, on what I, perhaps without foreseeing the consequences, called 'the death and legacy of Anarchism,' an expression that provoked, it seems, a scandal in many followers of the Idea and inspired personal attacks on me, which have not pained me, because they contained more devotion to the Idea than rancor toward its apparent detractors. Nevertheless, the interest and the polemic have nothing to do with the 'death' or 'life' of the theme being debated. In Italy during the fifteenth century, impassioned interest and fruitful polemics took place about the classical culture of Greece and Rome, but, tell me, did that culture revive because of all that interest and discussion? You will probably object that those cultures were alive because they stimulated a 'lively' interest, and that only their sources were dead. But in reality, what is now taking place is that it is becoming difficult for us mortals to understand the true meaning of the word *death* and even more difficult to understand its reality, the essential fact that constitutes it.

"Allow me, then, to clarify my point of view, without arrogance, but firmly: anarchism has died, just as the seed dies. What remains to be seen is whether it has withered in sterile soil or if, as in the evangelical parable, it has become a flower, a fruit, a tree—whether it has become new seeds. And I affirm—please pardon me for being so categorical, but I think it necessary if we are not to fall into a polite, empty salon discussion—I affirm, I say, that every political, social, and philosophical idea dies as soon as it comes to light and transforms itself, like a chrysalis, into action. That is the mission of the idea: to bring about events, transform itself (and that is the source of its grandeur) from the ethereal field of disembodied thought to the field of the material; to move mountains, as it says in the Bible, that beautiful but so badly used book. And for that reason, because the idea becomes an action and actions change the course of History, ideas must die and be reborn, not remain petrified, fossils, saved like museum pieces, like beautiful ornaments, if you like, but only useful for the glory of the erudite and for subtle, imaginative critics.

"That is the truth, I say it without boasting, and the truth is a scandal. It's like the light which hurts the eyes of those who habitually live in darkness. And that is my message, my friends. That you should leave here thinking, not about the idea, but the action. Infinite action, without limits, without hindrances or goals. Ideas are the past, action is the future, the new, that which is to come, hope, happiness."

Chapter 4

Worn away by time, my memories of that period have become uniform and have turned into details of a single picture. The impression each produced in me when it took place, its rough edges smoothed by the sandpaper of new suffering, blends with the other images, happy or tragic, to form a single, featureless plane. Like a languid dance looked at in the depth of a nineteenth-century provincial mirror, my memories acquire an aura of sanctity that transfigures and blurs them.

The house was closed, and at the door a servant kept all visitors out. We waited outside, clustered in the forward part of the garden. Occasionally we would see silhouettes walking by a window. On the other side of the wall separating the garden from the street, a crowd had gathered to pay its last homage to the tycoon. The dry cold and the luminous, serene air enabled the distant peal of bells to reach us cleanly. It was possible to hear the horses snort and the sounds of their hooves on the street. The door of the house opened. The servant stepped aside and allowed a canon dressed in funerary raiment to walk out. Two altar boys appeared and ran to line up. The first carried a long pole capped with a metal crucifix. The second balanced an incensory from which flowed perfumed spirals of smoke. The canon had his eyes fixed on his missal and intoned a sacred canticle which was chorused from within the house by deep voices. The procession began; behind the canon marched four priests, two by two. Then came the mace bearers from the town council wearing their medieval costumes, their wigs, and carrying their golden spool-shaped clubs. Finally came the coffin in which Savolta reposed, festooned and draped with brocades. Lepprince, Claudedeu, Parells, and three other men whose names I didn't know carried it. On the little balcony on the second floor we could see Mrs. Savolta, other ladies, and María Rosa Savolta wearing mourning, holding little handkerchiefs that quickly traveled to their eyes to absorb a tear shed for the tycoon.

Behind the coffin marched an unknown man wearing a long black overcoat and a bowler of the same color from under which fell blond, almost albino, curls. He had his hands sunk in his pockets and twisted his head from one side to the other, staring at all those present with blue eyes that stood out from his face, which was as white as wax.

.....

INSPECTOR VÁZQUEZ entered his office. His secretary tossed some papers on his desk to cover up the newspaper he'd been reading. "Who told you to try to pull a fast one?" grunted Inspector Vázquez. "Go on reading your paper and cut the crap."

"Don Severiano called. I told him that you were out of the office on business, and he said he'd call back."

"Did he call from Barcelona?"

"No, sir. Some girl, or the operator, maybe—she didn't mention her name—made the connection from someplace whose name I didn't catch. You couldn't hear a thing."

Inspector Vázquez hung his overcoat on a grimy rack and sat down in his sticky swivel chair.

"Give me a cigarette. Any other news?"

"A man wants to see you. Doesn't seem like one of the usual types."

"What does he want? Who is he?"

"He wants to talk to you. Won't say what it's about. His name is Nemesio Cabra Gómez."

"Fine. We'll let him wait for a while, just to give him a chance to shorten his speech. Are you going to give me a cigarette or not?"

The secretary got up from his table.

"Keep the pack. I've got a fresh one in my coat pocket, and besides, I shouldn't smoke so much, with my bronchitis."

.....

THE CROWD THAT COVERED THE SIDEWALKS and the roadway, and which had climbed the trees, lampposts and the gates outside houses, gave a muffled wail when the coffin appeared. Above the bare heads, the scattered police horses stood out. Sabers unsheathed, the mounted police maintained order. Every social class was represented in the crowd: men of rank wearing black suits with brand-new vests, military men in full dress, ordinary people attracted by the spectacle, and workers who came to bid their boss a final farewell. The varnished carriage moved forward pulled by six stallions decked with dark plumes and harnesses driven by liveried coachmen wearing plumed hats and postilions hanging from the stirrups who wore short trousers. They loaded the coffin on the coach, and the municipal band played Chopin's *Funeral March* while the coach began its slow circuit and the crowds crossed themselves and trembled. Governmental authorities led the mourners, followed by the partners, friends, and associates of the tycoon. Among the authorities was the strange individual with the long coat and black bowler and another personage dressed in gray who said a few quiet words to those nearest, nodded his head to their answers, and went away. It was Inspector Vázquez, in charge of the case.

.....

"WHAT'S THIS NEMESIO CABRA GÓMEZ LOOK LIKE?" asked Inspector Vázquez.

His secretary grimaced.

"Short, dark, skinny, filthy, unshaven . . ."

"Unemployed worker, I suppose," said the inspector.

"Looks like it, sir."

After leafing through the newspapers and seeing that they didn't allude to last night's event, Inspector Vázquez ordered the informer to be shown in.

"What do you want to talk to me about?"

"I've come to tell you things that will interest you, Mr. Inspector."

"I don't pay informers," warned Inspector Vázquez. "They just waste my time and never tell anything practical."

"It's no crime to collaborate with the police."

"It isn't profitable either," added the inspector.

"I've been out of work for nine months."

"So who feeds you?"

Nemesio Cabra Gómez smiled. He lisped slightly. He shrugged his shoulders. Inspector Vázquez turned to his secretary.

"Can we offer a piece of bread and a cup of coffee to an unemployed man?"

"No coffee left."

"Tell them to run some hot water over the grounds again," said Vázquez.

The secretary went out without seeming to abandon his sitting posture.

"What are you going to tell me?"

"I know who killed him."

"Savolta?"

Nemesio Cabra Gómez opened his toothless mouth.

"Someone killed Savolta?"

"It'll be in the afternoon papers."

"I didn't know . . . I didn't know. What a shame!"

.....

UNDER THE JANUARY SUN, the priests' litany for the dead and the coach and the crowd behind it advanced. A general trembling shook us, because we were all convinced that one of those present was the murderer. The church filled and the street as well, as far as the eye could see. The first pews were for the women, who were already there when we arrived. They wailed, prayed, and wavered on the edge of collapse. Then a silent and respectful multitude filled the naves. In the street, on the contrary, there was tremendous confusion. The confluence of all the financiers of Barcelona produced discussions, altercations, bargaining, opportunistic flirtations, attempts, and suggestions. The secretaries never stopped taking dictation and carrying notes from one place to another, elbowing their way through the crowd, frenetically trying to finish their business before anyone else.

Coming out of church, I ran into Lepprince.

"What are people saying?"

"Where?"

"Anywhere, here . . . in the newspapers, in the street. What does Cortabanyes say? I haven't been out of the house for two days now, practically. Just long enough to change clothes, take a bath, and eat something."

"Naturally, everyone's talking about Mr. Savolta's death, but nothing's been cleared up yet, if that's what you mean."

"Of course that's what I mean. Who do people think did it?"

"The assault came from outside. So those present are not under suspicion."

"I wouldn't leave anyone out, if I were the police, but I do agree that it was not a personal matter."

"You have a theory?"

"Of course. Like you and everyone else."

Claudedeu joined us. He was crying like a child.

"I can't believe it . . . so many years together and now, just look . . . I just can't believe it."

When he'd gone, Lepprince said, "I can't waste my time here. Come to my house tomorrow. After eight, all right?"

"I'll be there."

JUDGE DAVIDSON: Now I'd like to touch on a point that seems to me of special relevance. Did you know all the ins and outs of the Savolta company?

MIRANDA: Only what I'd heard.

JUDGE: Who was the majority stockholder?
MIRANDA: Savolta, of course.
JUDGE: When you say "of course," do you mean that Savolta owned all the stock in the company?
MIRANDA: Almost all.
JUDGE: To what extent?
MIRANDA: He owned seventy percent of the stock.
JUDGE: Who owned the remaining thirty percent?
MIRANDA: Parells, Claudedeu, and others connected to the company owned about twenty percent. The rest was owned by the public.
JUDGE: Had that arrangement always existed?
MIRANDA: No.
JUDGE: Give me a brief history.

.....

"THE SAVOLTA COMPANY," said Cortabanyes, "was founded by a Dutchman named Hugh Van der Vich in 1860 or 1865, if I remember correctly. I had barely anything to do with it, just as I have had barely anything to do with everything else that has happened around me. The corporation was formed in Barcelona, and the company was named after Savolta because at that time Savolta was Van der Vich's front man in Spain. The company was a swindle."

Cortabanyes was afraid. Ever since the New Year's Eve party, he experienced continuous chills, and his teeth chattered constantly. He called me in and began to tell me the story of the company as if he wanted to relieve himself of a weight. As if it were the prologue to a great revelation.

"After a time, Van der Vich went mad and left operation of the company in Savolta's hands. Savolta took that as an opportunity to appropriate the Dutchman's stock until Van der Vich died tragically, as everyone knows."

I'd read the romantic story when I was a boy. Hugh Van der Vich was an aristocrat from Holland who lived in a castle surrounded by thick forests. He went mad and acquired the habit of dressing up as a bear, prowling around his estates on all fours, and attacking peasant girls and shepherdesses. The legend of the bear spread. There were bear hunts in which more than thirty bears and six hunters died. One of the dead was Van der Vich.

"Van der Vich," Cortabanyes continued, "left a son and a daughter who went on living in the castle, which people claimed was enchanted. They said Van der Vich's soul wandered at night, catching any passersby in his claws, except for his children who left honey and dead mice out on the battlements for him to eat. The children had an incestuous relationship and lived in such an apathetic state that the authorities finally intervened. Both showed symptoms of madness. The son, Bernhard, was institutionalized in Holland and the daughter, Emma, in Switzerland. When the war broke out in 1914, Bernhard Van der Vich managed to escape, joined the German Army, and attained the rank of captain of dragoons.

"Bernhard died in a military operation in France, near the Swiss border. The Red Cross transported him, badly wounded, to Geneva. As they crossed the border into Switzerland, his sister shouted, 'Bernhard, où es-tu?' They never found each other: he died that same night on the operating table, and she, shortly after dawn. It's possible the whole story is nothing but a legend woven around this eccentric, wealthy family. The rich are different from other mortals, and it's only natural they attract the most bizarre rumors, the most outrageous fantasies."

MIRANDA: By the time the Van der Vich children died, Savolta and his group had taken over all the stock except a tiny number that remained in a Swiss bank under the name of Emma Van der Vich.
JUDGE: There were no other heirs?
MIRANDA: Not that I know of.
JUDGE: Did the company earn profits that could be considered high?
MIRANDA: Yes.
JUDGE: Regularly?
MIRANDA: Especially in the years preceding and during the war.
JUDGE: Not afterward?
MIRANDA: No.

JUDGE: Why?
MIRANDA: The entry of the United States into the conflagration lost the company its foreign clients.
JUDGE: Is that possible? Tell me, what product or products did the Savolta factory manufacture?
MIRANDA: Weapons.

.....

NEMESIO CABRA GÓMEZ WENT PALE. The secretary reappeared with a grayish cup of coffee and a loaf of floury bread which he deposited on the table. He then returned to his seat, where he remained with a distracted look on his face. Nemesio Cabra Gómez broke off a piece of bread, then dipped it in his coffee, making a repugnant paste.

"If you haven't come to tell me about Savolta," said Inspector Vázquez, "why have you come?"

"I know who killed him," said the informer, revealing the contents of his mouth.

"But who killed who?"

"Pajarito de Soto."

Inspector Vázquez thought for a few seconds.

"I'm not interested."

"It's a murder, and murders are police business, aren't they?"

"The case was closed days ago. You're too late."

"Then you should reopen it. I know something about the letter."

"The letter? The letter Pajarito de Soto wrote?"

Nemesio Cabra Gómez stopped eating.

"That interests you, doesn't it?"

"No," said Vázquez.

.....

AS WE'D AGREED, I went to Lepprince's house that evening. When the doorman, who knew me from my previous visits, saw me in mourning, he felt obliged to express his sympathy for Savolta's death.

"As long as the government doesn't take steps, there won't be any peace for decent people. What they've got to do is shoot them all."

In the foyer, I had a surprise. The pale man with the black bowler and the long coat I'd seen at the tycoon's funeral was there, standing outside the door. He stopped me.

"Open your coat," he said with a foreign accent and a threatening tone.

I obeyed, and he felt through my clothes.

"I don't carry weapons," I said, smiling.

"Name," he cut me off.

"Javier Miranda."

"Wait."

He snapped his fingers, and the butler, who pretended not to know me, appeared.

"Javier Miranda," said the man in the bowler. "Does he get in or not?"

The butler disappeared and returned a few seconds later. He said Lepprince was expecting me. The pale man stepped aside, and I walked in, feeling his menacing eyes on the back of my neck. I found Lepprince alone in the small salon we'd shared for so many hours.

"Who's that?"

"Max, my bodyguard. A deserter from the German Army, a man I can trust completely. Forgive him if he's bothered you. This is a delicate situation, and I've decided to set aside courtesy in favor of my personal security."

"But he frisked me!"

"He doesn't know you yet and doesn't trust anyone, not even his own shadow. A complete professional. I'll order him not to bother you from now on."

Just then shouts came from the hall. We went to see: the bodyguard was pointing his pistol at a man who was aiming his at the bodyguard.

"What's the meaning of this, Mr. Lepprince?" said the visitor, without taking his eyes off the bodyguard.

Lepprince quietly laughed at the absurdity of the scene.

"Let him in, Max. He's Inspector Vázquez."

"With his pistol?" asked Max.

"Well, isn't that nice," grunted the inspector. "This animal wants to disarm me."

"Yes, Max, let him in."

"You'll have to excuse him. He doesn't know anyone."

"Your bodyguard, I suppose."

"Quite right. I thought it advisable."

"No confidence in the police?"

"Of course I have confidence in the police, Inspector. But I thought I should take all possible precautions, even at the risk of going to extremes. I think the annoyances of these first few days will be made up for by future peace of mind. Not only my own, but yours as well."

"I don't like bodyguards. They're gunmen, troublemakers, and they work for money. I've never known one who didn't eventually sell out. In general they cause more trouble than they avoid."

"This case is different, Inspector. Believe me. A cigar?"

.....

"THOSE OF US who have the whole day for sleeping stay up at night, when good people rest. The city sleeps with its mouth wide open, Mr. Inspector, and we find out everything: what's happened, and what will happen, what's said, and what's kept silent, which is a lot in these hard times. I love order, Mr. Inspector, I swear it to you by my dead, may they rest in peace. And if you don't believe me, may God be my witness. I left my hometown because there was too much revolution there. Nowadays people don't respect the will of God, and He will have to send a great punishment down upon us unless we men of order and goodwill take action."

Inspector Vázquez lit a cigarette and stood up.

"I have to see about some business. Wait here if you like and then you can go on telling me these beautiful ideas of yours."

Nemesio Cabra Gómez got out of his chair.

"Mr. Inspector! Aren't you interested in what I know?"

"For the time being, no. I have more important things to take care of."

At the door, he called over his secretary and told him, sotto voce, "I'm going out for a moment. Keep an eye on this bird while I'm out. Don't let him leave. Oh, and I'm giving you back your cigarettes. I'll buy some now."

.....

THAT BY EXPRESS ORDER of my superiors I took charge of the "Savolta case" on January 1, 1918, immediately after Savolta's assassination. That the deceased Enrique Savolta y Gallibós, sixty-one years of age, married, born in Granollers (province of Barcelona), businessman, owned 70 percent of the stock in the company bearing his name, which produced weapons, explosives, and detonators in the industrial zone of the Hospitalet (province of Barcelona), and of which he was chief executive officer. That having investigated the events preceding his death, it was determined that it was perpetrated by workers organizations, also known as resistance societies, which probably carried out the assault in retaliation for the death of a journalist named Domingo Pajarito de Soto, which took place ten days or two weeks ago, and which was imputed, in the revolutionary circles of this city, to the intervention of one or more members of the aforementioned company. That investigations led to the arrest of . . .

.....

JANUARY PASSED and then February. I saw Lepprince only rarely. I went to see him a few times, but I had to go through a series of obstacles to get to him: the doorman, once amiable and excessively chatty, stopped me, asked my name, and called through the intercom to ask instructions. In the foyer, Max the bodyguard was waiting for me. He stopped frisking me, but he never took his hands out of his overcoat pockets. He showed me into the vestibule and warned the butler. The butler again asked me my name, as if he didn't know it, and asked me to wait a few minutes. My conversation with Lepprince was interrupted with irritating regularity: unexpected calls, furtive maids who handed him scrawled notes, a cringing male secretary with questions, Max, who would walk in without knocking and check the corners as if he were hunting roaches.

For all that, I went on frequenting the house on the Rambla de Cataluña. I often met Inspector Vázquez there. He would turn up unexpectedly, have a brief skirmish with Max, and walk into the salon. Lepprince would calm him with something: a cigar, coffee and cookies, a drink, and the inspector would sigh, stretch, seem to relax, and begin his chat, salted with crimes, tortuous paths, and crisscrossed trails. One day he told us that those suspected of Savolta's murder were already in Montjuïc. There were four of them: two young and two old men, all anarchists, three immigrants from the south, and one Catalan. In my mind I wondered how many painful shots in the dark had been perpetrated before these four criminals were found.

Sure enough, a few weeks before Vázquez told us about the arrest, I happened to be bored and it occurred to me to pass by the bookstore on Aribau street to kill an hour or so listening to Master Roca. But the bookstore was empty. Only the redheaded woman was there behind the counter. I walked toward the room in the rear, and she stopped me.

"Are you looking for a book?"

"Doesn't Master Roca come here?"

"No, he doesn't come anymore."

"I hope he's not ill."

She looked all around and then whispered in my ear:

"He's been sent to Montjuïc."

"Why? Did he do something wrong?"

"It's because of the Savolta murder. Know what I'm talking about? The next day, the repression began."

Master Roca fell ill in Montjuïc because of his advanced age. They released him relatively quickly, but he never came back to the bookstore, and I never heard anything more about him.

.....

"YOU CAN'T TREAT ME THIS WAY, Mr. Inspector, I'm a man of order. My only purpose was to help you. Why don't you pay any attention to me?"

Nemesio Cabra Gómez was nervous, twisting his fingers until the knuckles cracked.

"Be patient, I'll be right with you."

"Do you know how many hours I've been sitting here?"

"Quite a few, I think."

Nemesio Cabra Gómez threw himself over the table. The inspector was startled and covered himself with the newspaper while his secretary stood up and moved as if to run for the door.

"I've done a lot of thinking during these hours of anguish, Inspector. Don't abandon me. I know who killed Pajarito de Soto and Savolta, and I know who will be the next to fall. Interested or not?"

.....

I REMEMBER the last time I went to the house on the Rambla de Cataluña. Lepprince invited me to dinner. Once I'd gotten past the barriers, we sat down to have sherry in the little salon, where logs were burning despite the fact that spring had taken control of the city with its luminous colors and its exhilarating warmth. When we finished, we walked into the dining room. We were making general conversation by fits and starts with long silences. Finally, with dessert, Lepprince told me he was getting married. I wasn't surprised by the fact but by the secrecy that surrounded his relations until that moment. His fiancée, no need for me to say it, was María Rosa Savolta. I congratulated him and raised no objection except for the excessive youth of his future wife.

"She's almost twenty," replied Lepprince with his sweet smile (I knew she had just turned eighteen), "she's had a solid education and is a woman of refined culture. The rest will come in its own time. Experience is usually a series of nasty shocks, failures, and displeasures that embitter more than teach. Experience is good for a man, who has to fight, but not for a wife. May God permit me to deprive her of experience, if that means keeping her free of trouble."

I praised his words, which expressed great nobility, and then both of us sank back into a tense silence. The butler came into the dining room, excused himself for interrupting, and announced the presence of Inspector Vázquez. Lepprince had him shown in and asked me to stay.

"Excuse me for receiving you in the dining room, dear Vázquez," Lepprince hastened to say barely had the inspector walked in. "It seemed like a better idea than having you wait or ruining the end of an excellent dinner. Care to join us?"

"Thank you, but I've already eaten."

"Well, then, just have some dessert and a glass of muscatel."

"That would be a pleasure. I'm here because I think I should keep you informed about everything happening with regard to . . . your situation."

When he said "your," I understood him to mean Lepprince and his partners. He hadn't bothered to greet me and was just as disdainful of me as he'd been on the first day. It bothered me, but I thought it logical: in his profession neither civility nor courtesy had a place, and anything that got in his way (friends, secretaries, helpers, and bodyguards), he had to remove without second thoughts.

"You're referring to the attacks? Is there any news about the death of poor Savolta?"

"It was that I was referring to exactly."

The inspector paused, looking over the cruets and reading the wine label to himself. His contempt seemed to go beyond me and extend to Lepprince himself.

"Through . . . people who collaborate with the police in an indirect, nonofficial way, I've learned that Lucas, 'the Blind Man,' has come to Barcelona."

"Lucas the what?" asked Lepprince.

"The Blind Man."

"And who is this picturesque character?"

"A gunman from Valencia. He's worked in Bilbao and Madrid, although our reports about him are sketchy. You know what happens with this sort of person: people make a thief into a hero and imagine him to be everywhere, like God."

A servant brought a plate, silverware, and a napkin for the inspector.

"Why is he called the Blind Man?" asked Lepprince.

"One version has it that he squints when he stares. Others say his father was blind and sang folk songs down in Valencia. Pure legend, in my opinion."

"Despite the nickname, he would seem to have fine eyesight."

"As fine as a steel thread."

"Was it this Lucas who killed Savolta?"

Inspector Vázquez took some petit fours and gave Lepprince a significant look.

"Who knows, Mr. Lepprince, who knows?"

"Tell us more about your character, please. And eat, eat, you'll see these sweets are a real delicacy."

"I don't know if you realize it, Mr. Lepprince, but I'm speaking seriously. This gunman is a dangerous man and he's out to get all of you."

"By which you mean me, Inspector?"

"I was deliberately vague. If I had meant you specifically, I would have said so. I had this same conversation with Claudedeu early this morning."

"How dangerous is this man?" asked Lepprince.

"Here are some notes. I copied them myself from the files. Take a look at them, but you might not understand my handwriting."

"Oh, but I do. It says here that he's thought to have committed four murders."

"Two murders, strictly speaking. The other two are police who died in a gun battle in Madrid."

"And he escaped from the Cuenca jail."

"Yes. The *Guardia Civil* chased him through the mountains. Finally, I don't know why, they gave him up for dead and returned to barracks. A month later, he turned up in Bilbao."

"Does he work alone?" I asked.

"Depends. The Madrid reports say he's leader of a gang, without telling the exact number of members. Other reports say he's a lone wolf. That seems more consistent with his personality: he's a fanatic and extremely violent. If he's had partners, it's probably been a temporary arrangement to do a certain job."

Inspector Vázquez sliced a small petit four made of egg yolk and savored it slowly.

"A real delicacy, this little cake!"

"What would you recommend I do, Inspector?"

Vázquez didn't answer until he'd finished the last bits of the petit four.

"I would suggest . . . I would suggest you keep us abreast of all your activities, so that we can keep a close eye on you. It would be a good idea to prepare each and every one of your exits, in case and so that we force Lucas, the Blind Man, into doing something desperate. Men like that don't usually have much patience. If we give him the bait, he'll fall into the trap."

The maid announced that coffee and liqueurs were served in the little salon. Lepprince led the way, but Inspector Vázquez said he was in a hurry and left the house.

"It bothers him that I have my own bodyguard. He says it interferes with his work."

"And from his point of view it does."

"From his point of view, perhaps. But I feel more protected by Max than I would by all the police in Spain together."

"Well, I won't try to contradict you. But I do think that the Spanish police are extremely efficient."

"In that case, I feel doubly secure. But it isn't as though we were arguing about bullfighters. What's at stake here is my life, and I'm not going to use myself to prove who's better and who's worse."

.....

DOCTOR FLORS SCRATCHED HIS BEARD with his pencil case.

"What you're asking, Inspector, is very irregular. The patient is in a state of temporary calm which your presence could alter."

"What would happen if it were altered?"

"He'd become violent, and we'd have to give him cold-water showers."

"That wouldn't hurt anyone, Doctor. Let me speak to him."

"I really shouldn't, believe me. I'm responsible for the health of my patients."

"And I'm responsible for the lives of many people. I'm not asking you to do it for me, Doctor, but for the public good, which I represent. It's a serious matter."

Not very convinced, Doctor Flors accompanied the inspector through long corridors that didn't seem to lead anywhere. At the end of each corridor, the doctor made a ninety-degree turn and went down another corridor. The walls were painted green, as were the irregularly distributed doors. From time to time, at the right or left of the corridor—which disoriented Vázquez—there was a glassed-in porch that overlooked a rectangular garden, in the center of which there was a fountain surrounded by flowering rosebushes. Through the garden wandered a few patients, their heads shaved, wrapped in long striped bathrobes. The male nurse, by contrast, wore a thick black beard. The garden would suddenly appear on one side or the other, and on one occasion the inspector thought he was passing the same place for the second time.

"Didn't we see that statue of Saint Joseph before," he asked, pointing to an image that blessed them from a niche.

"No. You mean the statue of Saint Nicholas of Bari in the women's wing."

"Sorry, it seemed to me . . ."

"Your confusion is natural. The hospital is a labyrinth. It was planned that way in order to achieve the maximum isolation of its various parts. Like our garden?

"It will give me immense pleasure to show it to you at the end of your visit. The patients cultivate and tend it themselves."

"What's that man doing over there?"

"He's killing insect pests. He searches for their nests and then plugs them up with wax or clay. Wax is better, because the insects bore through the clay easily and get to the surface again after a few days. Interested in gardening, Inspector?"

"We had a little garden at home when I was a child. And a patio where my mother grew flowers. That was a long time ago."

They entered a corridor darker than the rest of the building, lined with thick doors that had no other opening but a small window protected by thick iron bars. An otherworldly hum filtered through the doors and flooded the corridor. Instinctively, the inspector walked faster, but Doctor Flors indicated that they had reached their destination.

.....

WITH APRIL CAME HEAVY SHOWERS and fickle weather. One afternoon, as Nicolás Claudedeu was leaving a meeting, it began to rain. A horse-drawn carriage was coming his way, so he hailed it. The coach stopped, and Claudedeu got in. Inside the coach was another man. Before Claudedeu could recover from his shock, the man shot him between the eyes. The driver whipped his horses, and the coach disappeared at the gallop, right before the astonished eyes of the police who were guarding Claudedeu and to the horror of the passersby. The body of the Man with the Iron Hand was found the next day in a municipal dump. Repression redoubled, but Lucas, "the Blind Man," would not let himself be captured. Interrogations went on for days, the lists of suspects reached six-figure lengths, whispered secrets and denunciations multiplied. The campaign spread to include not only the anarchists but the labor movement in general.

Text of Various Letters Found in Nicolás Claudedeu's House, Dated a Few Days Before His Death

Entered as Evidence: Document No. 8

▪

English translation by court interpreter Guzmán Hernández de Fenwick

Barcelona, 3/27/1918

Dear Sir:

It gives me great pleasure to communicate to you with regard to the individual in whose reports you are interested; Francisco Glascá, prior to the bombing on Consulado street, belonged to the *Action* group and had been arrested on other occasions for violent acts. He was currently working in the house of the owner, Mr. Farigola, and was a delegate to the union of the branch in question. He lives in an irregular relationship with a woman, according to his own statements, and has a daughter named Liberty, Equality, and Fraternity. His home address is on the list which you sent me and of which, according to what you said, you must have a copy.

On a sheet of paper that seems to be a rough draft:

See to it that things are carried out with discretion. As a last resort, but only as a last resort, you may have recourse to our friends V. H. and C. R. Thank you for the copy of the Madrid magazine *Spartacus*. These rumors must be nipped in the bud. What news do you have of Seguí? Be prudent, things are in an uproar.

(signed) N. Claudedeu

Barcelona 4/2/1918

Dear Sir:

It seems that the members of *Action* have taken the Glascá business personally. I'm afraid they may want to carry out reprisals, although

I doubt they'll dare to carry them out against you. I'm leaving for Madrid tomorrow without fail, and I expect to talk to A. F. You know already how little love he has for us, especially after the Jover matter. In his last visit, he told me that the trips Pestaña and Seguí are making to Madrid have something to do with the general strike; our attitude and that of the other members of the Owners League can speed things up and keep him from taking the appropriate measures. I don't even want to think of what morale must be in the ministry.

Doctor Flors opened a door and invited his guest to enter. Inspector Vázquez could not restrain a shudder as he stepped over the threshold. The cell was square, with a high ceiling, like a box of crackers. The walls and the floors were padded. There were no windows, no holes of any kind except for a peephole in the higher part that let in an uncertain light. Nor was there any furniture. The patient was hunkered down, his straight back leaning against the wall. His clothes were in tatters and barely covered his nakedness, which augmented his ruinous state. He hadn't shaved for weeks, and his hair had fallen out in an irregular way, revealing, here and there, a strip of stubbly skin. A dense and pestilential air was all there was to breathe in the cell. When the inspector entered, the doctor locked the door, and the policeman and the patient were left alone face to face. Vázquez was sorry he hadn't brought along his pistol. He turned to the door, and at the same time a tiny window opened, through which appeared the doctor's face.

"What do I do?" asked the inspector.

"Speak to him slowly without raising your voice."

"I'm afraid, Doctor."

"Don't worry, I'm right here in case something happens. The patient seems calm. Try not to excite him."

"His eyes are popping out."

"It's natural. Remember, he's insane. Don't contradict him."

Inspector Vázquez addressed the patient.

"Nemesio, Nemesio, don't you recognize me?"

But Nemesio Cabra Gómez did not seem to notice the presence of his visitor, even if he stared fixedly at him.

"Nemesio, remember me? You came to see me several times down at the station, remember? We always gave you a roll and coffee."

The sick man's mouth began to move slowly, and a stream of spittle flowed out. His voice was inaudible.

"I can't make out what he's saying."

"Get closer."

"I don't want to."

"Then get out."

"All right, Doctor, I'll get closer, but don't take your eyes off me."

"Stop worrying."

"Look, Doctor, I've got two men posted outside. If I don't come out in a while safe and sound, they'll come in and hold you responsible for whatever happens. I hope we understand each other."

"You wanted to see the patient. I advised you not to. Don't be such a crybaby."

The inspector went closer to Nemesio Cabra Gómez.

"Nemesio, it's me, Vázquez, remember me?"

He perceived a strangled voice, more like the chirping of a bird. He leaned forward and managed to understand.

"Mr. Inspector . . . Mr. Inspector . . ."

.....

SERGEANT TOTORNO ENTERED THE BOX, coughed discreetly, and, seeing that the two occupants paid him no attention, touched Lepprince's shoulder.

"Excuse me, Mr. Lepprince."

"What's going on?"

"I'm going to take a walk through the balconies, just to see if I find anything odd."

"Good idea."

"It'll give me a chance to stretch my legs. This theater stuff, as far as I'm concerned . . ."

"Go ahead, Sergeant, go ahead."

From the boxes on both sides emanated hisses demanding silence, and Sergeant Totorno walked out, banging his saber against the chairs. Max picked up the opera glasses and looked through them at the upper floors.

"Amateurs," he murmured, alluding to the sergeant.

"They do what they can," said Lepprince.

"Bah."

The curtain fell, there was applause, and the lights came up. Max stepped back in the box. Lepprince stood up and lit a cigarette before leaving. But when he opened the door to the corridor, a uniformed policeman blocked his way.

"I want to go to the bar."

"Inspector Vázquez's orders: you may not leave your seat."

"I'm thirsty. Tell Inspector Vázquez to come up here."

"He's not in the theater."

"Then let me go."

"I'm sorry, Mr. Lepprince."

"Then do me a favor, please?"

"Certainly, what is it?"

"Get an usher and tell him to bring me a lemonade. I'll pay for it here."

He went back to the box. It was hot. Max, in shirtsleeves, was shuffling cards.

"I'll stay back here, if you don't mind."

"Going to play solitaire?"

"Yes."

"Just as you wish. Don't you like the play?"

"I'll come forward at the end to see how it ends."

"What's your opinion of adultery, Max?"

"Don't have one really."

"Do you condemn it?"

"I've never thought about it. All that sex business, well . . ."

"All right," said Lepprince. "Play your solitaire. I hope you have good luck."

"Thanks."

Lepprince went forward to his seat. A chime sounded, announcing the beginning of the third act. It chimed again, and the lights faded while more gas flowed into the footlights. People hastily coughed and cleared their throats while the curtain went up. Someone knocked at the door of the box; Max opened: it was the policeman with a tray, a small bottle, and a glass.

"I went to get it myself."

"Thank you. Here, and keep the change."

"No, no."

"Mr. Lepprince's orders."

"Well, in that case . . ."

Informed by Max, Lepprince stepped to the rear and drank the lemonade.

.....

"DID YOU GET MY CALL, Mr. Inspector?"

"Yes, I did. That's why I'm here."

"A friend went to see you, right, Mr. Inspector?"

"A friend of yours, right."

"It was Jesus Christ, did you know that?"

Vázquez went back to the little window.

"I think he's delirious."

"What did I tell you . . ."

"Mr. Inspector, are you there?"

"Right here, Nemesio, what did you want to tell me?"

"The letter, Mr. Inspector, find the letter."

Vázquez again came close to the patient.

"Which letter, Nemesio?"

"It tells everything . . . the letter: find it, and it will tell you who killed Pere Parells. I'm not telling you, Mr. Inspector. It's Jesus Christ speaking through my mouth. The other day, I saw a glowing light that passed right through the walls; I had to close my eyes so I wouldn't go blind . . . and when I opened them, He was standing before me, just as you are now, Mr. Inspector, just like you, wearing the white shroud that Mary Magdalene gave him. His eyes gave off sparks, and His beard had luminous points like stars, and on His hands were the wounds, just as they were when He appeared to Saint Thomas, Doubting Thomas."

"Tell me about the letter, Nemesio."

"No. This is more beautiful than the letter, Mr. Inspector, and more interesting. I was prostrate, not knowing what to do, and all I could do was repeat: 'Lord, I am not worthy of having You enter my humble home,' and He showed me his Divine Wounds and his Crown of Thorns that looked like the Sun, and he spoke to me in a voice that came from all corners of the cell at once. It's true, Mr. Inspector, it came from all corners of the cell at once, and everything was light. And He said to me, 'Go find Inspector Vázquez, of the Social Brigade. Tell him everything you know, and he will get you out of here.' I answered, 'And how will I go to Inspector Vázquez when they won't let me out of here, Lord, when they have me locked up?' And He answered, 'I will go to the station and tell him to come, but you have to tell him everything you know.' And He disappeared, leaving me sunk in darkness, where I remain since He left."

Vázquez walked to the door.

"Let me out, Doctor, this is a waste of time."

"Wait, Mr. Inspector, don't go," said Nemesio Cabra Gómez.

"Go to the devil," shouted the inspector.

But the madman stood up and seized the inspector by his shoulders, forcing him to his knees. He then brought his face close to the policeman's ear and whispered a few words. Doctor Flors by then had entered and wrestled with the madman to free the inspector from the pincers that held him against the padded floor. Two male nurses came, and the three of them subdued Nemesio Cabra Gómez.

"Take him to the showers," ordered Doctor Flors.

Vázquez straightened himself out. He picked his hat and one of his jacket buttons off the floor.

"I warned you it wasn't worthwhile trying it."

"Perhaps," answered Vázquez.

Without speaking, they wound their way through the corridors that bordered the garden and said good-bye at the door of the sanitorium. Two guards were waiting in a car.

"Thank God, Inspector. We thought you weren't coming out."

"That's what you wanted, the two of you, for them to lock me up."

The two guards laughed at their superior's joke.

"Where does Javier Miranda live?" the inspector suddenly asked.

"Miranda?" asked his subordinates. "Who is he?"

"I can see you don't know where he lives. Let's go back to the station so you can find out."

.....

WHEN LEPPRINCE REAPPEARED in the box, the first shot rang out from the balconies. Lepprince, or the man everyone assumed was Lepprince, fell to the floor. Sergeant Totorno ran toward the higher seats, where the shot had come from. A figure ran for the exit. Sergeant Totorno blocked the way, and the figure spun on his heels and jumped over several rows of seats, making his way to the rail behind which the sergeant had taken cover. The fallen Lepprince, meanwhile, stood up; in each hand he held a pistol: it wasn't Lepprince but Max, who had taken his place while Lepprince drank his lemonade. He shot twice at the man who was standing upright before the railing. The man crumpled over the rail, then fell into the orchestra section. A shocked confusion raged in the theater, the play had stopped, and actors and audience fled, trampling each other and tripping over those who had fallen, only to be knocked down by those behind them. From the balcony came another shot aimed at Lepprince's box. Max had jumped into the adjacent box and answered the attack with a volley from his two pistols, firing both at the same time without stopping. A wayward shot wounded a spectator who began to howl. A body tumbled down the balcony until it was stopped by the seats. The terrorists, who could not have been more than five, were trapped between Max's pistols and the fire of Sergeant Totorno who, even though he was wounded, went on firing imprecise shots in all directions. The terorists tried to make their way toward the fire escape. The policeman who had brought the lemonade entered Lepprince's box with a shotgun, squeezed the trigger, and peppered the seats above. Sergeant Totorno fell to the floor. The terrorists, still on their feet, jumped over the sergeant's body and got into the corridor. Max, hidden behind a column, killed them. One was Lucas, "the Blind Man," who died at the outset of the gunfight with a bullet in his neck. Another of the dead terrorists had a bullet in his left shoulder blade and buckshot in his brain. Another had a bullet in his heart. The last two terrorists were wounded, one slightly, the other seriously. The brave Sergeant Totorno, in grave condition, lost two fingers of his right hand because of the shotgun blast. As for the spectator wounded in the right buttock by a stray shot, he was released from the hospital in a few days, and indemnified by Lepprince.

Chapter 5

That night, I went to the movies and afterward stopped off for a beer and a sandwich. Then I made my tedious way home, tedious because the weather was fine and no one was waiting for me, because I had nothing to do and was in no hurry to get anywhere. I lived in a small apartment on the top floor of a modern building on Gerona street. A friend of Serra-madriles found it for me shortly after I reached Barcelona. There was barely any furniture, and what I did have was of the worst quality: wobbly chairs, shaky tables, a wicker sofa, and a profusion of sun-eaten cretonne. The bedroom contained a narrow bed, little more than a cot, and a legless dresser with a cracked mirror. The other room was supposed to be a dining room, but since I ate in a cheap, neighborhood restaurant, I used it as a reading room. I had few visitors, and any other use I might have invented for it would have been superfluous. Finally, I had an empty storeroom without windows, a sink in the bedroom where I could clean up. The other sanitary services were in a separate room off a landing on the stairway; I shared them with an astronomer and an old maid. There was one good thing: the windows of the two rooms faced a little flower garden. Midway through 1919, the garden disappeared, and they began to build. A damn shame.

As I was saying, when I got home, it was late, almost midnight. As I inserted the key in the lock, I noticed the door wasn't locked. I chalked it up to my own carelessness, but it made me nervous.

I opened the door slowly: there was light in the dining room. I slammed the door and started to run down the stairs. A familiar voice called me by name—from behind me.

"Don't run, Miranda, no reason to be afraid."

I turned around. It was Inspector Vázquez.

"We came by a couple of hours ago. When you didn't come home, we took the liberty of opening the door and waiting in comfort. I hope that doesn't bother you."

"No, of course not. It's just that you scared the hell out of me."

"I understand. We should have warned you of our presence so you wouldn't end up finding out on your own, but what can you do? We'd almost forgotten about you."

I'd reclimbed the last steps and walked into the apartment. In the dining room stood two policemen in civilian clothes. A glance was all I needed to tell me they'd been through everything. I was certainly entitled to protest, and even to register a complaint, because, without a doubt, Vázquez had acted on his own, without the necessary judicial authorization. However, I said to myself, belligerence would only bring more complications and, anyway, it didn't really bother me that they'd turned the house upside down.

"Who's that in the photo?" asked Inspector Vázquez.

"My father."

"My, my, what would your father think if he knew the police were visiting you."

I supposed he wanted to intimidate me, but it backfired, and he actually lost the advantage of surprise.

"He wouldn't think anything: he died three years ago."

"Oh, sorry. I didn't know you were a widower."

"Orphan, to be more precise."

"That's what I meant, sorry again."

Now it was my turn: the inspector had made himself look foolish in front of his assistants.

"I'm sorry to have nothing to offer you, Inspector," I said with aplomb.

"No need for excuses, for heaven's sake. We never eat or drink on duty."

"Come, come, Inspector. I've come to admire your gastronomic good taste at the house of our common friend, Mr. Lepprince."

He looked flustered, and I was afraid I'd gone too far in my personal attack. But he deserved it. He wanted to interrogate me, taking advantage of our casual acquaintance, but that allowed me to make use, just as he had, of our previous personal relationship. Because I had no doubt that he had come more to accuse than to investigate and that he was trying to weaken me by this midnight visit and the presence, clearly unnecessary, of his two subordinates.

"We've come on a friendly visit," he said when he'd recovered. "Naturally, you don't have to let us in. We don't have a search warrant, so we have to appeal to your good nature. Of course, these explanations are superfluous since you're a lawyer."

"I'm no lawyer."

"No? Darn, I just can't get anything right tonight. I don't know what's wrong with me. . . . You're a law student then?"

"Wrong again."

"Anyway, help me out. How would you define yourself, professionally speaking?"

It was a fulminating counterattack.

"Administrative assistant."

"To Mr. Lepprince?"

"No. To Mr. Cortabanyes, the lawyer."

"Oh, now I get it. . . . I thought—see?—that since I saw you so often at Mr. Lepprince's house . . . But now I see I'm mistaken. An administrative assistant wouldn't be eating at Mr. Lepprince's table unless there were something more between them—how should I put it?—a friendly relationship, perhaps."

"You're doing all the talking. I haven't said a word."

"Nor should you, Miranda my friend, nor should you. You're right to keep quiet. Even a fish wouldn't get into trouble if he kept his mouth shut."

"I understand I'm the fish, but should I take it that you are the fisherman, Inspector?"

"Now, now, my dear Miranda. Why are we Spaniards so hostile? This is a little gathering of friends."

"In that case, please introduce me to these two gentlemen. I like knowing my friends' names."

"These two gentlemen have come with me merely to keep me company. Now that you're here, they will be leaving."

The two subordinates said good night and left without even waiting to be seen to the door. When we were alone, Inspector Vázquez adopted a more circumspect and at the same time more familiar tone.

"You seem surprised, Mr. Miranda, at my sudden interest in you. Nevertheless, there could be nothing more logical than such interest, not only in you but in any person related to the Savolta case, don't you think?"

"What do I have to do with the Savolta case?"

"An obtuse question, in my opinion, if we review the facts. In December of last year, an obscure journalist named Domingo Pajarito de Soto dies. A superficial investigation reveals an unquestionable reality: you are his most intimate friend. A few weeks later, Savolta is assassinated, and, strange to tell, you are one of the guests at the party."

"You suspect me of committing two crimes?"

"Calm down, that's not where I'm heading. But let's go on reviewing the bare facts: both deaths have or seem to have a connection, the Savolta company. Pajarito de Soto had just finished a job, for which he was paid, for the company. We have to ask: who put the journalist in touch with his last employers?"

"I did."

"Exactly: Javier Miranda. Second point: the relation between Pajarito de Soto and the company was carried through by one of the company's main figures. Not through the chief of personnel, Claudedeu, not through Savolta's direct intervention, but by the mediation of an individual whose functions in the company are vague: Paul-André Lepprince. I go to visit Lepprince, and who do I find at his side?"

"Me."

"Too many coincidences, don't you think?"

"No. Lepprince ordered me to find and contract Pajarito de Soto. From my contact with both arose a friendship with both, a friendship tragically cut short in the case of Pajarito de Soto, a friendship that still exists in the case of Lepprince. The explanation couldn't be simpler."

"It would be even simpler if there weren't so many obscure points."

"For example?"

"For example, that while you maintained this 'friendship' with Pajarito de Soto, you were also very friendly with his wife, Teresa."

I leapt to my feet, indignant.

"Just a minute, Inspector. I don't have to put up with this kind of interrogation. I'd like to remind you that you're in my home, and that you are not legally sanctioned to do what you're doing."

"And I'd like to remind you that I'm a police inspector and that I can not only get judicial authorization but an arrest order and have you brought down to the station in handcuffs. If you want to play the formalities card, play it, but don't start crying later over what happens."

There was a silence. The inspector lit a cigarette and tossed the pack onto the table by way of offering me one. I sat down, took a cigarette, and we smoked while the tension relaxed.

"I'm not a nosy landlady," the inspector went on in a deliberate tone. "I don't stick my nose into people's stinking private lives to find out if they're cuckolds, homosexuals, or pimps. I'm investigating three murders and one attempted murder. So I'm asking for, demanding, everyone's help. I'd prefer to be understanding and respectful, to work around formalities, routines, anything not to put anyone out more than is necessary. But don't abuse me, don't irritate me, and don't force me to use my authority because it'll come down on you like a ton of bricks. I'm fed up, understand?

Fed up! Fed up with being the laughingstock of all the little asshole gentlemen of Barcelona; fed up with that little prick Lepprince feeding me cake and liqueurs, as if we were celebrating his first communion. And now you come along, a nobody, very self-satisfied because you wag your tail and get scraps tossed to you in high society salons, and you want to imitate your masters and be a wiseacre with me, make me look ridiculous, as if I were the maid for all of you instead of being what I am and doing what I do: protecting you. You're all idiots, see? bigger idiots than the cows in my hometown, because at least they know how far they can go and where they have to stop. Want some advice, Miranda? When you see me walk into a room, even if it's Lepprince's dining room, don't go on eating, as if a dog had walked in: wipe off your mug and stand up. Have I made myself understood?"

"Yes, sir."

"That's better, act sensibly. And now that we're such good friends and understand each other so well, answer my questions. Where is the letter?"

"What letter?"

"What letter do you think? Pajarito de Soto's letter."

"I don't know anything about . . ."

"You don't know that Pajarito de Soto wrote and sent a letter the same day he was killed?"

"Did you say *he was killed?*"

"I said what I said, now answer the question."

"I heard the letter talked about, but I never saw it."

"Are you sure you don't have it?"

"Completely sure."

"And you don't know who has it?"

"No."

"And you don't know the contents of the letter."

"No, I don't, I swear."

"You may be telling the truth, but watch out if you're lying. I'm not the only one after that letter, and the others don't waste their time talking the way I do. First they kill you, then they search, without questions, understand?"

"Yes."

"In case you find out, suspect, remember even the most insignificant detail about the letter, tell me as fast as you can. Your life may depend on doing it right away."

"Yes, sir."

He got up, took his hat, and walked to the door. I accompanied him and gave him my hand, which he took in as cold a manner as possible.

"Excuse my behavior. We've all been nervous these past few months. Too many horrible things have happened. I don't want to get in the way of your work, you can see that."

"Good night," he cut me off.

I watched him walk down the stairs, I went back in, locked the door, and sat there meditating and smoking the cigarettes Vázquez had left behind until dawn. The sun was just rising when I fell asleep. I forgot to wind my alarm clock, so when I opened my eyes it was already past eleven. I called the office from a bar and claimed I'd received an urgent note. The truth wasn't very different from my excuse. I had a coffee, read the newspaper, had my shoes shined, and mentally repeated a confused monologue—though some of it I must have said aloud, judging by the mocking faces of the other people in the bar. I paid and left. I walked to Lepprince's house. The doorman told me he'd gone out about half an hour before. I asked if he knew where he'd gone, and he answered me, as if he were revealing a huge secret, that Lepprince had gone to Sarriá, to see Savolta's widow and ask for María Rosa's hand in marriage. We parted company like two conspirators. I went to Plaza de Cataluña and took the train. In Sarriá, I climbed the steep streets, as I had months earlier, when we buried the tycoon.

There were guards at the door of the mansion, a privilege provided by the authorities to honor the memory of the deceased. Their vigilance, however, was useless: the terrorists had other targets in their sights. I was allowed in once I had identified myself. The butler used a thousand arguments to keep me from trying to see Lepprince.

"This is a small family meeting, very intimate. Try to understand, sir."

I insisted. The butler agreed to inform Lepprince of my presence, but would not guarantee Lepprince would see me. I waited. Lepprince appeared in less than a minute.

"Something serious has to be going on for you to interrupt me when I'm involved in something so . . . private, so to speak."

"I don't know if what I'm going to tell you is serious. Being in doubt, I preferred a sin of commission to one of omission."

He showed me into the library. I described Vázquez's visit and his incisive tone, although I omitted any reference to the inspector's fury because it might have offended Lepprince.

"You were right to come."

"I was afraid I wouldn't find you later, when it might be too late."

"You were right, I assure you. But your fears are unfounded. Vázquez is suffering from hallucinations, brought on, I'm sure, by an excess of zeal. In France, it's what we call *professional deformation.*"

"That's just what we call it in Spain as well," said a voice behind us.

We turned around and saw Inspector Vázquez in person. The butler behind him was gesticulating silently, telling us he couldn't keep him out. Lepprince gestured for the butler to leave. The three of us were left alone. Lepprince took a box of cigars off a shelf and offered them to the inspector. Vázquez refused with a smile, and shot me a malevolent glare.

"Thank you, but Mr. Miranda and I have more plebeian tastes and prefer cigarettes—isn't that true?"

"I must admit I smoked the ones you left behind last night."

"Almost a full pack; you should take better care of your health . . . or your nerves."

He offered me a cigarette, which I accepted. Lepprince put the cigars back on the shelf and gave us a light. The inspector looked over the library and stopped at the window.

"This is much prettier in spring than it was the other time . . . in January, I mean."

He gave a half turn and leaned on the frame of the half-opened door, looking into the salon.

"Would you like me to have the panels opened so you can check to see if it's possible to shoot at the staircase from here?" said Lepprince with his usual suavity.

"As you might imagine, Mr. Lepprince, I reviewed that possibility on an earlier occasion."

He returned to the center of the room, looked around for an ashtray, and found one.

"May I ask the reason for your unexpected visit, Inspector?"

"Reason? No. Reasons. First, allow me to be the first to congratulate you on the occasion of your future matrimony with the daughter of the deceased Mr. Savolta. Although perhaps I'm not the first, but the second."

He was alluding to me. Lepprince made a small bow.

"Second, I want to congratulate you as well for your luck: you got away from the attack in the theater without a scratch. I heard all about it in great detail, and I must admit that I was mistaken when I doubted the efficacy of your gunman."

"Bodyguard," Lepprince corrected him.

"As you wish. None of that matters now, because my third reason for coming to see you is to say good-bye."

"To say good-bye?"

"Yes, to say good-bye, farewell."

"What is all this?"

"I've received irrevocable orders. I leave this very afternoon for Tetuán."

In the inspector's smile there was a trace of bitterness that moved me. It was then I realized how much I esteemed Inspector Vázquez.

"For Tetuán?" I exclaimed.

"Yes, Tetuán. Surprised?" he said, as if he'd just noticed I was there.

"I certainly am," I answered sincerely.

"And you, Mr. Lepprince, does it surprise you as well?"

"I am totally ignorant of the customs of the police force. In any case, I hope your transfer is beneficial."

"All places are beneficial or harmful, according to how we behave in them," pronounced the inspector.

He turned on his heel and left. Lepprince stood there staring toward the door with his eyebrow comically arched.

"Do you think we'll ever see him again?"

"Who knows? Life takes lots of strange turns."

"I can certainly believe that," he said.

Letter from Sergeant Totorno to Inspector Vázquez dated 5/2/1918, in which he describes the situation in Barcelona

Entered as Evidence: Document No. 7a

▪

English translation by court interpreter Guzmán Hernández de Fenwick

Barcelona 5/2/1918

Dear and Distinguished Chief:

I hope you will excuse my delay in writing to you, but because of the accident I had in the theater a month ago I was unable to hold a pen. Also, it did not seem prudent to dictate this letter to someone else, because you know how people are. I finally learned to write with my left hand. Please forgive my bad penmanship.

Not much has happened here since you left. They took me off active duty and transferred me to Passports. The inspector who took your place has ordered that Mr. Lepprince no longer be guarded. And that, together with everything else, makes it impossible for me to find out anything about Lepprince, despite my attempts to keep abreast of him, as you said I should before you left. I read in the newspaper that Mr. Lepprince married Mr. Savolta's daughter yesterday, and that by express order of the family practically no one attended the ceremony, coming as it did so close to the death of her father. They haven't gone on a honeymoon, for the same reason. Mr. Lepprince and his wife have changed address. I think they have their own mansion, but I still don't now where.

Poor Nemesio Cabra Gómez is still locked up. Mr. Miranda still works for the lawyer Mr. Cortabanyes, and is no longer seen with Mr. Lepprince. That aside, the city is very calm.

Nothing more for today. Watch out for those Moors, they're bad people and very treacherous. The boys and I here miss you.

A respectful salute.
(signed) Sgt. Totorno

Doloretas rubbed her hands together.

"We have to think of something," she said.

I yawned. Through the window, I could see how Caspe street was losing color in the homogeneous light of the early afternoon. There were lamps burning in some of the windows on the other side of the avenue.

"What's wrong, Doloretas?"

"We have to tell Mr. Cortabanyes that it's time to start using the gas heater."

"But, Doloretas, it's only October."

I took advantage of that accidental allusion to the date to tear two old pages off the calendar and remind myself of the speedy flight of empty days. Doloretas went back to typing a page spattered with erasures.

"Then you get chills and . . . and I don't know . . . ," she grumbled.

Doloretas had been working in Cortabanyes's office for many years. Her husband, a lawyer, died young without leaving his wife any income. His colleagues agreed to give work to Doloretas so she could earn some money. Little by little, as those young lawyers got more and more important, they stopped needing Doloretas's sporadic assistance and replaced her with full-time secretaries who were more efficient and dedicated. Only Cortabanyes, the least clever and clumsiest, went on giving her odd jobs, increasing her fee bit by bit until she became a fixed expense that Cortabanyes paid unwillingly but inalterably. Not that she was very useful or very rapid or that years of repeating the same tasks had created in her a minimum of experience: each demand, each file, each document went on being a mystery for Doloretas. But Cortabanyes's office did not require more. She, for her part, always did—well or badly—her job and was always loyal. She never tried to become a permanent fixture in the office. She never said, "See you tomorrow" or "I'll be back." She would leave saying, "Good-bye and thank you." She never dropped hints such as "If you have something, please remember me" or, more hypocritically, "Don't forget, you have me at your orders" or "You know where to find me." She would never turn up without calling first or use the phony excuse "I was just passing by and thought I'd say hello." Only "Good-bye and thank you." And Cortabanyes, whenever he saw a long document to copy looming on the horizon, would say automatically, "Call Doloretas," "Tell Doloretas to come tomorrow afternoon," or "Where the devil is Doloretas today?" Cortabanyes, Serramadriles, and I could never figure out what she did or how she lived when she wasn't doing work for the office. She never told us about her life or her troubles—if she had any.

Copy of the Notes Taken over the Course of the Ninth Statement Made by Javier Miranda Lugarte on February 6, 1927, before Judge F. W. Davidson of the Supreme Court of the State of New York

(Folios 143 and following)

▪

English translation by court interpreter Guzmán Hernández de Fenwick

Judge Davidson: Mr. Miranda, I'm happy to see you've recovered from the illness that kept you away from these sessions the last few days.

MIRANDA: Thank you, sir.
JUDGE: Do you think you're well enough to continue with your statement?
MIRANDA: Yes.
JUDGE: Could you tell us what sort of infirmity you just experienced?
MIRANDA: Nervous collapse.
JUDGE: Perhaps you'd like to request a postponement sine die?
MIRANDA: No.
JUDGE: I therefore remind you that you are appearing before me voluntarily and that you may refuse to continue with your statement at any time.
MIRANDA: I know.
JUDGE: Besides, I want to make clear that it is the intention of this court in virtue of the powers bestowed upon it by the people and the Constitution of the United States of America to discover the truth about the facts placed before it, and that the apparent harshness it has shown from time to time corresponds purely and exclusively to its desire to carry out its charge rapidly and efficiently.
MIRANDA: I understand.
JUDGE: In that case, we can proceed with the statement. It only remains for me to remind the witness he is still under oath.
MIRANDA: I know.

.....

THE HUMAN MIND has a curious, terrible power. At the same time that I recall moments of the past, I experience the sensations I experienced then, with such realism that my body reproduces movements, conditions, and disorders from another time. I weep and laugh as if the causes of the laughter and weeping existed again with the same intensity they had years ago. And nothing could be further from the truth, because I'm sadly aware that almost everyone who made me suffer or enjoy myself back then has remained behind, far away in time and distance. And too many, for God's sake, rest underground. This nervous depression that afflicts me (and which the doctors erroneously attribute to my sessions with the judge) is nothing more than the photographic (mimetic, we could say) reproduction of those sad months of 1918.

.....

ONE BRILLIANT MORNING in June, Nemesio Cabra Gómez heard the bolts that sealed his cell slide open. An orderly with a black beard and a white smock holding a length of rubber hose in his hand gestured for him to get up and come out. The orderly started walking and then stopped after a few steps.

"You first," he ordered, "and no tricks, or I'll give you a hiding."

And he waved the rubber hose, which hissed like a snake. They walked through the tortuous corridors. As they passed before the glassed-in porches that faced the garden, Nemesio Cabra Gómez sensed the burn of the sun and was dazzled by the light. He pressed himself to the glass to contemplate the sky and the garden, where another inmate was sealing anthills. The orderly hit him with the hose.

"Let's go, you: what's wrong with you?"

"I've been in that box for months."

"Well, no nonsense now or back you go."

That was the first notice he had that they were going to set him free. Doctor Flors confirmed it. He told Nemesio that the doctors had declared him cured and that he could return to normal life, but that he should avoid alcohol and other stimulants, that he should avoid arguments, that he should sleep as much as possible, and that he should visit a colleague (whose name and address he wrote down on a card) whenever he felt ill or, in any case, every three months until he was definitively discharged.

Since the clothes he wore when brought into the sanatorium were both worn out and full of gaping holes, Doctor Flors gave him a shirt, trousers, a pair of shoes, and a cloak donated by some charitable ladies. They packed up his new clothes and led him to the door.

Once he was free, he slipped into a nearby woods to try on his new wardrobe. The things Doctor Flors had given him were used and of different sizes. The shirt was too big, while the trousers were too short and so tight he couldn't button them. So he tied them around his waist with some twine. The shoes were tight, and he had no socks. The cloak, on the other hand, seemed fine, even if it was useless in that season of the year. He put his identification and the few personal objects he possessed in his pockets and tossed the rags into a thicket. Quite happy, he went back to the road and walked for a long while, until he came to the rails of a narrow-gauge train, or *carrilet*, and followed them, looking for the station. When he found it, he waited until the *carrilet* pulled in, got on, and hid in the lavatory to avoid paying for a ticket—he had no money.

In Barcelona, after all the passengers had exited, he slipped onto the platform, walked through the gate with the crowd, and then stood staring at the street, his eyes filled with tears because he was his own master once again.

Letter from Inspector Vázquez to Sergeant Totorno dated 5/8/1919, urging Totorno to stand fast

Entered as Evidence: Document No. 7b

▪

English translation by court interpreter Guzmán Hernández de Fenwick

Tetuán, 5/8/1919

Dear Friend:

Don't give up hope. If you feel yourself giving up, just think that the struggle for truth is the most noble mission a man can have on the face of the earth. And that is exactly what the mission of the police is.

Find out if Lepprince still has that German gunman Max working for him, but don't tell anyone about our correspondence. I congratulate you on your recovery. There is no physical defect that cannot be overcome by a strong will. Wouldn't it be more comfortable for you to use a typewriter?

Yours affectionately,
(signed) A. Vázquez
Police Inspector

Cortabanyes was right to shatter my illusions: the rich are only concerned with themselves. Their friendliness, their concern, and their show of interest are mirages. You'd have to be a fool to think their affection would last for long. And that happens because the links that can exist between a rich man and a poor man are not reciprocal. The rich man doesn't need the poor man: whenever he wishes, he can replace him.

I wasn't invited to Lepprince's wedding, which, to a certain point, was understandable. The ceremony took place in the strictest intimacy, not only out of respect for Savolta's memory but also because it would have attracted large crowds which might have been infiltrated by the criminal element. I hoped to go on seeing Lepprince after the marriage, but it wasn't to be. Lepprince had his own ways, which were as incomprehensible and disconcerting as he himself. The day I went to the Savolta house—when Inspector Vázquez left after telling us about his sudden transfer from Barcelona—Lepprince brought me in, either because he wanted to or felt obliged to, to say hello to his future wife and mother-in-law. He dragged me to the little salon on the second floor where the two women were awaiting his return and introduced me as if I were a great friend; he repeated the pompous term "prestigious lawyer" and made me, ignoring the protests my discretion imposed on me, toast their future happiness.

I still remember the impression María Rosa Savolta made on me then. During the months between that fateful New Year's Eve and this moment, a singular change had taken place in the young woman, whether because of her accumulated suffering, her being in love (which her eyes, words, and gestures could not dissimulate), or because of the prospect of the imminent and transcendent change that would better her life—marrying Lepprince. She seemed more adult, more reposed in her bearing, all of which revealed a greater serenity of spirit. She'd exchanged the naive expression of a girl just freed from the coziness of school for the serious style of a lady, exchanged the languid air of the perplexed adolescent for the magic aura of the anxious woman in love.

But I don't want to get excessively rhetorical: I'll omit the descriptions and pass directly to the events themselves.

Letter from Sergeant Totorno to Inspector Vázquez dated 6/21/1918, in which he provides information about several known figures

Entered as Evidence: Document No. 7c

▪

English translation by court interpreter Guzmán Hernández de Fenwick

Barcelona 6/21/1918

Esteemed and Respected Chief:

Please pardon my delay in writing you, but I decided to follow your thoughtful advice and spent these last weeks learning to use the typewriter, which is more difficult than it might seem at first sight. My brother-in-law lent me an Underwood, thanks to which I've been able to practice at night, although you can see the number of mistakes I still make.

I finally found out what you wanted to know—if Mr. Lepprince still had that gunman in his service—and the answer is yes he does, that he has taken him to his new home and has him along wherever he goes. Another bit of news that may interest you is that Nemesio Cabra Gómez was released a few days ago. I found out from a friend down at the station who told me they'd arrested Nemesio because he was making cigars out of tobacco from cigarette butts and putting a band on them, then selling them as genuine cigars. It seems Nemesio invoked your name, but it didn't help him, because they locked him up. My friend (the one from the station about whom I've already spoken) told me that Nemesio looks dead and has such an emaciated face that just looking at him makes you feel pity. Everything else goes on much as usual. Watch out for the Moors now—they like to attack from behind. Respectfully at your orders.

(signed) Sgt. Totorno

It's hard to suffer solitude patiently, more so when it's preceded by a period of friendship and pleasant company, which is what I'd had with Lepprince. So, one afternoon, fed up with the emptiness of my free time after work, I broke every rule of decorum and went to Lepprince's house, to the dear old apartment on the Rambla de Cataluña, whose linden trees formed an arch of green over the boulevard, imitating the landscape painting that adorned the mantle in the little salon.

The doorman with the white muttonchops came out to meet me and greeted me effusively; his presence restored life to me, as if in his big mouth, with its shiny gold teeth, were the symbol of the wedding bands. But he disabused me almost immediately: Mr. and Mrs. Lepprince had moved away. He was astonished that I didn't know and that I hadn't seen the FOR RENT sign on the balcony. He was sorry he couldn't give me any more information, but he himself, after so many years of faithful service, did not know the whereabouts of Mr. Lepprince, so generous, so kind, and so eccentric.

"However," he added in an attempt to console me, "I confess I'm almost happy he's gone because while I really liked the gentleman—even though he gave me some unpleasantness—I couldn't even look at that German or Englishman who killed so many people in the theater. This has always been a respectable house."

By then he'd taken my arm and was marching me back and forth in the entranceway.

"The gentleman gave me a shock when that woman came to live here. You know which one I mean: the one who climbed up the elevator cables like a wild monkey from Africa or like someone from America. Now, I'm the kind of guy who likes to understand everybody. Which is what I said to my missus, I said that even if he seems older than he is because of his style and seriousness, Mr. Lepprince is young, my dear, I said, and it's natural for him to be wild in some aspects of daily living. You know what they say about how a hair from a certain part of a lady's body can tie a man up tighter than steel handcuffs—you get me, right?"

"Yes, of course," I answered not knowing how I'd ever get away.

"The proof is that that business quickly passed. But that big guy with such milky white skin, I don't know what to tell you . . . I just couldn't stomach him. I know what I'm talking about, and you can see that I don't mince words. It isn't that, no sir, not that."

I'd skillfully led him toward the door, where I held out my hand to him in a sign of farewell. He grasped it with great emotion and, holding it between his own soft, sweaty hands, concluded, "For all that, Mr. Javier, I'm sorry he's gone. I was really fond of him, I mean it. And his wife, sir, was a saint. The legitimate wife, I mean, you understand me. A saint! I really liked that one, really."

I recounted my failure to Perico Serramadriles, who shook his head as if he were tied up and wanted to get rid of his glasses.

"The goose that laid the golden eggs is dead, Lord, the goose that laid the golden eggs is dead."

He repeated all that about the goose and the golden eggs so many times that he finally got me mad, and I shouted at him to shut up and leave me in peace.

"Don't fight, for heaven's sake," Doloretas intervened. "I'm ashamed just listening to you. Two young men like you thinking about money all the time instead of working and building yourselves a future, for God's sake."

LETTER FROM INSPECTOR VÁZQUEZ TO SERGEANT TOTORNO DATED 6/31/1928, IN WHICH HE REQUESTS MEANS TO INTERVENE IN BARCELONA LIFE FROM HIS PLACE OF EXILE

Entered as Evidence: Document No. 7d

▪

English translation by court interpreter Guzmán Hernández de Fenwick

Tetuán 6/31/1928

Dear Friend:

I received your attentive letter dated June 21, and it was very useful to me. I have no doubt whatsoever about the existence of a conspiracy of immense proportions whose victim, in this instance, was poor N. Do what you can so that notice of his arrest reaches me in an official way (a bulletin or a newspaper article would do) so that I can intervene by arranging his freedom. Humanitarian sentiments move me to proceed as I am, and you know very well, Totorno my friend, that such is the case. If my influence is still worth anything (something I find more difficult to believe with each passing day), I will use it to relieve all that abuse and humiliation.

I applaud your progress with the typewriter. Life is an unrelenting struggle. Courage! Always advance!

Yours sincerely,
(signed) A. Vázquez
Inspector of Police

Work went on, monotonous and unproductive. Summer arrived punctually and gave no signs it would ever leave. My apartment, located directly beneath the roof, was exposed to the sun all day long and seemed more like an oven than anything else. At night, the heat barely abated, but of course the humidity increased: objects acquired a viscous patina, and I, used to the dry climate of Castile, suffocated and melted. I began to suffer from insomnia. And when I finally did fall asleep, I was beset by nightmares. Usually, I would feel the presence of a bear next to me in bed.

The danger of sharing my bed with a beast didn't make me nervous, because the bear in my dreams was peaceful and tame, but I just couldn't stand having him so near me in that room filled with burned air. I would wake up dripping with perspiration and have to run to the sink to splash handfuls of water on my face. Feeling the cool liquid running down my back and chest briefly consoled me.

To avoid the bear's company and my restless, tiring half-sleep, I would read without stopping until very late. When my eyes finally closed, I would sleep badly and little. In the morning, I would wake up very tired, and this hypnotic state would last all day until—an irony of my constitution—I would recover my lucidity and vigor at nightfall.

During that time, Perico Serramadriles and I got into the habit of going swimming. In the time between the noon break and going back to work in the afternoon, we would go out to the beach on trolleys overflowing with ugly, sweaty people. We ate at the seaside, delicious sandwiches and great paellas we'd buy in the shacks. We soon gave up the paellas, however, because they were too expensive and too heavy—they put us into a torpor that interfered with work. On more than one afternoon, the two of us fell asleep in the office at the same time. Not that it mattered much, because Cortabanyes's few clients were away on vacation, and the calm of the office was only disrupted by the obstinate flies that Doloretas flailed at with a rolled-up newspaper.

Letter from Sergeant Totorno to Inspector Vázquez dated 7/12/1918, in which he explains how he carried out the task Vázquez set for him

Entered as Evidence: Document No. 7e, Appendix 1

▪

English translation by court interpreter Guzmán Hernández de Fenwick

Barcelona, 7/12/1918

Admired and Distinguished Chief:

Excuse my slowness in carrying out your always welcome orders. As you know, in my current situation I am quite distant from the world of the station, and that makes the pleasure I would take in carrying out your well-considered orders more difficult to accomplish. But after carefully thinking the matter over, I found a way of having the news about the unfortunate Nemesio's being locked up sent to you. To that end, I managed to have the information about your having been transferred made known to him. At this very moment, Nemesio knows that you are in Tetuán and, unless I am sadly mistaken, he will move heaven and earth to get in touch with you in order to have you intercede in his case. It seemed a good plan to me: what do you think?

Thank you for your interest in my progress with the typewriter. You were always a beacon for us on the difficult road of duty. But as you see, my technique still leaves a lot to be desired. Nothing more to report: I remain at your orders.

(signed) Sgt. Totorno

Letter from Nemesio Cabra Gómez to Inspector Vázquez on the Same Date in Which He Describes His Sad State

Entered as Evidence: Document No. 7e, Appendix 2

▪

English translation by court interpreter Guzmán Hernández de Fenwick

Barcelona, Year of our Lord 1918,
Day of Grace July 12

My dear sir and brother in Christ Our Lord:

Jesus Christ, through one of His Angels, has informed me you are currently in Tetuán, a fact that plunged me into sadness and despair, although I did recall His words:

> And he will scourge us for our iniquities, and will have mercy again, and will gather us out of all nations, among whom he has scattered us. (Tobit, 13-5)

Now that my soul has been sweetened and my spirit made tranquil, I have decided to write this letter so that you may participate, as does Our Lord, in the great calamities that for my sins have befallen me. You should know then, Mr. Inspector, that when those learned men noticed that I had been cured of my illnesses by the intercession of the Holy Spirit, they allowed me to return to the paths of the Lord, where the wheat and the tares are so intertwined. Thus it is that through my own fault and blindness I came to fall into evil ways, which have led me to this prison, just as before I landed in that nauseating cell which you came to know and which it was only possible for me to leave with the help of the Most High. Which means, to tell the truth, that I have bettered my condition, because here they treat me like a human being and don't beat me or give me showers of ice-cold water, don't torture or threaten me, and I cannot complain about their behavior toward me, which is charitable and worthy of God's mercy. But the fact is that I possess great truths which have been revealed to me in dreams by a cloud or a flame or I don't now what (by Divine Grace), and I can only communicate those truths to you, Mr. Inspector, and to do so I must be set free from this my material prison where I am shackled. Do something for me, Mr. Inspector. I am not a criminal or a madman, which is what they make me out to be. I am only the victim of the evil one's temptations. Help me and you will be rewarded with spiritual gifts in this life and Eternal Health in the Eternal Life to come.

I speak daily with Jesus Christ and beg him to save you from the Moors.

Yours truly,
N.C.G.

P.S. You will receive this missive from the hands of a messenger. Don't ask him any questions or look him directly in the eye, because you might contract an incurable illness. Farewell.

JUDGE DAVIDSON: Were there any more attempts on the life of Lepprince after the incident in the theater?
MIRANDA: No.
JUDGE: Is it logical to suppose that the terrorists would give up getting revenge so quickly?
MIRANDA: I don't know.
JUDGE: That would not seem to be their tactics, according to my information.
MIRANDA: I've said I don't know.
JUDGE: Following the reports in my power, during 1918, there were in Barcelona eight hundred and seven so-called social attacks, whose list of victims reads as follows: dead business owners, four; wounded, nine; dead workers and employees, eleven; wounded, forty-three. This list does not include material damages caused by numerous fires and dynamite explosions. In May, there was a massive looting of food stores that continued for several days and that only the declaration of a state of martial law could stop.
MIRANDA: Those were crisis years, no doubt about it.
JUDGE: And doesn't it seem odd to you, given the nature of those months, that there wouldn't be further attempts on Lepprince's life?
MIRANDA: I don't know. I don't think my opinion about it matters.
JUDGE: Let's change the subject. Could you tell us to what you attribute Inspector Vázquez's sudden exile?

MIRANDA: It wasn't an exile.
JUDGE: I'll rephrase that: could you explain Vázquez's sudden change of post?
MIRANDA: Well . . . he was a police officer.
JUDGE: I know that. I mean the real motives for removing him from the Savolta case.
MIRANDA: I don't know.
JUDGE: Couldn't the sudden cessation of attacks be related to the departure of Inspector Vázquez?
MIRANDA: I don't know.
JUDGE: Finally, was the attack on Lepprince prepared as part of a charade that covered up other actions?
MIRANDA: I don't know.
JUDGE: Yes or no?
MIRANDA: I don't know. I don't know.

.....

I SANK INTO A DEPRESSION: my solitude deepened, day by day, hour by hour, minute by minute. If I took a walk to calm my tormented spirit, I would fall into a strange trance that caused me to blank out and to take long strides without consciously choosing any route. Sometimes I would wake up and realize I was lost in a suburb, not knowing how I'd managed to get to such an unusual place—I'd have to ask passersby the way back. Other times, when I'd just begun my stroll, I'd find myself at an intersection and, not knowing which street to take, would simply stand there, as motionless as a statue or a beggar, until hunger or fatigue obliged me to go home. If I drifted away from known or familiar places, I would be assailed by a fatal disquiet, I would tremble like a man about to be executed. Tears would come to my eyes, and I'd have to go home and lock myself within the four walls of my apartment. There, I would try to find relief from my sense of abandonment in weeping which would sometimes go on the entire night. It happened more than once that I would wake up and find my cheeks moist and the sheet soaked. I thought seriously about suicide, but I rejected the idea, more out of cowardice than for any attachment to life. I could no longer stand reading, and if I went to see a film or a show, I would have to leave the theater almost as soon as the performance began because it was impossible for me to stay in one place. Finally, I'd stopped going out with Serramadriles, and our relationship shrank to mere formal courtesies.

Request Sent From Inspector Vázquez To The Minister Of The Interior Dated 7/17/1918, In Which He Intercedes On Behalf Of Nemesio Cabra

Entered as Evidence: Document No. 7f

▪

English translation by court interpreter Guzmán Hernández de Fenwick

Don Alejandro Vázquez Ríos, Police Inspector of Tetuán,
states, with all due respect and consideration
for Your Excellency:

That he has received a letter from an individual named Nemesio Cabra Gómez dated 7/12/1918. That Cabra Gómez is currently incarcerated by governmental order in the jails of the Barcelona Police Station. That some months ago the author of this letter happened to be in the aforementioned police station where he had occasion to meet and have dealings with the aforementioned Nemesio Cabra Gómez. That the author of this letter noted in him symptoms of mental disorder, symptoms that later were confirmed and caused Cabra Gómez to be treated in one of the sanatoria that exist in our country for that purpose. That later, in view of his partial recovery and in view of the fact that he gave no signs of being dangerous, Nemesio Cabra Gómez was released and allowed to rejoin society in order, through work and contact with other people, to recover his mental equilibrium and sanity. That a few weeks ago, Cabra Gómez was arrested for the supposed manufacture of false cigars. That Cabra Gómez is mentally retarded, not legally responsible for his acts, and that his incarceration can only worsen his illness and make it incurable. For which reason, with all due respect and consideration for Your Excellency, the author of this letter begs that you set the aforementioned Nemesio Cabra Gómez free at your earliest convenience in order that he reenter society and bring his recovery to a successful conclusion. I hope Your Excellency will grant this request out of the goodness of your heart. May God bless you.

(signed) Alejandro Vázquez Ríos
Police Inspector
Tetuán, July 17, 1918

To: His Excellency, the Minister of the Interior
Ministry of the Interior, Madrid

ARTICLE CUT FROM AN UNKNOWN BARCELONA NEWSPAPER
HANDWRITTEN DATE: 7/25/1918

Entered as Evidence: Document No. 9a

▪

English translation by court interpreter Guzmán Hernández de Fenwick

Appointments

Don Alejandro Vázquez Ríos, who carried out the duties of inspector of police with admirable brilliance here in Barcelona, later to carry on the same labors in Tetuán, has been named Inspector of Police in Bata (Guinea).

Those of us who recall with gratitude and affection his residence among us and who had occasion to admire his intelligence, his tenacity, and his humanity, which far exceeded the mere execution of his duties, wish him a pleasant residence in that beautiful city and congratulate him with all our hearts for his well-deserved appointment.

.....

I BEGAN TO DRINK EXCESSIVELY as soon as I left the office, in the deluded hope that alcohol would deaden my senses and make my waking hours more bearable. The results were totally counterproductive, because my sensitivity was heightened, time seemed not to pass, and I was assailed by tormenting hallucinations. I would wake up tense, floating in the waves of delirium. My stomach burned, and I would feel as though a ball of cotton had been stretched out to block both my throat and mouth. My hands would reach for objects without finding them, my swollen muscles would not respond to the orders of my brain. I was afraid of going blind, and until the light bulb in my room restored the familiar images of the objects in it, I could not take a calm breath. Sometimes I would wake up firmly believing I'd gone deaf and throw things on the floor to see if hearing the noise would allay my fears. Other times, I'd feel I'd lost the power to speak, and I had to talk and hear my voice to be sure I was all right. I stopped drinking, but my sick state persisted. One night, I woke up shaken by chills. My temples throbbed, my eyes ached, and my forehead was burning to the touch. I felt more alone than ever and decided to return home to my family. Cortabanyes gave me an indefinite leave of absence and promised to keep my job for me until I either came back or definitively resigned, although he regretted he could not go on paying me while I was away—it had been a bad year and his income did not allow for any superfluous expenses. I was not offended: Cortabanyes had his good side and his bad side, and one went with the other. I also made an agreement with the owner of my building: he agreed not to rent my apartment to anyone else as long as I kept paying the rent, a job I turned over to Serramadriles.

I took the train, and two days later I was in Valladolid. My mother received me coldly but my sisters were mad with joy. You'd think the king was visiting them. They spoiled me, fed me the choicest dishes at all hours of the day. They said I didn't look well, that I should put on some weight, and that I had to sleep and eat so I would regain my color. Going home comforted me and restored my peace. Soon news of my arrival spread through the city. Every day the house was filled with old acquaintances and people I'd never seen before. They were all interested in me, but more interested in life in Barcelona. I told them about all the anarchist attacks, a subject that filled the local newspapers, exaggerating the details and, of course, exaggerating my own participation in them—I was always a major actor.

Nevertheless, the warmth around me was fictitious. All the ties of affection I'd had with my childhood friends were broken. Time had changed them. They seemed old to me even though they were my age. Some were married to vulgar young girls and adopted paternalistic airs that amused me at first and irritated me later. Most of them had reached a mediocre social status which they would never leave, and were so self-satisfied they seemed about to burst. With new friends, things were even worse. They had a visceral aversion to Cataluña and everything Catalan. Their contacts with sharp, pretentious, and chauvinistic merchants had created an image of the Catalan which for them was an absolute truth. They mimicked the Catalan accent, mocked it, made fun of Catalan regionalism, and in exasperation criticized Catalan separatism, overwhelming me with counterarguments as if I were the standard bearer for Catalan defects. They pretended, I think, that I defended subversive, antipatriotic ideas so they could give free reign to their hostilities. And if I didn't identify myself with their point of view, they felt cheated and went on with their diatribes, paying no attention to my silence and my acquiescence. If I tried to go into the fine points of their arguments because I thought them badly focused or too impassioned, they took offense and redoubled the force of their attacks with missionary zeal and holy anger.

The girls were ugly, badly dressed, and their conversation was insipid. The ennui that invaded me after being with them made me nostalgically recall my chats with Teresa. More and more jokes were made about my being single, and the mothers fluttered around me, looking at me as if they were appraisers and speaking to me with the honeyed words of matchmakers.

My family lived in misery, not only because we lacked material means but for a certain conventlike air that surrounded them. Their Carthusian style made them stint on everything, not only luxuries but anything that might simply be a pleasure. The house was always dark because sunlight was sinful and "ate up the carpets." The food was tasteless to save money on seasoning. Their way of measuring everything was "a pinch" of whatever it happened to be. My sisters were like nuns and floated through the house like souls in purgatory, hugging the walls and trying not to be noticed. They hated going out, and contact with people turned them into pathetic puppets. They suffered to hide their timidity and their inability to face the world around them.

Despite the flattering attention my being a novelty brought me, I began to be weighed down by the city. I thought about what my life would be if I were to stay much longer; I'd have to find a job, reconstruct a circle of friends, live with my family, give up women, yield to local customs. I made a careful list of the pros and cons and decided to go back to Barcelona. My sisters begged me not to go until after Christmas. I agreed, but I wouldn't stay any longer. The second day of the new year, tired of passing for a dandy and of not being understood, I packed my bags and took the train once again.

Letter From Sergeant Totorno To Inspector Vásquez Dated 10/30/1918, In Which He Provides Information And Advice

Entered as Evidence: Document No. 7g

▪

English translation by court interpreter Guzmán Hernández de Fenwick

Barcelona 10/30/1918

Dear Chief:

Please excuse my slowness in writing to you, but few things have happened which could be of interest to you. And then a few days ago something did happen that seemed important to me, which is why I now write you with such urgency. The fact is they've arrested N.C.G. again, this time for begging in the cathedral completely naked. Once again, he's with us, this time sentenced to six months confinement, crazier than ever. The interesting part is that they seized his personal effects, as usual, among which, as a friend (of whom I've spoken in earlier letters) from the station told me, were *unimportant papers* and other things. I suspect those unimportant papers might be very important, but I don't see any way of getting to them. What do you suggest? You know you always have me at your orders.

Watch out for those blacks, they're all cannibals and worse. Respectfully yours,

(signed) Sgt. Totorno

Letter From Inspector Vázquez To Sergeant Totorno Dated 11/10/1918 In Response To The Above

Bata, 11/10/1918

Dear Friend:

Your letter reached me in bed. I'm afflicted by a strange sickness that is eating me up. The doctors say it's a tropical fever from which I will recover as soon as I depart this inhospitable place, but I'm not so sure I'll ever recover. I lose more and more weight every day, I'm the color of wax, my eyes are sunken, and my face is covered with splotches that look very suspicious. Every time I look in the mirror I'm horrified to note the advances of the sickness. I don't sleep, and my stomach rejects all the food I force down with great difficulty. My nerves are out of order. The heat is unbearable, and I have that incessant drumming which seems to spring from everywhere at the same time deep in my brain. I don't think we'll ever see each other again.

As for N.C.G., they should poison him like a mad dog. Yours,

(signed) Vázquez

Part Two

Chapter 1

It was 9:30 on a stormy December night; a heavy downpour had just begun. Rosa López Ferrer—better known as Rosita the Idealist, prostitute by profession; twice arrested and jailed: once for complicity in the sale of stolen goods and once for concealing an individual sought and later arrested for terrorist acts—swished some wine around in her mouth and noisily spat it out, spattering a customer who had been contemplating her in silence for a long while.

"Every day you put more water and junk into this wine, you bastards!" she screeched at the top of her lungs, rebuking the owner of the tavern.

"I hope the duchess here isn't annoying you," answered the owner, imperturbable after checking to see if anyone besides the silent customer had witnessed her accusation.

"Be more polite to the lady," responded the silent customer.

Rosita the Idealist looked at him as if she hadn't noticed his presence before, even though the silent customer had been perched on a low stool for over two hours without taking his eyes off her.

"And what's this got to do with you, rat?" Rosita spat at him.

"Excuse me, I only wanted to see justice served," said the customer.

"Well, go see justice served out on the street, freak!" said the owner, leaning halfway over the bar. "Maggots like you give the place a bad name. You've been here all afternoon and haven't spent a cent. You're so ugly you'd scare a wolf away, and besides, you stink."

Despite this insult, the customer evinced no more sadness than that which naturally emanated from his face.

"All right, you don't have to get that way. I'll leave."

Rosita the Idealist felt sorry for him.

"It's raining. Don't you have an umbrella?"

"No, but don't worry about me."

Rosita turned toward the bartender, who wouldn't take his irate eyes off the customer.

"Look, he doesn't have an umbrella."

"So what? Water sure won't do him any harm."

Rosita insisted.

"Let him stay until the rain lets up."

Suddenly uninterested in the matter, the bartender shrugged his shoulders and went back to his chores. The customer sank back onto the stool and returned to his mute contemplation of Rosita.

"Have you eaten?" she asked.

"Not yet."

"Not yet since when?"

"Since yesterday morning."

Taking advantage of the owner's distraction, the good-hearted prostitute stole a slice of bread from the bar and passed it to the man. Then she held out a platter with slices of salami on it.

"Take some while he's not looking," she whispered.

Just when the man's hand shot toward the platter, the bartender caught them in the act.

"By Jesus, I'll cut your heart out, you crook!"

He came around the bar, waving a kitchen knife. The man hid behind Rosita the Idealist—after stuffing the salami slices into his mouth.

"Out of the way, Rosita, I'm going to cut him apart!" the owner was shouting. And he would have carried out his threat if the arrival of a new, astounding customer hadn't interrupted him. The stranger was a man of medium height and advanced age, lean, with gray hair, and a serious mien. He was elegantly dressed, and his demeanor, as well as the quality and cut of his clothes, announced his wealth. He was alone and stopped on the threshold to take a curious look at the bar and its occupants. It was obvious he was not a regular at dives like this. The bartender, Rosita, and the man she was protecting supposed he was just trying to get out of the rain because his topcoat and hat were soaked through.

"What may I get you, sir?" said the bartender solicitously, hiding the knife under his apron and walking toward the door with a little bow. "Please come in, it's raining cats and dogs."

The new customer looked doubtfully at the bartender and his apron, out of which the shining blade of the carving knife was peeking. Then he took a few steps, took off his hat and coat, and hung them on a greasy hook. Then, with no further preambles, he walked right over to the astonished customer his providential arrival had just saved.

"What's your name?"

"Nemesio Cabra Gómez, serving God and your honor."

"Well then, let's sit down at a table where no one will bother us. We have to talk business."

The bartender humbly approached.

"Please forgive me, sir, but this man just stole a salami, and seeing that you're such good . . . "

The new customer gave the bartender a grim look and took some coins out of his pocket.

"Take it out of this."

"Thank you, sir."

"Bring some food for this man. No, nothing for me."

Nemesio Cabra Gómez, who had followed the course of events without missing a single detail, rubbed his hands and brought his pallid face close to Rosita's.

"One of these days I'll be rich, Rosita," he said in a very low voice, "and I swear by the Virgin of Mercy that on that day, I'll take you away from all this and help you lead a decent life."

The generous prostitute couldn't believe her eyes. Did these two men, so completely different, really know each other?

.....

Perico Serramadriles waved a Reform Republican Party membership card in front of my face. That was the fifth party my colleague had joined.

"God only knows," he said. "God only knows what they do with the money we give them."

Perico was in the mood for a chat, but I wasn't. When I came back from Valladolid, I reentered the office with Cortabanyes's tacit acquiescence. He'd also had the tact not to say a word about what was obviously a crashing, shameful failure. My return took place under the auspices of his apathy, which dissimulated his affection and substituted for it—to my advantage.

"Look, the process is as simple as this: you join a party, any party, and they start in: Pay this, pay that, vote this way, vote this other way. And then they tell you things like: We really screwed the conservatives, we really screwed the radicals. And I ask myself, what is all this leading to? You're the same one day as another, prices go up, salaries stay put."

Perico Serramadriles, vibrating to the rhythm of current events, had become a revolutionary: he wanted to sack the convents and palaces exactly in the way two years ago he was calling for the use of fire and sword to put down strikes and demonstrations.

To tell the truth, the situation of the country that year—1919—was the worst we'd ever been in. Factories were closing, unemployment was on the rise, and black waves of immigrants from the abandoned countryside were flowing into a city that could barely feed its own children. The new arrivals swarmed in the streets, hungry and phantasmagoric, a few of them dragging their poor possessions around in little bundles, while the majority simply walked around with their hands in their pockets. All begged for work, a place to stay, food, cigarettes, and money. Their skinny children ran around half-dressed, accosting passersby; prostitutes of all ages constituted a pathetic throng. And naturally, the unions and the resistance groups had unleashed a tragic wave of strikes and physical attacks; meetings were held in movie houses, theaters, plazas, and streets; the masses attacked the bakeries. Confused rumors from Europe told about events in Russia that lifted the spirits and spurred the imagination of the disinherited. New emblems appeared on the walls, and Lenin's name was repeated with obsessive frequency.

But as for the politicos, if they were nervous, they covered it up. Through sheer demagoguery they hoped to attract the poor to their side with promises that contained equal doses of blood and generosity. Bread was scarce, but there were plenty of words, and the poor, with nothing else to do, nourished themselves on vain hopes. And beneath that painful, shouting facade of ambitions, hatred germinated and violence fermented.

Against that desolate background, the image of Perico Serramadriles stood out on that dark February afternoon.

"Know what I'm saying, kid? The politicians only try to get ahead at our expense," he said, nodding his head affirmatively and seriously to corroborate this highly original observation.

"So why don't you quit?"

"The Republican Party?"

"Of course."

"Oh," he exclaimed, disconcerted. "Which one would I join then? They're all the same."

As for me, what can I say? I wasn't concerned with any of it, indifferent as I was to everything unrelated to my own situation. I think I would have received the most chaotic revolution, wherever it came from, as a resurrection as long as it brought a slight change to my gray life and closed horizons, my agonizing solitude, and my leaden ennui. Boredom, like a rust, corroded my work and my free time. Life ran through my hands like a filthy stream of water.

Nevertheless, for better or worse, a fortuitous event was going to change my life.

It all began one night when Perico Serramadriles and I decided to take an after-dinner walk. Winter was yielding to incipient spring; the weather was unstable but mild. It was a serene, warm mid-February day. Perico and I had eaten in a restaurant close to

Cortabanyes's office because a client who turned up at the last minute had forced us to stay late. So at eleven we were on the street, beginning our walk with no fixed destination or preconceived plan. By common agreement, we went into Chinatown, which at the time was coming out of its winter lethargy. The sidewalks were teeming with ragged, sinister-looking people all searching that sordid zone of corruption for some fleeting consolation to ease their daily sorrows. The drunks were singing and staggering around, the prostitutes, standing in the greenish light of fluttering street lamps, were offering themselves shamelessly from doorways; pimps posted on the corners struck menacing poses and flashed knives; the poor Chinese in their silky robes hawked exotic products, trinkets, unguents, hot sauces, snakeskins, and minutely carved figurines. From the bars came a solid mass of voices, music, smoke, and the smell of frying. Occasionally a scream would pierce the night.

Barely speaking, Perico and I went deeper and deeper into that labyrinth of alleys, ruins, and trash, he peering into everything avidly, I unaware of the pathetic show taking place around us. By chance or by some mysterious plan, we came to a spot that was strangely familiar to me. I recognized the houses, the irregular cobblestone street, some shop, a smell, a light—something that woke up sleeping memories. By contrast to the streets we'd just gone through, this area was deserted and silent. We were near the port, and a light mist charged with salt and tar made the air dense and breathing difficult. A foghorn bellowed and the somber waves of its groan remained, vibrating at ground level. I went along with greater and greater confidence, faster and faster, dragging the surprised and frightened Perico at my heels. An instinctive, irrepressible force was pushing me, and I would have gone on alone even if I'd known that a dark destiny (perhaps death) was waiting for me. But Perico was too disconcerted to break free of my determined influence, and, besides, he was afraid to go back and get lost. When I stopped, he caught me up to me, out of breath.

"Mind telling me where we're going? This is a horrible place."

"This is it. Look."

And I pointed to the door of a gloomy cabaret. A dirty, broken sign announced ELEGANT VARIETY SHOW and included a price list. We could hear the feeble notes of an out-of-tune piano.

"You don't really want to go in there, do you?" he asked, fear etched into his face.

"Of course, that's why we came. I'm sure you've never been here."

"Who do you think I am? Of course I've never been here. You have?"

Instead of answering, I pushed open the door and we walked in.

"MATILDE! Where the devil are you?"

"Did you call me, ma'am?"

The lady spun around startled.

"What a scare you gave me!" and she burst into jovial laughter. She'd expected the maid to appear from the door that connected the salon with the hallway. "What were you doing standing there like someone in a trance?"

"Waiting for your orders, ma'am."

The lady threw back a long blond tress that fell like golden rain down her back. The salon's mirrors reflected the glitter of her hair, sparkling in the rays of the spring sun at its zenith. Her attention attracted, the lady contemplated the mirror and examined the reflected image of the salon: framed in that way, it seemed to her like a distant, perfect work of art. She saw the glass doors opening onto an ample porch that ended in a staircase with a stone banister descending toward an undulating esplanade of new grass. Before, the esplanade had been a thick forest of old trees, but her husband, for reasons she never managed to understand, cut down the haughty poplars and the melancholic willows, the majestic cypresses and the coquettish magnolias, the paternal lime tree and the smiling lemon trees. Now the esplanade was filled with flower beds: narcissus, anemones, primroses, hyacinths, tulips imported from Holland, roses, and peonies, without forgetting the discreet, long-suffering, faithful geraniums; there was also an irregular pond of terra-cotta and ceramic, in the center of which four rose-marble angels poured water in the four cardinal directions. For an instant, the vision from the winter garden brought her memories of her happy childhood, of her languid adolescence; she saw her father strolling in the garden, leading her by the hand, showing her a butterfly, reprimanding a grasshopper which had frightened the girl with its jumpy flight. "Bad bug, get out of here! Stop frightening my little girl." Days long gone. Now the house and garden were different, her father was dead . . .

"Matilde! Where the devil are you!"

"Did you call me, ma'am?"

María Rosa Savolta examined the contradictory figure of the maid with a severe eye. What was this being of primitive coarseness with the shape of some prehistoric monument, beetle-browed, buck-toothed, and bearded, doing in a salon where all the objects sought to outdo each other in delicacy and elegance? And who put that starched cap on her, those white gloves, that apron fringed in lace? And poor Matilde, as if she had followed the course of her mistress's thoughts, lowered her eyes and entwined her bony fingers, expecting a reprimand, elaborating a quick excuse. But the lady was in good humor and burst into a giggle as light as a bird's warble.

"My good Matilde!" she exclaimed and then, recovering her seriousness, "Do you know if they confirmed my appointment with the hairdresser?"

"Yes, ma'am. At five, just as you said."

"Heaven grant us time enough to do everything." Her eyes fell on her own image in the mirror in the center of the reflected salon. "Matilde, do you think I've put on weight?"

"No, ma'am, not a bit. Ma'am, if you don't mind my saying so, I think you should eat more."

María Rosa Savolta smiled. Pregnancy still hadn't betrayed her thin figure. Despite the fact that in Spain full-figured women continued to dominate fashion, movies and illustrated magazines were introducing a new female ideal with softer angles, narrow waist and hips, and small bust.

JUST AS WE ENTERED the cabaret, the piano music stopped. The woman pounding the keys got up and in a squeaky voice announced the imminent appearance of a comedian whose name I have forgotten. The few customers in the cabaret paid her no attention, being more interested in us. Perico and I slipped between the empty tables on tiptoe and took seats next to the dance floor. Immediately we were set upon by two mature females, who threw their arms around our necks and smiled with a forced rictus.

"Looking for company, you handsome devils?"

"Don't waste your time, ladies. We're broke."

"Shit, all of you say the same thing!"

"Well, it's the truth," corroborated Perico, somewhat astonished.

"If you have no money, you should stay home," said the other by way of reprimand. And turning to her friend, "Let's go, don't waste your charms."

Paying no attention, the woman who'd grabbed Perico pulled up her skirt.

"How do you like those hams, sonny?"

Poor Perico almost fainted.

"I already said you wouldn't get a cent out of us," I repeated.

They gave us the finger and left, mockingly shaking their ruddy backsides. Perico took off his glasses and dried the sweat dotting his forehead.

"Cute little whales!" he said in a low voice. "I thought they were going to swallow us."

"They're only trying to earn an honest living."

"Do you really think they ever do?"

"Lots of men come here who aren't fussy. Crude guys."

"I don't think that even if I were drunk I could . . . with a monster like that. Did you see what she did? Lifting her . . . my God!"

A few hisses shut us up. The comedian the piano player had announced in such hyperbolic tones was now on stage. He was a poor devil who looked more like a lunatic than an actor, who sadly and mechanically recited a long series of jokes and quips, some political, the rest indecent, most of which went over the heads of the audience, which was not used to looking for double meanings and relatively obscure allusions. In any case, the obscenities got a few laughs, and the lunatic's performance achieved an ephemeral success rewarded with brief but sincere applause. Once the comedian left the stage, the lights went up, and the piano player played a waltz. Two couples went to the floor to dance. The women were prostitutes from the cabaret; the men, a sailor and a pimp, both with brutal faces.

"Would you mind telling me why the hell you brought me here?" I was amused by my friend's reaction. He was horrified, and I, to the contrary, was calm, as I was years before with Lepprince, when for no apparent reason he brought me to this very spot. Except that now I was master of the situation, and Perico was playing the part I had then.

"Leave if you want."

"Walk home alone through this part of town? Go on, I'd never get out alive!"

"Then stay, but I'm warning you: I'm going to watch the whole show."

The program was starting again. The pianist stopped playing, the lights went down, and a spotlight illuminated the dance floor. Leaving her piano, the woman walked right into the center of the cone of light, requested silence several times, and when the shifting back and forth of chairs and the whispering died down, shouted:

"Distinguished guests! I have the honor to present to you a Spanish and international act, applauded and celebrated in the best cabarets of Paris, Vienna, Berlin, and other capitals, an act which years ago had tremendous success right here and is returning now after a triumphant tour. I now present to you, ladies and gentlemen: María Coral!"

She ran to the piano and banged out some blood-curdling

chords. The floor remained empty for a few seconds, and then, as if she'd popped out of the ground or from the dark corner of a dream, María Coral appeared—the gypsy, wrapped in the same black cape dotted with phony jewels she'd worn two years ago, that night when I met Lepprince . . .

"Do you know Mr. Lepprince?"

"Mr. Lepprince . . . No, I never heard his name before," said Nemesio Cabra Gómez without taking his eyes off the stew he'd just been served.

"I don't know if you're lying or telling the truth," replied his mysterious benefactor, "and I don't really care." Out of the corner of his eye, he looked at Rosita the Idealist and the bartender, who were dying to hear what they were saying, and he lowered his voice: "I want you to follow my instructions to the letter and nothing more, understand?"

"Of course, sir. Just tell me what to do," answered Nemesio, his mouth full.

The mysterious benefactor went on talking in hushed tones. He was obviously nervous, looking at his watch—a heavy gold item that attracted the covetous eyes of everyone in the tavern—several times during the interview, and frequently turning to look toward the door. When he finished speaking, he got up, gave Nemesio some money, hastily waved to the others, and walked out, unconcerned about the storm pouring down on the city. No sooner had he left than Rosita, transformed into pure sugar, threw herself on Nemesio, and said in honeyed tones, "Nemesio, honey, you two were really talking up a storm!" And the bartender nodded agreement from behind the bar with a good-natured smile, as if to announce that all his clients were men of the world.

Nemesio finished off his dinner without saying a word, and when he'd finished wiping his plate clean, set about leaving the tavern.

"Going so soon, Nemesio?" asked Rosita. "Can't you see it's pouring?"

"Yeah, cats and dogs," corroborated the bartender.

"A good night to snuggle up between the sheets . . . with someone you like," concluded Rosita.

Nemesio dug into his pocket, took out a coin, and gave it to Rosita.

"I'll come back for you."

And he dashed out into the street, his toothless mouth wide with laughter.

FOLLOWED BY HER FAITHFUL MATILDE, María Rosa Savolta walked into the kitchen. A cook expressly hired to show off his art and five women recruited for that special day were busy at work. Myriad aromas mixed together, the air exuded fat, and an infernal heat dominated the place. The cook, assisted by a young maid, red and perplexed, shouted orders and curses indiscriminately, only interrupting himself to take long drinks from a bottle of white wine he kept on one side of the oven. A matron as large as a hippopotamus beat a white dough with a whisk. One of the women cooks passed by, miraculously balancing a wobbly pile of plates. The clash of pots and pans was like a medieval tourney or pirates boarding a ship. No one noticed the presence of the lady, so the maelstrom went right on. Because of the oppressive heat, the women had rolled up their sleeves and unbuttoned their smocks. A coarse, solidly built maid plucking chickens had the space between her heavy breasts lined with feathers, like a nest. Another showed bosoms white with flour; elsewhere a girl was holding a skimmer filled with fresh lettuce against her firm peasant breasts. Their shouts were deafening. The maids fought and taunted each other, rounding off their short phrases with nasty laughter and obscene exclamations. And reigning over that orgy, like the billy-goat at a witches' sabbath, the sweaty, drunk, exultant cook leapt, danced, ordered, and blasphemed.

María Rosa Savolta felt she was about to faint. She began to perspire and said to Matilde, "Let's get out of here. Draw my bath."

Alone in the tranquility of her bedroom, she calmed down and stared into the garden, where a light breeze made the grass wave and shook the delicate stems of the flowers. The statues flanking the pavilion seemed to be conjured into life by the sun and the perfumed wind that came down the leafy slope of Tibidabo. María Rosa Savolta pressed her forehead against the glass and, forgetting the party and the insane preparations, drifted into a contemplative state, lulled by the virile, possessive caress of the sun. She had never felt this way, not even in her happy years at boarding school. She sighed. She didn't have much time. She went toward the bathroom, where the water was flowing. The room was filled with steam and the perfume of bath salts.

"I'll take care of the rest, Matilde, there's no time to waste. Go see if the hairdresser's here and make me some lunch. Nothing much . . . something light: some pastry, a little fruit, and a lemonade. Or better, a glass of cocoa. Oh, I just don't know! Whatever you say, it's all the same, as long as it's not too heavy. That kitchen upset my stomach. You know what I like. Get going, why are you standing there? Can't you see I'm going to take a bath?"

She waited until Matilde was gone, bolted the door, and got undressed. The bath was very hot and the vapor choked her. Carefully, slowly, she sank into the water until it covered her shoulders. Her skin was burning. An electric shock ran through her thighs and stomach.

No doubt about it, she thought. Everything tells me I'm going to be a mother.

DOÑÃ EMILIA THE HAIRDRESSER was putting the finishing touches on María Rosa Savolta's coiffure as the afternoon declined behind the lace curtains. The hairdresser was a forty-year-old woman, a widow, skinny, with long features, bovine eyes, and irregular, prominent, rakelike teeth that gave her an annoying lisp. She'd been a hairdresser before she married and again after becoming a widow, after five years of unhappy marriage with a lazy, egocentric, spendthrift she had stoically put up with while he was alive and on whom she now took revenge by bragging about his memory. She would talk about him constantly with the unconscious, cruel fury of an overdone romanticism that made the man seem ridiculous to her involuntary audience. The good woman was a chatterbox, and she took full advantage of the immobility to which her clients were condemned.

"These fashions," she was saying to María Rosa Savolta after a long disquisition in which she'd meandered through every possible subject with the same daring Doctor Livingstone had when he plunged into the African jungle, "are nothing more than follies to make women look ridiculous and make men spend money. Jesus, what will the French think up next! Thank heaven Spanish women have always had a solid idea of elegance and common sense to spare, otherwise . . . I couldn't tell you, Mrs. Lepprince, how silly we'd look. Because look, as my Fernando, may he rest in peace, used to say"—she crossed herself with the curling iron—"as he used to say, and he had common sense, of a kind many politicians would like to have, that there's nothing like the classic, the discreet—a well-cut dress, without fantasies or geegaws, cleanliness, and a nice hairdo, and, for grand occasions, a simple jewel or a flower."

The faithful, gaping Matilde listened to the hairdresser's peroration, nodding her countrywoman's head and whispering low: "You're so right, Doña Emilia, you're so right," while she held out hairpins, combs, little mirrors, nail clippers, curlers, curved combs, and rollers. María Rosa Savolta was amused by the noisy chatter which kept alive the obscene lies that rogue Fernando implanted in his wife's simple brain, so that she, ugly as she was, wouldn't spend a penny on clothes.

Suddenly, María Rosa Savolta called for silence with a wave of her hand and a quiet *shh!* She had just heard some footsteps she recognized in the hall. Paul-André had come home. Just as he'd promised, he left the office early to supervise preparations for the party. María Rosa made Doña Emilia hurry, and when she—scandalized that someone could prefer anything to the liturgy of the hairdo—finally declared her work complete, María Rosa, without giving Emilia a chance to brag, without praising Emilia's handiwork, slipped on her dressing gown again and went into the corridor. She then tiptoed to her husband's office and silently cracked the door open. Lepprince was seated at the table, his back to the door, and didn't see her. He'd taken off his jacket and put on a comfortable silk robe. María Rosa called him.

"Darling, are you busy?"

Lepprince jumped and hid something in the ample folds of his robe. His voice sounded ill-humored.

"Why didn't you knock before coming in?" he asked, and then, realizing it was his wife, he recomposed his face, smoothed his furrowed brow, and put on a smile. "Excuse me, sweetheart, I was completely distracted."

"Am I interrupting?"

"Of course not, but why aren't you dressed? Don't you know what time it is?"

The first guests won't be coming for more than two hours."

"Yes, but you know how I hate last-minute contretemps. Today everything has to work perfectly."

María Rosa feigned a pout of unjustly wounded sensibility.

"Look who's talking. You haven't even shaved. You should see yourself: you look like a savage."

Lepprince raised his hand to his chin, and in doing so allowed his robe to come open, revealing the burnished butt of a revolver. María Rosa saw it and her heart jumped. But she said nothing.

"I just need a few minutes, my love," said Lepprince, who hadn't noticed. "So, if you don't mind, leave me alone for an instant. I'm expecting my secretary so I can take care of a few details before the party. Some things just can't wait, as you know. Did you want something . . . "

"No . . . nothing, darling. But don't take too long," she said, closing the door.

Returning to her bedroom, she passed Max on his way to Lepprince's office. She smiled at him coldly and he bowed deeply, clicking the heels of his patent leather boots.

.....

THE PIANO BEGAN to thresh out some notes that sounded strangely distant, as if heard through a wall or in a dream, and the cabaret took on an unreal atmosphere because of the influence and magic of María Coral's dazzling beauty. I saw Perico Serramadriles sit up in his chair and stop paying any attention to the picturesque world in which we'd immersed ourselves. An unusual silence took over the place, the tense silence that accompanies the contemplation of something forbidden. It seemed—at least to me it seemed—that the slightest noise would have shattered us, as if we'd been transformed into weak glass figurines. María Coral went around the floor like an optical illusion, like a nonspecific inspiration. Her crudely made-up face emanated a paradoxical purity, and her perfect teeth, which her scornful smile revealed, seemed able to bite flesh at a distance. As she spun around and swirled her cape, she partially revealed fleeting fragments of her body: her breasts, as round and dark as pitchers; her fragile, infantile shoulders; her agile legs; and her adolescent waist and hips. A sensation of disquiet ran through the audience, as if even the most vile could feel the lacerating pain of that superhuman, inaccessible beauty.

When her performance was over, the gypsy waved, gathered up her cape, slipped it over her shoulders, blew a kiss to the audience, and disappeared. A few hands clapped weakly, and then silence reigned again. The lights went on and illuminated a group of surprised people, cadavers lined up for a trial in which the crime to be judged was the sadness and solitude of their own souls. Perico Serramadriles wiped the sweat off his brow and neck with his wrinkled handkerchief for the thousandth time.

"Man, what . . . what . . . what a thing!"

"I told you we wouldn't be wasting our time coming here," I responded, feigning nonchalance although I felt deeply upset. In my mind I kept repeating that this woman had been Lepprince's and now she might belong to someone else. And I obstinately, obsessively repeated to myself that to live without being able to open the door to pleasures like that was worse than dying.

Going home was sad: neither Perico nor I said much, I, because I found myself in a whirlwind of confused emotions, he, out of respect for my mood, which he intuited. It's hardly necessary to say I barely slept that night, and the brief tag ends of sleep or half-sleep my exhausted body fell into were plagued by convulsive nightmares.

The next day, I felt I was shipwrecked in a world whose vulgarity I couldn't identify and whose routines I could not adapt myself to despite all my efforts. Perico Serramadriles vainly tried to coax me out of it, and Doloretas wondered about my health, thinking I'd caught cold. All the thanks they received for their concern were my grunts. At nightfall, while I was unwillingly chewing a leathery sandwich in an inhospitable greasy spoon, I decided to go back to the cabaret and either renew my life—or lose it in the attempt.

IT WAS SHORTLY BEFORE DAWN when Nemesio Cabra Gómez entered the tavern. The air corrupted by the harsh smoke of cheap tobacco, the smell of humanity, and spilled wine made him reel: he was extremely tired. The tavern appeared empty, but Nemesio, as soon as he got used to the light, walked directly toward some greasy burlap curtains. The bartender, who watched everything with his sleepy eyes, shouted to him.

"Where do you think you're going, rat?"

"I just want to have a word with someone, Don Segundino. Really, I'll be gone in a minute," begged Nemesio.

"The person you're looking for hasn't come in."

"Excuse me, but how do you know when I haven't said who it is?"

"Because I can smell it, see?"

While he meekly received these insults, Nemesio crept forward until he'd reached the filthy curtain. He made a final bow, lifted one corner of the rag, and instantly went into the back room without giving the bartender a chance to stop him. The room was lit by an oil lamp hanging from the ceiling over a table. The table was round, with a large circumference, and seated around it were four men with heavy black beards, wearing thick gray flannel jackets and visored caps pulled down over their eyes. They smoked yellowish, crudely rolled cigarettes. None was drinking. One member of this gloomy company was holding a complicated mechanism, on top of which there was a kind of alarm clock which he was winding with a meticulous slowness. Another read a book, while the remaining two talked in low voices. Nemesio Cabra Gómez stood next to the door, silent and shy, until one of the men noticed and greeted him.

"Comrades, just look at the disgusting bug that's gotten in here."

"Looks like a worm to me," one said, looking toward Nemesio with small eyes separated by a scar that ran from his left eyebrow to his upper lip.

"We'll have to use a good insecticide," observed another as he opened a four-bladed jackknife.

Each of them addressed Nemesio in this way, and he made a servile bow to each comment and stretched his toothless mouth even wider. When the group had finished speaking, a sepulchral silence reigned in the room, broken only by the phlegmatic tick-tock of the clockwork.

"What are you looking for?" one of the men reading asked. He was young, emaciated, with a sickly gray look to him.

"A bit of conversation, Julián,' answered Nemesio.

"We don't talk to worms," said Julián.

"This time it's different, comrade: I'm working for the good cause."

"The apostle has spoken!" mocked one of them.

"You can't say I've ever betrayed you," Nemesio weakly protested.

"You wouldn't be alive if you did."

"Haven't I helped you several times? Who warned you, Julián, when they were going to search your house? And you, who gave you those identification papers and that disguise? And I only did all of that out of friendship, didn't I?"

"The day we discover why you really did it, you'd better be preparing for your funeral," said the scarred man. "All right, enough's enough. Tell us why you're here and then get out."

"I'm looking for someone . . . not to get him in trouble, I swear."

"You want information?"

"What I want is to warn him of a great danger. He'll thank me for it. He's got family."

"What's his name?" Julián cut him off.

Nemesio approached the table. The lamplight illuminated his shaved skull and his ears acquired a purple transparency. The conspirators concentrated their menacing eyes on him. The clockwork device whistled and stopped. In the street, a clock struck five.

THE BUTLER ANNOUNCED THE ARRIVAL of Mr. and Mrs. Pere Parells. María Rosa Savolta, her face flushed, ran to meet them, then kissed Mrs. Parells effusively and Pere Parells more timidly. The old financier had known María Rosa since she was born, but now things had changed.

"I didn't think you'd come!" exclaimed the young hostess.

"My wife's foibles," answered Pere Parells, trying to hide his nervousness. "She was afraid we'd be the first to arrive."

"But, my dear, don't speak to us as if we were strangers you'd never met before," said Mrs. Parells.

María Rosa blushed mildly.

"I only wanted to show my respect for you . . . "

"Of course, darling," Pere Parells chimed in, "it's only natural. María Rosa is young, and we're a pair of old fogies, can't you see?"

"Good heavens, don't say that!" protested María Rosa.

"What are you talking about, Pere?" agreed Mrs. Parells, feigning anger. "Speak for yourself. In my heart, I feel like a girl."

"That's the idea, Mrs. Parells, the only thing that matters is to be young at heart."

Mrs. Parells made her bracelets tinkle and patted María Rosa's cheek with her mother-of-pearl fan.

"You can say all that because you don't know anything about the afflictions of old age."

"Don't be so sure, ma'am, I felt quite ill this morning," said María Rosa, blushing and staring at the hem of her dress.

"Are you serious, child? We'll have to talk this over at a better time. Are you sure? Great news! Does your husband know?"

"What are you two talking about?" asked Pere Parells.

"Nothing, my dear, nothing. Why don't you go tell dirty jokes? And be careful what you drink, you know what the doctor said!"

As his wife put his arm around María Rosa's waist and walked away with her, Pere Parells entered the grand salon. An orchestra was playing tangos, and a few young couples were dancing cheek-to-cheek to the rhythms imported from Buenos Aires. Pere Parells detested accordions. A servant appeared with a tray of cigarettes and cigars. He took a cigarette and lit it at the lighter held out to him by a little page boy dressed in purple velvet. Pere Parells smoked and contemplated the crowded salon, the myriad servants, the finery, the jewels, the music, the lights, the quality of the furniture, the thickness of the rugs, the value of the paintings, the splendor. He frowned, and his eyes were veiled with sadness. He saw Lepprince walking toward him, smiling, holding out his hand, his tuxedo impeccable, his shirt made of silk, his buttons diamonds. Instinctively, he tugged at his shirt cuffs, straightened his back, which was becoming bent with age, smiled, carefully trying to hide his missing, recently pulled, molar, and snapped his cigarette in a sudden, uncontrollable twitch.

IT WAS EARLY, and the cabaret was empty when I walked in. A cloth covered the piano, and the chairs were stacked upside down on the tables to make space for the broom a huge woman was beating against the floor. She was wearing a flowered robe furrowed with sewn-up rents and, wrapped around her head like a turban, a handkerchief with an herb pattern. An unlit butt hung from her lower lip.

"You're early, sweetie. The show doesn't start until eleven."

"I know. I wanted to see whoever it is who runs all this."

She went back to sweeping, filling the air with dust and fuzz.

"The boss lady must be around. What do you want her for?"

"I have to ask her some questions."

"Police?"

"No, no. Just a personal matter."

She came toward me and pointed the broom handle at me. I recognized her as one of the girls who'd attacked us the night before.

"Say, aren't you the big spender who invited us to get lost last night?"

"Well, I was here last night."

She burst out laughing and the butt fell out of her mouth.

"Tell me why you want to see her, be a good boy now."

"I can't. It's personal."

"All right, Mr. Banker. You'll find her back there making drinks. Got a cigarette?"

I gave her one, and she went back to her sweeping. The cabaret, empty and dark, had an air of filth and desolation to it that defied description. The dust raised by the woman stuck in my throat. As usually happens with me in situations like this, all the energy that brought me to the very brink of the situation seemed to drain out of me. I hesitated, and only the fact that I'd arrived at the end and knowing the sarcastic woman was watching pushed me forward.

Just as she said, the manager, who was none other than the old piano player, was busy behind the curtain with jugs and bottles. What she was doing was very simple: she was refilling the bottles of known brands with a liquid she poured from the jugs through a rusty funnel. The phoniness of the wine served in the cabaret was so obvious to the taste and so indifferent a matter to the clientele that her operation made no sense. I took it to be a touching matter of principle.

When I was next to her, she noticed my presence, finished filling the bottle she had between her knees, and dropped the funnel. She was out of breath, and her expression could not have been less friendly.

"What do you want?"

"Sorry for bursting in at this inopportune moment," I said by way of introduction.

"Too late to be sorry, so now what?"

"Well, it's like this. There's a young woman working here, dancer or acrobat, named María Coral."

"So what?"

"I'd like to see her if it's possible."

"What for?"

I thought that if I'd been rich I would have been spared all this scorn and humiliation, that all I'd have to do would be to insinuate my desires and slip some cash into the piano player's hand so that the machinery would begin to function with speed and smoothness. But my circumstances were quite different, and I knew that my descent into the underworld had only begun. Time would show me just how accurate my premonitions were.

"Why don't you help me lift up this jug?"

"But of course," I said, trying to win her over.

Under her inexpressive eyes, I proceeded to fill an empty bottle.

"Heavy, isn't it?"

"Sure is. Weighs a ton," I said, huffing and puffing.

"Well, I get to do this same thing every day. And at my age."

"You need someone to help you."

"You said it, big boy, but how do I pay him?"

I didn't answer and went on filling the bottle until the liquid overflowed the funnel in hoarse bubbles and flowed onto the floor.

"Sorry."

"Don't worry. You're just not used to it yet. Fill this one."

I did what she said, and she sat down in a chair to watch me work.

"I don't know what the hell you men see in that kid," she

commented, as if speaking to herself. "She's stubborn, lazy, dumb, and with a heart of stone."

"You mean María Coral."

"Yes."

"Why do you talk about her that way?"

"Because I know her and women like her. Don't expect anything good from her: she's a snake. Of course, you can do whatever you like, it makes no difference to me."

"Will you tell me where I can find her?"

"Sure, honey, don't suffer. If I told the other one, I can tell you too. He was more generous, I won't deny that, but I like you. You're nice and seem like a good kid. At my age, I value good manners as much as gold."

I HAD TO REFILL three more bottles before she gave me the address I wanted so badly. As soon as I had it, I thanked her, said goodbye to the two women, and went to look for María Coral.

A cold, moist wind came up, sweeping through the streets, making the streetlights shake, and scaring off the passersby. The habitués of the night had deserted the sidewalks and taken refuge in the bars, in the coziness of coal stoves and wine. People kept silent, and only the wail of the wind gave a voice to the late hours. Nemesio Cabra Gómez opened the tavern door, and a gust of wind and dust walked in with him. The customers in the dive fixed their sullen eyes on the ragged ghost.

"It would be you, rat! Look what you've done to the floor, which I just mopped!" the bartender spat at him.

"All I want is a little hospitality," said Nemesio. "Who can sleep on a night like this? I'm stiff with cold."

A brandied voice came from the back of the tavern.

"Come on over here, friend, I'll stand you a drink."

Nemesio walked toward the unknown man.

"I really thank you for your kindness, sir. It's easy to see you're a good Christian."

"Me, a Christian? An atheist through and through, you should say. But this isn't a night for arguments, it's a night for wine. Bartender, a drink for my friend!"

"LOOK, SIR," said the bartender, "I don't want to stick my nose in your affairs, but this bird is just dead meat. If you take my advice, you take him by one arm, I'll take him by the other, and we'll both throw him out before he does something wrong."

"Give him a drink and don't make a mountain out of a molehill."

"Whatever you say, but I'm warning you. This man will bring you bad luck."

"You're that dangerous?"

"Don't pay any attention to them, sir. They have it in for me because they know I have friends in high places and that I can testify about their evil lives."

"You have friends in the government?"

"Higher than that, sir, much higher. And these people live in sin. It's the struggle between the light and the darkness: I am the light."

"Don't let him start with his crazy stories," said the bartender, placing a glass of wine under Nemesio's nose.

"He doesn't look very dangerous. A little nuts, nothing more."

"Just watch out, sir, just watch out."

THE ADDRESS THE PIANO PLAYER GAVE ME turned out to be in territory I'd never explored. I knew so little about the neighborhood that I might as well have been in a foreign city. I had to ask for help several times before I found the place which, luckily, was not far from the cabaret. Three ideas ran through my mind while I searched for the gypsy: the first, naturally, was to wonder if I'd find her at home; the second was to wonder what I'd say, how I could justify my interest in seeing her; and the third was: who was it who had taken an interest in the whereabouts of the acrobat shortly before I did? There were no answers for questions one and three: time and luck would answer them. As to the second, well, no matter how many times I turned it around, I could find no answers. I remember drinking a glass of rum at a stand along the way to buck up my spirits; instead it made me annoyingly warm and dizzy to the point of nausea. I remember little more about that anguishing walk.

I finally found the address and saw it was a miserable boarding- or rooming house that, as I suspected at first and confirmed later on, was also a brothel. The entrance was narrow and dark. There was a cripple sitting in a sort of sentry box.

"Where are you going?"

I told him, and he explained which floor it was, which door to take, and the room number as well, all without asking a question. I thought he might have expected a tip, but I was so flustered I didn't give him a cent. I climbed the worn-out steps, occasionally lighting my way with a match and sometimes feeling my way along. The gloominess of the place, instead of depressing me, made me brave, because it showed that María Coral was not enjoying a position that would allow her to disdain me. In the depth of my soul, instead of feeling compassion for that poor woman, I was happy about her sad fate. When I rethink thoughts like that I'm ashamed of my egoism.

I reached a door that said JULIA'S ROOMS-TO-LET and below that, next to the doorknob PUSH. I pushed, and the door opened with a squeak. I found myself in a vestibule dimly lighted by an oil lamp burning in a saint's niche. The only furniture in the vestibule was a terra-cotta umbrella stand. To the right and left there were dark hallways lined with doors whose numbers were written on them with chalk. I lit a match, my last, and walked first down the right-hand corridor and then the one on the left. I finally stopped in front of number eleven and knocked, first softly and then with greater insistence. No one answered: the silence was only broken by the gurgling of a faucet and the out-of-place song of a goldfinch. The match went out, and I waited for a few seconds that seemed like hours. I saw two possibilities: that the room was empty or that María Coral was with someone (the man who had been in the cabaret before I was, no doubt) and that both of them, surprised in their intimacy, were maintaining a scrupulous silence. In either case, elemental logic dictated a discreet withdrawal, but I wasn't acting out of logic. All through my life, I'd experienced the same thing: that I behave timidly up to a certain point, and when I go beyond it, I lose control of my actions and commit the most tactless follies. Both extremes, unadvisable because of their distance from the center and balance, have been the cause of all my misfortunes. Often, in these moments of reflection, I tell myself it's impossible to fight against one's character, and that I was born to lose all my battles. Now, maturity has calmed me down somewhat, but it's too late to rectify the mistakes of my youth. Hindsight has only brought me the pain of recognizing my failures without being able to amend them.

What would have become of me if in that moment I had walked out, suffocated my preposterous impulses, and forgotten the insane idea that dragged me along? I'll never know. Quite a few deaths might have been avoided; perhaps I wouldn't be where I am. I only know that when I opened the door to that room, I also opened the door to a new life for myself and for all those around me.

"AND THAT'S HOW IT WAS," said Nemesio Cabra Gómez, "how I found out what my only mission was in this world. The angel disappeared, and so great was the light his body produced that for a long time I was sunk in the most absolute darkness even though I'd lit the lamp. Right then and there I abandoned my house and my hometown, took a train without paying for a ticket—because you should know that for my movements I use the airy condition—and came to Barcelona."

"Why Barcelona?" asked the unknown man, who seemed to follow Nemesio's story with amused attention.

"Because it's here that more sins are committed daily. Have you seen the streets? They're the hallways of hell. The women have lost their decency and without blushing offer for practically nothing what they should be guarding with the greatest care. The men sin, if not in deeds at least in thought. Laws are not respected, authority is mocked everywhere, children abandon their parents, the churches are empty, and attempts are made to take human life, which is God's greatest creation."

The unknown man gulped down his wine and refilled his glass from an almost-empty bottle. With the butt he'd been smoking, he lit up another cigarette. His eyes were bloodshot, his lips black, and his face swollen.

"And don't you think, really, that misery is the cause of vice?" he said in a barely audible voice.

"What?"

"Don't you think it's this damned poverty that forces these women . . . ," he interrupted himself, worn out by the effort, and fell forward onto the table, smashing his forehead against the wood and knocking over both the bottle and the glass, which broke into smithereens.

Conversation stopped, and a sepulchral silence reigned in the tavern. All eyes fixed on the exotic couple made up of Nemesio Cabra Gómez and his drunken friend. Nemesio, noting the uncomfortable position they were in, softly shook the man's shoulder.

"Sir, let's take a walk. You need some air."

The man raised his head and stared at Nemesio, making an effort to understand.

"Let's get out of here, sir. We've been here quite a while and it's unhealthy. The air is foul with so much tobacco and so much frying."

"Bah!" answered the man, shaking a huge fist that hit Nemesio in the stomach. "Leave me in peace, you preacher of the straight and narrow, you operetta saint."

Conversation in the tavern resumed, but in a lower tone, and the customers still took furtive looks at the table where this picturesque dialogue was taking place. A chorus of guffaws celebrated the punch Nemesio received and from which he was recovering with grotesque gasps and labored breathing. Hearing the laughter, the unknown drunk stood up again, leaning on his hands, focused his blazing eyes on the crowd and said:

"And what are you idiots laughing at? If you had your heads screwed on right, you'd be crying! Look, look at yourselves, miserable, ragged ghosts! You laugh at me, but you don't see that I'm just what you'd see if you looked in the mirror."

Again the crowd roared with laughter.

"Looks like you found a perfect partner, Nemesio!" someone shouted from the back of the room.

"One nut and one drunk! A great show!"

"That's right, keep on laughing!" continued the drunk, pointing his finger straight at them and losing his balance in the process. He would have fallen, but Nemesio propped him up. "Go on laughing at me, if that makes you feel more like men! But one day you'll see things the way I see them now. I wasn't always like this. I went to school, I read a lot, but in the long run it didn't do me any good. Like you, I led the high life, that's right, I had faith in my fellow man, and made jokes about those life had defeated. But finally the veil fell off my eyes."

"Pull down his pants!"

And two thugs got up to carry out the order. Nemesio stepped in front of the drunk.

"Let him talk," he said in a supplicating voice not devoid of a certain dignity. "He's an honorable man of great culture. You can learn a lot from him."

"He should shut up and not spoil our evening!"

"Right, get him out of here!"

"No! I won't get out. I still have a couple of things to say to you. Nemesio here says your dissolute behavior is the result of the poverty eating away at you, making your wives and children sick. And I tell you that isn't true. All of you suffer misery, hunger, ignorance, and pain because of *them,*" here he pointed toward a hypothetical group outside the tavern walls, "because of *them,* the ones who oppress you, exploit you, betray you, and, when they have to, kill you. I could tell you stories that would make your hair stand on end. I could tell you the names of illustrious people whose hands are red with the blood of workers. Ah! You won't see those hands because they're covered with kid gloves. Gloves imported from Paris and paid for with your money! You think you're paid for the work you do in their factories, but it's a lie. They pay you so you won't die of hunger and can go on working from sunup to sundown until you drop. But the money, the profit, no! They don't give you that. *They* keep that for themselves. And they buy mansions, automobiles, jewels, furs, and women. With their money? Fat chance! With your money! And you, what are you doing about it? Look at yourselves and tell me what you're doing about it?"

"And what about you, what are you doing about it?" asked someone. And no one laughed. They were all listening with feigned indifference, with uncomfortable sarcasm. Anxiety had taken control of the crowd.

"Forget me. I'm a wreck. I tried to fight in my way, and I failed. Know why? I'll tell you why: because I believed in beautiful words and false friends. Because I cherished the hope I could soften their filthy hearts with arguments. Vain illusion! I tried to open their eyes to the truth, and I was crazy to try it. They have their eyes open from the day they're born: they see everything and know everything. I was blind, ignorant . . . but no more. That's why I talk this way. And now, friends, listen to my advice. Listen to my advice, because it's not me talking to you but bitter experience. This is it: don't drown your suffering in wine," his voice suddenly became firm, fiery, "drown it in blood! Flood the sterile furrows of your abandoned fields with *their* blood. Wash off your children's filth with *their* blood. Let not a single head remain on any of *their* shoulders. Don't let them talk, because if you do, they'll convince you. Don't let them make a single gesture, because they'll cover you with money and buy your will. Don't look at them, because you'll want to imitate their elegant manners and you'll be corrupted. Feel no pity, because *they* feel none. They know how you suffer, how your children die of malnutrition and lack of medical care, but they laugh, they laugh in their luxurious salons, next to their fireplaces, drinking the wine from your vineyards, eating the chickens from your farms seasoned with the oil from your fields. And they keep warm with your clothes, live in your houses, and watch the rain fall on your shacks. And they disdain you because you can't speak the way *they* speak, because you don't go to the theater or the Lyceum, because you don't know how to use silverware. Kill, yes, kill! Don't leave a single one alive! Kill their wives and children. Finish, finish *them* off . . . forever . . . "

The exhausted drunk stopped talking and fell forward onto the table, breaking the dense silence that followed his speech with a heartrending sob. The people in the tavern were petrified, seeming to search for anonymity, invisibility, silence, and calm.

After a few seconds, the owner of the bar came over to the drunk being looked after by Nemesio, coughed, and said in an affectedly firm tone:

"Get out. I don't want problems in my place."

The drunk went on crying between convulsions and did not respond. Nemesio got behind him, slipped his arms under the man's armpits, and pulled him up.

"Let's go, sir. You're very tired."

"Get him out, get him out!" shouted the other people in the bar in one voice. Some looked fearfully toward the door. Others made threatening gestures at the drunk. Nemesio tried to resolve the situation peacefully.

"Calm down, calm down, for God's sake. We're on our way, right, sir?"

"Right," the drunk finally murmured, "let's go. Oh . . . , help me."

The bartender and Nemesio got the drunk to his feet. He was slowly recovering his strength and balance. The crowd pretended not to notice what was happening, so Nemesio and the drunk walked the length of the tavern without being bothered. The night was cold, dry, without moonlight. The drunk shivered.

"Let's walk a bit, sir. If we stand still here, we'll freeze to death."

"I don't care. Go away and leave me alone."

"Don't say that. I can't leave you like this. Tell me where you live, and I'll bring you home."

The drunk shook his head. Nemesio made him walk, which the drunk did uncertainly but without falling.

"Live near here, sir? Should we take a cab?"

"I don't want to go home. I don't ever want to go home. My wife . . . "

"She'll understand, sir. We've all gone overboard once in a while drinking."

"No, not home," the drunk insisted sadly.

"Then we'll walk. Don't stop. Want my jacket?"

"Why are you so concerned about me?"

"Because you're the only friend I have. But keep walking, sir."

PERE PARELLS, with a glass of sherry and a cigarette, came upon a circle of guests composed of two beardless young men, one old poet, and a lady of masculine appearance who turned out to be the cultural attaché of the Dutch embassy in Spain. The poet and the lady were comparing cultures.

"I have noticed with some bitterness," the lady was saying in fluid Spanish with a barely perceptible foreign accent, "that the upper classes in Spain, unlike their counterparts in the rest of Europe, do not consider culture something to be proud of but almost as a defect. They think it proper to boast about their ignorance of and lack of interest in art and confuse refinement with effeminacy. In social gatherings, no one ever talks about literature, painting, or music; museums and libraries are deserted, and anyone who has any liking for poetry tries to hide it as something shameful."

"How right you are, Madame Van Pets."

"Van Peltz."

"You are so right. Recently, last October, I read my poetry in Lérida, and would you believe that the hall at the Ateneo was half empty?"

"Just as I was saying, here people disdain culture out of some badly understood idea of masculinity, the same thing that happens—please don't take offense—with hygiene."

"Two of our most glorious literary figures, Cervantes and Quevedo, knew days of pain in prison," observed one of the young men.

"The Spanish aristocracy has lost its chance to achieve universal renown. By contrast, the Church, in that sense, has been much more intelligent: Lope de Vega, Calderón, Tirso de Molina, Góngora, and Gracián all derived benefits from the ecclesiastical condition."

"A historical lesson every nouveau riche should think about," noted Pere Parells with a twisted smile.

"Bah," exclaimed the poet, "we can't count on them. They go to the Lyceum to snore because they've got to show off their jewels, and they buy expensive paintings to look well, but they can't tell Wagner from a music hall routine."

"Well, well, let's not exaggerate," said Pere Parells, remembering in his heart of hearts the titles of music hall shows he'd especially liked. "A time and place for everything."

"Which is why," went on Madame Van Peltz, who was not going to tolerate frivolous digressions, "artists have turned against the aristocracy and created this naturalism we're suffering through and which is nothing more than a mad desire to throw themselves into the arms of the people by praising their instincts."

Pere Parells, not really accustomed to such conversations, detached himself from the group and sought refuge with some industrialists he knew slightly. The industrialists had cornered an obese, smiling banker and were pouring out their anger to him.

"Don't tell me the banks haven't decided to sit back on their asses!" exclaimed one of them, aiming his cigar at the banker.

"We proceed with caution, my dear sir, with exquisite caution," replied the banker without losing his smile. "You must realize that we aren't managing our own money but the savings of others, and what for you would be acts of bravery for us would be irresponsible fraud."

"Bullshit!" bellowed the other industrialist, whose face was passing from red to white with shocking speed. "When things are going well, you all swell up with money . . . "

"And then start squeezing!" added his friend.

" . . . and when things go the other way, you turn your backs . . . "

"On their asses, on their asses!"

" . . . and pretend to be deaf. You'll ruin the country and still pretend you've behaved like good businessmen."

"Gentlemen, I earn my salary, which doesn't change from month to month," the banker responded. "If we do things as we do them, it is not for personal profit. We administer money entrusted to us."

"Bullshit! You're speculating on the crisis."

"We've also had our share of disasters, don't forget, so don't make me remind you of some dramatic cases."

"Ah, Parells!" said one of the industrialists, noticing the presence of their friend. "Come over here and break a lance in this joust! What's your opinion of the banking system?"

"A noble institution," Pere Parells temporized, "even though its restrictions, respectable though they may be from any point of view, keep it from acting with the decision and daring we would like to see."

"But don't you think they've simply sat back on their asses?"

"Well, on their asses, when you say on their asses . . . I don't know. Perhaps they give that impression."

"Parells, you're trying to worm out of this one."

"That's true," nodded the financier, feeling morally tired and wishing he could be out of all the fighting.

"Don't run off now, damn it. Is it true that the Savolta company is collapsing?" the first industrialist teased him in order to reanimate what was to him a pleasant chat.

"Who says so?" Parells cut him off with such swiftness that his questioner could not throw a veil of irony over his words.

"You know, people are talking."

"Really? And what are they saying, if you don't mind telling me?"

"Don't play dumb."

"Is it true the stock is being sold off?"

"Sold off? Not that I know of."

"People say Lepprince wants to get rid of the stock his wife inherited from her father, is that true? People are talking about a certain company in Bilbao, interested in buying . . . "

"Gentlemen, you're having visions."

"And isn't it true that a bank in Madrid refused to buy some of your paper?"

"Ask them at the bank. I don't know what you're talking about."

"Bah, these fops won't tell us anything."

"True," said Pere Parells, winking at the banker, "you forget that we always turn our asses toward you."

He patted the industrialists on the back, flashed a smile of complicity at the always beaming banker, and went back to circulating through the salon. He wanted to go home, slip into his robe and slippers, and rest in his armchair. Toward the back of the room, near the library door, he could make out Lepprince, who was giving a waiter orders. He walked decisively toward him, waiting until the waiter had gone.

"Lepprince, I have to speak to you urgently."

"SIR, TELL ME YOUR ADDRESS, and I'll take you," insisted Nemesio Cabra Gómez. "You'll see how much better you feel tomorrow."

The drunk dozed off hanging onto a lamppost. Nemesio shook him as hard as he could, and the drunk opened his eyes and squinted.

"What time is it?"

Nemesio looked for a clock on the street but didn't find one.

"Very late. And so cold it'll peel your skin off."

"It's still early. Come on, I've got to send a message."

"At this time of night? Everything's closed."

"Not what I'm looking for. A mailbox. Let's go to the post office."

"Is it on the way to your house?"

"Yes."

"Let's go then."

Nemesio had the drunk hang an arm over his shoulder and held him up. Nemesio had a weak constitution, so the two of them lurched from side to side, tripping so often it was a miracle they didn't fall down. A bell struck three.

"Five o'clock," exclaimed the drunk. "Still early, what did I tell you?"

"Couldn't we leave that letter for tomorrow?"

"Tomorrow could be too late. What I have to do is simple, see? Mail a letter. Here's the letter. A simple sheet of paper with writing on it, but ah! Ah, my dear friend! Lots of heads will roll when this letter reaches its destination. If it doesn't, time will tell. What time is it?"

"Don't know, sir. Careful with the curb."

They kept on walking until they reached the post office, an operation that took them half an hour, despite the fact that they weren't even half a mile away. Several times Nemesio had to stop and catch his breath and rest, sitting down on the base of a portico. During those pauses, the drunk would take the opportunity to sing as loudly as he could and to urinate in the middle of the street. Once they reached the building, they looked for a box. The drunk felt the walls and tried to slip the letter through any space he'd find between two stones. Finally Nemesio found what they were looking for.

"Give me the letter, sir. I'll mail it."

"Not a chance! You shouldn't even see who it's addressed to."

"I won't look."

"You can't trust anyone. This letter is very important. Where's the mailbox?"

"Right here, just open the little door."

He helped the drunk to slip the letter through the slot and tried to see to whom it was addressed, but the envelope had suffered a great deal, and the wrinkles and stains made it difficult to read. All he could see was that it was addressed to someone right in Barcelona. Once the deed was done, the drunk seemed to calm down.

"I've done my duty," he affirmed solemnly.

"Then let's go to your house."

"Let's go. What time is it?"

Walking more swiftly now, they went toward the Ramblas. It began to drizzle, but it stopped after a few minutes. It felt warmer, and the wind died down. Drunks and drifters were asleep on the benches. Wagons loaded with vegetables and pulled by Percherons passed by heading for the Borne. A dog barked between Nemesio's legs, and he had to jump up on a bench to avoid being bitten. In sum, it was a journey without incidents worthy of mention. When they reached the corner of the Ramblas and Unión street, the drunk parted company with Nemesio.

"Don't follow me, I'm sober now, and I'd prefer to go on alone. I live right here, at that entryway," he pointed vaguely down on the street. "You go to bed and sleep in peace. I've given you enough trouble tonight. You don't know how much I thank you for what you did for me."

"Sir, you don't have to thank me for anything. We haven't had such a bad time of it after all."

The drunk had fallen into a deep state of melancholy.

"Yes, perhaps you're right. It was even amusing at times. But now everything will have to change. Life doesn't permit any let-ups."

"What do you mean?"

"I'm going to ask a favor of you. Can I trust you?"

"Completely."

"Then listen: I have a bad feeling, a foreboding. If something happens to me, listen now, if something happens . . . understand?"

"Sure, if something happens to you . . . "

"Look for a friend of mine whose name I'm going to tell you

as soon as you find out something's happened. Find him and tell him someone murdered me."

"Murdered?"

"That's right, that the people he knows about killed me. Tell him to take care of my wife and child and that he shouldn't abandon them, that he should take pity on them. My friend's name, listen carefully now, is Javier Miranda, Will you remember that?"

"Javier Miranda, yes, sir. I won't forget."

"You find him and tell him everything you heard me say tonight, see, if something bad happens to me. And now, don't hang around here, get going."

"You can trust me, sir. I swear by everything on High that I won't let you down."

"Good-bye, friend," said the drunk, clasping Nemesio's hand.

"Good-bye, sir, and take care of yourself."

They separated without another word, and Nemesio saw him walk away with slow but steady steps. He thought it indiscreet to keep spying on the drunk, so after a while he turned and went his way. When he reached the corner of the Ramblas, he was blinded by the lights from an automobile that was turning into Unión street. An unformed thought hit Nemesio's brain, something that disturbed him, even though he couldn't define it. He went on walking and turning over the idea in his head until it dawned on him: that automobile had been following them. It had been parked outside the tavern, later in front of the post office, and finally it had seen them make their way through the vegetable carts going up the Ramblas. He hadn't taken much notice then, but now, after hearing the drunk's final words, those mysterious facts, those coincidences, took on a tragic meaning. Nemesio turned around and began to run back, turning into Unión street and continuing until some shouts made him stop. About one hundred yards away, dimly illuminated by the uncertain light of the street lamp, a circle of people wearing bathrobes swirled around. Others, who hadn't found anything to put on, appeared at balconies in nightclothes. Two policemen made their way through the curiosity seekers. In a few moments, the previously deserted street came alive. Nemesio cautiously approached.

"Excuse me, ma'am, what happened?"

"A car ran over a young man. They say he's dead."

"Who was it, does anyone know?"

"A journalist who lived right here, in number 22, with his wife and child. Just imagine what bad luck! Killed two steps from his house."

"It wouldn't have happened," said a neighbor lady from a low window, "if he'd spent his nights at home as he should have instead of gallivanting all night."

"Don't speak that way of the dead, ma'am," said Nemesio.

"You keep quiet, because you look like the same sort of man," retorted the woman at the window.

The police pushed the people aside and called for a doctor and an ambulance. Nemesio hid behind the lady who'd given him the information, and took advantage of the guards' distraction to disappear surreptitiously.

Chapter 2

I opened the door to María Coral's room and was greeted by an acrid smell and the same absolute darkness I'd had in the hall. At first I thought the room was empty, but I concentrated and was soon able to detect labored breathing and weak noises that sounded like groans of pain. I called her name: "María Coral! María Coral!" but received no answer. The moans went on. I'd used my last match trying to find the room number, so I quickly felt my way back to the vestibule and took the little oil lamp burning in the saint's niche. Then I went back to the room: my eyes were used to the darkness so it wasn't hard for me to distinguish the shape of an iron bed with the figure of a woman on it in the back of the room. It was María Coral, and, thank God, she was alone. I thought she was sleeping and having a nightmare. I went to her and took her hand: it felt icy and extremely moist. I brought the lamp close to the gypsy's face, and a tremor ran through my body: she was as pale as death, and only a slight tremor in her chin and her heartrending groans indicated she was still alive. I took her by the shoulders and tried to make her regain consciousness. It was useless. I slapped her a few times, but that only made her moans more anguishing and her pallor more intense. María Coral was dying. I shouted for help, but nothing suggested anyone else was in the house. I was confused, flustered, and didn't know what to do. I thought about picking the gypsy up and carrying her somewhere she might be cured, but I immediately rejected the idea: I couldn't walk out at night hauling the body of a dying woman. I knew no doctors. One name repeatedly came into my mind: Lepprince. I resolutely walked out of the room, closed the door, put the lamp back in its place, and went jumping and tripping down the stairs. The doorman observed me from his guard box with some curiosity: this must not have been the usual way visitors to the boardinghouse left. I asked him where I could find a telephone. He said in a nearby restaurant and asked me if something was wrong. From the door, I said no, and in two seconds was in the restaurant, which was not really a restaurant but a filthy eating house where a dozen thugs were eating away at two communal pots of thick soup. They told me where the phone was, but then I realized I didn't know Lepprince's number. I had to do something, so I called Cortabanyes's office, certain the old lawyer would still be in his lair, if only so he wouldn't have to go home to an empty house. I dialed and waited with my heart in my mouth. When someone answered, I gave a sigh of relief.

"Hello?" It was Cortabanyes's unmistakable voice.

"Mr. Cortabanyes, it's Miranda speaking."

"Oh, Javier, how are you?"

"I'm sorry to be bothering you at this hour."

"Don't worry, my boy, I was just pottering around the office before dinner. What did you want?"

"Give me Lepprince's telephone number, please."

"Lepprince's telephone number? Why? Is something wrong?"

"A serious matter, Mr. Cortabanyes."

The lawyer hemmed and hawed and played dumb, no doubt to gain time and weigh the advantages and disadvantages of revealing the fact that he knew both Lepprince's telephone number and his address.

"Can't you wait until tomorrow, my boy? This is no time to be calling people. Besides, I don't know if I have that number. He moved . . . you know, when he got married."

"It may be a matter of life or death, Mr. Cortabanyes. Give it to me, and I'll explain everything later."

"I don't know, let me think if I have the damn number. My memory just gets worse and worse. Don't push me, Javier my boy."

Seeing his hesitation and knowing that these delaying tactics could go on all night (Cortabanyes could resolve issues, and his opponents wouldn't know what they'd talked about), I decided to tell him the entire story. Besides, I supposed that Cortabanyes already knew it anyway, and that I wouldn't be revealing any secrets to him.

"Look, Mr. Cortabanyes. Lepprince had an affair with a young woman who used to work in a cabaret. She was associated with two killers Lepprince hired a couple of years ago for some not-very-legal jobs. By the merest chance I found her, and I think she's seriously ill. If she dies, the police will investigate, and certain facts might come out, facts compromising for Lepprince and the Savolta company. Understand?"

"Of course I understand you, my boy, of course I understand. Are you with the young woman now?"

"No, I had to telephone from an eating house near the place where I found her."

"And she's alone?"

"Yes. At least she was a minute ago."

"Did anyone see you enter or leave the boardinghouse?"

"Only the doorman, who doesn't seem to be a particularly curious person."

"Listen, Javier, I don't want you to get mixed up in this mess. Give me the address of the boardinghouse, and I'll find Lepprince. Don't go back there, but stay nearby and make note of whoever enters or leaves. We'll be right there, all right?"

"Yes, sir."

"Just do what I told you and stay calm."

He copied the address, hung up, and I left the eating house. Following his instructions, I took up a position opposite the boardinghouse, and there I stood, smoking one cigarette after another and counting the seconds. Almost an hour must have gone by before I heard a voice calling me from a corner without saying my name. I didn't recognize the person calling, but I went. Hidden around the corner was a black car, a limousine. The person who'd called me told me to come over to the car. The window curtains were pulled, so I couldn't see who was inside. When I was next to the car, the door opened and I got in. Lepprince and Cortabanyes were waiting for me. The chauffeur's place was empty, so I concluded that it was the driver who'd called me over. On the passenger's side in the front was Max. Lepprince sat me down on one of the folding seats, and without even saying hello asked, "Are you sure it's María Coral?"

"Absolutely. I saw her perform just yesterday."

"And the strongmen?"

"Not a sign of them. They didn't perform with her, and I haven't seen them anywhere."

"All right," he concluded in an expeditious tone. "Show Max and my driver the way. We'll wait here. Hurry up."

"We'll need a flashlight. There's no light in the boardinghouse."

"Max, take a flashlight. Now all of you get going."

Max got out of the car, took a flashlight out of the trunk, waved to the chauffeur, and the three of us started walking. I led them, but before we reached the boardinghouse door, I stopped.

"Let's pretend we've just been out drinking. If the doorman asks any questions, let me do the talking."

The nodded, and we walked in. The doorman barely glanced at us, and we went into the vestibule. Max handed the flashlight to the driver and took out the pistol he'd kept half covered under the folds of his topcoat. There was no one in the vestibule—if there had been, they would have died of shock at seeing us. In the flickering light of the saint's oil lamp we would have presented a rather disconcerting tableau. The driver turned on the flashlight and handed it to me. Without saying a word, I led Lepprince's men to María Coral's room. Nothing had changed: the gypsy was still groaning in her bed, still breathing with difficulty. The flashlight made the room seem even smaller, its decrepit condition even more shocking: the plaster was falling off the wall, and there were so many stains on the wallpaper it was impossible to see its color or design. There were cobwebs hanging in the ceiling corners, and the furniture consisted of a pine table and two chairs. In a corner there was an open cardboard valise: María Coral's clothing (but not her cape or the plumes she used in her cabaret act) was heaped all around it. A skylight over the bed opened onto an interior courtyard as narrow and dark as the rest of the building.

I shined the flashlight on María Coral's face, and the sight of her sharp features, her half-closed eyes, and her bluish lips upset me even more than they did the first time. Without realizing it, I began to tremble as if I had the palsy. Max, who noticed my state, touched my elbow to get me out of the way. I stood aside, and he and the driver stood María Coral up. She was wearing a ragged nightgown soaked with sweat. We couldn't bring her out that way. I took off my overcoat and draped it over her shoulders. The poor thing was unaware of anything going on around her. Before we left, Max pointed to a threadbare velvet bag on a table. I picked it up and put it in one of the overcoat pockets. Max grabbed María Coral's feet, the chauffeur picked her up under the shoulders, and we walked out into the hall and crossed the vestibule. I peered down into the landing. Seeing no one, I called my companions. The four of us then went down the tortuous stairway without meeting anyone. At the bottom step, I whispered into Max's ear.

"We can't walk by the porter like this. Stand her up and we'll pretend we're drunk."

I put out the flashlight and walked right over to the little guard box where the good fellow was still passing away the dead hours. I said hello, trying to place my body between him and the entranceway that led to the street. I slapped him on the back and put some coins on his table by way of tip. But he looked around me to get a look at the strange group made up of two men carrying along an unconscious woman, then he fixed his vacuous eyes on me and sank back into the lethargy of his senseless vigil. I joined the others and walked to the car. On the way, I told myself it must be a strange sort of boardinghouse when the doorman shows no sign of surprise when such bizarre things take place right in front of him.

Max and the driver laid María Coral on the back seat as Lepprince and Cortabanyes changed to the jump seats. With Max and the driver in their places, the motor started to purr softly. Through the window, Lepprince said, "Go home and don't talk about this with anyone. You'll be hearing from me soon."

He closed the window, and I watched the car pull away with no idea where they were going. I'd forgotten to take back my coat, and the night was cold. I turned up my jacket collar, plunged my hands in my pockets, and started walking quickly.

NEMESIO CABRA GÓMEZ PACED BACK AND FORTH, looked at the monumental clock over his head, and invariably stopped to stare into the display windows of El Siglo. The big stores had packed their windows with the most attractive merchandise they'd ever had, and, as if the quality of their products wasn't enough of a lure, they'd hung them with colored streamers, silver paper, holly, and other Christmas motifs. A constant stream of customers went in and out of the department store. Those who walked in carrying nothing walked out loaded with packages, but those who were already carrying packages came out buried under a brightly colored, jolly pyramid. No one seemed to mind that all those bundles turned them into voluntary, part-time stevedores. Some well-to-do ladies came with their maids or houseboys, but most preferred to carry the weight of these future thrills for themselves. Nemesio observed them with envy and a touch of sadness. On the marquee of the store, huge letters read: MERRY CHRISTMAS AND A PROSPEROUS 1918.

Nemesio again looked up at the clock: 6:40. The meeting was set for 6:30, but he was more than used to waiting and did not get impatient. Besides, the scene was amusing. A young mother leading a child by the hand came up to Nemesio, smiled, and gave him a few cents. Nemesio counted the pennies, bowed in gratitude, and muttered, "May God bless you." Then he recommenced his pacing to stave off the afternoon cold. Ten more minutes passed. At ten minutes to seven, Nemesio heard someone whistle to him from a horse-drawn cab. He went over, and a hand signaled him to get in. He obeyed, and the cab started moving. The curtains were drawn so he could not see in which direction they were going.

"What news do you have?" asked the man sitting opposite him.

Despite the semidarkness inside the carriage, Nemesio recognized the distinguished gentleman he'd talked business with a few days earlier.

"I found your man, sir. It was difficult, because he didn't seem to have many friends, but with patience and by keeping my eyes open . . . "

"Forget the preamble. Get to the point."

Nemesio swallowed hard and once again considered the propriety of telling the truth. He was afraid that when the distinguished gentleman heard the news he would lose interest and order him to stop the search, which would mean the loss of his economic expectations. But he couldn't lie because the gentleman would discover the truth sooner or later, and Nemesio, through experience, feared the reprisals of the powerful more than anything in the world.

"You'll see, sir, that you won't like what I have to tell you. You won't like it a bit."

"Tell me and get it over with, damn it."

"He was murdered, sir."

The gentleman gave a start and sat back with his mouth wide open. It took him a few seconds to recover his ability to speak.

"What did you say?"

That he was murdered. Poor Pajarito de Soto was murdered."

"You're sure?"

"I saw it with these eyes doomed to the grave."

"You saw how they killed him?"

"Yes . . . well, not exactly. I walked him home, but he wouldn't let me go to the main entrance with him. As I went away, I saw an automobile go by; at first I didn't think much of it, but later, thinking things over, it seemed to be the same car that had been following us the whole night. I ran back, sir, and he was already dead, stretched out right in the middle of the street."

"Was anyone else there?"

"When he was killed, no, sir. You know how little charity there is in the world today. By the time I got to him, a good-sized crowd had gathered, but that was after the accident."

"And he was dead?"

"Dead as a doornail, sir. Not even breathing."

The gentleman remained silent for a few minutes, which Nemesio used, listening to the noises on the street, to figure out where they were. He heard the clang of a trolley and the noise of motors. The coach moved forward slowly. He deduced they hadn't left the central business area; probably they were having difficulty going up Paseo de Gracià.

"Did you two talk about anything before he was killed?"

"Yes, sir. We talked all night. At the beginning, Pajarito de Soto was excited because of the wine."

"Drunk?"

"A little drunk, yes, sir. He really raised a ruckus in the bar where I found him."

"What do you understand by a ruckus?"

"He started out by complaining about everything and said a lot of people would have to be killed."

"Mention any names?"

"No, sir. He said a lot of people would have to be killed, but he didn't make a list."

"Did he explain why?"

"He said they'd tricked him and that they would trick everyone unless they were killed first. Actually, it all seemed a bit exaggerated to me. I don't think anyone has to be killed."

"What else did he say?"

"Not much. The people in the bar made him shut up, and we

left. Out in the street, he stopped talking about killing people. He sang and urinated."

"And he went on that way until you left him near his house?"

"No, sir. Before we parted company, he'd calmed down and seemed very sad. He told me he'd probably be killed. It must have been a premonition, don't you think?"

"No doubt," the gentleman corroborated.

"He did ask me a favor, although I don't know if I should mention it."

"Of course you should, idiot, that's why I'm paying you."

"Well, he asked me to tell a friend of his if something bad happened to him."

The gentleman seemed to recover part of his lost vitality.

"Did he tell you the friend's name?"

"He did, sir, but I don't know if I should . . . "

"Stop saying these stupid things, Nemesio. The friend's name?"

"Javier Miranda," whispered Nemesio.

"Miranda?"

"Yes, sir. Know him?"

"What does that matter to you?" the gentleman cut him off. Then he stroked his chin with his gloved hand. "So it's Miranda, eh? Yes, I know him, certainly. He's Lepprince's dog."

"What's that, sir?"

"Nothing that matters to you." He tapped his walking stick on the roof of the carriage, which had stopped for an instant. "That's all, Nemesio. You've done a pretty good job. You can get out now and forget we ever set eyes on each other."

He handed some money to Nemesio and leaned over to open the door. Nemesio had been expecting a similar finale, but he couldn't keep his face from expressing all the sadness that overwhelmed him. The gentleman misinterpreted Nemesio's mien.

"What's wrong with you? You want more money?"

"Oh no, sir. I was thinking that . . . "

"What, what?

"Aren't we going to go on, sir? Aren't we going to see this thing through to the end? They killed a poor man, sir. It's a huge crime."

"I'm not the one to dispense justice, Nemesio. The police will take charge of the case and punish the guilty party as he deserves. I was only interested in getting a little information, and that, unfortunately, is now impossible to get."

"And what about this Miranda? Don't you want me to find him? I can do it. I have good friends everywhere."

"Don't lie, Nemesio. You could lose a homing pigeon. Besides, I'm the one giving the orders. Get out, please."

Nemesio decided to play his last card.

"I haven't told you everything, sir. That night there was something more."

"Oh, yes? So you wanted to carry on by yourself, is that it?"

"Don't take offense, sir. We poor people have to fight to survive."

"Look, Nemesio, you've been very clever, but this filthy business doesn't interest me anymore. Even if there was something else, it doesn't matter to me."

"It's of great interest, sir. Of the greatest interest."

"I told you to get out. Don't try to play games with me, understand? You never saw me and don't know who I am. Don't be fooled by my apparent tolerance. Be careful if you don't want to end up like Pajarito de Soto."

He opened the door and unceremoniously pushed Nemesio, who stumbled around before he regained his balance. Just then the El Siglo stores were closing their doors. The coach had simply gone around the block several times. Nemesio tried to follow it, but the crowds closed around him, keeping him from moving rapidly. He counted the money the gentleman gave him, put it in his trouser pocket, and elbowed his way through the throng.

LAWYER CORTABANYES had stuffed two chicken croquettes into his mouth, and his fat cheeks began to move energetically. He looked around for a napkin so he could wipe his fingers, and once he'd found the object of his search at the end of a long table, he strode toward it with his hand held out, trying not to dirty anyone's clothes. A lean gentleman, with white hair and a bulbous nose, across whose chest was a sash of some military commendation unknown to the lawyer, got in his way. The gentleman with the sash was baffled, and the lawyer, in trying to explain himself, spit out tiny chunks of croquet that landed on the man's military decoration. The gentleman patted Cortabanyes on the back.

"*Bon appétit!*"

"Thank you, thank you. Excuse me, but I don't remember your name."

Cortabanyes enjoyed huge parties. With their superficial courtesy and formality, he felt sure of himself, safe from direct questions, from professional inquiries and insidious propositions. He liked to start a light conversation, leave it, listen to every little group, and make a joke or a frivolous remark. He liked to observe, deduce, guess, discover new faces, evaluate those on their way up and those whose power was declining, judge tacit pacts, salon betrayals, and social crimes.

"Casabona, Augusto Casabona. Pleased to meet you," said the man with the sash.

Cortabanyes shook his hand, and both suddenly stood stockstill, not knowing what to say.

"What do you think," the gentleman finally muttered, "what do you think, Cortabanyes my friend, of this latest rumor circulating around here?"

"Never say the latest rumor, my dear Casabona, because by now it can't be."

"Ha, ha, what wit, Cortabanyes my friend," said the man, who suddenly became as serious as someone under sentence. "I mean the rumor that our friend Lepprince will be the next mayor of Barcelona."

Cortabanyes's obese structure shook in silent giggles.

"There are so many rumors, Casabona!"

"Yes, but some have to be true."

"That's just what I tell myself when I play the lottery: some number has to win. But it's never mine."

"Well, Cortabanyes my friend, I can see you're avoiding the topic, a fatal sign that you know more than you let on. Don't try to fool me now."

"My dear Casabona, if I knew something, I'd tell you. But the truth is I know nothing. I've heard that same rumor, I won't lie to you, but I paid no more attention to it than what I pay to all other rumors, that is, not very much."

"Nevertheless, you must recognize, Cortabanyes my friend, that the news, if it turns out to be true, would be a bombshell."

At parties, Cortabanyes wasn't afraid of other people's indiscretion. He didn't earn anything for answering, and he could just as easily keep silent. However, he decided to make the awkward Casabona suffer.

"A bombshell, you say? Just between us, the image is not a happy one."

"I didn't mean . . . You've got a fine understanding, Cortabanyes my friend. The profound sympathy I feel for our common friend, Lepprince, is clear. It was for that reason alone that I brought up the theme, because I wanted to ask a small favor of Mr. Lepprince, nothing of any importance. If he could see his way clear . . . "

Cortabanyes savored the man's anxiety.

"And tell me, Casabona my friend, what do you do?'

"Oh, I have a little stamp shop on Fernando street, you've probably passed it a thousand times. If you like stamps, you have to know it. Modesty aside, I can truthfully say I've had the most valuable examples in my hands, not to mention my clientele, among whom you could find the best people, not only in Barcelona, but in all of Europe."

"Please excuse my lack of interest, Casabona, but my modest means don't allow me to take interest in anything but movable stamps."

"Movable stamps," exclaimed the man, growing pale and

squeezing a giggle out to ingratiate himself with the lawyer. "Ha, ha! What a wit, Cortabanyes my friend. I could never think up one that good, word of honor, I never could have thought up one that good. Movable stamps, right? I have to tell my wife about it," he bowed. "Excuse me," and he went on singing low.

Cortabanyes saw him disappear among the little groups chatting while the orchestra took a break. The musicians were drinking champagne and raised their glasses in thanks, first in the direction of Lepprince, then toward María Rosa Savolta, who returned the compliment with a graceful bow and a plethoric smile. Next to her, Mrs. Pere Parells was also smiling and bowing, a parasitic participant in the homage being paid to her hostess. Cortabanyes looked around for more croquettes. Dinner was late. However, instead of croquettes he found Lepprince, who was waving to him from the library door and gesturing to him to join him. Because of the distance and his tired eyes, the lawyer could not tell if Lepprince's face expressed satisfaction or annoyance.

THE LIMOUSINE STOPPED on Princesa street, near the San Juan salon, in front of a new, three-story building with sash windows. Through the caramel-colored plate glass door, a light was visible in the vestibule. Above the door and perpendicular to the wall, a sign said: MERIDA HOTEL CONFORT.

Lepprince and Max got out of the car, and the Frenchman pulled the bell cord, which was protruding from a hole in the lintel. Inside a buzzer rang, and soon the men heard the swish of slippers coming toward them. A hoarse voice kept repeating, "I'm coming, I'm coming." Then a bolt slid back, and the glass door opened as wide as a safety chain would let it. Lepprince and Max exchanged an ironic look. Half a sleepy face observed them through the crack.

"What do you want, gentlemen?" asked the half face.

"I'm *Monsieur* Lepprince, remember me?"

The half face's half-open eye suddenly recovered its normal size.

"Ah, *Monsieur* Lepprince, excuse me for not recognizing you! I was asleep, and I'm dopey when I wake up. I'll open up right away."

The door closed, then there was the noise of a bolt sliding, and the door was open. The hotel receptionist was wearing a gray wool bathrobe over his wrinkled suit.

"Come in and forgive me for receiving you in this robe. I didn't think anyone would be coming at this time of night and had let the fire in the stove burn down, but I'll light it again right now. A treacherous night, isn't it?"

"Carlos, we have a certain someone you already know with us."

Carlos clasped his hands and raised his eyes to the ceiling.

"Oh, the young lady's back! How nice, *monsieur*!"

"I hope you have a room free."

"There's always a room in my hotel for *Monsieur* Lepprince. It won't be the same one as last time. If you had given me a little advance warning . . . But, no matter. I have another, an inside room, a bit smaller, but very discreet and quiet. *Très, très mignom*."

Lepprince and Max went back to the limousine, where Cortabanyes was waiting.

"You can stay here," said Lepprince. "It won't take us long."

"Not a chance, my boy," replied the lawyer. "I wouldn't stay here alone on a street this dark. Besides, the cold is killing."

Lepprince and his driver removed María Coral from the car, then Cortabanyes got out. The four men and their burden entered the hotel, and the receptionist closed the door and locked it again.

"The young lady is sick," Lepprince explained. "We'll bring her to the room and then send for a doctor. I'll remain here with her and of course take care of the expenses."

The manager, who had frowned when he saw the gypsy's lifeless form, recovered his smile.

"This way, gentlemen, follow me. Allow me to lead the way. Careful with that first step."

Carrying a lamp, he shone it on the staircase first and the hall later. When he reached thc last door, he took a key out of his pocket and unlocked it. The room, like the rest of the hotel, was clean, but smelled moist.

"It's a bit cold. If you'll allow me, I'll just light the stove. The room's not very big, so it will be cozy in no time."

While Lepprince and his driver stretched María Coral out on the bed, the manager lit a fire. When he'd finished, Lepprince handed him some money and waved him out of the room.

"Thank you, *monsieur*. If you need me, I'll be downstairs. Don't hesitate to call me."

Lepprince took the overcoat she still had on off of María Coral and covered her with the sheets. Max checked the window and took a look at the scene outside. Cortabanyes rubbed his hands next to the stove.

"Go and get Doctor Ramírez," said Lepprince to his chauffeur. "His address is number 6 Salmerón street, first floor. Before that, drop Mr. Cortabanyes off at his house. Max will go with you because he knows the doctor. Max, tell him that it's urgent and that he's not to ask questions. If he asks them anyway, you know what to answer. And try to keep him from telling his wife anything. If he's not at home and out taking care of some sick person, find out where he is and bring him here no matter what. I'll talk to you tomorrow," he concluded turning to Cortabanyes.

The three men left. Lepprince, alone, sat down on the edge of the bed and pensively contemplated María Coral's face.

DURING THE MORNING, the sky continued cloudy, and a fine rain floated in the air. The cars passed by, leaving a black furrow on the pavement, and the hooves of the horses splashed water to and fro. From the window I could see a double row of umbrellas passing up and down the street. The day did not inspire happy thoughts, and my tranquility of the night before—the tranquility of having left María Coral in good hands—dissipated. As I shaved, I reconsidered the events in the clear light of day, and I was not satisfied by the analysis. In the first place, Lepprince had behaved in a strangely cold manner with me, especially considering that we hadn't seen each other for several months. He was reluctant to leave the car and had sent in his place his gunman and his chauffeur. This driver was something new for me: Lepprince had always bragged he could drive his car better than anyone else and got a huge pleasure from doing it. Who was that disagreeable, simian person? A new bodyguard? Why did Lepprince hide behind the curtains in his limousine? Why did he have Cortabanyes accompany him—after all, his presence was completely unnecessary, and he was, foreseeably, annoyed to be in that situation? And finally, why had he just abandoned me there? There was enough room in the car for me. What had they done with María Coral?

I quickly ate breakfast and went to the office with the intention of buttonholing Cortabanyes the moment he walked in and making him tell me everything. But I didn't get the chance: even though I was early, Cortabanyes had come even earlier and was in his office with a client. Yet another mystery to add to the list: Cortabanyes never appeared before ten or ten-thirty, and my watch said a quarter to nine.

I was pacing back and forth in the library, chain-smoking. At ten minutes after nine, Doloretas walked in and began a conversation about the problems created by the rain. Noting my monosyllabic, irrelevant responses, she stopped talking, took the cover off her typewriter, and began to work. At a quarter to ten, Perico Serramadriles appeared. He brought a copy of a satirical newspaper and tried to show me some seditious cartoons. I paid no attention, and he withdrew to his office. At ten, I heard Cortabanyes's voice calling me into his office. I was there in a flash. The untimely visitor was Lepprince.

"Come in, Javier my boy, and sit down," said Cortabanyes.

Lepprince got up and stopped me with a gesture.

"Don't sit down, it's not worth the effort; you and I are leaving right now."

"How is María Coral?"

"Fine," said Lepprince.

"Are you sure?"

Lepprince smiled condescendingly. My tone must have seemed impertinent to a man who was not used to having his word questioned.

"That's what the doctor said, Javier, and I have every confidence in him. In any case, you'll soon be able to see for yourself, because you're going to visit her this morning."

"Where is she?"

"In a hotel. She doesn't need anything; anyway, you needn't worry so much about her health. What she had wasn't serious."

He patted me on the back, stared me straight in the eye, and smiled. My fears of the morning vanished. I took my overcoat, which Lepprince had brought and draped over one of the armchairs in the office, and we both went out to the street. The limousine approached majestically, stopped next to us—we stayed out of the rain—and the chauffeur got out with an umbrella in his hand which he used to cover Lepprince. We got in. Max was in the car. We got out in front of the little hotel on Princesa street. I felt a bit humiliated.

"I hope this is not a bad moment for a visit," I whispered into Lepprince's ear as we crossed the tiny vestibule.

"Don't be silly. Look, no sooner had María Coral regained consciousness than she wanted to know, logically enough, where she was and what had happened to her. We explained it all to her, and naturally that included your participation in last night's events. She wouldn't stop pestering me until I promised to bring you to see her as soon as I could."

"Really? Is it true she wants to see me?" I asked with such joy that Lepprince burst out laughing. I blushed right to the roots of my hair. The feelings that had overpowered me were beginning to frighten me.

We reached the door, and Lepprince knocked. A woman's voice invited us in. The woman who answered the knock was a nurse. María Coral was resting in bed with her eyes closed, but she wasn't sleeping, because she opened them when she heard us enter. Color had returned to her cheeks, and her eyes had recovered some of the liveliness I remembered from other times. I walked over to her bed, not knowing what to say. She stretched out a white hand which I clasped. She did not let go immediately.

"I'm happy to see you all better," I said with an infatuated voice.

"You saved my life," she said with the hint of a smile.

Lepprince and the nurse had gone out into the hall. I felt even more inhibited and lowered my eyes so I wouldn't feel María Coral's fixed on my own.

"Mr. Lepprince," I added, "came instantly to help you. That's certainly what saved you."

"Come closer, I can't hear you."

I brought my face close to hers. She was still squeezing my hand.

"There's something I'd like to know," she whispered.

"What's that?" I asked, imagining and fearing the question.

"Why did you come to my room last night?"

I'd guessed correctly. I felt myself blush again. I looked for some expression in her eyes or voice, but I could detect nothing but curiosity.

"Don't misunderstand," I began to say. "The other night a friend and I went to the cabaret and saw your act. I recognized you, went back with the intention of saying hello to you, and they gave me your address. When I knocked at the door and no one answered, I thought you'd gone out or didn't want any visitors, but suddenly," I added, changing the facts conveniently, "I seemed to hear a groan. I opened the door and saw you in bed in an alarming state. I called Lepprince, and you know the rest."

"That explains the *how* but not the *why*."

"The *why?*"

"Why you wanted to see me."

I seemed to see a tiny, malicious light glinting in her eyes, so I looked toward the floor again.

"When I saw you in that filthy boardinghouse, I feared the worst."

María Coral released my hand, sighed, and closed her eyelids over the beginnings of a tear.

"What's the matter? Do you feel ill? Should I call the nurse?" I exclaimed in alarm—but relieved at the same time.

"No, it's nothing. I was thinking about that boardinghouse and everything that's happened. Now it seems so far off, and look, only a few hours have gone by. I was thinking . . . oh, what does it matter?"

"Please, tell me what you were thinking."

She turned her face to the wall so I wouldn't see her weep, but her muffled groans betrayed her.

"I was thinking that soon I'll have to go back there. I'd rather die . . . Please don't laugh at me! . . . I'd rather die in this nice clean hotel surrounded by good people like you."

I couldn't go on listening: I fell on my knees at her side and again took her hands in mine.

"Don't say that, I forbid it. You'll never go back to that horrible place, never go back to that cabaret, never go back to the vile life you've lived until now. I don't know how I'll do it, but I'll find some way for you to lead the decent life you deserve. If necessary . . . if necessary, I'd do anything for you, María Coral."

She turned her face and looked at me with such sweetness that it was my eyes that filled with tears. With her free hand, she caressed my hair and cheeks and said, "Don't speak that way. I don't want you to suffer because of my luck. You've done enough as it is."

The door opened and I jumped to my feet. Lepprince and the nurse came in followed by a mature man, heavy, bald, and well-shaved who smelled like a facial massage. Lepprince introduced him as Doctor Ramírez.

"He's come to examine María Coral."

Doctor Ramírez gave me a frank smile.

"Don't worry about the girl. She's strong and there's nothing wrong with her. She's a bit weak, but that will pass quickly. Now, if you don't mind, you'll all have to leave the room. I'm going to give her a sedative so she'll sleep. She needs rest and good food: there's no better medicine in all the world."

Lepprince and I left the hotel. The rain had stopped, but the sky was still overcast and the air saturated with humidity.

"After these rains," said Lepprince, "spring will be here. Have you noticed the trees? They're ready to bud."

CORTABANYES MET WITH LEPPRINCE, and both went into the library. The lawyer was in an excellent mood, but not the Frenchman.

"I just spoke with a voter," said Cortabanyes. "An influential man, owner of a stamp shop. I think his name is Casabona."

"I have no idea who he is."

"You invited him to the party."

"I don't know ninety percent of the people who came, and I suspect they don't know me either."

"Well, this one knows you, and quite well. . . . He asked me when you'd be mayor so he could ask some favors of you."

"Mayor? Rumors certainly do fly. What did you say to him."

"Nothing concrete. But it would be a good idea to buy a few stamps from him: you have to butter up the electors," laughed Cortabanyes.

Lepprince cut off the lawyer's conversation with a gesture of impatience.

"Have you spoken recently with Pere Parells?"

"No, is something bothering him?"

"He started pestering me with tales about those stocks," grunted Lepprince.

A waiter opened the library door and stood stock-still on the threshold. Lepprince fulminated him with a glance.

"Excuse me, sir. Madame wants to know if dinner should be served."

"Tell her yes and stop bothering me," Lepprince sent him on his way. Then to Cortabanyes, "Who could have told him such a thing?"

"Him? You mean Pere Parells? Not me."

"Me either," said Lepprince stupidly. "But the fact is that he's heard something, and that shows there are information leaks."

Cortabanyes straightened his tie and pulled the threadbare cuffs of his shirt.

"What can we do about it?" he said in absolute calm.

"Don't take that tone with me, Cortabanyes!" roared Lepprince.

"What tone is that, my boy?"

"Cortabanyes, for the love of God, don't play dumb. We're both in this thing up to our necks. You can't abandon ship now."

"Who said anything about abandoning ship? Come, come, calm down. Nothing's gone wrong. Just think a minute. What's happened? Parells heard a rumor: Casabona, the stamp man, heard another. So what? You aren't mayor, and the shares in the Savolta company haven't been sold. All that's happened is that two false rumors are circulating. Nothing more."

"But Parells believes them. He's furious."

"He'll get over it. What other choice does he have?"

"He can do us a lot of harm if he decides to."

"If he decides to, sure, but he won't. He's old and alone. Since the deaths of Savolta and Claudedeu, he's had no strength. It's all show, believe me. And we need him on our side. He provides prestige, everybody thinks highly of him. He's . . . how shall I put it: tradition, the Lyceum, the Virgin of Montserrat."

Lepprince crossed and uncrossed his legs and twisted his fingers around all the while staring fixedly at the lawyer. He snorted and said, "All right, I'm calm now. What do we do now?"

"What did you say to him when he told you the rumors?"

"I told him he was an idiot and to go to hell. Yes, I know! I wasn't very diplomatic, but it's too late now."

"Son, you are pigheaded," Cortabanyes reproached him good-naturedly. "You don't deserve what you have. Try to remember you're a rich man, a public personality, that you just can't throw a fit every time something or someone gets in your way. You have to be as cold as ice, my boy. You're rich, don't forget it: you have to be conservative above all things. Moderation. Never attack. It's the others who have to attack. You only have to defend yourself, and very little at that. We don't want them to think their attacks can hurt you in the slightest."

Lepprince lowered his head and sat stock-still. Cortabanyes patted him on the back.

"Ah, you youngsters are so impulsive!" he declared. "Come on, arouse those spirits, we're being called to dinner. That will help things. See to it that Pere Parells gets an important seat at the table and be courteous with him. Later you'll take him aside, give him a cognac and a cigar, and make up with him. If necessary, you'll ask him to forgive you, but he must not leave this house with his head full of black clouds. Understand?"

Lepprince nodded.

"Well then, get up, wash your face, and let's head for the dining room. You can't come late: it's your party. And promise me you won't lose your temper again."

"I promise," said Lepprince in the lowest of voices.

NEMESIO CABRA GÓMEZ was hungry. For an hour he'd been wandering the silent streets, and the cold had seeped right into his bones. He passed by a cheap restaurant and stopped to peer through the windows in the door. It was almost impossible to see inside because of the grease and the steam, but it was easy to hear the roar of a party. It was the feast of Saint Sylvester, New Year's Eve. He counted the money he had left and calculated he could still buy himself a decent meal. The door opened to allow a fleshy man on holiday to exit with a young woman who had a fresh, plump body and was wearing an acrid perfume. Nemesio stepped aside and hid in the shadow. An unnecessary effort, because the man wouldn't have seen him even if he'd thrown himself at his feet, occupied as he was in trying not to fall down and in feeling up the woman. She in turn tried to elude her client's gross caresses without ceasing to smile and to pretend to be happy. But what Nemesio could not avoid was that the vision of the woman flooded his eyes, while his nose was attacked by her sensual perfume and the smell of fried fish coming from the restaurant.

Those temptations overwhelmed his prudence. He pushed the door and walked in. The place was a chaos. Everyone was talking at the same time, the drunks sang—each one his own song and each at the top of his lungs, with the drunk's tenacity in wanting to be heard. Nemesio contemplated the scene from the entrance: no one seemed to notice him, things looked fine. But soon events contradicted his optimism. Slowly but surely, the voices got lower and lower, the drunks fell silent, and in a matter of seconds the most absolute silence dominated the restaurant. Then something else happened: the customers who'd been crowding around the bar moved to both sides of the place until they created an avenue lined with expectant faces at one end of which stood Nemesio and at the other a muscular man with a beard wearing a filthy sheepskin jacket and a beret.

Nemesio needed no more information to deduce that his situation was not the one he desired. He turned, opened the door, and started to run. The man in the jacket and beret came out after him.

"Nemesio!" he roared in a voice that sounded like a cannon blast. "Nemesio, don't run away!"

Nemesio galloped through the streets, dodging around passersby and jumping over obstacles, never turning his head, certain that the man in the jacket was hot on his heels and would follow him until he caught him. He ran even more quickly, was hit with a pail of water tossed from a window, lost a shoe. He became weaker, his lungs ached. He heard that voice again.

"Nemesio! It's useless to run, I'll catch you anyway."

He still hopped along for a bit, his vision clouded, he grabbed onto a stone bench and slowly slipped until he was sitting on the ground. The big man in the jacket caught up to him huffing and puffing, seized him by the shoulders, and pulled him to his feet.

"Tried to get away, eh?"

Each time the man loosened his hold, Nemesio's legs crumpled and he began to fall. The huge man sat on the bench and waited until Nemesio caught his breath. While he waited, he opened his jacket to pull out a flower-patterned handkerchief to dry off his sweat. As he did so, he allowed Nemesio a glimpse of the butt of his pistol.

"I didn't do anything, I swear by the Holy Trinity," gasped Nemesio hugging the bench. "I've got nothing to be ashamed of."

"Oh, no? So why did you run?"

Nemesio breathed deeply and shrugged his shoulders.

"No one has any faith in his fellow man these days."

"You'll tell us all about it later. Now, get up and come with me. And don't do anything silly. The next time you try to run away I'll plug you. And you know it."

Chapter 3

Lepprince was right: spring was announcing itself by infusing a fragrance into the air that had something to it of the pleasant vertigo of madness. For two days (now, in memory, the most beautiful in my life), I went to the hotel on Princesa street to visit María Coral. The first day, I brought her flowers. Now I can laugh when I recall how many doubts, how many hesitations I had to overcome, how much daring I had to gather to buy that modest bouquet and with what a blush I gave it to her, fearful I would look too sweet or vulgar, fearful she wouldn't like those flowers, that they would arouse in her a bad, counterproductive memory, that she would have already received a bigger, more expensive bouquet (from Lepprince, naturally), and that my gift would only serve to prove how poor, how lowly I was. A knot forms in my throat when I relive the scene when I gave her the flowers, when I recall the seriousness with which she took them, without jokes or bitterness, with a simple gratitude that showed not only in her words but also in her big, shining eyes, and in her hands, which took up the flowers and brought them to her face, how they then put the bouquet on the bed, and took my own and clasped them briefly but expressively. We spoke little; I had too little or too much to say to her to bear a conversation; I went away, I strolled until very late. I remember I was sad, that I cursed my luck, that I was happy.

I returned the next day. My flowers, in a crystal vase, were on top of a desk. María Coral looked well and was very animated. She told me they had forbidden her to keep the flowers in the room between dusk and dawn because flowers in darkness consume the oxygen in the air. I already knew that, but I let her tell me, in complete detail. I brought her some candy. She scolded me for spending so much money, opened the box, offered it to me, and I ate one. Then Doctor Ramírez came and devoured three in an instant. With his mouth full of chocolate, he took her pulse and smiled.

"Child, you're in better health than I am."

He told her to get out of bed and open her nightgown so he could auscultate her. I went out into the hall and waited for the doctor, who confirmed the diagnosis: María Coral was fine, she could get up whenever she pleased, lead a normal life, even go back to work if she wished. Those words, far from making me happy, were like daggers in my heart. I cut short my visit and went home. I wanted to think, but my head was a whirlwind. I constructed a thousand wild projects, but not once did I deal with the essence of the problem. I slept little and badly. In the morning, my ideas were tinged with pessimism, as is usual after a disturbed night. At work, I behaved like a bumpkin: I got everything backward, lost papers, and tripped over the furniture. Cortabanyes was the only one who didn't seem to realize I was upset. The others stared at me with curiosity, but having already learned their lesson, they kept silent and cleaned up after me. As soon as work was over, I ran to the hotel. The old manager stopped me in the vestibule.

"If you're here to see the sick lady, don't bother going up. She left at midday."

"She left? Are you sure?"

"Of course, sir," he exclaimed, pretending my doubts offended him. "I wouldn't lie to you."

"And she didn't leave a note for me? My name is Miranda, Javier Miranda."

"She left no notes for anyone."

"But tell me, did she leave alone? Did someone come for her? Did she say where she was going?"

The manager excused himself with a gesture.

"Sorry, sir, but I'm not authorized to reveal anything about guests of the hotel."

"It's that . . . this case is different, it may be important, do me a favor."

"Sorry, sir, I told you the lady left no messages," he repeated with a craftiness I found suspicious.

I thought things over quickly, not knowing very well just what those things were.

"May I make a telephone call?"

"Of course, sir," answered the old man with the condescension of someone who hasn't yielded on a major point and is happy to yield on something small. "Here it is."

He walked a few steps away, and I called Cortabanyes to ask for Lepprince's address or telephone number. I doubted he'd give it to me, but I was ready to force him somehow, although I had no idea what kind of pressure I could put on the lawyer. My plan, in any case, was worthless because no one answered. I hung up, said good-bye, and left. The first thing that occurred to me was to go to the cabaret. Why? And what would I do when I did locate María Coral? I thought about it, but I wasted no time looking for answers to questions that had no answers. I walked a few steps, and a car pulled up next to me. A familiar voice called me.

"Sir, oh, sir."

I turned: it was Lepprince's chauffeur, waving to me from the car window. The curtains were drawn, so I supposed Lepprince was inside. I stopped.

"Get in, sir."

I did, and I found myself sitting in a luxurious box of red leather, illuminated by a little lamp in whose oscillating light I could see the smiling face and elegant figure of Lepprince. The car started moving again.

"What became of María Coral?" I asked.

"Hello, Javier. That's not the proper way to begin a conversation with a friend, is it?" The Frenchman reprimanded me with his perpetual, benevolent smile.

NEMESIO CABRA GÓMEZ began to walk, followed by the colossus wearing the beret, who never took his eyes off him. They passed through dark alleys which Nemesio, a habitué of the slums, recognized with no difficulty. This disturbed him, because it meant his captor was not concerned that Nemesio could later reconstruct the path and find the place he was being led to. The only reason could be that he wasn't going to allow him that opportunity.

He looked for a clock: the streets they walked through weren't very crowded, and the noise of parties came from eating houses and patios. If twelve midnight were to come, the people would pour out onto the streets to congratulate each other, drink, and celebrate the New Year. That would offer a hypothetical opportunity for escape. Where the hell was a clock? They passed a church, and Nemesio raised his eyes: standing out from the bell tower was a white sphere with roman numerals. The arrows indicated eleven o'clock. That detail would help him later on in his deductions. The giant gave him a shove.

"You can pray later, when the time comes."

Nemesio dawdled to gain time at the risk of even more shoves, but his efforts were useless. Standing in front of a store that was closed, the titan gave him an order.

"Knock: twice, pause, three more times."

"Listen, Julián, you've made a mistake. This is all a misunderstanding. I'm not what you think."

"Knock."

"Just think that you're going to have a burden on your conscience unless you listen to reason. Do you want to be a Caiaphas, the priest who judged Christ?"

"If you don't start knocking, I'll use your head as a knocker."

"You won't listen to me?"

"No."

Nemesio knocked just as his kidnapper had told him, and soon an oilcloth curtain was raised, a grim face asked who they were, and the door opened, causing some bells hanging from the lintel to ring. Nemesio found himself in what looked like a photographer's studio. At one end of the place there was a camera with a bellows set on a tripod. From the camera hung a black hood and a ball attached to a cable. At the other end of the room was a majestic chair, a golden column, some stuffed pigeons, and several bunches of paper flowers. On the walls were portraits the darkness made difficult to see clearly, but which suggested engaged couples or children about to take first communion. The three men did not speak. The one who'd opened the door lowered the curtain, lit a match, and led the new arrivals to a narrow staircase hidden from ordinary visitors by a counter. They went down the stairs; the match went out, and they went on feeling their way until they came into a room that must have been the darkroom, to judge by the basins filled with dark liquids and other pieces of photographic apparatus. At a table where an oil lamp was burning sat two men, the same ones who had held a mysterious conversation with Nemesio ten days earlier in the back room of a tavern. Nemesio knew them and they knew him. The giant wearing the beret, called Julián by everyone, pushed Nemesio toward the table and then sat down next to his comrades. The one who'd let them in also sat down. The four of them stared at the prisoner, and no one said a word. Nemesio lost his nerve.

"Don't look at me that way. I know what you're thinking, but you can't always go by appearances."

"The hen only cackles when she's laid an egg," said one of the men.

"Take a good look at me, you've known me for years," Nemesio insisted as he measured the space that separated him from the stairs—he'd be shot before he got there. "I'm a poor devil, poor as a church mouse. Look at my ribs," he raised his rags and showed a flaccid skin and prominent ribs, "you can count all my bones, as the Lord's Sacred Books say. So, tell me, living the way I live, would I always be so hungry if I were an informer? What good would it do me to make enemies of you, betray my own people, and have vengeance taken against me? What have they done for me? What do I owe the police?"

"Shut up, parrot," said Julián. "You're not here to make speeches but to answer a few questions."

"And to answer for your acts," added another, who by his manner seemed to be the chief.

A cold sweat soaked Nemesio's loose skin. Again he measured distances, tried to remember where the objects scattered around the photographic studio were located, objects which, if the moment came, could impede his escape; he tried to remember if the man had locked the door of the studio with a key. It was too risky, and he told himself that the gamble wasn't worth it.

"Tell us what happened, but don't lie or hide anything . . . you know why."

"I swear by the Most High that what I told you was the truth. I've got nothing to add but what you already know: they killed him."

The man with the scar slapped his hand on the table, making bowls and dishes jump.

"But who killed Pajarito de Soto?"

Nemesio gestured as if to beg pardon.

"I don't know."

"Why did you come around asking for him?"

"A distinguished-looking gentleman found me about two weeks ago. I didn't know him, and he didn't know me. He didn't say who he was. He assured me I had nothing to fear, that he wasn't the regular or secret police, that he hated violence, and that he only wanted to avoid an execrable act and unmask some criminals."

"And you believed him?"

"You believed me."

"That's true," said the one with the scar, who seemed the most equable. "Go on."

"The distinguished gentleman asked me if I knew Pajarito de

Soto (may he rest in peace), and I said no, but that it wouldn't be any problem for me to locate him. 'I'm counting on that,' said the gentleman, then I said, 'Why do you want him?' 'I have grounds to believe that he's in danger.' 'Well, what's he done?' 'I don't know,' he says, 'and that's exactly what you have to find out.' 'Why me and not the police?' 'I'm the one asking the questions,' he said, 'but I'll tell you that I don't have strong enough reasons to go to the police and besides . . . ' 'What?' I ask. 'Nothing.' And he fell into a somber silence. Seeing he wouldn't go on, I asked him: 'And what do I have to do once I find this Pajarito de Soto?' 'Nothing,' he repeated. 'Follow him everywhere and keep me informed of his activities.' 'And how will I get in touch with you?' 'On Christmas Eve, at six-thirty, you'll wait for me right outside El Siglo. Will you have time to find my man?' 'Don't worry, sir.' We agreed on a price—not a very high one, to tell the truth—and we parted company."

"Who was that distinguished gentleman?" asked the man with the scar.

"I didn't know then and I don't know now. May God strike me dead if I'm lying."

"And you who brag about knowing everything, you haven't been able to ask around?" said Julián mockingly.

"You know the circles I move in. That gentleman moved in a sphere different from the one I live in. Poor me, I don't have contacts like that and won't have in a thousand years. May I sit down? I haven't eaten."

"Keep standing. You'll have time to rest soon."

A chill ran down Nemesio's back, but a certain calm began to possess him despite his fears: those conspirators seemed more disposed to dialogue than action.

"Should I go on?"

"Yes."

"I'd never heard of this Pajarito de Soto, so I thought he was new in these parts. After asking around here and there, I found you, and you told me."

"Because you assured us that you wanted to prevent something bad from happening to him."

"And that was the truth."

"But no sooner did you lay your eye on him than he was murdered."

"I got there too late, it seems."

"Liar," Julián cut him off.

"Quiet," ordered the man with the scar. Then to Nemesio, "Listen. Pajarito de Soto was an idiot who created more problems than anything else. But he was a man of goodwill and worked for the cause. We can't let his death go unpunished. It would be easy for us to eliminate you, but it wouldn't do any good because it would only make the murderer laugh. We have to aim higher, understand? We have to aim at the head, not at the feet. We have to find out who had him killed, and you're going to do it."

"Me?"

"Right," said the man with the scar with mortal calm. "You. Listen and don't interrupt. Until now, you've sold us to the rich for money, but now the tables are turned: this time you're going to sell them, and the price is your life. We're giving you a week. Don't fail, but above all, don't try to fool us. You're more clever than you seem, you circulate nicely among whores and tramps, but don't confuse us with them and don't think you're that smart: we're not that scum. In seven days, we're going to meet again, and you're going to tell us who did it and why, what happened at the Savolta company, and just what this business is all about. If you do what we say, nothing will happen to you, but if you don't, if you try to trick us, you know what you'll get."

As if sealing the scarred man's words, all the clocks in the city struck twelve. Those bells would ring for a long time in Nemesio's head. The streets filled with shouting crowds; the sounds of trumpets, whistles, drums, and rattles filled the air. In the distance, in the residential neighborhoods, some fireworks exploded.

"Get out," said the scarred man.

Nemesio said good-bye and left the place.

.....

"SO WE'LL SOON HAVE a small Lepprince," chirped Mrs. Parells.

The ladies, who preferred gossip to dancing, sipped lemonade or sweet sherry clustered in the music room. María Rosa Savolta's cheeks went from snow-white to bright red. From this circle of women flowed a cascade of comments, advice, and congratulations.

"With such good-looking parents, the child will be a gem!"

"You're going to have to eat a lot, child, you're all skin and bones."

"Just suppose it's twins . . . "

"Say what you will, but this child's going to be pure Catalan."

Still laughing, María Rosa Savolta, dazed by the shrieks and kisses, begged for silence.

"Lower your voices, for heaven's sake! My husband will find out."

"What? You still haven't told him?"

"I'm keeping it as a surprise, but for God's sake, I wouldn't want someone else to tell him before I do."

"Don't worry, child, the information won't leave this room," they said in one voice.

A man had secreted himself into this seraglio and kept a smiling silence. Lawyer Cortabanyes made it a practice to frequent feminine gatherings, because he knew that through doggedness and patience, it was possible to find out many things there. That night his theory proved to be accurate. The lawyer ruminated his croquettes and calculated the consequences of what had just been revealed to him. A lady covered with ostrich feathers slapped him with her fan.

"Spying on us, you rascal?"

"Madam, I simply came in to pay my respects."

"Well, you have to give us your word as a gentleman that you won't repeat anything of what you've heard."

"I shall consider it a professional secret," said Cortabanyes, and turning to María Rosa, "Allow me to be the first member of my sex to congratulate you, Mrs. Lepprince."

The lawyer bent over to kiss the future mother's hand and, carried forward by his extraordinary volume, fell onto the sofa, flattening María Rosa, who squealed with fear and amusement. The ladies came to the aid of their hostess: some pulled on Cortabanyes's arms, others on his legs, still more on the tails of his shabby tuxedo. Finally they managed to pull him off the sofa and send him rolling into the piano. He fell full-length against it, striking every key. Then the pulling and pushing began again, and the game was repeated, with the docile, round lawyer being tossed from hand to hand by the gleeful circle of matrons.

THE LIMOUSINE MADE ITS WAY through the streets, but with the curtains closed I could not see where we were going. Lepprince offered me a cigarette, and we smoked without exchanging a word for a good part of the ride. At a certain moment, the whine of the engine and the angle of the car led me to suppose we'd begun going up a steep hill.

"Where are we?"

"We're almost there," answered Lepprince. "Don't worry, this isn't a kidnapping."

Going around a sharp curve, I fell against Lepprince. The force of gravity then pulled me back to a vertical position, but I instantly found myself tossed to the other end of the seat. I raised the curtain, but saw nothing but night, bushes, and pine trees.

"Satisfied now?" asked Lepprince. "Then lower the curtain. I like to travel incognito."

"We're in the country."

"That's obvious," he said.

After a while, not without submitting us first to a continuous series of curves and hard braking, the car stopped, and Lepprince indicated that we'd arrived. The chauffeur opened the door, and I heard violin music, a waltz. That's right, out in the country.

"What is this place?"

"The casino. Get out."

How stupid of me not to have realized it! The truth is that I'd never been—nor did I ever dream I'd be there—at the Tibidabo Casino. Of course I knew the place. I'd often gone into ecstasy contemplating, from a distance, its seignorial cupolas, its lights; imagining the place, calculating how much money was being bet at roulette and at the poker or baccarat tables.

"Do you object?" asked Lepprince.

"Not in the slightest."

We walked into the casino. The staff seemed to know Lepprince well, and he in turn greeted them by their nicknames. Surrounded by a cloud of servants, we were shown to the dining room where a table had been reserved for us in a discreet corner. Lepprince ordered the dinner and the wines without asking me, as he usually did. While we waited to be served, he asked about me, about my work and my projects.

"I was told you'd gone back to Valladolid—it is Valladolid, isn't it? I was afraid it was true and that we'd never see each other again. Luckily, I see you changed your mind. Know something? I think Barcelona is an enchanted city. It has something—how shall I put it?—something magnetic. Sometimes it's uncomfortable, disagreeable, hostile, and even dangerous, but what can you do? It's impossible to give it up. Don't you think so?"

"You may be right. I came back because I realized that in Valladolid there was nothing for me to do. Not that I have so much here, I admit that, but at least I have some freedom of action."

I thought he was expressing interest in my affairs merely out of courtesy and that I was not the object of our interview, but his concern seemed so genuine, and I was so in need of a friend to whom I could tell my problems, that I told him everything, everything that had happened to me since the last time we'd seen each other, before his wedding, everything I'd thought, desired, hoped for, and uselessly suffered. My tale lasted through the entire meal, and I fell silent when the check came, which Lepprince signed without looking at it. We then went into a salon where we had coffee and cognac.

"Everything you've just told me, Javier, saddens me deeply," he said, picking up the broken thread of our conversation. "I had no idea your situation was so painful. Why didn't you come to me? What are friends for?"

"I tried. I went to see you at home, but the doorman told me you'd moved, and either he didn't know or wouldn't tell me your new address. I thought I could find you through Cortabanyes or that I'd write you at the factory, but I was afraid of annoying you. You didn't give any signs of life, and I suspected you wanted to sever our relations . . ."

"How can you say things like that, Javier? I'd be offended if I thought you really mean what you're saying." Here he paused, tasted his cognac, sat back in the armchair, and closed his eyes. "Nevertheless, you had good reason to think so. I recognize I behaved badly. Sometimes, unintentionally, we commit small injustices." Here his voice became a whisper. "Forgive me."

"Please . . ."

"I know, I know what I'm saying about myself. I turned my back on you without realizing it, I was disloyal. And disloyalty is a bad thing, I mean it. At least let me give you an explanation. No, don't interrupt me, I want to give it to you." He stopped to light a cigar and then went on in a lower voice. "You already know that when I married María Rosa Savolta I came into possession, not legally but in fact, of the stock in the company that the deceased Savolta left to his daughter. Those shares, together with those I already had, made me, virtually, into the owner of the company, especially when you realize that Claudedeu left his stock to his wife, a half-deaf, elderly lady incapable of participating in the business world. While this has advantages you can easily imagine, it also entails a really overwhelming quantity of work. And that isn't all. There is another reason, less solid but no less real: when I married María Rosa, my social position changed. I became a member of one of the most prominent families in the city and went from being a parvenu to being a public man with all the social compromises that implies—which, I confess, at times is a heavier burden than the business responsibilities I mentioned."

He smiled, took a long puff on this cigar, and slowly exhaled the smoke.

"These have been hard months, Javier, difficult to bear. But the waters are finally returning to their course. I feel tired and need a breath of air, I want to live my life again, see my old friends from before again, resume our chats, our dinners, remember?"

A knot formed in my throat, and I couldn't articulate a single sound. I nodded affirmatively.

"And I'll begin by taking care of you, don't worry. But first . . . ," he stared me straight in the eye; I knew that we were finally coming to the real subject of our interview, and I held my breath. My heart was pounding, my hands were cold, moist with sweat. I drank a drop of cognac to calm my nerves. "But first I want to ask your advice. You know what I'm talking about, right?"

"María Coral, I suppose."

"Exactly." He was silent for a time, and when he spoke again, I noted a slightly grandiloquent and false tone in his voice, a tone that vibrates in the voices of actors when the curtain goes up and they begin to recite the script. "Let's start at the beginning. Has María Coral ever told you her story? No? It's only natural. Her pride wouldn't let her. Poor, unhappy thing! She didn't want to tell me anything either, but I wheedled it out of her until I knew everything. When I left her . . . ," he gestured with his open hand, as if he were pushing a memory away from himself. "Now I realize I behaved in an ignoble way, but what can you do? I was very young, even though she thought I was already a man," he sighed and went on with no transition. "María Coral joined up with her *partenaires,* the two strongmen. They went on performing in different cities, in shows of the lowest quality, church festivals, who knows what, until the two killers were imprisoned for some crime—a minor robbery, a brawl. María Coral had to leave town and perform alone. When her pals got out of jail, they decided to leave the country. You remember that years back they got involved in social things—a bit compromised the two of them were. It's possible that when they were arrested their story came out, and they, fearing perhaps they would be involved in some scandal or perhaps induced by the police themselves, thought it more prudent to head for the border. They didn't tell María Coral anything, and, in any case, she couldn't have gone with them because she was still a minor. So the poor girl had to go on earning a living without help or protection. In her tour, she came to Barcelona where you found her, half-dead of hunger and sick. And that's where this brief, sad story ends."

"Ends?" I asked, certain that Lepprince would understand my meaning.

"That's what we have to talk about," he said, jumping from melancholy to more practical matters."You know that I, in a certain way, had contracted a debt with María Coral. Not a formal debt, of course, but I just told you that disloyalty is odious to me. I want to help her, but I don't know how."

"Well, with your position and fortune it shouldn't be difficult."

"More difficult than you'd imagine. Naturally, it wouldn't be a problem to me to give her a little money and send her on her way, but what do we gain with that? Money doesn't last long these days. After a few months or a year at most, things would again be the way they are now, and we wouldn't have achieved anything. Besides, María Coral is a child; it isn't only money she needs but protection. Don't you agree?"

"Yes," was the only thing I could say.

"Well then, what to do? Keep her, get her an apartment, a little store? Impossible. I can't. Everything becomes known sooner or later, and who would believe my generosity is disinterested? I can't see myself the subject of rumors. Think about my wife, whom I adore, what would she think if she knew I was keeping a minor with whom my name was already connected when I was single? Not a chance."

"Why not find her a job? That way she could earn her living honorably," I proposed in good faith.

"A job? For María Coral?" Lepprince laughed quietly. "Think, Javier, what kind of job could I get her? What does María Coral know how to do besides somersaults? Nothing. So where would we put her? Dishwasher? In a factory or shop? You know what working conditions are in those places. It would almost be better to let her go back to the cabarets."

It was true, I couldn't imagine María Coral subjected to a back-breaking schedule, to iron discipline, or the abuses of foremen. The mere idea enraged me, as I told Lepprince, who only smiled and smoked in silence, looking at me tenderly and ironically. Since I said nothing and he guessed I was upset, he added after a time:

"It looks like all doors are closed to us, eh?" and I guessed from the tone of his voice that we'd reach the point he so desired to reach.

"Why all this mystery? I'm sure you've already thought up a solution."

He laughed quietly again.

"I'm not trying to be mysterious, dear Javier. I just wanted you to follow my line of thought. Yes, I have thought of a solution, and the solution, to put it clearly, is you."

I choked on the cognac.

"Me? What can I do?"

Lepprince leaned forward, always staring me in the eyes. Then he put his hand on my forearm.

"Marry her."

EVERYONE KNOWS that there is only one link between honorable people and criminals, and that link is the police. Nemesio Cabra Gómez wasn't stupid and knew that if those above could get their hands on those below by means of the police, those below could also use the same means, even though it would take more effort and a lot of tact. So, after thinking it over carefully, he reached the conclusion that he would only by able to give the information demanded of him in exchange for his life if the police gave it to him. The plan he developed involved considerable risk, but considering the stakes, there was no time for hesitation. Accordingly, early the next morning, January 1, Nemesio walked into the police station and asked to speak with the inspector. Nemesio knew people at the station. When need or threats pushed him into it, he had no misgivings about doing small services for the authorities, although until that point he had never been involved in political matters, having prudently limited his activities to the area of street crime which in no way compromised him. Until then, things had gone well, and even if he'd earned no one's respect, he'd at least managed to get both the police and the underworld to leave him in peace.

"Good morning and Happy New Year, officer."

The officer scrutinized him with distrust.

"What do you want?"

"I'm Nemesio Cabra Gómez, and it's not the first time I've been here."

"That's obvious," said the officer mockingly.

"Don't misunderstand me. I mean that I've done good work for the authorities in the past," Nemesio humbly corrected himself.

"So what do you want? To do some more good work?"

Nemesio nodded.

"All right, what's it all about?"

"Something important, officer. With all due respect, please allow me to reserve my information for another level of authority."

The officer turned his head to one side, narrowed his eyes, raised his brows, and scratched his mustache.

"The Minister of the Interior is in Madrid."

"I want to speak with the chief inspector of the Social Brigade," Nemesio cut him off, seeing that the mockery would never end.

"Inspector Vázquez?"

"Yes."

The officer, bored with idle chatter, shrugged his shoulders.

"Third floor. I don't suppose you're armed."

"Frisk me if you like. I'm a man of peace."

The officer did search him, gestured with his thumb for Nemesio to pass, and the informer walked to the third floor. There he asked for Inspector Vázquez. The secretary told him Vázquez hadn't arrived yet and asked him to take a seat in the hall. After a long while, the inspector came. He seemed in a bad mood. More time passed, and finally the secretary showed him into a large but messy office which the light of a clear winter day illuminated with official opacity. The details of the interview between Inspector Vázquez and Nemesio are transcribed in another part of this report.

"MARRY HER? Me? Marry María Coral?"

"Don't shout. No need for everyone to find out," whispered Lepprince, never losing his smile.

Luckily, the orchestra was still playing, so my words mixed with the music. No one seemed to notice.

After my brusque reaction, I fell silent. The proposition seemed totally absurd to me, and if it hadn't come from Lepprince himself, I would have rejected it out of hand. But Lepprince was never frivolous, and if he spoke to me in those terms, it was because he'd coldly thought it all over beforehand, right down to the last detail. With that certainty, I decided it would be better not to spurn the idea, but to remain calm and allow him to present his plans.

"Why should I marry her?"

"Because you love her."

If the dome of the casino had crashed down on my head, it would not have left me any more disconcerted or shocked. I was prepared to hear any reason, any suggestion, but that . . . that went beyond the limits of the foreseeable. My first reaction, as I said, was one of absolute shock. Then a sudden indignation came over me, and finally I again sank into a kind of paralysis. But this time my consternation was not caused by the strangeness of what Lepprince had said but for the revelation it entailed. Could it be true? Could it be love, that overbearing sentiment which had pushed me to search for María Coral, the irresistible impulse that dragged me to the cabaret, to the boardinghouse, to her lugubrious room, against all logic, with the stupidity of a force of nature? And my anguish during these past days, my doubts, my ridiculous timidity, my blind obstinacy not to accept an inexorable destiny, could it be . . . ? No, I didn't want to think it. It seemed as if an abyss was opening at my feet, and that I was wavering on the edge in horror. I lacked the courage to face up to a possibility like that. Lepprince, however, had all the courage he needed to face the incongruities of life. How I envied, how I still envy his fortitude in those situations!

"Javier, have you fallen asleep?"

His calm, friendly voice brought me back from my caviling.

"Sorry. You've left me so . . . so confused."

He laughed openly, as if my confusion were childish.

"You're not going to tell me it isn't true."

"I . . . barely know her. What makes you suppose . . . ?"

"Javier," he chided me, "we're not schoolboys. There are things that are obvious. I understand your doubts, but facts are facts. They stand there, as obvious as one of these columns. What I say is that by denying them we don't resolve them."

"No, no, it's all crazy. Let's forget it."

"All right, just as you wish," said Lepprince as he stood up. "Excuse me for a moment, I just remembered a call I have to make. Don't run away now."

"Don't worry."

He'd left me alone on purpose so I could straighten out the tangle in my head. I don't know what conclusions I reached in those few minutes, but when he came back I was just as confused as I was at first, although I was much calmer.

"Sorry it took so long, what were we talking about?" he asked with affected irony.

"Look here, Lepprince, I'm in a total state of confusion. Don't push me."

"I already said we'd forget all about it."

"No, now it's too late. You're right: it's useless to deny the facts."

"Ah, so you admit you love María Coral."

"No, it isn't that . . . no. I mean that's the source of my confusion. I just don't know what I feel, understand? I don't deny that I feel something for her, an intense feeling, it's true. But I barely know her. Is it love or just a passing infatuation? Besides, love is one thing and getting married is something else very different. Love is a puff of air, something ethereal. . . . Matrimony is something very serious. Not something to be decided on some happy whim."

"Don't decide it on a happy whim. Take all the time you need and proceed according to your own judgment. After all, you're not going to marry me," he joked, "so you don't have to explain everything to me."

I'm coming to you as a friend and adviser," I carefully stated in deadly seriousness. "In the first place, who is María Coral? We know practically nothing about her, and the little we do know wouldn't recommend her as a candidate."

"That's true, she has a wild past. It's also clear to me and to you that her only desire is to forget that past and lead a decent life. María Coral is a good person. In any case, that's something you'd have to decide for yourself. God keep me from giving you advice that would make you reproach me later."

"All right, let's leave that aside and turn to something else. What can I offer her?"

"A good name and a respectable life, but above all, you yourself: an honest, sensitive, intelligent, and educated person."

"Thanks for the compliments, but I was talking about money."

"Ah, money . . . money, money, money . . . "

We were interrupted by the arrival of Cortabanyes, who was walking around the salon, dragging his feet as if he were wearing leg irons. Cortabanyes stood out from the crowd because of the shine of his wrinkled suit covered with stains and his general air of neglect. To complete the picture, he was chewing the butt of an extinguished cigar.

"Good evening, Mr. Lepprince. Good evening, Javier my boy," he mumbled as he passed. Lepprince stood up and took his hand. I was struck by that gesture of deference which, later on, I would remember. "How's that bomb factory of yours going?"

"Upward, always upward, Mr. Cortabanyes."

"Then you must be making rockets, not bombs."

I blushed to hear such a dreadful joke, but both Lepprince and a few indiscreet eavesdroppers chorused it with laughs. I supposed they laughed out of good feeling for the lawyer.

"And your practice, Mr. Cortabanyes, how is it doing?"

"Badly, Mr. Lepprince. But I don't want to bore you. You're young and will be wanting to talk about women, as is natural."

"Wouldn't you like to chat with us?"

"No, thank you. I think people are waiting for me to play a few hands of gin rummy. Not for money, of course."

"Only chick-peas, is that it, Mr. Cortabanyes?"

"Uncooked chick-peas, yes, sir. Look, I've got a handful right here, see?"

As he said that, he pulled a handful of chick-peas from the bulging pocket of his jacket. Several rolled across the floor, and a waiter got down on all fours to catch them.

"Well, then. You get on with telling each other stories, and I, who have no stories to tell, will cuddle with my cards."

He went off dragging his feet on the carpets, greeting people left and right, while the waiter ran after him with the recaptured chick-peas.

"I didn't know Cortabanyes frequented the casino," I said to Lepprince.

A HORSESHOE-SHAPED TABLE had been installed in the mansion's ample dining room to seat all one hundred guests. By the light of the candelabra, the silver, the china, and the carved crystal all glittered. A long row of flowers put a note of life and color into the picture. The guests feverishly looked for their names on the place cards. There were races, confusion, shouts, gestures, wounded sensibilities.

María Rosa Savolta cut her husband off just as he was entering the dining room.

"Paul-André, I want to talk to you for a second."

"But, dear, everyone's at table, can't you wait?"

"It has to be now. Come here."

And taking her husband by the hand, they crossed the salon, empty now except for the musicians, who were putting their instruments away, straightening out their music, wiping their sweaty brows, and getting ready to join the servants for a cool drink.

"Come in and close the door," said María Rosa, entering the library. Her husband obeyed her without dissimulating a grimace of impatience.

"Well then, what's going on."

"Sit down."

"The devil! Will you tell me just exactly what's bothering you?" shouted Lepprince.

María Rosa began to pout.

"You never spoke that way to me before," she whined.

"For the love of God, don't cry. Forgive me, but you've made me nervous. I'm fed up with mysteries. I want this evening to be a success, and these contretemps disturb me. Look what time it is: it's getting late, our guest of honor may arrive at any moment and find us still eating dinner."

"You're right, Paul-André, you think of everything. I'm a fool."

"Come then, don't cry anymore. Take my handkerchief. What was it you had to tell me?"

María Rosa wiped away a tear, handed the handkerchief back to her husband, and took his hand.

"I'm expecting a child," she announced.

Lepprince's face expressed infinite surprise.

"What?"

"A child, Paul-André, a child."

"Are you sure?"

"I went to the doctor a week ago with Mama, and this morning he confirmed it. There's no doubt."

Lepprince released his wife's hand, sat down, pressed the tips of his fingers together, and let his eyes trace the outline of the rug.

"I don't know what to say . . . it's something so unexpected. These things, when you first learn them, always surprise you."

"But aren't you happy?"

Lepprince raised his eyes.

"Of course I'm happy, very happy. I always wanted a child, and now I have one. Now," he added in a hoarse voice, "nothing can stop me."

He shook his head and stood up.

"Come along, we'll announce it here and now."

He kissed his wife on the forehead, and, their arms about each other's waists, they entered the dining room. The guests, taken aback by the lateness of their hosts, had begun to whisper until the women in on the secret, interpreting the disappearance of the young couple, spread the news that justified this unusual absence. Everyone fell silent, and all eyes turned to the door. There was a smile of pleasure on every face. When Mr. and Mrs. Lepprince made their entrance, they were received with warm and heavy applause.

INSPECTOR VÁZQUEZ was not interested in knowing who killed Pajarito de Soto. The murder of Savolta was occupying all his attention and almost all his energy. It was not a simple murder investigation he held in his hands but the entire social order, the security of the nation. Inspector Vázquez was a methodical, tenacious policeman, little given to displays of imagination. If someone had buried the Pajarito de Soto matter, then it would stayed buried. For the moment, he had other concerns. Besides, Nemesio Cabra Gómez did not look trustworthy. He limited himself to treating him with a certain respect and to turning a deaf ear to all the nonsense this inopportune confidant would impart.

For Nemesio it was like an ice-cold shower. He just did not

expect a reception of that sort and abandoned the station with his tail between his legs. The intrusion of the Savolta murder into his affairs might prove fatal to him. "Savolta, Savolta," he kept repeating to himself. "Where have I heard that name before?" The morning cold cleared his brain. He remembered the final words uttered by the man with the scar: "In seven days, we're going to meet again, and you're going to tell us who did it and why, what happened at the Savolta company, and just what this business is all about." What relation was there between Savolta and Pajarito de Soto? Would Savolta's death be the result of Pajarito's? Lost in these reflections, he reached his own neighborhood. Carts unloading goods for the recently opened shops were coming and going. Women carrying big baskets were going in and out of the market. The eating house was empty. Nemesio pounded on the bar with the palm of his hand.

"Hello, for God's sake! Isn't there anybody here?"

He had to wait a while until a boy wearing an apron appeared, rolling a heavy barrel.

"What can I do for you?"

"I'd like to see the boss."

"The boss? He's sleeping like a pig."

"It's a very important matter. Wake him up."

"You wake him up—if you're tired of living," said the boy impertinently as he pointed to a narrow, moist staircase that led to the living quarters.

"Is that the kind of manners they teach nowadays?" grumbled Nemesio as he walked up. A concert of unmistakable sounds led him through the narrow corridor to a low door, out of alignment with its own hinges. He knocked softly with his knuckles. The noises didn't stop. He pushed open the door and walked in.

The bartender's bedroom was a dark, badly ventilated attic with no other furniture in it but a chair, a clothes rack, and a bed, which at the time was occupied by the bartender and a whore who was snoring. Once he was used to the bad light, Nemesio could make out the bearded, beetle-browed face of the man and his herculean, hairy arms, which were wrapped around the whore. She had a chubby face, reddish skin, and prominent breasts that poked out over the blanket and seemed to observe Nemesio like two naughty piglets.

Feeling his way, the intruder went around the bed to be next to the bartender. He shook his shoulder. Seeing that this had no effect on him, Nemesio called him by name, slapped him a few times, and finally ended up throwing a glass of water—which turned out to be a glass of wine—into the bartender's face.

As usually happens with deep sleepers, his awakening was so instantaneous that one of his flailing arms hit Nemesio and threw him against the wall.

"What's going on? Who's there?" he shouted.

"Just me, don't be afraid," said Nemesio.

The bartender's bulging eyes identified the intruder.

"You!"

The whore had awakened and was covering her naked flesh as best she could.

"Sorry to bother you, but the matter that brings me here is serious. Otherwise, I never would have dared . . ."

"GET OUT OF HERE!!" bellowed the bartender.

The whore, out of shock, a dream, or shame, was weeping.

"Don Segundino, for the Virgin's sake, tell him to go away!" she begged.

The bartender felt around under the pillow and pulled out a revolver. Nemesio retreated to the door.

"Don Segundino, don't get upset, it's a matter of life or death."

The bartender fired a shot in the air. Nemesio knocked over the chair where male trousers and female underwear were promiscuously piled, jumped, ran out into the hall, and flew down the stairs.

"Don't say I didn't warn you . . . ," muttered the boy in the apron. But Nemesio was already in the street and running past the women, who pulled themselves and their baskets back as the bolt of lightning went by.

.....

I gulped down my third cognac, lit up what I assume was my thousandth cigarette (I never liked cigars), sighed, and looked at Lepprince. Fatigue was overwhelming me; I would have fallen asleep in the casino armchair if I weren't making a supreme effort to concentrate.

"You were saying your problem is money," said Lepprince.

"Money . . . ? Yes, that's true. I can barely make ends meet now, how could I ever get married?"

"My friend, money is never a problem. More cognac?"

"No thanks, please. I've already drunk too much."

"Do you feel ill?"

"No. Just a bit tired. Go on."

"As you probably understand, I too have thought about the economic aspects of the situation. I didn't tell you before, but I have a proposition for you. Now, I don't want you to take this the wrong way. One thing has nothing to do with the other. The proposition does not depend on your marrying María Coral . . . and vice versa. Don't even think for a minute that I'm trying to cocrcc you."

I made a gesture that could mean anything. Lepprince put out his cigar, and a waiter exchanged his ashtray for a fresh one. Lepprince then made sure no one was listening to us.

"What I'm going to tell you is strictly confidential. Don't say anything, I know I can count on you"—he cut off my protests of discretion. "What I'm going to tell you is only a possibility, and I want you to understand that to avoid future disillusionment. In sum, I'll tell you that serious propositions have been made to me by groups I can't identify at the moment urging me to enter politics. At first, they tried to attract me to their respective parties. Naturally, I refused. In the light of my unwillingness, they changed tactics. To make a long story short, they want me to be the next mayor of Barcelona. That's right, don't look so shocked: mayor. I don't have to explain to you the importance of such a position. You already know it perfectly well. They don't know it yet, but I can tell you now that I think I'm going to accept their offer and announce my candidacy. I think, without being immodest, that I can do a good job for the city and, indirectly, for the nation. I am a foreigner and almost a new arrival. That might seem like an obstacle, but it's actually an advantage. The people are fed up with parties and political chicanery. I am impartial, not married to any group: my hands—understand?—are not tied. That's where my strength lies."

He paused to weigh the effect his words had produced on me. In truth, I must not have given any impression whatsoever, because by then things were moving at a rate that far exceeded my comprehension. I thought that if Lepprince were saying these things, they had to be true, but I refrained from making any comments.

"All of what I'm saying is the preamble to what comes now. The possibility—and please note that I'm talking only about possibilities—will require an intensive preparation on my part, a preparation into which I've thrown myself to the degree my other responsibilities allow. Nevertheless, I don't want to mix things, simply because I want to keep them in order. So, I've decided to create a kind of office . . . a secretariat we could call it, dedicated exclusively to my political activities. To organize and run that secretariat, I need a person I can count on. Naturally, there could be no one better than you."

"Just a minute," I said, shaking off my somnolence. "If I'm understanding you correctly, you want me to go into politics."

"Into policics? No, at least not in the sense in which you're taking it. I want you to do for me what you do for Cortabanyes: efficient work in the background."

"I would have to leave his office."

"Of course. Would you be sorry?"

"No . . . I was just thinking about Cortabanyes. I wouldn't want to hurt him in any way. Despite everything, I owe him a lot."

"I like hearing you say that. It proves you've got a conscience and, above all, that you're already thinking affirmatively about my proposition."

"I didn't mean that."

"All right, all right, don't worry about Cortabanyes. I'll talk to him."

He suddenly stood up, relaxed his facial muscles, stretched his legs, and, revealing a fatigue much like my own, yawned.

"You've finally managed to infect me with your sleepiness. Let's go. Enough for one night. We'll go on talking. Think it over and don't make a snap decision. Oh, I forgot," he said, taking a wallet out of his pocket and a card out of his wallet, "this is my address. I'll also give you my office number so you can find me at any hour of the day or night."

The limousine drove us back to the city. We'd talked a lot, but we hadn't settled anything.

Chapter 4

WE WERE MARRIED on a spring morning at the beginning of April.

Why? Why did I make such a reckless decision? I have no idea. Even now, after having so many years to think them over, my own acts are still an enigma to me. Did I love María Coral? I think not. I think I confused (my life consists of a continual confusion of feelings) the passion that young, sensual, mysterious, and unfortunate young woman inspired in me with love. Probably my solitude, my boredom, my being aware that I'd wasted almost all of my youth so pitifully also influenced me. Desperate acts and the various forms and degrees of suicide are the patrimony of sad young men. Lepprince was the one who ultimately tipped the balance with his solid reasons and his persuasive promises.

Lepprince wasn't stupid: he was aware of the unhappiness around him and wanted to remedy it to the degree his capabilities, which were many, allowed. But we musn't exaggerate: he wasn't a dreamer who aspired to change the world, and he certainly didn't feel guilty about the problems of others. I said he admitted, to himself, a certain responsibility, not a certain guilt. It was out of responsibility that he decided to help María Coral and me. And he judged this to be the best solution: María Coral and I would marry (if and when we would give our mutual consent); that way the gypsy's problems would be resolved in the most absolute way, and the Lepprince name would not be involved. I, for my part, would stop working for Cortabanyes and start working for Lepprince, with a salary commensurate with my future needs. That way, Lepprince did not have to resort to charity: I would earn my living and that of María Coral. The favor came from Lepprince, but not the money. It was better for all of us and more dignified. The advantages María Coral derived from this arrangement are too obvious to list. As for me, what can I say? It's certain that without Lepprince's intervention, I would never have decided to take such a step, but, rethinking things, what did I have to lose? To what could I aspire? At best, a brutalizing, ill-paid job, a woman like Teresa (to make miserable, just as Pajarito, poor man, had done to his wife), or a stupid soubrette like the ones Perico Serramadriles and I chased in the streets or at dances (and with whom I would dehumanize myself to the point of putting up with their vegetable, chattering company without resorting to violence). My salary was miserable: it barely allowed me to subsist; it costs a lot to maintain a family; a future of permanent loneliness horrified me—even today, as I write these words, it still horrifies me . . .

"To tell the truth, man, I don't know what to say. The way you put it, so matter-of-factly . . ."

"You don't have to reveal great truths to me, Perico; all I want is your opinion."

Perico Serramadriles swallowed some beer and wiped off the foam that clung to his incipient mustache.

"It's hard to give an opinion about such an unusual case. I've always held the opinion that marriage is a very serious thing and shouldn't be decided on the spur of the moment. And now you yourself say you're not really sure you love this girl."

"What is love, Perico? Have you ever known true love? The longer I live the more I think love is pure theory. A thing that only exists in novels and movies."

"That we haven't found it doesn't mean it doesn't exist."

"I'm not saying that. I'm saying that love in the abstract is the product of idle minds. Love doesn't exist unless it materializes in something corporeal. A woman, I mean."

"Obviously," admitted Perico.

"Love doesn't exist; all that exists is a woman with whom we fall in love under certain circumstances for a limited time."

"Well, if you put it that way . . . "

"Tell me: how many women have crossed our paths that we might have fallen in love with? Not a one. What were they? Clothes pressers, seamstresses, daughters of minor employees like us, future Doloretases *in potentia*."

"I don't see why it has to be that way. There are other women."

"Sure, I know all about it: princesses, beauty queens, movie stars, refined, cultured, sophisticated women. . . . But those women, Perico, are not for you and me."

"In that case, follow my example: don't get married," said my highly rhetorical friend.

"Now you're just showing off, Perico. You say that today and feel like a hero. But the sterile years will pass, and one day you'll feel alone and tired, and the first one to cross your path will eat you alive. You'll have a dozen kids, she'll get fat and old in the twinkling of any eye, and you'll work until you drop just to feed your kids, pay the doctor bills, dress them, get them a bad education, and make them into honest, poor office workers like us, all so that the species of the miserable will be perpetuated."

"I just don't know . . . you paint everything so black. You think all women are the same?"

I kept my mouth shut because the long-buried memory of Teresa passed before my eyes. But her image did not change my arguments. I evoked Teresa and for the first time I asked myself what Teresa had meant in my life. Nothing. A frightened, unprotected little animal who aroused a naive tenderness in me like an anemic, hothouse flower. Teresa was miserable with Pajarito de Soto and miserable with me. All she got from life was suffering and disillusion; she wanted to inspire love but garnered only betrayal. It wasn't her fault, or Pajarito de Soto's, or mine. What did they do to us, Teresa? What witches presided over our destiny?

.....

WHEN THE APPETIZERS, the entrée, the fish, the fowl, the fruit, and the dessert were finished, the guests left the table. The men gasped for air and patted their bellies with happy resignation. The ladies mentally bade farewell to the dishes they'd refused with great effort, dissimulating their eagerness under a rictus of disgust. The orchestra went back to the bandstand and played the first notes of a mazurka, which no one danced. Conversation, suspended for a long while, became general again.

Lepprince looked for Pere Parells among his guests. During dinner he'd watched him: the old financier, taciturn and sulky, barely ate anything and answered the questions asked by his dinner companions with dry monosyllables. Lepprince became nervous and gave Cortabanyes a questioning look. From the other end of the table, the lawyer answered him with a gesture of indifference, as if it were a matter of little importance. After dinner, he and Lepprince met.

"Go to him, go now," said the lawyer.

"Wouldn't it be better to wait until later? In private perhaps?" insinuated Lepprince.

"No, right now. He's in your house and won't dare to make a scene in front of everyone. Besides he's eaten little and drunk more than usual. You can get whatever he knows out of him, and that's important for us. Go on."

Lepprince found Pere Parells alone, near the orchestra, immersed in his own thoughts. He was pale, and his bloodless lips trembled slightly. Lepprince did not know whether to attribute those symptoms to irritation or to the digestive disorders of old age.

"Pere, would you mind talking with me for a few minutes?"

Parells made not the slightest effort to conceal his annoyance; his only answer was silence.

"Pere, I'm sorry I was a bit brusque with you. I was nervous. You know how things have been going lately."

Without turning to face Lepprince, Parells responded.

"Do I really know? Tell me, how are things going?"

"Don't dig in your heels that way, Pere. You know better than I how things are."

"Do I indeed?" said the old man with unrelenting sarcasm.

"Since the war ended, business has been flat, I agree. I don't know how we're going to resolve all our problems, but I'm convinced we will resolve them. There are always wars. I don't think we have any reason to be nervous as long as we're united and work together to restructure the business."

"When you say *work together* you mean work with you, of course."

"Pere," Lepprince insisted patiently, "you know that I need your help, your experience now more than ever. . . . It isn't fair for you to blame me alone for what might happen; why is it my fault the Americans won the war? You yourself favored the allies . . ."

"Look, Lepprince," Parells stopped him without changing position or looking into his young partner's face, "I made this business out of nothing. Savolta, Claudedeu, and I, through our work, without stopping to take a breath, stealing time from sleep, forgetting we were tired, we made the business what it was until a short time ago. The business matters to me. It's my whole life. I've seen it grow, bear its first fruits. I don't know if you understand what something like that means because when you walked in it was all there. But no matter. I know conditions are unfavorable, I know all our work is on the point of going under. Savolta and Claudedeu are dead, I feel old and tired, but I'm not so stupid," here the tone of his voice changed, "I'm not so stupid that I don't know things like that can happen. I've seen lots of failures in my life, so I'm not shocked about my own. Moreover, even if it were certain we were going to fail, and even if I do feel as worn-out as I do, I wouldn't hesitate to start all over again, to dedicate all my hours and energies to the company."

He paused. Lepprince waited for him to continue. "But, and take careful note of what I'm saying to you," the old financier went on calmly, "I would destroy what means so much to me before I'd allow certain things to happen."

Lepprince lowered his voice until it was a whisper.

"What do you mean?"

"You know better than I."

Lepprince looked around. Some of the guests had noticed them and were watching with unabashed curiosity. Ignoring Cortabanyes's advice—to speak to Parells in public—he suggested they retire to the library to speak alone. Unwillingly at first, then with sudden firmness, Parells accepted. That tactical error would precipitate the tragedy.

"Explain just what you mean," said Lepprince once they were safe from public view.

"You explain!" screamed Pere Parells, forgetting the decorum he'd maintained until then. "Explain to me what's going on and what's been going on these past years. Explain to me what you've been hiding from me until today, and then perhaps we can begin to talk things over."

Lepprince turned red with rage. His eyes shone, and his jaw was tight.

"Pere, if you think I've been juggling the books we can go over to the office right now and look them over."

Pere Parells looked Lepprince directly in the eye for the first time that night. The defiant eyes of the two partners met.

"I'm not just talking about the accounts, Lepprince."

Parells knew he'd said too much, but he couldn't control himself. Too much to drink, all the rage he'd held in for so long made him say what he thought, and he listened to his own words as if a third person were saying them. But what he heard did not seem badly put to him.

"I'm not just talking about the accounts," he repeated. "For a long time now, I've been noticing serious anomalies inside and outside the business. I had certain investigations carried out on my own."

"And what did you find out?"

"I'd rather not divulge that information. You'll know what it is at the proper time."

Lepprince exploded.

"Listen here, Pere. I came here to clear up what I thought was a simple misunderstanding, but now I see that things are taking a direction I simply will not allow. Your allusions are an insult, and I demand an immediate explanation. And as for your fears about the future of the business, well, you can get out whenever you please. I'm willing to buy your stock at whatever price you'd care to name. But I don't want to see you anymore at the office, understand? I don't want to see you anymore. You're old, you're senile, you can't think straight. You're a useless wreck, and if I've put up with your absurd interference until now it's been out of respect for what you were and to honor the memory of my father-in-law. But now I'm fed up, once and for all, fed up."

Parells turned white, then gray. He seemed to choke and brought his hand to his heart. A savage glitter flooded Lepprince's eyes. The old man recovered slowly.

"I'll bury you, Lepprince," he muttered with a strangled voice. "I swear I'll bury you. I've got more than enough proof."

ROSITA THE IDEALIST, the generous prostitute, was coming back from the market, grumbling and cursing out loud about the high price of everything. Cabbage leaves and a loaf of bread protruded from her basket. She stopped to buy goat milk and cheese. Then she went on her way, stepping around puddles. *The streets of the poor are always wet,* she was thinking. Along the gutters ran a blackish, shining, and putrefied water that poured into the drains with a lugubrious gurgle. She spat and blasphemed. Sitting on a tiny stool, with a little metal plate at his feet, a blind man strummed out a sad chant on his guitar.

"Congratulations on your little outings, Rosita," said the blind man with a crowlike cackle.

"How did you recognize me?" she asked, coming closer.

"By your voice."

"And what do you know about my outings?" she said, resting her empty hand on her hip.

"Just what people are saying," answered the blind man, stretching forward a hand and feeling around. "Would you let me?"

Rosita shook her head no, as if the blind man could see her.

"Not today, Uncle Basilio, I'm not in the mood."

"Come on, just a little, Rosa. God will reward you."

"I said no, and no is no."

"You're worried about this business with Julián, eh, Rosa?" asked the blind man with his idiotic grin.

"What does it matter to you?" she growled.

"Tell him to watch his step. Inspector Vázquez is looking for him."

"Because of the Savolta thing? He didn't do it."

"Sure, but he'll have to convince Vázquez," declared the blind man.

"Well, he won't find Julián. He's well hidden."

The blind man strummed the guitar again. Rosita the Idealist went on her way, stopped, went back, and gave Uncle Basilio a piece of cheese.

"Here, take it. It's fresh cheese, I just bought it."

The blind man took the cheese from Rosita's hands, kissed it, and put it in his jacket pocket.

"Thanks, Rosa."

The two of them remained silent for an instant. The the blind man, in an indifferent tone, said. "You've got a visitor, Rosa."

"Cops?" asked the prostitute in fear.

"No. That squealer . . . you know. Your lover boy."

"Nemesio?"

"I don't know any names, Rosa. I don't know any names."

"You wouldn't have told me if I hadn't given you the cheese, right, Uncle Basilio?"

The blind man put on a miserable face.

"I just didn't remember, Rosa. Don't be that way."

Rosita the Idealist walked through the dark doorway of the building in which she lived, took a careful look into the corners, and, seeing no one, made her difficult way up the steep stairs. She was puffing when she reached the fourth floor. On the landing she saw a huddled shadow.

"Nemesio, get up out of there. You don't have to hide."

"Are you alone, Rosita?"

"Can't you see?"

"Here, let me help you."

"Get your hands off the basket, you pig!"

She put it down on the floor, dug through the pleats of her skirt, took out a key, and opened the door. Nemesio walked in behind her and closed the door again. The apartment consisted of two rooms separated by a curtain which concealed an iron bed. In the first room there was a table with a heater attached to it underneath, four chairs, a chest, and a camp stove. Rosita turned on the light.

"What do you want, Nemesio?"

"I have to speak to Julián, Rosita. Tell me where I can find him."

Rosita made a disdainful gesture.

"I haven't seen Julián for months. He's got another girl."

Nemesio shook his head sadly without raising his eyes from the floor.

"Don't lie. I saw both of you walk into this very building last Sunday."

"Oh, so you're spying on us, eh? And who's paying you, if you don't mind telling?" asked Rosita as she emptied the basket, her voice a blend of indifference and scorn.

"No one's paying me, Rosita, I swear. You know that for me, you . . ."

"That's enough. Get out."

"Tell me where Julián is. It's important."

"I don't know."

"Tell me. It's for his own good. Someone killed a man named Savolta, Rosita. I don't know who he is, but he's a big shot. I suspect Julián is mixed up in the affair. I'm not saying he did it, but I know he's got something to do with Savolta. Vázquez is in charge of the case. I've got to warn Julián, don't you see? It's for his own good. It doesn't matter one way or the other to me."

"It must matter, otherwise you wouldn't be making such a fuss. But I don't know anything. Get out and leave me in peace. I'm tired, and I've still got a lot to do."

Nemesio studied Rosita's face with a mixture of pity and respect.

"You're right. You don't look so hot. You're tired and it's still morning. That's no good. This life's no good for you, Rosita."

"So what do you want me to do, fool? Sell stories to the cops?"

When Nemesio left, he had the feeling something bad was going to happen.

LEPPRINCE TOOK CARE of speaking with María Coral. I didn't have the nerve to do it, and I was happy for his mediation. It took him three days to give me the answer, but the tone of his voice was festive when he told me that the gypsy would be happy to marry me. Almost at the same time we began the preparations for the wedding, my work with Lepprince began. I was finally leaving Cortabanyes's office. Doloretas shed a few tears when I left, and Perico Serramadriles patted me on the back with affected camaraderie. Everyone wished me good luck. Cortabanyes was a bit cold, perhaps jealous that I would leave him for someone else (a feeling many bosses allow themselves with regard to their employees, over whom they think they have certain proprietary rights).

At the beginning, the work Lepprince assigned me made me dizzy. Then with time, as happens with all jobs, I ended by sinking into a soft, grayish routine in which the number and format of a document counted for more than its content. (Besides, until Lepprince's political projects became clearer, my work consisted merely in the selection and classification of newspaper articles, letters, pamphlets, reports, and texts of varous kinds.) No sooner had María Coral agreed to the marriage than we proceeded to transform her into the worthy bride of a young and promising secretary to the mayor. We visited the best shops in Barcelona and fitted her out with the latest-style clothes and shoes from Paris, Vienna, and New York. I began, following Lepprince's advice, the project of refining María Coral, since the gypsy's style left a lot to be desired. Her vocabulary was obscene, her manners rough. I taught her to carry herself elegantly, to eat properly, and to converse discreetly. I gave her a superficial but sufficient culture. The gypsy responded to this program with an interest that moved me. She was astonished, as well she should have been. She was, after all, living a fairy tale. She made notable progress, because she possessed a lively intelligence and an iron will, befitting someone who lived in such turbulent places with the lowest levels of human scum. The underworld is a good school.

The months that preceded our wedding were a whirlwind of activity. Aside from María Coral's education, arranging our home cost me hours of pleasing labor. I decorated our house according to the most modern style; there was nothing missing, neither the necessary nor the superfluous: we even had a telephone. I bought or chose everything myself. The frenzy of the preparations kept me from thinking, and I felt almost fortunate. I bought new clothes, carried my books and other possessions from my old apartment to my future home, fought with bricklayers, painters, carpenters, decorators, and tailors. The time flew by, and I was taken by surprise on the eve of the wedding.

To tell the truth, my dealings with María Coral during those febrile days had been frequent, but for some unconscious though foreseeable reason, we'd kept our contacts at a formal, almost bureaucratic level, that of student and teacher. Even though the imminence of our marriage must have been floating in the air of our relations, we both pretended to know nothing about it, and we behaved as if, once my educational labors were finished, we would have to separate and never see each other again. I showed I was efficient and courteous; she, submissive and respectful. There was never an engagement with such an air of fastidious decorum. Far away from our respective families, tutors, and moral or social obstacles (I was rootless; María Coral a common cabaret performer), we behaved paradoxically with greater circumspection than if we'd been surrounded by a wall of modest mothers, faint-hearted chaperons, and strict guards.

One morning in April we were married. No one attended the ceremony except Serramadriles and a few of Lepprince's employees (ones I didn't know), who signed as witnesses. Lepprince did not attend the church ceremony, but he was waiting for us at the door. He shook hands with me and did the same with María Coral. He took me aside and asked if everything had gone well. I said it had. He admitted he was afraid the gypsy would change her mind at the last minute. It's true that María Coral did hesitate before saying, "I will," and her voice was almost imperceptible and tremulous. The priest's blessing closed like a door over her assent.

Then we went on our honeymoon. It was Lepprince's project, and he'd organized it in secret. I didn't want to go along with such a foolish idea, but he gave me the train tickets and the hotel reservation, insisting with such firmness that I simply could not say no. After a tiring journey, we reached our destination. On the train, we didn't speak. The other passengers saw we were newlyweds, gave ironic looks, and, at the first opportunity, left the compartment alone to us.

The place Lepprince selected was a spa in the province of Gerona, which we reached in a broken-down coach pulled by four half-dead nags. It consisted of a seignorial hotel surrounded by a few houses. The hotel had an extensive, well-tended garden in the French style, filled with cypresses and statues. At the end of the garden was a small woods with a path that led to the thermal baths. The view was splendid and rural, the air of the greatest purity.

We were received with disproportionate cordiality. It was teatime, and in the garden, sitting at cast-iron and marble tables protected by colored parasols were families and small groups. There was a tranquility in the air that warmed my heart.

Our rooms were on the second floor of the hotel, and, to judge by those I saw later, they were the most sumptuous and expensive. We had a suite—bedroom, bath, and sitting room. The bedroom and sitting room had windows that opened onto a terrace with rosebushes in blue ceramic vases. The furniture was superb and the bed, wider than it was long, was covered by a canopy that held up the mosquito net. In each one of the rooms there was an electric fan that kept the air fresh and fluttered strips of paper that frightened away the insects that came in from the garden.

María Coral stayed in the suite to unpack, and I took a walk outdoors. As I passed by the tables, the gentlemen stood up to say hello, the ladies nodded their heads, and the young girls stared timidly into their steaming cups of tea—as if they were reading a romantic future in the leaves. It amused me to respond to these ceremonious greetings with a tip of my Panama hat.

Pere Parells's wife and other ladies signaled to all the guests whose eye they could catch and whispered back and forth, accompanying their chatter with malicious giggles or severe gestures of repulsion according to whatever was being said. The arrival of the old financier silenced them.

"We're leaving," said Pere Parells to his wife.

"What!" exclaimed the ladies. "You're not leaving now, are you?"

"We are," said Mrs. Parells, as she got to her feet. The years had taught her not to ask questions and certainly not to contradict. Theirs was a happy relationship. In the vestibule, she asked her husband if something was wrong.

"I'll tell you everything right away. Now, let's go. Where's your coat?"

A young maid brought various overcoats until the old couple identified their own. She begged their pardon for her awkwardness, alleging she was new to the house. Pere Parells accepted this incongruous excuse and asked her to get him a cab. The maid didn't know what to do. Pere Parells suggested she consult the butler. The butler was equally perplexed. There were no taxis in that neighborhood. Perhaps down in the plaza they would find a taxi stand or a carriage stop.

"And couldn't you send someone?"

"Sorry, sir, but the entire staff is busy with the party. I'd be happy to go myself, but I have express orders not to leave the house for any reason. I'm sorry, sir."

Pere opened the door and walked out into the garden. The stars were shining, and the breeze had died down.

"We'll take a little stroll. Good night."

They crossed the garden. A man was standing guard next to the entrance gate. Pere and his wife waited for him to open the gate, but he didn't move. So Pere tried to open it himself but couldn't do it.

"It's locked," said the man. He didn't look like a guard, to judge by his manners, although, at the same time, he was dressed like one.

"So I see. Open up."

"I can't. Orders."

"Orders? Whose orders? Has everyone gone crazy?"

The man, wearing a striped waiter's vest, showed Pere his identification. "Police."

"So what does this mean? Are we under arrest or something?"

"No, sir, but the house is under guard. No one can enter or leave without authorization."

"Whose authorization?"

"The chief inspector's."

"And where is the chief inspector?" howled Pere Parells.

"Inside, at the party. But I can't go get him, because he's incognito. You'll have to wait. Orders are orders. Got a cigarette?"

"No. And will you please open this gate right now? Do you know with whom you're dealing? I'm Pere Parells! This is ridiculous, understand? Ridiculous! What are all these precautions about? Are you afraid we're going to steal the silverware?"

"Pere," said his wife calmly, "let's go back to the house."

"I don't want to! I'm fed up with that house! We'll wait here until they open the gate!"

"As long as you're thinking of staying awhile, I'll just slip off to the bathroom," said the policeman. "I'm just about wetting my pants."

The old financier and his wife went back to the vestibule and spoke with the butler, who spoke with Lepprince. Finally, a guest who was wandering through the rooms with a solitary, circumspect air joined them.

"My wife is feeling ill, and we'd like to go home. I suppose that's still not a crime. I'm Pere Parells," he said in a cutting tone. "Please do me the favor of having the gate opened."

"Instantly," said the inspector. "Allow me to accompany you, and please excuse the annoyance. We're expecting the arrival of some people whose presence obliges us to take these uncomfortable precautions. Believe me, it's as big a bother for us as it is for you."

The policeman at the gate was urinating behind a bush when the three of them arrived.

"Cuadrado, open the gate!" ordered the inspector. Cuadrado buttoned his trousers and ran to carry out the order. In the street, Pere Parells felt a shiver of indignation.

"Shameful!"

There were police stationed on the sidewalks, and at every corner there were mounted *Guardia Civiles* wearing swords and three-cornered hats. Whenever the police spied the old couple, they scrutinized them from head to toe. On the hill just above the plaza, they heard muffled noises, and the ground began to shake. They stepped back against a garden wall. Up on the hill came horses and coaches. The police posted on the sidewalks brought their hands to their holsters, alert for the slightest irregularity. The mounted men guarding the corners unsheathed their sabers and presented arms. The coaches came closer, the horses' hooves echoed against the cobbles. Trumpets blared. Some neighbors, astounded by the unexpected commotion, poked their heads out of windows, only to be violently called back inside by the police stationed inside the house. There were armed men even in the treetops. The fog gave a ghostly aspect to the procession.

Pere Parells and his wife, paralyzed with astonishment and

huddled against the wall, saw pass before their eyes a regiment of cuirassiers and several carriages flanked by hussars whose lances tore leaves off the lower branches off the trees. Some coaches had their curtains lowered, others did not. In one of the last coaches, Pere glimpsed a face he recognized. The galloping procession left the still-frozen couple covered by a cloud of dust. Pere recovered from his stupefaction and said in a low voice, "This is too much."

"Who was it?" asked his wife, with a slight tremor in her voice.

"The king. Let's go."

"INSPECTOR VÁZQUEZ, you must hear me out. Just listen to what I have to tell you and you won't be sorry. A crime is always a crime."

Inspector Vázquez threw the papers he was reading down on the desk and focused a fulminating stare on his ragged confidant, who was rubbing his hands together and balancing first on one foot, then on the other in a desperate attempt to be noticed.

"Who the hell let this bird into my office?" bellowed the inspector, addressing the peeling paint on his ceiling.

"There was no one here, so I took the liberty . . . ," explained his confidant, advancing toward the desk covered with newspapers and photographs.

"I swear by Christ's blood, by the eternal salvation of my . . . !" Vázquez started to say, but he stopped when he realized he was using the same religious terminology as his annoying visitor. "Why can't you leave me in peace? Get out!"

"Inspector, I've been trying to speak with you for five days now."

There were only two days left of the seven the conspirators allotted Nemesio, and he hadn't found a single clue related to Pajarito de Soto's death. The Savolta murder had cut him off, and the police were concentrating on solving that crime to the exclusion of all others. Also, his efforts to find the conspirators and warn them of the fact that Inspector Vázquez was looking for them in connection with the Savolta affair had been met by an absolute rejection from every one of the sources he'd approached during those five unlucky days.

"Five days?" said the inspector. "They've seemed like five years to me! Let me give you some advice, buddy. Get out and stay out. The next time I see you snooping around here, I'll have you locked up. You've been warned. Now get out of my sight!"

Nemesio walked out of the office and down to the ground floor filled with dire foreboding. But he was soon distracted by an unexpected incident. As he reached the bottom stair, Nemesio detected unusual movement: there were shouts, and policemen were running in every direction. *Something's going on. I'd better get out of here now.* He was trying to do just that, when a uniformed policeman grabbed him by the arm and dragged him to the far corner of the room.

"Out of the way."

"What's going on?"

"They're bringing in some dangerous prisoners."

Nemesio waited, holding his breath. From his corner, he could see the entrance, and, parked in front of it, a paddy wagon. A double file of armed police formed a path from the wagon to the building. They brought the prisoners out of the wagon. Nemesio tried to run, but the policeman still held him by the arm. The silence was only broken by the clinking of chains. The four prisoners entered. The youngest was weeping; Julián had lost his beret, had a black eye and bloodstains on his sheepskin jacket, held a manacled hand against his ribs, and his legs gave way as he walked; the man with the scar looked serene, although he had deep circles under his eyes. Nemesio thought he'd die.

"What did they do?" he whispered in the ear of the policeman guarding him.

"It looks like they're the ones who killed Savolta."

"But Savolta died at midnight on New Year's Eve."

"Shut up!"

He didn't dare say that he'd been with the prisoners at that precise moment in the photographer's studio, that Julián had brought him there by force. He was afraid of being implicated in the matter, so he obeyed and kept silent. Uselessly, however, because the man with the scar had seen him. He nudged Julián with his elbow, and when Julián caught sight of Nemesio, he shrieked, in a voice that seemed to boil out of his guts, "You finally sold us out, you son of a bitch!"

One of the guards hit him with the butt of his rifle, and Julián fell to the floor.

"Take them away!" ordered an individual dressed like a poor man.

The sad procession passed by Nemesio. Two agents were dragging Julián by his armpits, blood pouring out of him. The man with the scar stopped opposite Nemesio and gave him a freezing scornful smile.

"We should have killed you, Nemesio. But I never thought you'd do this."

He was pushed forward. It took Nemesio a few seconds to regain his composure. He tore himself violently away from the policeman holding his arm and ran back up the stairs. In the hall, he ran into Inspector Vázquez.

"Inspector, it wasn't those men! I swear. They didn't kill Savolta."

The inspector looked at him as if he were seeing a cockroach walking over his bed.

"But . . . you're still here?" he said, turning bright red.

"Inspector, this time you'll have to listen to me whether you want to or not. Those men didn't do it, those men . . ."

"Get him out of here!" shouted the inspector, pushing Nemesio aside and striding forward.

"Inspector!" implored Nemesio, while two powerful agents dragged him bodily toward the door. "Inspector! I was with them, I was with them when Savolta was killed. Inspector!!"

CORTABANYES MET WITH LEPPRINCE in the library. Lepprince was pacing nervously, his face serious, and his gestures brusque. Cortabanyes, nursing his laborious digestion, heard explanations sprawled in an armchair, attentive to Lepprince's words, his eyes half-open, his lip hanging. When Lepprince finished, the lawyer rubbed his eyes with his fists, taking his time before speaking.

"Does he know more than he says, or is he saying more than he knows?"

Lepprince stood stock-still in the center of the room and looked Cortabanyes up and down.

"I don't know. But this is no time for word games, Cortabanyes. Whatever he knows, he's dangerous."

"Unless he's got nothing concrete in his hands he isn't. He's old and alone, as I've already said. I really doubt that at this time in his life he's going to embark on an adventure that will do him no good. If he only suspects, he'll keep quiet. Today he was excited, but tomorrow he'll see things in a different way. It's to his benefit not to make trouble. We'll convince him to retire and resign himself to the pleasant labor of clipping coupons."

"And if he's got more than the mere suspicion going through his head?"

Cortabanyes scratched the few hairs he had on his bumpy cranium.

"What can he know?"

Lepprince began pacing again. The lawyer's calm restored his confidence but maddened him at the same time.

"Why the hell ask me!? Do you think he'll just tell us?" He stood still, his mouth open, his eyes fixed, and one hand in the air. "Wait! Remember . . . ? Remember Pajarito de Soto's famous letter?"

"Yes, do you think Pere Parells has it?"

"It's a possibility. Someone had to receive it."

"No, it isn't probable. All that happened a long time ago. Why would Parells have kept quiet for three years and only now . . . ? Because business is bad," he answered himself, as he usually did. "It's a hypothesis. But I doubt it. Especially, and we've argued this point a thousand times, it isn't certain the letter ever existed. The only proof was what that lunatic said who told Vázquez."

"Vázquez believed him."

"Sure, but Vázquez is a long way from here."

Lepprince added nothing more, and both men were silent until Cortabanyes said, "What do you think you'll do?"

"I still haven't decided."

"I'd advise you to be . . ."

"I know, calm."

"And above all, no . . ."

A huge commotion came from the salon next door. The orchestra stopped playing, trumpets sounded, and horses stamped their hooves in the garden.

"They're here," said Lepprince. "Let's be with everyone else, we'll go on talking later."

"Listen," said the lawyer before Lepprince reached the library door.

"What do you want?" answered Lepprince impatiently.

"Is it absolutely necessary for you to keep Max with you at all times?"

Lepprince smiled, opened the door, and joined his guests. The voice of the butler asking for attention imposed an expectant silence in which the high-sounding announcement echoed.

"His Majesty the King!"

WE HAD DINNER in the hotel dining room, and afterward took a walk through the various salons. In one, people were dancing to an orchestra playing waltzes, but since the guests at the spa had come to cure illnesses than to amuse themselves, there were only a few clumsy dancers. In another salon, where a fire was blazing, some matrons with complicated hairdos and huge stomachs were chattering. The third room was reserved for gambling. When we got back to our rooms, the unnaturalness of the situation became obvious to us, our movements became awkward, and we dragged ourselves aimlessly around. Finally María Coral broke the silence with some simple and logical words, which in those circumstances sounded like a declaration of principles.

"I'm sleepy. I'm going to bed."

It was a motion, and I seconded it without comment. I took my pajamas and robe out of the wardrobe and went into the bathroom. There I calmly changed, giving María Coral time to do the same. When I'd finished, I lit a cigarette and smoked it, thinking it would help me meditate. But it wasn't the case: it burned, leaving my head as empty as it had been during the past weeks. In the bathroom it was cold; I noted that my extremities were stiff, and my back had a tremor. It was foolish to stay there, sitting on the edge of the tub, fleeing from nothing in no direction. I decided to face facts and improvise appropriate behavior as I went along. I opened the door and walked out. The bedroom was in darkness. The light from the bathroom allowed me to see the silhouette of the bed. I put out the light and felt my way. I had to go around the bed, tracing the edge because María Coral was on the side closest to the bathroom door—I wasn't going to climb over her. Her breathing seemed regular and deep, and I concluded she was asleep. I told myself it was better that way and took off my robe and slippers and slipped between the sheets. I closed my eyes and tried to go to sleep. It wasn't easy; before I drifted off, I had time to think over a long list of banalities: that I hadn't wound my watch, that I didn't know if Lepprince had paid the hotel in advance, that I didn't know how to tip the staff, that I hadn't sent my clothes out to be washed. I don't know how long I slept, but no doubt it was a short, light sleep because I woke up suddenly with my head clear and my nerves tense. Next to me, I felt the presence of a warm body, and my fingers held the pleats of a silky nightgown. The situation called for one kind of action or another, but both God and the devil seemed to have abandoned the battleground. There are moments in life when we know that everything depends on quick intuitions and abilities; I was in one of those moments, but in my head there was a blur instead of ideas. I heard the bells of a distant clock: two o'clock. I experienced the same sense of helplessness as an exhausted camper lost in a thick woods who sees the sun setting and realizes he's been in that same place before. Finally I fell back to sleep.

Against all expectations, I woke up in a good mood. It was a radiant morning: the sunlight came in through the spaces in the curtains and formed circles on the floor, turning it into a Lilliputian stage. I jumped out of bed, went into the bathroom, shaved, brushed my hair, and dressed, carefully choosing the most appropriate clothes for that solemn spring day. When I finished, I went back to the bedroom. María Coral was still asleep. She had an unusual way of sleeping: stretched out on her back, with the covers pulled up to her chin, and her hands on top of the covers. I remember the way dogs roll over on their backs and raise their legs to have their bellies scratched by their masters. Was this the right moment? I hesitated, and, in these cases, as everyone knows, hesitation means giving up. Or a defeat. I opened the curtains, and the sun poured in, not leaving even a corner in darkness. María Coral half opened her eyes and emitted some complaining noises, half grunt, half deep breath.

"Get up; look what a beautiful day it is," I exclaimed.

"Who told you to wake me up?" was her reply.

"I thought you'd want to enjoy the sun."

"Well, you thought wrong. Have breakfast sent up and close the curtains."

"I'll close the curtains, but I won't order breakfast. Right now I'm going down to have breakfast in the garden. If you want, you can join me; if not, fend for yourself."

I closed the curtains, took my stick and hat, and went down to the dining room. The French doors were wide open, and a few people were sitting at the tables on the terrace. Only some old people chose to take the sun inside, protected from the air, which was cool and even painful because of its incredible purity. An intermittent breeze swayed the bushes in the park.

"Would you like to order breakfast, sir?"

"Yes, please."

"Hot chocolate, coffee, or tea?"

"I'd like café au lait, if the coffee's good."

"It's excellent, sir. Would you like croissants, toast, or some rolls?"

"A bit of everything."

"Will you be breakfasting alone, or shall I also serve madam's breakfast?"

"I'll be alone. . . . No, just a moment, bring the same thing for my wife."

As I was ordering, I saw María Coral walk in, still sleepy and ill-humored. But her appearance didn't fool me: she'd come down to have breakfast with me. I stood up, helped her be seated, told her what I'd ordered, and buried myself in the newspaper. The ordeal of the night was over, and yet an electric charge floated in the air and presaged new anguish. I decided to speed things up. After breakfast, I suggested to María Coral that we go up to our suite "to take a little rest." She stared at me.

"I know what you want. Come for a walk, and we'll talk."

We strolled silently through the garden, and when we came to the end, we sat down on a stone bench. The stone was cold, the leaves on the trees were rustling, a bird was singing; I'll never forget that scene. María Coral told me she'd thought things over and that the situation demanded absolute clarity. She declared she'd married me out of self-interest, that no feeling of any kind had entered into her decision. Her conscience was clear because she supposed I wasn't the victim of any hoax and that I myself had married her as a way of getting ahead; therefore, what was blameworthy in such a marriage was compensated for by the fact that in entering into it she'd avoided having its anguishing circumstances lead her to situations a thousand times worse.

"We've begun in reverse," she added. "Most people get to know each other first and then get married. We're married, and we barely know each other."

Starting from that basis, and above and beyond the formality of our union, we should proceed like sensible people. A premature intimacy could only lead us to tensions and misgivings. It would only nurture hatred and rancor. Besides, she considered herself a decent woman (she said it humbly, lowering her eyes, while a slight blush passed over her smooth cheeks). To give herself to me would seem like a kind of prostitution.

"I know that my life does not authorize me to demand respect. It's true I worked as an acrobat in the most sickening shows, but away from my work, I was always proper."

The need to be believed burned in her eyes. A tear formed in her eye like an unexpected visitor, like the first breeze of spring, like the first snow, like the first flower to bloom.

"If I went with Lepprince, it was for love. I was a girl, and his personality and his wealth dazzled me. I didn't know how to be his equal. I killed myself trying to please him, but I could see the irritation in his gestures, his words, and his eyes. When he threw me out, I accepted it as fair. He was the first man in my life . . . and the last, until now. I will always respect you, if you respect me. If you want my body, I will not refuse you, but you may be sure that you will be vilifying me if you take me. And it's quite possible I will run away from you. If that happens, you will be responsible for the rest. You decide: you're the man, and it's only logical you should give the orders. But just realize that whatever you decide, you'll have to live with it."

"I accept your conditions," I exclaimed.

She bent over and kissed my hand. That's how our days passed at the spa. At the time I thought they were pleasant; now I consider them happy. Better that way. There are events that are happy when they take place and become bitter in memory, and others, insipid in themselves, which with time take on a nostalgic hue of happiness. The happy days last only briefly; the second kind fill our whole life and provide solace when disaster strikes. I, personally, prefer them. María Coral and I carried out our pact to the letter. Our relationship was of a geometric correctness; on my side at least there was no violence or effort in observing all the clauses. María Coral turned out to be a silent, discreet partner, one with whom I barely exchanged half a dozen insignificant comments over the course of a day. We would take separate walks; if by chance we ran into each other in the labyrinthine garden, we would stop briefly and exchange a few words before going back to our independent strolls. The words we exchanged were cordial.

We ate lunch and dinner together merely out of social propriety and because it was more comfortable for María Coral if I chose the dishes: the menu, with its French names, upset her.

"I wonder if you ever ate anything but sausage sandwiches," I said to her one day.

"Maybe, but at least I don't try to give the impression that I've only eaten caviar and lobster," she retorted.

I would laugh at her rough-and-ready comebacks, because it was in those instants when María Coral showed her best side, her true personality of a poor, frightened girl. At the time, she was nineteen. She didn't realize it, but until then no one understood her as I did. And for my part, even though I wouldn't confess it even to myself, I held the hope that the opaque tenderness I felt for her would one day, not in the distant future, have its reward. The spa setting, so calm, favored those kinds of daydreams. Tranquility reigned with undisputed ubiquity. María Coral and I were the only young members of that ailing community. Many guests, as I found out from a waiter, never left their rooms; some never left their beds, expecting to end their days in that spot. And except for the two of us, no one ever reached the end of the garden, unless it was in a wheelchair or hanging onto the solicitous arm of a staff member.

Among those wrecks, I made friends with an old mathematician, who claimed to have invented several revolutionary engines, which, incomprehensibly, the government ignored. He went on about perpetual motion and its application to pumping water out of the lower strata by the movement of those very strata. The incoherence of his arguments and a certain stutter in his voice gave his terminology a distant, poetic dimension, like a fairy tale. I also discovered a dusty politician from the Radical Party who was hell-bent on making me admire his scandalous amatory adventures, which without a doubt were the fruit of his imagination over the course of his long stay at the spa, the fruit of solitude, like the sprouting of a vine in the cracked walls of an abandoned cloister. One afternoon, just before sunset, we happened to be on the terrace, he and I, half asleep. The garden seemed to be deserted.

Suddenly, María Coral emerged from a cypress grove cut to form an arch. She was walking by herself with a decisive air. The politico put on his glasses, scratched his goatee, and nudged me with his elbow.

"Young man, did you see that beauty?"

"That lady, sir, is my wife."

Chapter 5

DAWN WAS BREAKING; the clear, cloudless sky poured a tenuous but defining light over the deserted streets. The automobile parked with two of its wheels resting on the sidewalk; two men, wrapped in their topcoats against the morning damp, got out. In unison, they looked at their watches. Without saying a word, they approached a uniformed policeman standing guard at the entrance to a house. The patrolman came to attention in the presence of the other two. One of them took out a small sack and offered tobacco and paper to the others. The patrolman accepted, and for a moment they all stood there rolling cigarettes.

"Did any of you see it?" asked the one who'd offered tobacco to the patrolman.

"No, Inspector. We heard the explosion and came running."

"Any witnesses?"

"We haven't found any yet, Inspector."

Through the windows of the neighboring houses, curious faces scrutinized them through shutters and curtains. The watchman appeared, staggering. He was obese, getting on in years, and dragged his stick as if it were a piece of his own crude body which had somehow come loose. His mustache was limp, sad, stained with nicotine, his eyes swollen, and his nose bright red.

"A nice time for you to be turning up," said the man who'd offered the tobacco.

The watchman kept silent and hid his face under the visor of his cap.

"Give me your name and number. You're in for it."

"It's that I sort of fell asleep, sir. At my age . . . you know . . ."

"Asleep? Drunk you mean! You stink to high heaven, man, to high heaven!"

While the inspector wrote down the negligent watchman's information, a noisy ambulance appeared, and two sleepy attendants got out. They opened the rear door and took out a folding stretcher which they proceeded to set up on the sidewalk with fatigued motions. When they finished, they picked it up and dragged their way to the police.

"Is this the place?"

"Right. Who called you?" asked the inspector.

"I did, sir," said the patrolman.

"Is anyone hurt?" asked one of the ambulance attendants, scratching his unshaved chin.

"No."

"So why did you call us?"

"We've got a dead one. Follow us," said the inspector, walking through the entranceway.

RETURNING TO BARCELONA put us face-to-face with a reality we'd almost forgotten. Being away made me more sensitive, so no sooner did I step out of the train than I noticed a tension in the air, the result of the crisis. The station was crowded with beggars and unemployed men eagerly offering their services to the travelers. Ragged children ran along the platforms stretching out their hands, peddlers cried out their wares, the *Guardia Civil* kept the crowds pouring off the trains in order and formed the immigrants into miserable squads. Ladies from charitable organizations followed by servants carrying baskets handed out bread to the needy. On the walls there was graffiti of all sorts, most of which called for violence and subversion. On the way home, we witnessed a small demonstration by workers demanding higher salaries. They stoned a car: a lady got out, blood running down her face; she screamed hysterically as she took refuge in a doorway.

My stay at the spa had been an interlude; now, back in Barcelona, the tragedy began again with the same violence and hatred, with no joy, no purpose. After years and years of constant, cruel struggle, the antagonists (workers, owners, politicians, terrorists, and conspirators) had lost any sense of proportion, had forgotten why they were fighting, and had renounced any gains they might have made. More united by our antagonism and anguish than separated by ideological differences, we Spaniards were a confused throng climbing down an inverted Jacob's ladder whose steps were revenge for revenge and whose plot was a confused skein of alliances, denunciations, reprisals, and betrayals that were taking us to the hell of intransigence founded on the fears and crimes engendered by despair.

As soon as we set foot in our new apartment, María Coral set about making the changes that would give our shared life the liberty and security she intended to impose on me. Not without anger on my part—her changes broke up my well-planned distribution of the furniture—she proceeded to move my bed (why not hers?) from the common bedroom to a dark storeroom. She generously ceded me half of a two-part wardrobe, and she allowed me to take a small easy chair, two other chairs, and a floor lamp. Her total disregard for the harmonic unity of the house irritated me, but after thinking it over, I concluded that it was better this way. Our relations were still as calm as a frozen lake. Now we saw each other less; almost never, to tell the truth, but her presence in the house was palpable despite her efforts to the contrary: a sound, a perfume, a light at the bottom of a door, a song on the other side of a wall, a sigh, a cough.

I went back to my work in the small office Lepprince had set up in a building not far from Cortabanyes's offices. The work was monotonous, methodical, often boring. My only company was an old maid, who typed, in sullen silence, the handwritten note cards I passed her, and a boy, who ran around town and came back at nightfall with the newspapers, magazines, pamphlets, and flyers he picked up God alone knew where.

Thus passed away the office hours. The rest were the same as before, with slight variations. One afternoon, I came home and heard María Coral calling me from her room. I asked permission to come in, and her complaining voice granted it.

She was in bed, sweaty and trembling. She was ill, and her appearance reminded me of how she looked the night I found her half-dead.

"What's wrong?"

"I don't know, I feel awful. With this heat, I must have slept uncovered and caught a chill."

"I'll call a doctor."

"No, don't call any doctor. Go buy me some herbs and make me an infusion."

"What kind of herbs?"

"Any kind. They're all good. But don't call the doctor. I don't want anything to do with doctors."

"Don't be backward. Herbs and concoctions don't do anything."

She shut her eyes and clenched her fists.

"If you don't mind doing me the favor I'm asking, do it please," she said between her teeth, "but if you're going to insult me and give me lessons, you can just get out."

"All right, don't get angry. I'll bring you your herbs."

I went to an herb shop, and asked the lady for an infusion good for colds, and she gave me a packet of ground-up, dry leaves that smelled good but did not reassure me in the slightest. I boiled them up in a pot and gave the mixture to María Coral. When she'd drunk it down, she fell into a breathless stupor and began to perspire so intensely I was afraid she was going to melt away. I wrapped her in two blankets and stayed at her bedside reading until her breathing returned to normal and she drifted into a peaceful sleep.

Around midnight, she woke up with a start that made the book jump out of my hands and almost caused me to fall on the floor.

She began to whimper and wave her arms, and even though her eyes were wide open, she wasn't seeing anything, as I proved by passing my hand in front of her face. I sat on the edge of the bed and held her shoulders. María Coral rested her head next to mine and began to cry. She went on weeping for a long time, then she calmed down and went on sleeping. I watched over her until dawn, when I too fell asleep. When I woke up, she was no longer in bed. I searched the house and found her in the kitchen. She was eating bread and cheese, sitting on a bench.

"What are you doing here?" I asked in surprise.

"I woke up hungry and came to get something. You were sleeping like a baby in the armchair. Did you spend the whole night there?"

I told her I had.

"That was very nice of you, thanks. I'm all right now."

"Maybe. But it would be better if you went back to bed and kept covered up. Are you sure you don't want me to call a doctor?"

"I'm sure. Go to work; I'll look after myself."

I did go to work. When I came home, María Coral wasn't there. She came in late, greeted me coldly, and went to her room without giving me any explanation. I didn't want to ask her anything. After all, she wouldn't have been able to tell me anything about what intrigued me most—the reason why she cried. A nightmare? A natural release caused by the infusion? I decided to forget the incident; even so, for a long time, whenever I thought of María Coral, I saw her in that situation, crying on my shoulder.

NEMESIO CABRA GÓMEZ left the path and walked into the thickets and brambles. The place wasn't particularly rural, but the night made it seem isolated and gave it an air of danger the light of day would have banished. Falling down and getting up again, Nemesio left strips of his already ruinous clothes on the branches and bushes. The land was rising into a pronounced hill, and the amateur climber began to pant and cough, but he didn't stop. The very cold and humid night would allow no moonlight through. On his hands and knees, Nemesio scrambled up the side of the mountain until he reached an open, flat area where he stopped. He crouched down in the weeds and waited, shaking with cold and fear until he saw an indecisive light on the horizon. Then he got up, crossed the flat area, and hugged the reddish stone wall without being seen by the guards. The castle slept. The light grew brighter. Staying close to the outer wall, he reached a guard box enclosed and flanked by battlements on top of which the silhouettes of two men huddled in their greatcoats began to stand out against the gray of the morning. Nemesio crawled across the open space and stood up once he'd reached the cover of the wall. A few yards beyond began the terrifying ditches around Montjuïc prison.

Along the path that led to the castle guard box came a chaplain riding sidesaddle on a donkey. He identified himself, and the sentinels opened the door for him. From his hiding place, Nemesio saw two horse-drawn carriages arrive: one was filled with civilians, the other with soldiers. It was day now, and the city became visible to the hidden man. In front of him, he saw the docks, to his right stretched the industrial Hospitalet zone, blinded by the smoke pouring from the chimneys; to his left, he could see the Ramblas, Chinatown, the old town, and above that, almost behind him, the bourgeois, seignorial Ensanche neighborhood.

Inside, the castle came to life: commands were given, bugles resounded, and drums were beaten; there was running, the banging of heels, the clanging of bolts, locks, chains, and bars. A side door opened, and the procession appeared. The troops led the way, the condemned men followed, and the chaplain and the authorities closed the march. The man with the scar strode forward with a serious air, his eyes on the ground, concentrating on his own thoughts. Julián followed him, very pale, his eyes sunken, stumbling, as if his guards, knowing of his imminent and inexorable end, hadn't bothered to dress his wounds. The young fellow Nemesio had seen weeping at headquarters was no longer weeping: he must have told himself he no longer belonged to this world. He walked like a robot, and his bulging eyes seemed to drink in the blue morning air.

Nemesio couldn't contain himself. He stood up, abandoned his hideaway, and shouted. No one paid him any attention, and his shout was drowned out by the tattoo beaten out on the drums. They bound the eyes of the condemned men, and the priest passed next to them muttering a prayer. The firing squad had already formed. An official gave the pertinent orders, there was a loud report, and Nemesio fainted.

When he recovered consciousness, the sun was high in the sky. Walking through the brambles, not even feeling the thorns, he reached the path. He sat down on a stone bench. A carter bringing food supplies to the castle garrison found him there at nightfall. Seeing him half-naked and bleeding, his gaze lost in the infinite and his mouth hanging open, he assumed Nemesio was ill. He informed the garrison, and a detail was sent out to find him. The doctor declared him insane, and Nemesio Cabra Gómez was led, still without having spoken an intelligible word, to the San Baudilio de Llobregat Sanatorium. He would spend more than a year there, consumed by his remorse and the images he'd witnessed. More than a year would pass before Inspector Vázquez, reviewing the file on the Savolta affair and reconstructing the intricate relationships which had led to his own exile, remembered that strange character and went to visit him.

María Rosa Savolta gave a little shriek and dropped her cup of coffee on the rug. Without changing expression, Lepprince pushed a button several times. In a short while, the butler appeared, wearing a robe and struggling to remove his mustache net, which had tangled itself around his ears.

"Did you ring, sir?"

"Pick that up," said Lepprince, pretending not to see the mustache net.

The butler removed the cup, the saucer, and the teaspoon, and then covered the smoking, dark stain with a napkin. He left and returned with more coffee. Then he bowed and again left.

"Excuse me, how awkward I am! I don't know what's happening to me. I get so distracted. I'm really sorry."

"No reason to excuse yourself, my dear," Lepprince cut her off sharply. "It could happen to anyone."

Saying that, he shot me a furtive glance, and I, recalling his words, changed the subject. We were in the splendid mansion Lepprince had bought on the flank of Tibidabo. The invitation came by mail one afternoon, and logically, caught María Coral and me by surprise. But it was no mistake: Mr. and Mrs. Lepprince have the honor to invite Mr. and Mrs. Miranda to dinner at their house next Wednesday, etc. María Coral gave every sign of not wanting to go.

"I'm not going to play a part in this comedy. Good evening, madam, splendid dinner, madam," she imitated, walking through the room and wiggling her hips exaggeratedly, in sluttish fashion. "Dry shit!"

"Don't be that way. It isn't so much to ask. Lepprince wants to see us, so he's invited us, that's it. He hasn't heard from us in ages. When you think about it, we've been ingrates; after all, we owe him a lot, don't you think?"

"Don't start wallowing around like a pig. You do an honest day's work for your pay."

"Don't be silly," I replied without raising my voice, trying to convince her. "On my own, I never would have reached a position like the one we're enjoying. Besides, right now it doesn't seem appropriate to make radical statements but to accept an invitation, have a nice time, and good night, sleep tight."

"Well, I'm not going," declared María Coral.

Of course, we were there right on time. I felt I'd been somewhat violent and feared María Coral would make one of her unforeseeable remarks. But my fears were unfounded because nothing happened. Lepprince gave us a hearty welcome, and María Rosa Savolta was cordial and simple. She kissed María Coral on both cheeks and stated, in front of everyone, that I'd chosen a "charming, very beautiful, and very distinguished wife." Horrified, I looked at María Coral, thinking she'd take advantage of the compliment to unloose one of her tavern insults, but nothing of the sort happened. The gypsy blushed, modestly lowered her eyes, and remained distant and timid all night. Lepprince took me aside and offered me a glass of dry sherry.

"Well . . . tell me all about it . . . I'm dying to hear about you two."

We were in a smallish room where Lepprince had set up his office. Hanging on one wall was a picture I instantly recognized: it was the genuine reproduction which had adorned the mantle in the apartment on the Rambla de Catuluña. The same bridge over the same river and the same peace.

"Now that you're working for me, I see you less than when you worked for Cortabanyes."

"Well, everything follows a pattern, like this river here. Life gently follows its course."

"You don't seem overly exuberant."

"But I am. I have no complaints. And all thanks to you."

"Don't be silly."

"I'm not being silly. I'll never forget how much María Coral and I owe you."

"Not a word. Besides if you two owe me anything, now you'll have the chance to pay me back with interest."

"Is there something we can do for you? Consider it done."

The problem, in short, was María Rosa Savolta. While her married life was happy, she couldn't put her past misfortunes behind her: the dramatic death of her father and the risks Lepprince had run had left their mark on her still tender soul. From time to time, she suffered depressions that sank her in a swamp of anomie; nightmares disturbed her rest, and she was constantly plagued by unfounded fears. At present, the situation wasn't serious, but Lepprince, always concerned for his wife's well-being, was afraid that if she continued in her disturbed state, her symptoms would get worse and lead her to a condition bordering on insanity.

"God in heaven!" I exclaimed when I heard that word.

"There's no reason to be prematurely alarmed. It may be a

passing thing brought about by an accumulation of unfortunate events."

"I hope so. What does the doctor say?"

"I don't want him to see her, for the time being. It would be torture to subject her sanity to the cold analysis of a professional. In any case, I don't trust modern therapy: keep after the sick until they become conscious of their illness, what cruelty! Isn't it a thousand times more humanitarian to leave them in ignorance about their affliction in the hope that tenderness and calm will have their healing effect?"

I agreed.

"But what role would we have in all this?"

"A role of vital importance. You two are young, newlyweds, you only inspire happiness and the joy of life. Besides, you are not connected to the business, the Savolta family, and that nucleus of high Barcelona society, the scene of her suffering. You're fresh, purifying air. Which is why I'm depending on you two as her best medicine. Can I count on you?"

"Count on both of us for anything."

"Thank you. I expected you'd say that. Oh yes, one last thing: she shouldn't see anything, not even suspect that you know about what I've just told you. Don't tell María Coral; you know how women are—incapable of keeping a secret. The two of you should try to be affectionate but never compassionate."

The butler announced dinner. María Rosa and María Coral appeared after we'd been there for a while. María Rosa excused their tardiness.

"I've been showing the house to our guest. Women things."

"The house is beautiful," said María Coral, "decorated with exquisite taste."

Well, well, I thought, *and where did this girl get those manners?* I secretly laughed, imagining what María Rosa Savolta's face would have looked like if she'd witnessed the act her invitation had inspired. But these are minor details.

Lepprince had recovered his usual, relaxed manner and was joking as he swiftly bore the bulk of the conversation. When dinner was over, he dismissed the servants, and, in a small adjacent room, he himself served coffee with an amusing lack of skill—which he exaggerated a bit to make the rest of us laugh. His wife tried to help him, but he kept her back with false professional pride. He winked at me, laughed under his breath, and gave free reign to the good humor his daily responsibilities forced him to cover up. Once he'd carried out his labors as a host, he lit a cigar, made an exclamation of well-being, and went back to our conversation, asking about certain details of my work. I explained it all to him and he said, "Don't think you're laboring in vain, Javier. In November, as you know, there will be elections, and it's likely I'll be a candidate."

"That would be great!" I exclaimed.

"It's even possible that you and I may have to make a trip to Paris to locate some documents relative to my nationality."

I thought I'd faint. Paris! The women protested at this discrimination, and Lepprince, caught between two fires, laughed and begged mercy. They wouldn't leave him in peace until he promised to study the possibility that the four of us might make the trip. The two women applauded enthusiastically.

It was late. María Rosa Savolta seemed tired, dropped her cup of coffee, became upset, begged us to forgive her, and after saying good night affectionately to me and kissing María Coral once again, she went off to her room accompanied by her solicitous husband. Left alone, I commented to María Coral, "A charming couple, don't you think?"

"Bah."

"What's wrong with you? I thought you rather liked the conversation."

"That man gets on my nerves. Who does he think he is? He knows all, answers every question. He's nothing but a hick, believe me. A hick with money who wants to impress people. And his wife, well, you won't deny she's unbearable. As common as a . . ."

"María Coral! Don't say those things . . ."

Lepprince's return interrupted our argument. He was smiling

and begged pardon in his wife's name for her sudden departure.

"María Rosa is delicate and has to rest. She begs your pardon, and asks me to say good-bye for her."

We exchanged clichés. Lepprince accompanied us to the vestibule. In the garden, the black limousine was waiting for us, the sleepy chauffeur at the wheel. On the way home, I mentioned to María Coral, "It's strange, but I haven't seen Max all night. Could he have been fired?"

Perhaps it was only a false impression, but it seemed to me the driver paid ironic attention to what I said.

ON THE LANDING, they met another policeman who came to attention, as had the one standing guard in the street. There were two doors to the landing: one was closed and the other wide open. The inspector went to the open door and sniffed an acrid odor he immediately identified. He came back to the landing and again checked his watch.

"What time did it happen?" he asked the policeman.

"I don't know precisely, Inspector. At the time, we didn't think to look at our watches. We were on patrol when we seemed to hear an explosion. We ran here and saw smoke coming from the window, heard screams, tremedous screams. We called for the watchman to open the downstairs door, but he didn't appear, so we knocked out the lock with our rifle butts. We came up and found this. There was one dead man. We called you and ordered an ambulance. I have no idea of how much time all that took, but it couldn't have been more than twenty or thirty minutes."

"Where did the screams come from?"

"From the house, Inspector, from the house itself. An older couple lives here with their maid. The maid wasn't home. The woman wasn't hurt, but was screaming.

"Is the woman still here?"

"No, sir. She went to a neighbor's house." He pointed to the closed door. "We thought we could let her go because she seemed so terrified. Would you like us to get her?"

"No, not for the time being. Has the maid come back?"

"No, Inspector. She won't be back for a few days. It seems she went to her hometown on Saturday for some celebration or other. The annual hog slaughter, I suppose."

"All right. Stay on guard. We're going in."

Aside from the smell of gunpowder, the house gave no signs of violence. The vases and other decorations in the foyer and the hall were undamaged.

"No doubt it was a small bomb," commented the man with the inspector, "otherwise the shock wave would have broken all this china."

The inspector nodded his head. They reached a thick, dark door at the end of the hall.

"This it?"

"Yes, I think so."

"This is an oak door. It stood up through everything," said the inspector's companion, checking the hinges appreciatively. "Solid construction. They don't build them like this anymore."

The inspector opened the door, and the two men walked in. The ambulance attendants waited in the hall. The room, which must have been an office, was in a terrible state. The furniture had been knocked over, the pictures knocked down, the rug burned right in the middle and blackened right out to the edges; the wallpaper, pulled off by the force of the explosion and the flying material, hung in strips, revealing patches of plaster. Under the mahogany desk, almost covered by papers, was the lifeless body of a man. The inspector leaned over him.

"He's got no blood on his face or clothes."

The inspector's companion, who must have been an explosives expert, was measuring distances with a tape.

"He must have seen the bomb and jumped back. The bomb went off on the floor, here where the rug has almost disappeared. The shock wave turned over the desk, and the body was pinned underneath, protected by the mahogany."

"In that case, he could easily have escaped, no?"

"In my opinion, yes. I don't think he was killed by the bomb.

A heart attack seems more likely. The bomb wasn't very big. Look at the ceiling: the plaster and the light fixture aren't even damaged."

A voice from the hall asked, "May we come in?"

Two men entered without waiting for an answer. One was middle-aged, the other old. The old man, with a tangled, gray beard and thick tortoise-shell glasses, was carrying a doctor's bag. The middle-aged man was dressed in black. He was the examining magistrate, and the other the forensics expert.

"Hello, gentlemen. What's happened here?" said the examining magistrate, who must have just arrived in Barcelona.

The doctor kneeled next to the body and poked at it. Then he asked for a basin.

"There was no way to find the duty officer down at the jail," commented the magistrate. "He went out two hours ago to have a coffee and still hadn't come back when I came over here. There's no hope for this country!"

"Doctor, what did he die of?" the inspector asked the doctor as he came back, drying his hands on his handkerchief.

"What do I know? Of the bomb blast, I guess."

"But there are no visible wounds on the body."

"No?"

"Didn't the photographer come? In England, they always take photos at the scene of the crime," said the magistrate.

"No, sir, we don't have a photographer. This isn't a wedding."

"Listen here, I'm the one who says what has to be done. I'm the examining magistrate."

One of the ambulance attendants poked his head in.

"Can we take away the cold cuts, or are we supposed to wait until he starts rotting?"

"Sir, let's show more respect!" the magistrate berated him.

"As far as I'm concerned, you can have him," said the doctor.

"At least make a drawing, an outline," said the magistrate.

"I can't draw, with or without a pen," said the inspector. "What about you?" he asked the explosives expert.

"Me either," he answered distractedly. He'd taken some tubes out of his pocket and was filling them with powder and splinters using a tiny spatula.

"Nothing can be touched until the officer in charge comes," protested the magistrate, seeing that the attendants were pulling the cadaver up by the arms.

"We aren't going to spend the whole morning here," they answered back.

"If I say so, you will," declared the magistrate. "Or I'll have you all up on charges."

THE ORCHESTRA LAUNCHED into the "Royal March," and His Majesty, Don Alfonso XIII, entered the salon, accompanied by his wife, Queen Victoria Eugenia, their retinue, and guards. The king was wearing a cavalry uniform, and the lights sparkled on his gold embroidery. The guests, standing, gave him warm and prolonged applause. Lepprince stepped forward from the company and ran to greet the monarch. The king, with a good-natured smile, clasped his hand and patted him on the back.

"Your Majesty . . ."

"What a pretty house you've got, my boy," said Don Alfonso. Lepprince kissed Doña Victoria Eugenia's hand. María Rosa Savolta, paralyzed by a sudden attack of timidity, could not step forward from the crowd until her husband waved insistently. Finally, the fearful young woman walked to the monarchs and bowed to their august persons. Instantly, the retinue broke ranks, and the king, the queen, and their escorts mixed with the other guests.

"You do me great honor by coming to my house," said Lepprince, addressing the king less formally, dropping the pompous "Your Highness" from his speech.

"Dear friend!" answered the monarch, hanging onto Lepprince's forearm. "I don't want you to think I don't know that my presence will help you win votes for the municipal elections in November. But your mediation is important because I want to win over the Catalans. I have no idea how I stand in these remote parts." Then the two of them burst into laughter.

"Have you two been married long?" Doña Victoria Eugenia asked María Rosa. "No children yet?"

"I'm expecting, Your Majesty," answered the bashful María Rosa, "and I wanted to ask you and His Majesty to be godparents to our child."

"But of course!" exclaimed the queen. "I'll talk to Alfonso right away, but you can count on it. I have two of my own."

"I know, Your Majesty. I've seen their pictures in the magazines."

"Yes, of course."

Our visits to the Lepprince mansion became more frequent at that time. Although it was already late spring, the summer heat still hadn't made itself felt. I felt happy in the company of Lepprince and those two women, who were so beautiful and so different. I don't think I would have changed places with anyone if such a thing had been in my power. Among the pleasant memories I have of that period—all compacted now into a single happy moment—there is one that stands out with special clarity. Lepprince, always nervous, always searching for new emotions and new vistas, had suggested we go out to the country one Sunday. As we used to say then, we'd go picnicking.

"We spend too much time cooped up in our offices," he argued to overcome his wife's objections. "We need pure air, contact with nature, and a little physical exercise."

So it was settled. They would bring the food and pick us up at our place at ten in the morning.

At ten, the limousine was at our door, and in it, Lepprince and his wife. We got in, and the car pulled away. As soon as we left the city, we began to go up and up steeper and steeper hills that made the limousine's motor roar but did not slow it down. I was sitting on a jump seat, facing the rear, and I could see through the back window that another car was following us. I thought nothing of it at the beginning and didn't mention it to the others. However, after an hour, and despite the turns and counterturns and all the complexities of our route, the car following us hadn't given up the pursuit. A bit alarmed, I pointed it out to Lepprince.

"Yes, I know a car is following us. Nothing to be afraid of. But please excuse me from telling you what it's all about. It's a surprise I arranged for all of you."

I didn't say another word and contemplated the countryside. We were passing through a thick forest of pines and ilex, and the dappled sun filtered through the branches. As the trees thinned out, there came into view a very leafy, very wide valley surrounded by other mountains and forests. We began to go downhill and finally reached the valley. We drove around some more until we found a clearing covered with herbs, bushes, and clover. Its appearance satisfied us: it was flat and wide, and on one of its edges there flowed a spring of icy water that was pure and tasty. We ran to fill our cups and taste it because it seemed medicinal. As we drank, the second car pulled up, and I understood what the surprise was that Lepprince had for us, because the mysterious automobile was none other than Lepprince's old red *conduite-cabriolet.*

"Ah, well, well, so that's what it was," I shouted in delight, as if the car were an old friend. "And who's inside?"

"Can't you guess?" asked Lepprince. "Max."

The two cars stood at one end of the clearing. A few yards away, the chauffeur set about unfolding a tablecloth and distributing over its white linen surface plates, knives, forks, spoons, bottles, and pans. Max, sitting under a pine tree, his bowler over his face, took a nap. The rest of us wandered around the meadow trying to find four-leaved clovers, following the flight of birds, studying curiosities of all sorts: a caterpillar, a beetle. A cricket sang in the bushes and the spring gurgled; the thick leaves, tossed by the mild breeze, produced the murmur of a sacred, distant symphony. María Rosa Savolta seemed worn-out and sat down on the grass—not without her husband first spreading a handkerchief out to protect her from dirt, moisture, and insects.

"What peace!" exclaimed Lepprince, standing next to his wife, spreading his arms as if he wanted to gather the landscape up in them. María Rosa Savolta, protected from the sun by her parasol, looked up to contemplate her husband. The diaphanous light attenuated by the filter of the foliage gave his figure an air of mystical ecstasy.

"It's true," I agreed. "We city dwellers have lost the sense of plenitude nature confers."

But Lepprince was fickle and couldn't fix his attention for very long. Suddenly he shook his head, clicked his tongue, and shouted, "Come on, Javier, that's enough rapture. Didn't I say I had a surprise for you?"

Saying this, he made a prearranged sign, and the chauffeur, who had finished setting out our meal, got into the red car and drove it slowly to where we were.

"Get in," said Lepprince, when the chauffeur had stopped and gotten out.

"Where are we going?"

"Nowhere. The game here is that you're going to drive."

I saw a teasing expression in his eyes, mixed with tenderness, and an insolent challenge: one of his characteristic expressions.

"You're joking."

"Don't be a coward; you've got to try everything once in this life. Especially strong emotions."

I was never able to say no when Lepprince asked me to do something. I got into the driver's seat and awaited his instructions. María Rosa Savolta, who was following our movements with good-natured pleasure, seemed to guess the nature of our intentions.

"Hey! What are you two doing?"

"Don't get excited, honey," shouted her husband. "I want to teach Javier how to drive this thing."

"But he's never done it before."

I somehow managed to put on a resigned smile and shrugged my shoulders, saying in effect that I was just following orders.

"We'll have a good laugh, you'll see!" Lepprince said.

"You'll kill yourselves! That's all you'll do," and she turned to María Coral for support. "Tell them something, to see if they listen to you more. They're both stubborn."

"Let them go, they're old enough to make their own decisions," answered María Coral, who seemed excited by the idea of an improvised circus act.

Meanwhile, Lepprince gave me instructions, as did the chauffeur—each contradicting the other and assuming I understood their strange jargon. Seeing she couldn't dissuade her husband, María Rosa Savolta decided on a new tactic.

"My friend," she said to María Coral, "at least we can pray for God to protect these madmen."

"You pray if you like, ma'am; I'm going to join my husband."

And in a flash she was next to the car, jumping into the back seat. And there she stayed, curled up, since there was room only for a valise and not for a person. Lepprince, happy as a lark, was turning the crank, while I clutched the steering wheel with both hands. We'd taken off our jackets, and with the first shudder of the motor, my straw hat rolled to the ground. Lepprince shouted, "Hurrah!" tossed his English cap into the air, and got up on the running board when the car began to move. The chauffeur shouted something to me, but I couldn't hear what he was saying. Lepprince fell headfirst into the car and began to kick his legs, asking for help, laughing his head off. I tried to keep the car under control, but it went around and around in circles. For one second I would see María Rosa Savolta kneeling on her handkerchief, with her hands pressed together, looking down, and in the next I would see the chauffeur waving his arms and shouting mechanical advice. By then, Lepprince was right side up and had grabbed the steering wheel. With him pulling on one side and me on the other, the car began to go in a zigzag, chasing the chauffeur as if it had a mind of its own. In one of its pirouettes, it ran over my hat, and then, for no apparent reason, it gave an asthmatic wheeze and stopped. Lepprince jumped out and started it again. I said, "Oh no! Oh no! That's good enough for today."

To which he responded, "Just a little more."

He was saying that when the car gave a jump and began to go, slowly at first, but then more rapidly, with only María Coral and me on board.

"Do something, Javier! Stop this thing!" she shouted from the rear.

"Exactly what I'd like to do!" I answered, trying not to drive toward the trees, hoping the car would stop on its own. Lepprince and the chauffeur ran, sometimes behind us, sometimes in front, colliding with each other, and shouting at the same time. Only Max, under his pine, on the cool grass, seemed to nap, unconcerned with the tragedy unfolding on the meadow.

Finally, to my great surprise, I managed to get the vehicle to follow, more or less, the route I set for it. When it did stop, I joyfully leapt out and helped María Coral down. Lepprince was out of breath when he reached us.

"I did it!" I tried to cover up the nervous tremor running through me. He laughed.

"You've begun well. I didn't do any better the first time. Now it's a question of practicing and losing your fear."

I've recounted this apparently trivial incident in some detail because it was to have an importance in the future, as we shall see.

During our lunch and over the course of our return trip, my deed was the only subject of conversation. Lepprince was in an excellent mood, María Rosa Savolta had gotten over her fright, and María Coral, as I could see out of the corner of my eye, admired me. During those spring months, on our frequent trips to the country, I got better and better, until I had mastered—if I may put it so immodestly—the elements of driving.

"A CLOCKWORK MECHANISM?" asked the magistrate.

The expert whistled and rubbed his hands.

"No, it's not that. It's too early to draw any conclusions, but I think it's an Orsini bomb—you know, those spherical bombs with detonators that function when the bomb hits any solid body. Easy to use, no fuse, no machinery, perfect for the amateur.

They're the most popular. They always go off," he concluded, as if he were a bomb salesman.

The magistrate went out on the balcony. There wasn't a soul on the sidewalk except the policeman standing guard at the entry. In the distance, there was the ding-dong of a ragman's bell.

"It would be thrown from the street. The victim's balcony was open."

"Why would he? In the early morning, it's cold," observed the magistrate.

The inspector shrugged his shoulders and got out of the way for the magistrate, who was calculating the distance between the balcony and the street.

"It's quite a distance, don't you think?"

"Right, that's true," admitted the inspector. "Unless, which is highly improbable, a ladder was used."

"Or if the person who threw it was standing on top of a carriage," noted the expert. "A carriage or, even better, a car."

"Why would a car be better?" asked the magistrate.

"Because a carriage isn't as steady. The horses could move and cause the person on top to lose his balance and seriously risk falling down with the bomb in his hands."

"True, a nice point," recognized the magistrate enthusiastically. "We'll have to reconstruct the crime. As far as motive is concerned, what do you think, Inspector?"

The inspector looked askance at the magistrate.

"Who knows? His enemies, his heirs, the anarchists . . . There are thousands of possibilities, damn it all."

The officer from the jail, who had arrived meanwhile, showed his drawing. The bomb expert passed judgment on it with a smile of superiority. The ambulance attendants had taken the victim's body away. The forensics man left, promising to have his report ready as soon as possible. When the drawing was finished, the magistrate and the officer left. The inspector and the bomb expert were alone again . . .

"How about a coffee?" asked the inspector.

"Good idea."

Down in the street, they found two men arguing with the officer on guard.

"What's going on here?" asked the inspector.

"These gentlemen insist on going into the house, Inspector. They say they're friends of the dead man."

The inspector studied the two men. One was young, elegant, and self-confident, the other, an older, fat, and sloppy man who never stopped shaking and waving his arms around.

"My name is Cortabanyes, I'm a lawyer, and this gentleman is Don Paul-André Lepprince. We're friends of Mr. Parells."

"How did you find out about what happened?"

"His widow just called us, and we came as quickly as we could. I beg you to pardon our manners and our butting in, but you can easily imagine how this unexpected news affected us. Poor Pere! Just a few hours ago we were speaking with him."

"A few hours ago?"

"Mr. Parells attended a reception in my house," said Lepprince.

"And he said nothing to you, and you noted nothing suspicious in his behavior?"

"I don't know, we wouldn't know," whined Cortabanyes. "We're very upset."

"May we go up to see the widow?" asked Mr. Lepprince, who did not seem upset in the slightest.

The inspector thought it over.

"All right, go up to see the widow, but don't go into the house. The widow is in the apartment over there. We have a guard on duty who can tell you which it is. I'll be away for a few minutes. When I get back, we'll speak. Wait for me."

The policeman guarding the landing made a face when he saw Lepprince and Cortabanyes appear. His orders were not to let anyone in without express authorization from his superiors, which is what he told the two men. They replied that the inspector had asked them to stay for questioning because they were the last people, except for his wife, to see the deceased alive. Despite the officer's doubts, they courteously but firmly pushed him aside and walked directly into the victim's apartment. Once inside the old financier's office, Cortabanyes began to tremble.

"I can't, I can't," he sobbed. "I just don't have the strength."

"Now, now, Cortabanyes, I'll do it, but we can't miss this opportunity. Help me pick up this desk. Look, there are no bloodstains or anything like that. Push, I can't do it alone."

They pushed the desktop back, and the desk turned upright. The drawers weren't locked, and Lepprince began to go through them while the lawyer watched, paralyzed, livid, his mouth hanging open.

Poor Parells! Who would have said that when we said good-bye that night it would be the last time! For reasons I wouldn't understand for a long time, he didn't like me, but that didn't keep me from esteeming him greatly, not only for his intelligence but for his distinguished personality, his courtesy, his culture. . . . There just are no more men like him.

We were together for the last time at the party Lepprince gave, that memorable party the king attended. María Coral and I had been invited. When we arrived, ill at ease, fearful, and expectant, we did not know that social event would mark the end of one stage in our lives. After the party, nothing was the same. But there, in the mansion's luxurious salons, amid perfumes, silks, and jewels, known faces, industrialists and financiers, sordid reality seemed very distant and its dangers warded off as if by magic.

"To Deauville? Very kind of you, sir, but you'd have to speak with my husband about that."

"For the love of God, María Coral," I reprimanded her in one of the rare moments in which we were free of pests, "would you stop behaving like a cocotte?"

"A cocotte?" Then, making up for her ignorance with her considerable perspicacity, "You mean a high-class whore?"

I nodded, still frowning.

"But Javier, that's what I am!" she answered gleefully, responding with a smile to the wink of a decrepit but still foppish general.

My wife's exotic beauty caused a stir as soon as we entered the house. In her presence, the most mature, the wisest gentlemen would imitate the flirtatious mannerisms of an operetta rake. I felt a mixture of vanity and jealousy that drove me mad.

"Well now, how's life treating you, my boy? Quite sought after, I see," said Cortabanyes, who came looking for me with one of his clients hanging on his heels.

"Here I am," I said, pointing to María Coral, who at that moment was chatting with a canon, "wasting my time and my dignity."

"If you can lose it, that means you have it!" declared the lawyer. "And how's your work going?"

"The mills of God grind slowly, but they grind exceeding small," I answered, trying to make a joke.

"Well, those mills will have to work faster, my boy. Tonight things of transcendent importance are going to occur."

"Such as?"

"You'll see soon enough," he said, lowering his voice and sealing his lips with a finger.

"And what do you think," chimed in the client, unwilling to interrupt his own conversation, "of the Moroccan war?"

Cortabanyes gave me a signal, and I intervened to get this load off his back.

"A really bad situation."

"You're telling me!" said the client, seizing onto a new audience the way a shipwreck victim clings to a board. "It's intolerable! A handful of shitty blacks beating the pants off a country that once upon a time conquered the New World."

"Times have changed, my dear sir."

"Not the times," protested this screaming bore with a vehemence that contrasted with the general indifference, "but the men. There are no politicians like the ones we used to have. What became of Sagasta and Cánovas del Castillo?"

The arrival of the king interrupted our talk. The guests ran to kneel at the feet of our illustrious guests, and Cortabanyes took the opportunity to join us.

"See them? Like hens at feeding time." He shook his head with a desolate air. "This way we'll go nowhere. Remember when the mob wanted to lynch Cambó?"

I said that I did remember. Now Cambó was Minister of Finance in Maura's government.

The king greeted everyone amiably and listened to panegyrics and petitions with bored indifference, marching through the salon seriously, his shoulders slightly bent, prematurely old, a little shadow of melancholy in his sweet smile.

"THERE ARE PAPERS on the floor. Look through them, don't waste time. You'll have a chance to bawl at the funeral."

Cortabanyes kneeled down and began to leaf through the papers scattered here and there.

"Poor Pere! We knew each other for more than thirty years. He was a good man, a solid man, incapable of being disloyal. I still remember the day his son died. His name was Mateo. . . . What an ill-starred family! Pere wanted his son to be a perfect gentleman, so he sent him to study at Oxford. They saved every cent they could to pay for Mateo's studies. At Oxford, he came down with pneumonia, and it killed him. He came back to die here, in this very house."

"Why are you telling me all these tearful tales?" grunted Lepprince.

"Look," said Cortabanyes, showing the papers on the floor as an explanation. "This is what Pere was reading when he was killed."

Lepprince took what the lawyer handed him—a letter yellowed by the years and use—and began to read:

My dear parents:

The news that you're both well fills me with joy. I can't complain, although the rigors of winter, which never seems to end, keep me from getting over this cough that continues to bother me. Yes, here, as in the novels, it always rains. . . .

The letter was dated March 15, 1889. Lepprince left it on the floor, and read the beginning of the next letter:

Dear Father:

Don't let this letter fall into my mother's hands. My health is getting worse, and for a week now I've had frequent attacks of fever. The doctors say there's no reason for alarm and attribute everything to this climate, which is so harsh. Fortunately, it's only a short time now until examinations begin, so soon I'll be home to spend vacation with you. You can't imagine how much I miss you. Alone and ill in this admirable but strange country, I only think of Barcelona. . . .

"Hell!" exclaimed Lepprince. "Help me put this desk the way it was."

They turned the desk over, trying not to make any noise. Cortabanyes was weeping noisily.

"Let's go," said Lepprince. "It's not here. I suspect that damned letter never existed."

Chapter 6

SPRING PASSED. A glaring, leaden, and humid summer grasped the city and the souls of its inhabitants. The climate overwhelmed María Rosa Savolta's fragile constitution, and her advanced pregnancy made her even more sensitive to the rigors of summer. The collapse of her health aggravated her nervous condition. María Coral and I stopped visiting the mansion and only saw the Lepprinces on our Sunday excursions. Soon these too ceased, and we lost contact with María Rosa and Paul-André. María Rosa never left the house, rarely venturing out of her bedroom. From time to time, she would startle the servants with her ghostly appearance—silent, suffering, her face immutable, her eyes fixed, stupefied. She wandered the house, dragging her feet, wrapped in her long peignoir, unkempt and pale, with the touching fatalism of a fish swimming along the edge of its bowl.

Separated from the Lepprinces, María Coral and I found ourselves cut off from society, locked into our own narrow world of polite formalities, our intangible, ambiguous relationship. A boiling rancor was born in me, a reaction against my situation, a rancor that at the time I couldn't comprehend and that now, with the perspective and calm provided by the passing years, I see clearly: it was the result of myriad repressed feelings and prematurely abandoned illusions. Day by day, my exasperation grew. I began to be rude with María Coral and treat her with an irony as coarse as it was cutting. At first, she pretended not to notice, but then she counterattacked. She had a lively wit and she could compose retorts effortlessly. We would argue over trivial things and insult each other until we were exhausted. One night in June, on the festival of Saint John to be precise, things reached a climax.

We fought, and I threw as many reproaches in her face as I could think of. I was very excited, and the dialectical battle was tilting in my favor: María Coral was breathing heavily, her eyes were filled with tears, and her shoulders sagged. She looked like a boxer on the ropes. Finally, with a broken voice, she begged me to stop, to stop hurting her. My brain must have been cloudy, because I redoubled my attack. María Coral got up from her chair and left the room. I followed her through the halls; she went into her bedroom, closed the door, and bolted it. I was possessed: I stepped back, took a running start, and slammed my shoulder against the door. A panel broke, splinters flew everywhere, and the hinges bent.

María Coral was standing in front of her bed, clearly afraid. I took her in my arms, embraced her, and kissed her. To humiliate her? Who knows? She offered no resistance, and made not the slightest movement, as if she were in a trance or dead. I fell on my knees at her feet and clasped her waist. Then she knocked me backward with her knee. I jumped to my feet. María Coral was stretched out on the bed, her arms and legs spread, her eyelids sealed, her breathing rapid. If I had had the slightest bit of sense, I would have put my tail between my legs and walked out of the room; after all, I was holding all the winning cards. But I wasn't thinking. I went to the bed and put my hand on her tense body. María Coral didn't move a muscle.

"I already told you that if you try this, I won't fight you," she murmured between her teeth. "But you know what will happen afterward."

I withdrew my hand and stared at her.

"How can you say that? Has anything changed since that afternoon? All these months of living together haven't weakened your resolve in the slightest?"

"I haven't changed. You, however, have changed. So, decide."

"How can you be so self-centered? Don't you think you owe me something?"

"Are you trying to give me the bill?"

"No. I only want you to see how badly you treat me. I married you, accepted your conditions, and respected them. When you were sick, I took care of you, as any good husband would. You live on the money I make. Isn't that enough?"

She sat up, closed her legs, and leaned on her arms.

"Do you believe that? How can you be such an idiot? You still think you're being paid for your work and that you're being helped out of friendship? Haven't you realized yet what the truth is?"

"What truth? What are you suggesting?"

María Coral hid her face between her knees and burst into tears, weeping as I hadn't seen her weep since her illness.

"How dumb, how blind, how helpless you are!"

Then she said this:

"It all began in the hotel on Princesa street, where I was getting over the illness that didn't kill me thanks only to your intervention. The doctor had given me a clean bill of health, and it was only a matter of hours before I left the hotel and went back to my job in the cabaret. Lepprince came to my room alone, against his custom. After a long preamble, he told me a stupid story of loneliness, incomprehension, and failure that centered on his wife. He hates her. He married her for her money, to take control of the business—what did you think?

"Then the propositions came: I could go back to what we had before, he would set me up in a flat, pay the rent. I didn't give in at the beginning. These last years have been hard, and I've learned how to make deals. The offer was generous but not totally safe: Lepprince is fickle, and with the confused way things are going, who could assure me he wouldn't be murdered a month or a year later? So, I put my own clauses in the contract: I didn't want money, or an apartment, not even a shop, or a block of stock. I wanted a well-established, decent, hard-working husband.

"Lepprince laughed a lot, and said, 'If that's all, it's a deal.' When he said that, he already must have been thinking of you. It hasn't been a bad deal for you: you work for him and keep me, so that he has me practically for nothing. When you volunteered to be my future husband, I was genuinely curious. What kind of man could accept such a shameful deal? Three possibilities for you passed through my mind: a cynic, a complete fool, or someone desperate, drowning in debt. What I never imagined is that you were an idealist who believed in love. When I realized the truth, I was really sorry for you and even now respect you.

"Given those conditions, as you can easily understand, I could never be yours. During these months, I've tried hard to hide the truth from you so as not to embitter your life. Now that's no longer possible, because you know how I am. The list of men who have passed through my life is infinite. I had to run away from my hometown or they would have stoned me to death. I joined up with the strongmen from the circus. To pay them for the food I ate, I had to work and satisfy the needs of both of them. They would take turns, one night each, but they'd often get drunk and forget that arrangement. They frequently beat me. Then Lepprince came along, and then lots of others.

"With only one man have my relations not been ignoble: you. Which is why I set the conditions you know so well and why I cried in the garden at the spa. My life is a hell. When you leave here for work, you take my peace with you. A few minutes later, Lepprince comes with Max. Sometimes he stays only for an hour; other times longer. He talks my ear off about himself, his business, his political aspirations, and, most recently, his child, about which he's got lots of illusions. When he stays for a long time, he usually eats here, sleeps a siesta, and reads or writes letters in the afternoon. He even brings a secretary with him. If it gets late and he's afraid you'll come back, he calls his men and has them give you extra work. See how simple things are when you have money and power? I think that if, despite all his precautions, you'd turned up unexpectedly, Max would have shot you dead. Those people have no heart."

"And you, do you have a heart?"

"I don't know. I feel confused."

I got up without saying a word. I left the room, walked out the door, and left the house. In front of the building, right in the middle of the street, a bonfire was burning to celebrate the feast of Saint John. Fireworks were exploding and skyrockets were flashing in the sky; bands were playing; people dressed up, some wearing masks, were wandering in all directions. Still totally stupefied, I wandered the city amid the general uproar and ended up on the Ramblas, which looked like a dance hall, a circus, and a madhouse. Groups of citizens were raising hell, well supplied with all kinds of noisemakers; swarms of soldiers were dancing in circles, and an infinite number of heads covered with paper hats passed in every direction. Even the policemen on duty sang and tossed firecrackers at the prostitutes passing by. As I, crushed and out of my head, was contemplating that happy spectacle of a city having a party, a hand fell so heavily on my shoulder that it made me bend my knees.

"Javier, what are you doing here?!" I heard someone shout—the din was deafening.

At first I didn't recognize the man who'd slapped me down because he was hidden behind a grotesque papier-mâché nose. Then I identified him.

"Perico Serramadriles!"

"What's this, joining the party?" His eyes were bloodshot and glassy, and his breath stank of wine.

"Man, if you only knew . . ."

"What's wrong with you? You look like you're on the way to a funeral. Tell me about it."

"No, I don't want to butt in. Got company?"

"Sure, a mob actually."

He pointed toward a group that was jumping around, shrieking. The girls, very young, very healthy-looking, ruddy, and chubby, were doing a comic cancan, raising their skirts up to their knees and pursing their lips in a vulgar, provocative way.

"Go on with your friends, Perico, I don't want to ruin your party."

"Bah, let'em go, I'll catch up to them later. Let me set something up with them, and I'll be back with you in a minute."

He talked things over with the calmest of the dancers, tossed a general kiss to the girls, and came back.

"Now, tell me everything, Javier. We were always friends, although for a while now you've forgotten me."

"It's true, but let's not talk in the street. Let's go somewhere quiet, all right? I'll buy you a drink."

We looked for a place where the din might be softer and found a sad, half-empty bar, where only two drunks, wearing threadbare uniforms of veterans of the 1898 Cuban war, were humming low, holding on tightly to each other so they wouldn't fall, staggering their way among the tables. We sat in a corner and ordered a bottle of wine and two glasses. The first taste made me sick to my stomach, because I hadn't eaten anything since midday, but little by little the wine settled my stomach, and I began to feel better, more sure of myself, and more able to face life.

"Oh, Perico, today," I began, "I found out something that just about killed me."

"What?"

"I found out my wife's got a lover."

"Your wife? You mean María Coral?"

"Of course."

"What? You mean that's why you're so sad?"

"You think it's nothing?"

He looked at me as if he were seeing a ghost.

"No, man, it's . . . it's that I thought you knew."

"Knew what?"

"That . . . about your wife and Lepprince."

"Hold it! You mean you knew?"

"But, Javier, everybody in Barcelona knows it."

"Everybody in Barcelona? So why didn't you tell me?"

"We all thought you knew when you got married. Do you mean to tell me you just found out today? Are you serious?"

"I swear by my mother, Perico."

"That's one for the books! Waiter, more wine."

The waiter brought more wine. We drank straight from the bottle.

"Does this mean you don't know anything about the casino either? But it was even in the papers. No names, naturally, but the allusions were clear enough. The left-wing press, of course."

"The casino?"

"I can see you're in never-never-land. Lepprince slapped his . . . your wife in the Tibidabo Casino. She tried to stab him with a knife she'd hidden in her bag. The police were going to arrest her, but Cortabanyes stepped in."

"That happened? My God! And why did Lepprince slap her? What had she done?"

"I don't know. Probably jealousy."

"So there's probably another man involved?"

"I'd say so. . . . You're not much of a candidate for Lepprince's jealousy, if you'll pardon me for saying so."

"Go on, say whatever you like. What difference does it make to me what you say when I'm probably the joke of every bar?"

"Not exactly, Javier. Most people take you for a scoundrel, and no one suspects you didn't know the truth."

"So much the better."

For a while, the two drunken singers had been snoring on the floor. Outside, on the street, the uproar was still going strong. Perico put his hand on my forearm.

"I was all wrong about you, Javier. Forgive me."

"There's nothing to forgive. After all, you've done me a favor: I'd rather be a scoundrel without dignity than a stupid cuckold."

"Don't be so sad. There's a solution to every problem."

"Maybe, but I don't see what the solution to my problem could be."

"You'll think one up tomorrow. Know what we're going to do tonight? We're going on a spree. Up for it?"

"Yes. I think's it's a very wise measure."

"Then let's stop talking. Pay and let's have some fun. We'll join up with my pals. You'll see what a sensational group they are . . . and what tramps we've picked up."

I paid and we left. We elbowed our way through the mob. Following Perico Serramadriles, who turned to see where I was from time to time and waved like a robot for me to speed up, I reached a lugubrious house on Arco de Santa Eulalia. The entry door was open, and Perico went in with me right behind him. We lit a match and began to climb a staircase with high, narrow, and worn-out stairs. I don't know how many turns we made or how many matches we wasted until we reached the roof, which was poorly illuminated with Japanese lanterns and decorated with paper chains. Serramadriles's friends were gathered there. There were seven men and four women—make it thirteen or fourteen counting the two of us. The men were in the sleepy stage of drunkenness, while the women had reached the highest stage of euphoria. The result was that the women threw themselves on us as soon as we appeared on the roof and began pulling at our arms and coattails so we'd dance with them.

"Girls, girls," Perico was saying through a giggle, "how can you dance without any music?"

"We'll sing," which they promptly did at the top of their lungs, each one in her own key, jumping and running around, spinning Perico around like a top. One of them threw her arms around my waist and stuck to me, her mouth to my chin, looking me in the eye with the fixity of a lunatic.

"Who're you?"

"The biggest cuckold in Barcelona."

"Quite a joker, eh? What's your name?"

"Javier. What's yours?"

"Graciela."

Graciela was very maternal: she gave me a drink as if she were giving a bottle to a baby, and after each swallow she nestled me against her plump breasts. One of the sleepy drunks dragged himself over to where we were and put his hand up Graciela's skirt. She shook her hips as if she were scaring off flies with her tail.

She never stopped laughing, and her good humor spread to me. I bent down to where the drunk was and took off his mask: a sickly, miserable forty-year-old appeared and forced a toothless smile onto his face.

"Solid hams, eh?" I said, just to say something.

"You bet," he answered, pointing to the place where he'd placed his hand, which I imagined clutching a rough, tense calf. "And what vistas there are. Come and see, come on."

I stretched out next to the drunk, and we both looked up Graciela's skirt. There was nothing to see except for a black bell inhabited by opulent shadows.

"My name's Andrés Puig."

"I'm Javier, the biggest cuckold in Barcelona."

"Oh, how interesting."

"Are you two going to spend the night down there?" asked Graciela, tired of our prospecting.

"My wife, see, is a strange case: with me, nothing. . . . Understand? Nothing."

"Nothing," repeated the drunk.

"But with everyone else . . . know what she does with everyone else?"

"Nothing."

"Everything."

"What luck! Introduce me to her."

"Why not? Right now."

"I couldn't. I'm so drunk that I couldn't do it."

"Don't worry, my friend. My wife is the kind that can revive the dead."

"Really? Tell us, tell us."

"I'll tell you how I met her: she worked in a cabaret. The worst cabaret in the world. She would come out onstage naked, covered with big colored feathers. Two strongmen would toss her in the air and catch her, and with each toss she dropped one feather. At the end, you could see everything."

"Everything?"

"Isn't that what I just said? Everything."

"Holy cow. What a birdy she must be."

"I couldn't even begin to tell you."

About that night, I remember fighting with Andrés Puig about which of us was to have exclusive rights to Graciela's favors. I won. I remember the girl's hesitation in the face of my imploring and also my daring ("For God's sake, not right here.") followed by a confused decision that had no imploring to it ("Let's go to my house; my folks are asleep.") to which, inconsistently, I paid no attention. I remember I drank whatever was left in all the bottles and that I had a subsequent attack of verbal diarrhea, which left me calm.

It was dawn when I got home. When I left, I had no intention of ever returning, but my steps led me back unconsciously. I was very happy, whistling a tune, when, as I opened the door, a sinister smell made me retreat to the other end of the landing. Later I understood that only the fact that I still had Perico's papier-mâché nose on had saved me from certain death from gas. I began to run down the stairs in desperation, but suddenly an idea came to me. I ran back up, took a deep breath, and went into the house. I thought I'd faint. I could barely see the furniture, the cloud was so dense. I was running out of air, so I went to a window and broke it with my fist. It wasn't enough: I ran to the other end of the hall and broke another window to get cross ventilation. Then I turned off the gas and ran into María Coral's room. She was lying on the bed, her long hair spread over the pillow. She was wearing the same nightgown she'd worn the first night we slept together at the spa, so far off and so painful in my memory.

But that was no time for meditation. I wrapped María Coral in a coverlet, picked her up in my arms—weakened by drink—and with a superhuman effort ran down the stairs into the street. The cool dawn air restored me. I looked for a coach, but the streets were deserted. At the corner, the bonfire had burned down to a few coals. At the next corner, breaking through the morning mist that snaked its way from the port to the mountains, there appeared a landau pulled by two white horses. I stopped it and asked the driver to take us to the hospital right away. It was a matter of life or death, I argued, hoping against hope that María Coral hadn't died yet. The driver told me to get in. Inside the landau was a man stretched out, wearing a cape and evening clothes.

"Just get in, this guy won't even notice," said the driver pointing his whip at his boss.

I got in and deposited María Coral on the front seat, while I sat on the rear seat with the sleeping gentleman, whom I unceremoniously pushed aside—this situation demanded resolve. I had barely sat down when the coachman snapped the reins, and the landau raced forward. The gentleman opened his eyes and stared at my papier-mâché nose.

"What's this, having a party, eh?"

I pointed to María Coral's body wrapped in the coverlet. The man wearing the cape and evening clothes observed her body carefully, squeezed his bloated face into a sneer of intelligence, and tapped me with his elbow.

"What a punch you've got, man!" he exclaimed before he fell asleep again.

Chapter 7

I'D ONLY BEEN AWAY from Perico Serramadriles for two hours when we ran into each other again. While just as accidental, this second encounter was far more dramatic. I was waiting in the hospital corridor for the doctor's diagnosis—I assumed María Coral was going to die—when Perico appeared: he'd fallen down a flight of stairs dead drunk and landed on his head. His head was covered with bandages, and his face was unrecognizable because of all the bruises. Even so, his company affected me like a sedative. We sat down on a bench, smoked his last cigarettes, and watched the sun come up through the windows and, as the hours passed, witnessed every conceivable form of human pain parading up and down the corridor.

"In a certain sense, Javier, I envy you. You've reached a level of emotional intensity that makes life no longer nauseating and monotonous."

"That emotional intensity, as you call it, hasn't given me anything but disgust. I frankly don't think I'm anyone to envy."

"Well, even with all I know, I think I'd trade places with you with pleasure. Of course, all this is just hot air because things are the way they are, and no one likes his own life. . . ."

"Yes, and it's the only one you have to live."

A young doctor passed by, his robe covered with bloodstains.

"What are you two doing here?"

"I've busted my head," said Perico.

"And you've been fixed up, right?"

"Yes, just look."

"Then go home. This isn't a casino."

"All right, I'm leaving."

"And you, what did you bust?"

"Nothing. My wife had an accident, and I'm waiting to find out what's going to happen."

"Well, you stay, but don't get in the way of the stretcher bearers. Nice night! And they call all this celebrating Saint John's night."

And off he went, cursing and waving his arms.

"I'd better go," Perico said. "I'll pass by your house later to see how things turn out. Be brave."

"I just don't know how to thank you for being with me like this."

"Forget it and come to see us over at the office one of these days."

"I promise I will. How's Cortabanyes, by the way?"

"Same as ever."

"And Doloretas?"

"Ah, you don't know? She's very sick."

"What's wrong with her?"

"I don't know. She's being treated by some ancient doctor, and it'll be a miracle if he prescribes the right medicine for her."

"I wonder what she lives on if she isn't making those messy copies of hers."

"Cortabanyes gives her a few cents once in a while. Why don't you pay her a visit? You could cheer her up. You know she loves you like a son."

"Don't worry, I will."

"Good-bye, Javier, and good luck. If you need me, you know where to find me."

He left, and time slowed down. Finally a doctor appeared who asked me into his dump of an office.

"How is she, Doctor?"

"By a miracle, she survived, but she's in really serious condition. She needs care and lots of affection. You know there are sicknesses whose cure depends more on the will of the patient than on science. This is one of those cases."

"Yes, I'll take care of her."

"Tell me the truth, now. Are you sure this was just an accident?"

"Completely sure."

"Do the two of you . . . get along? Do you have any problems?"

"Oh no, Doctor. We haven't even been married for a year yet."

"And yet it looks as though you were out celebrating the holiday last night while your wife stayed home: is that right?"

"She had a headache, and I had to attend a party—for business reasons. We were sorry to be apart, but there were no bad feelings. I'm telling you it was an accident. It's incomprehensible, I can see that, but that's the way all accidents are."

The doctor was summoned because the flood of party victims was still pouring in; at least my problems with him were over. At around midday, Max appeared.

"Mr. Lepprince says: how is the lady?"

"Tell Mr. Lepprince my wife is fine."

I thanked Lepprince for having the sense not to have come to the hospital himself, but I thought some other messenger might have been more appropriate.

"Mr. Lepprince says he will pay the bills."

"Tell Mr. Lepprince that I don't want to deal with that matter just yet. Anything else?"

"No."

"Then be on your way, and tell Mr. Lepprince that if there's any news I'll be in touch with him."

"I understand."

For the next few days, I heard nothing from Lepprince or his men, except for a brief visit from Mr. Follater, who brought a box of candy, told us about the sickness his own wife had had some years before and that the entire office was praying for the swift recovery of my wife. But all that took place later. Late that morning, the doctor called me in again and asked if I wanted to see María Coral. I said I did. He said I shouldn't talk to her or touch her, and then showed me into a room through whose windows sunlight was pouring. It was a long, narrow room, like a Pullman car; it had a high ceiling and contained a double row of beds, each occupied by a patient. The room was completely silent, so the groans, moans, and sighs all seemed louder than they were. We walked between the two rows of beds, and the doctor pointed to one of the beds. I walked over to it and saw María Coral: her skin was yellowish, almost green; her hands, on top of the covers, seemed like the feet of a dead bird; her breathing was slow and irregular. I felt a knot in my throat and gestured to the doctor that I wanted to leave. In the corridor, he said, "It would be better if you went home and tried to get some rest. Her convalescence will be long and will require all your strength."

"I'd like to stay here. I won't get in the way."

"I understand your concern, but you should follow my advice. Do it for her."

"All right. I'll just give you my telephone number. Don't hesitate to call."

"Don't worry."

"And thank you for everything, Doctor."

"I did nothing more than my duty."

In my life, so full of betrayals and lies, that magnanimous personality was like a beacon in a dark sea.

The empty house broke my heart. I walked through the rooms, ran my hands over the furniture, and, one by one, recorded in my mind every one of the tiny objects that personalized our home, associating a memory with each one. I wondered what would happen now, what strange turn our lives would take. And I anguished over the causes that could have led María Coral to attempt suicide. Soon the mystery would be cleared up. That same afternoon, after a fleeting, nervous nap, I washed up, shaved, and went back to the hospital. The place had changed: the corridors were empty, the doctors chatted slowly, the odd nun slipped through the half light in the galleries carrying a tray of vials and instruments. The hospital no longer looked like a market and had recovered the academic, serious atmosphere it had in normal times. I found the doctor in his office. He told me about María Coral's condition, that it was satisfactory, and allowed me to visit her, begging me to be prudent and, at all costs, optimistic. I walked into the room by myself and fearfully made my way to my wife's bed. Her eyes were closed, but she wasn't asleep. I called her name, she looked at me, and a smile played over her lips.

"How do you feel?"

"Tired and with a stomachache."

"The doctor says you'll be as good as new soon."

"I know. And you, how are you?"

"Fine. Still a bit shaky."

"You must have been shocked, eh?"

I stared at the floor so she wouldn't see the tears I couldn't hold back pouring from my eyes. Then I remembered I was supposed to cheer up the patient and thought of a joke.

"This month the gas bill's going to be astronomical."

"For the love of God, don't mention gas. How can you be so thoughtless?"

"Sorry, I just wanted to make a joke."

"And why the devil do we have to make jokes right now?"

"The doctor said . . ."

"They can say whatever they like. They know nothing about nothing. We have more important things to discuss."

"Really?"

María Coral fell back into a state of prostration that alarmed me. But it only lasted a few seconds. She again looked at me with the fixity of a dead person.

"Javier, do you love me?"

To my great surprise—I thought I still had my doubts from before, the doubts that had once scandalized Perico Serramadriles when I told him about my impending wedding—the words came out on their own.

"Yes, I've always loved you. I loved you the first time I saw you, I love you more than ever now, and I will love you forever, whatever you do, until the day I die."

María Coral sighed, closed her eyes, and whispered, "I love you too, Javier."

The door to the room opened, and the doctor was coming over with the obvious intention of telling me to get out. I hastened to say good-bye to María Coral.

"Good-bye. I'll be back tomorrow as soon as visiting hours begin. Want me to bring you anything?"

"No, I have everything. Do you have to go so soon?"

"I have to. Here comes the doctor."

He was next to us and interrupted the farewell, which made me happy because I felt as though I had a swarm of ants in my body.

"Our little patient has to rest now, Mr. Miranda. Tomorrow is another day. Please be so kind."

"Don't worry about me, Doctor," said María Coral, raising her voice as we left. "Now I know I'll get completely better."

Outside, I breathed deeply. I'd confessed the truth, and it produced both a great relief and an uncomfortable disquiet in me.

In the days that followed the unlucky feast of Saint John, María Coral's health improved rapidly. Her mood was excellent and soon she was allowed to get up and take walks through the gardens surrounding the hospital. It was warm, and the sky was clear blue, without the trace of a cloud. During those peaceful strolls, we talked about trivial matters, trying not to touch on intimate subjects or to allude to the past or our situation. Since Max's visit, we'd heard nothing about Lepprince. Perico Serramadriles called from time to time, taking an interest in us. One day, as we were getting ready to take our walk, the doctor appeared and told us that María Coral's condition was satisfactory and that the next day she would be released.

"Buck up, ma'am," said the doctor with the best of intentions. "Tomorrow you'll go home and be able to go back to your life *just as it was before*."

Once he'd left us alone, María Coral began to feel ill, and a shadow passed over her face.

"What do we do now, Javier?"

"I don't know. We'll think of something. Count on me," I said to calm her down, although I shared her fears. Since the Saint John's festival, I hadn't been in the office, payday was coming, and we had no money. What would we do? We walked in silence through the paths flanked by hedges and flower beds. The patients, in their wheelchairs, waved to us blandly. Suddenly, María Coral stopped in front of me.

"I've got an idea!"

"Let's hear it."

"We'll emigrate to the United States."

"Emigrate?"

"Yes, that's it: we'll pack our bags and go to live in the United States."

"Why the United States?"

"People have told me marvelous things about the United States. I've always dreamed of going there. It's a country full of possibilities for young people. The salaries are high, there is freedom, you can do whatever you like, and no one asks you who you are, what you're thinking, or where you come from."

"But my dear girl, they speak English there, and we don't know a word . . ."

"Nonsense! It's full of immigrants from everywhere. We aren't going to give lectures, and besides, a language is something you can learn, right?"

"Sure, of course, but what kind of work will I do if I don't know how to talk?"

"Anything. You could be a cowboy."

"What a mad idea! Cattle!"

"Well, there are other possibilities, not counting cattle. What do you think of this? You can learn English when we first get there, until you can develop on your own; in the meanwhile, I'd support the two of us. I can go back to my old circus act."

"Never!"

"Bah, don't be ridiculous. Think what a great idea it is: we could go to Hollywood. There they'd hire me as an acrobat for fight scenes and cowboy movies. You could work in the movies as well—you don't have to speak any language to do that."

I couldn't hold back my laughter as I imagined myself transformed into a movie actor wearing a ten-gallon hat and galloping through the desert at top speed.

"I'm too ugly," I argued.

"So's Tom Mix," interjected a very serious María Coral.

She was so enthusiastic about the idea that I didn't want to disillusion her. That night, alone at home, I thought, calculated, and did my accounts. I was surprised by dawn, no closer to a solution than I was at the beginning. That afternoon I went to get María Coral and brought her home in a coach. I'd filled the room with flowers, but the weight of latent memories depressed her. She got into bed, and, with the help of a sedative prescribed by the doctor, fell into a restorative sleep from which she didn't awaken until late in the day.

In the afternoon, Perico Serramadriles came to visit. He brought a bouquet of carnations and tried by every means at his disposal to seem natural and relaxed, but the conversation ran on square wheels. I knew what was passing through my friend's mind and did nothing to smooth out the situation because any attempt to do so would be useless. I remembered the impression María Coral made on me the first time I saw her in the cabaret: the immoral, mysterious aura surrounding her made the unfortunate woman a being men only looked at as a body created for the pleasure of the wealthy and daring. Perico Serramadriles, too simple, lacking the cynicism of experience, did not dare to break the barrier of appearances, and his weak character cowered in the presence of a legend made flesh. The interview was short and tense. When we said good-bye, I knew we would never see each other again. When I went back to María Coral, still thinking Perico's thoughts, I looked at her as if she were a fruit forbidden to a poor lawyer's assistant, a delicacy reserved for the tables of the Lepprinces of this world. I was in a violent mood; María Coral was irritated.

"What's wrong with your friend? Why did he look at me as if I were some strange animal?"

"He's timid," I answered, so I wouldn't hurt her.

"You know very well that it's something else. He's afraid of me."

I wanted to say, "And so am I," but I didn't. I felt like the lion tamer who walks into the cage, knowing that no one else would want to go in with him and conscious that one day, suddenly, the lions could tear his throat out with one bite. The die was cast, as Cortabanyes would say, but how long could this entente last?

A FEW DAYS after Perico's visit, feeling housebound, I decided to visit Doloretas. I told María Coral, and she was not put out in the slightest.

"I'll stay home, if you don't mind. I'm still a bit weak. Don't stay long."

Doloretas lived in a sad, dark building on Cambios Nuevos street. The stairway was narrow and dark. The paint was peeling off the walls, the metal banister was rusty, and the whole building had an unhealthy reek of stews and greens. I knocked; on the other side, a peephole slid open, and a high-pitched voice asked, "Who's there?"

"A friend of Doloretas, Javier Miranda."

"Oh, I'll open up right away."

The door opened, and I walked into a gloomy, unfurnished foyer. The woman who'd opened the door was young and obese. With one hand she was holding up the corners of her apron to form a pocket. In the pocket were a few handfuls of peas.

"Excuse me for receiving you this way, eh? But I was shelling some peas."

"No need for apologies, ma'am, I understand perfectly."

"I'm a neighbor of Mrs. Doloretas, eh? and I keep company with her from time to time while I cook, as you see."

As she spoke, she guided me through a narrow corridor that ended at a square room in the center of which was a table with a heater attached underneath and an armchair. On the table was a basin filled with peas and a folded sheet of newspaper where the pods were piled up. Doloretas was lying in the armchair, covered with a blanket despite the heat. When she saw me, her dull eyes brightened.

"Oh, Mr. Javier, how kind of you to remember me."

It was difficult for her to talk because the right side of her face was paralyzed.

"How are you, Doloretas?"

"Not well, my boy, in a very bad way. As you see."

"Don't lose hope, ma'am, in a few days you'll be back at the front line in the office."

"Oh, Mr. Javier, don't try to raise my hopes. I'll never go back to the office. You can see the condition I'm in."

I really didn't know what to say because, to be frank, she couldn't have looked worse.

"I only asked God for one thing: *Lord, grant me good health . . . and lots of it, since you've taken everything else away from me.* But as you see, God's decided to inflict one last test on me."

"That's not fair, Doloretas. You'll get better, you can be sure of it."

"No, no. I've always had bad luck. Why, when I was a child I lost my parents and suffered many privations . . ."

The neighbor shelled her peas, mechanically rocking her large body back and forth. It was getting dark on the street, and, as usually happens in coastal cities in summer, with nightfall came a rise in atmospheric pressure: a wave of heat rolled over us. The pea pods produced a light, distant squeak as they were opened, like the screams of insects.

"Then everything seemed to get better: I met Andreu, who was the best of men—and so hardworking!—may he rest in peace. We got married, and since we were both young and good-looking, people took notice of us, everyone looked at us. . . . Excuse me for telling you these things, you'll say I'm a crazy old woman. . . . Andreu, see, wasn't from Barcelona. He came here to study, and when he met me and we got married, he decided to live here. He wasn't afraid of work and had lots of energy. But he didn't have contacts. Then he made a friend named Pep Puntxet. Andreu was very enthusiastic about his friend, and the two of them began to work together like madmen. Pep Puntxet knew lots of people, and, with one thing and another, they started to earn good money. I didn't like that man and said so to my husband: 'Be careful, Andreu, be careful, this Pep just doesn't sit well with me.' Andreu, poor man, only wanted to work and make money so I wouldn't lack for anything. What happened was that Pep Puntxet was a scoundrel who fooled him and got him involved in dirty business and ran off with the money as soon as things turned bad. Andreu was left holding the bag, surrounded by all his enemies. 'Be careful, Andreu, be careful. Don't get into a tizzy, dear, we'll pay our debts and start over.' Andreu was too good and didn't have an evil bone in his body. One night . . . one night I'd made a nice stew because I knew he'd be hungry when he got back. But the hours passed, and the stew got cold. Then some men came from the police. They asked me questions and told me, 'Come with us, ma'am, your husband's in the hospital.' When we got there, he was already dead, poor Andreu. They told me he'd had an accident, but I know very well he was killed by Pep Puntxet's enemies."

She was crying. The neighbor dried her tears.

"Don't think about it, Mrs. Doloretas, all that happened a long time ago."

Doloretas didn't stop crying.

"Oh, Mother of God. Life's filled with suffering, and very little happiness. Happiness fades fast. Suffering lasts . . . ," said the neighbor.

"I know," said Doloretas, "I know you've married, Mr. Javier, a very nice, very distinguished young lady. Do the right thing: be wise and pray a lot to God to preserve your health and your life. Pray a lot so your wife doesn't have to live the life I've lived."

When I left the house, I was depressed and thought that even my shadow was too heavy for me to bear. I stopped at a bar and drank a cognac while I meditated on Doloretas's words. Her story was the story of the people of Barcelona.

The way María Coral looked at me when I came home made me think she'd seen me crawl in on my hands and knees.

"What's wrong, Javier? Did you see a ghost?"

"Yes."

"Tell me about it."

"It was a very strange ghost: a ghost from the future brought back to life. Our own ghost."

"Hey! Stop right there! None of that lawyer bull; say what you mean."

"This isn't lawyer bull, María Coral. I'm confused and have to think things over."

I left her there, locked myself away in my room (because of her convalescence, we still slept apart), and didn't come out until dinnertime. María Coral was in a bad mood because of my impolite behavior. I told her what I meant: we were walking a tightrope, surrounded by wild animals; we couldn't rely on our own strength to survive. The crisis was staring us in the face; things were in a bad way; there were few jobs to be had. We couldn't just throw everything away, jump into a stormy sea, and cling only to the slippery log of our good intentions. We should use our heads, control our romantic impulses, not take big chances. Security, María Coral, security was everything. I said it thinking more about her than about myself, she had to believe me. I knew a few more things about life which she, because she was so young, couldn't even imagine . . .

She did not let me finish my speech. She shoved the dishes and silverware to the floor, stood up, knocking her chair over in the process, her face purple with rage, her body quivering. Not even when we were arguing on Saint John's night did she look like that.

"I know what you're trying to tell me, no need to say one more word! Why did I believe in you? How could I let myself—again—believe a man?"

She burst into tears and tried to leave the dining room. I grabbed her arm.

"Don't be that way, now, let me finish."

"Why bother, why bother . . . I understand what you don't dare to say out loud." She hissed out the words and looked at me with hatred. "You're the same as Lepprince . . . the same as Lepprince, except that he has money and you're nothing but a miserable good-for-nothing."

She pulled herself free, walked out of the room, and then her door slammed so loudly I thought it was a cannon going off. She'd locked herself in my room (the door to hers was still broken) and refused to come out, no matter how much I begged.

The next day I went to work. I was certain that María Coral's angry outburst would calm down with time. I was still trying to find the definitive solution to our problems when I saw Lepprince's limousine coming down the street toward me. I stopped and watched it stop outside the door to our building. Two figures I instantly recognized despite the distance got out: Lepprince and Max. The limousine turned around and passed by me again. Our problems no longer existed because a problem ceases to be one if it has no solution. In the present instance, there was no longer a problem, only an irreversible reality. With my heart broken, I went to work.

When I got back that evening, María Coral wasn't home. I stretched out on the bed without eating dinner, chain-smoking, until I heard steps in the foyer. María Coral was tripping over the furniture, and her unsteady walk and a sporadic, shameless hiccup told me she'd been drinking heavily. Nevertheless, with the weak hope of recovering the fragments of lost happiness, I got up and went to her room. But someone had repaired the door and the bolt resisted my attempts to push my way in. I called her as sweetly as I could.

"María Coral, are you in there? It's me, Javier."

"Don't try to come in, sweetie," her facetious voice, mixed with laughter, answered. "I'm not alone."

I went pale. Could it be true or was it merely her childish way of showing off? I bent down and peered through the keyhole. But before I could find out anything, I was knocked over by a slap someone gave me on the back. I turned around and found Max, smiling, standing in the center of the hall, pointing his revolver at me.

"Don't like nosy children," he said with stinging mockery.

I went back to my room and waited. For interminable hours, I heard Max's steps in the corridor, the giggles and games coming from María Coral's bedroom, the complaints of our decent neighbors, then a confused noise of people leaving. I imagined my wife, naked, bidding farewell to her lover from the landing . . . I finally fell asleep and dreamed I was in Valladolid, and my father was bringing me to school for the first time.

Beginning with the next day, our lives went on as they were before that memorable feast of Saint John, with the difference that we were now living in a theater without scenery, and we behaved like actors without an audience, feeling ridiculous that we were playing parts for each other, parts from which we could not escape. The shameful scenes were repeated with a certain frequency during the first weeks, although I never ran into Max again. Both they and I took pains to be more decorous in that sense. Then the parties began to diminish in number, duration, and degree of intensity: barely once a week. Lepprince was getting old. I would visit Doloretas every day and stay at her place until very late, in part to escape from the tragic caricature my home had become and in part because Doloretas's infinite string of calamities consoled me in my own misfortunes. The situation went on all summer until one day, in mid-September, everything changed.

I was coming home at night with the strange sensation that something new was waiting for me and so it was. The door was unlocked. I supposed María Coral had returned earlier than usual, and I called her from the doorway. No one answered. There was light in the dining room, so I went in. A big surprise: instead of María Coral, I found Lepprince sitting there. He looked tired, even sick. He had deep furrows on his face and dark circles under his eyes.

"Come in," he said.

"Waiting for María Coral?"

Lepprince smiled bitterly and looked at me with that profound gaze of irony mixed with tenderness, the same look he'd given me three years before when I was just a kid and had asked him point-blank, "Mr. Lepprince, who killed Pajarito de Soto?"

"I hope you don't think I'd be that tactless, Javier."

"Well then, why are you honoring this house with your presence?"

"You can well imagine I wouldn't have come if it weren't something serious."

I feared the worst and my expression changed. Lepprince saw it and made a languid gesture.

"It's not what you think. Calm down."

"What's going on?"

"María Coral ran away."

I remained silent, confused, trying to assimilate the magnitude of the message.

"Why are you telling me these things?" I answered. But my retort did not sound sincere because a tremor in my voice gave me away. Once again, Lepprince had chosen his target well and had hit the mark.

"What do you want from me?"

He took out his silver cigarette case and offered me a cigarette of a brand I'd never seen before. We smoked in silence until he spoke again.

"You've got to find her and bring her back."

He snuffed out the cigarette he'd just lit, put his fingertips together, and stared at the floor.

"How can I bring her back when I have no idea where she is?"

"I know where she is."

"So why come to me?"

"She ran away with Max."

I was dumbfounded.

"I can't believe it!"

"This is no time for explanations. Listen carefully to what I'm going to tell you, and let's not waste any more time."

He picked his attaché case up from the floor, opened it, and took out a revolver, a box of shells, and a folded sheet of paper. He put the revolver and the bullets on one end of the table and then proceeded to unfold and spread out the paper, smoothing down the surface with the side of his hand.

"Bring a lamp, a piece of paper, and a pencil."

I went to my room and brought the floor lamp I used for reading in bed. It was hot. Lepprince had taken off his jacket, and I did the same. We put our heads together under the lamp. Lepprince pointed to a spot on the map.

"This is Barcelona, see? Here's Valencia, and here on the other side, France. Madrid is over here. Understand? No, it would be better if I turned the map around. Or better still, come here, next to me, so we don't get all tangled up."

CHAPTER
8

THE HOARSE ROAR of the engine suddenly ceased, leaving a kind of emptiness in my head. I'd been hearing it all night, since I took off like a shot from Barcelona on the trail of the fugitives. According to Lepprince's calculations, I should have caught up to them that very morning. María Coral and Max did not have their own vehicle. They'd taken a train, a *carrilet,* and perhaps a light, two-wheeled carriage. Even making the best time, it was impossible for them to have gone further than Cervera. I, on the other hand, had the *conduite-cabriolet,* which I'd learned to drive on our Sunday outings back in the spring.

"As you pull into Cervera, you'll see a red-brick restaurant, the name of which I don't remember. Max will pass through there. If they haven't arrived yet, wait for them."

How could Lepprince be so sure of the route they'd follow and the stages in it? I'd asked him about that several times, but all he'd say was, "This is not the time for explanations: write it down and shut up."

I checked the notebook for the thousandth time: stop at the restaurant and wait. Be careful.

I took the pistol Lepprince had given me and stuck it into my belt, trying to cover its shocking presence with my jacket. I walked toward the reddish restaurant. The first light of day made the enormous mass of the city perched on its rock rise up before me. The countryside was silent, the cloudless sky presaged a hot day.

When I reached the building, I stopped, hugging the wall. I peeked through a big, steamed-over window. I could make out a large dining room with a long counter to the rear. The chairs were stacked upside down on the tables. Behind the bar, a figure whose proportions and movements were not those of Max was working away. I pushed open the door and walked in.

"Good morning, sir. You're an early riser."

"I'm not an early riser; I just haven't gone to bed yet."

The man went on with his work: he was placing a double row of saucers on the counter, and on top of each saucer, a large cup and teaspoon.

"In that case, would you like dinner or breakfast?"

"A sandwich, whatever you've got, and a café au lait."

"You'll have to wait. The coffee's not ready yet. Sit down and rest. You look tired."

I sat next to the window. From there I had a sweeping view of the entire room, and through the window I could see the highway that snaked its way through the orchards from the foothills of Montserrat. Driving that steep road at night had been quite a feat, and now my nerves were starting to show the effects. I relaxed, and the objects around me began to sway rather sweetly.

"Sir . . . sir! Your sandwich and coffee."

I woke up with a start and went for my gun. The man put a plate and a steaming cup under my nose. I'd fallen asleep right on the table.

"I'm sorry I scared you."

"I fell asleep."

"So I see."

"Was I out for a long time?"

"Barely fifteen minutes. Why don't you take a room upstairs and go to bed? You can't even stand up."

"Impossible. I have to keep going."

"Excuse me for butting into your business, but I think you're making a mistake. You're traveling by car, right?"

"Right."

"Well, you shouldn't drive in the condition you're in."

I sipped the coffee. The boiling hot liquid put a little life back into me.

"I have to go on."

The man gave me an ironic look.

"Well, let me inform you that Max and the girl passed through here more than three hours ago."

"What?"

"That Max and the girl must be far away by now. You've got a long trip ahead of you. Go to sleep, and you'll catch up with them tomorrow."

He turned and went back to the counter, grumbling under his breath, "Where's all this going to lead?"

"Listen! How do you know I'm looking for Max and the girl."

"You're the guy Mr. Lepprince sent, aren't you?"

"And who are you?"

"A friend of Mr. Lepprince. You don't have to take your gun out; if I'd wanted to hurt you, I had plenty of chances before now."

He was right, and besides, this was no time to be delving into mysteries.

"Which way did they go?"

"What do you mean *which way did they go?* Don't you have a notebook with the route marked in it?"

"Yes."

"Then why ask questions? Finish your breakfast, and I'll make your bed."

My eyes wouldn't stay open.

"The car . . . ," I murmured.

"I'll get it all ready and have the tank full. When you wake up, you can get right back on the trail, all right?"

"All right . . . and thanks."

"Don't thank me. We both have the same boss. When you get back, tell them I did a good job."

"Don't worry."

Dragging myself, I went upstairs where there were rooms for travelers. I slept deeply, better than I had for months, until the man woke me up. I washed, paid the bill, and went racing off. The sun was going down. The car was shining in front of the restaurant. I got in, said good-bye to the man, and drove off. I traveled all night and in late morning reached Balaguer.

"In Balaguer, you'll ask for Uncle Burillas, at the carriage station."

The station was an esplanade carpeted with manure. At one end there was a big building made of adobe. I walked over. The sun was beating down on the plaza, making me an easy target for even an average shot, so I walked as quickly as I could. The building, which was an office, a stable, and a waiting room for travelers, was closed. A sign said CLOSED. I heard a horse neigh and walked around to the other side of the building. Someone was shoeing a Percheron in the stable. Outside there was a carriage without a horse chained to a ring in the wall. I went to the blacksmith, an old, powerfully built, and surly man, who did not deign to look up at me. I waited until he was finished.

"Uncle Burillas?"

The old man led the Percheron to the stable and closed the door. He still had the hammer he'd used to nail on the horse's shoe in his hand.

"Who you lookin' fer?"

"Uncle Burillas. Is that you?"

"No."

"Where can I find him?"

"Go screw yourself. Dunno."

He began to walk to the office. I followed him at a respectful distance, trying to stay out of range of his hammer.

"Did you see the carriage from Cervera pull in?"

"No carriages, s'late." He pointed to the sign. "Dontcha know how ta read? Closed."

"I know there are no more carriages. I was asking about the one from Cervera."

"No carriages, no horses, no cattle. No bother me."

He went into his office and slammed the door. The sign danced in front of my eyes. I walked out and wandered the streets of

Balaguer, afraid I'd have a run-in with Max. After a fruitless search, I saw a line of boys being led down the street by a servant. The servant seemed like a decent sort, so I stopped him.

"Excuse me, but do you know Uncle Burillas?"

The servant looked at me with obvious disgust.

"I've never heard that name before, sir."

He went on his way, followed by the boys. One of them slipped out of line.

"Ask over in Jordi's tavern."

I found the tavern and asked the owner. He shouted, "Joan, a gentleman asking for you!"

A short, solid man, wearing the purple stocking cap favored by the locals, got up from a table and abandoned the noisy domino game he was playing with three other men.

"What did you want?"

"Lepprince sent me."

He scratched his chin, looked me up and down, looked at the ground, looked me over again, and asked, "Who?"

"Mr. Lepprince."

"Lepprince?"

"Yes, Lepprince. You are Uncle Burillas, aren't you?"

"Of course, who else would I be?"

"And you know Mr. Lepprince, don't you?"

"Then why ask questions?"

He repeated his looking-around routine and finally began to laugh with his eyes shut.

"Come, Mr. Lepprince, let's go outside."

I followed him. Outside, he went back to his reticent looks.

"How's my brother-in-law's business going?" he finally asked.

"It's going fine," I answered so as not to prolong the conversation.

"It's been going fine for six years," he laughed again. "I don't know what would happen if it went badly, damn it to hell."

"These things take their time, but I'll try to speed them up when I get back. Don't you have news for me?"

He became very serious. Then he laughed again for a good while until he became serious once more.

"Max and the girl were here. They passed through hours ago, looking for transportation. They wanted to rent a carriage, but they just couldn't get one."

"So they're still here?"

"No, they left."

His laughter came and went, and since he only spoke or listened in his periods of absolute normalcy, it looked as though we'd be there for hours.

"How did they get away?"

"In a car."

"Whose?"

"The company's."

"Which one?"

He laughed again. "The power company. They went in a car that belongs to the engineers. They must have gone down to the power station."

"Toward Tremp?" I said, remembering one of Lepprince's notes.

"Even further. Maybe all the way to Viella. They were in a big black car. Be careful if you're thinking of going there, Mr. Lepprince. The highway is very dangerous, and if you crash into the ravine, you'll kill yourself."

"Thanks, I'll be careful."

"Do whatever you like, but remember about my brother-in-law."

"When did they leave?"

"Early, early."

"Early in the evening or early in the morning?"

"Don't know."

I left, just to avoid an attack of fury. After a few minutes, I was en route again. Soon, just as Uncle Burillas predicted, the highway became narrow and curved into passages carved into the living rock by the river. The highway swung around a peak high above the black, turbulent waters, in effect following irregular, very dangerous curves. After midday, tired, hungry, and stiff, I could make out the Tremp swamp. It was hot. I left the car in the shade of some trees, took off my clothes, and swam in the icy water. The car showed signs of overheating, so I decided to give it a rest and give myself one at the same time. I stretched out in the shade of a weeping willow and fell asleep. When I woke up, the sun had already set. I went to the power station. Some workers told me that a company car had passed that way but hadn't stopped. They supposed it was going for La Pobla de Segur, Sort, or perhaps Viella.

I ate dinner and set out again. The night was dark, and the temperature was extremely low. When the moon came up, I could see the snow shining on the peaks. Although my teeth were chattering, I thought it better not to stop because the cold kept the motor from overheating. The car was dying: the front mudguards had fallen off; the spare tire rolled down the precipice, lost forever; the external horn was hanging by one screw and banged against the windshield; the brake barely responded to foot pressure; and the vehicle left a black trail in its wake.

At daybreak I came to a little town I'd never seen before. At the entrance to the village stood a rather large house made of gray stone and surrounded by a fence. On the fence was a sign with the letters P. F. M. I identified the letters as the name of the power company, the very one that employed the engineers Uncle Burillas mentioned. I stopped, got out, and opened the gate. In the garden, a man was watering the plants. I asked if a black company car had passed that way. He said the car was there, at the house, and that the engineers were resting. I asked to see them. One was awakened, and he came out to see me. I identified myself, mentioned Lepprince, and asked the appropriate questions.

"Yes, we brought a German and his wife here. A charming couple. What? No, no, we haven't been here for a long time, two hours at most. They must still be around here somewhere, right. They planned to go on to Viella or maybe even further, I don't know. They didn't talk much. Correct but reserved, right. No, I don't think they'll be leaving right away. There's no other way to get out of here except a coach that passes once in a blue moon—or they could rent a team of mules. She, the German's wife, seemed sick, which is why we agreed to drive them. And that's why I don't think they'll be going on, at least for now. Yes, that's everything I can tell you. Again, we didn't talk much. No, you're welcome, it was no bother. Always glad to be of service."

I left the car where Max couldn't find it and walked into the town so I wouldn't be noticed. The village was very small and picturesque, located in a small valley with little vegetation because the zone was so arid, and surrounded by high mountains, some bare and some treed, the highest peaks covered by perpetual snows.

The village didn't have more than a hundred inhabitants, although constant emigration made getting accurate figures difficult. The houses were all one-story, brownish, with thick walls and narrow, irregular windows that looked like cracks. The chimneys smoked.

My plan to sneak in unnoticed was quickly ruined. I suddenly found myself surrounded by curious citizens who'd been taking the sun. I tried to get information from them. They told me the foreigners were staying in *Oncle* Virolet's house—he had empty rooms because his sons had gone to Barcelona.

"All of them go and get jobs with the company. Only we old-timers stay behind. The company pays well, and, anyway, the town's too small for the young."

I made them tell me more about the couple.

"The lady looked sick," they all agreed, "and that's why they had to stay. The blond gentleman wanted to leave at all costs, but she refused. Those of us who saw her agreed, and we advised them to rest for at least two days. The climate here is very healthy."

I asked if there were another place in the village where I could rent a room. They showed me to the house of a Mrs. Clara, an old lady who raised chickens in her dining room. For an absurdly low price, Mrs. Clara rented me a room with a slanting roof into which a sofa was brought. I asked if I could wash up and was given a basin, a pitcher of water, and a four-part mirror. When I looked at myself in the mirror, I saw that my cheeks were sunken, my chin receding, and that I had violet circles under my eyes. A violent trembling seized me, and I felt febrile. I went to bed and spent the afternoon and the evening huddled under the blankets. Mrs. Clara brought me broth, fresh eggs, crackers, and some wine. My sleep was infested by nightmares. I woke up refreshed but saddened by the visions that had so mercilessly pursued me and had prophesied violent death.

The incidents that took place on the road and my subsequent collapse kept me from formulating a plan of action or even imagining the nature of our encounter. Since I didn't want to make things up as I went along, I spent the day entangled in the most absurd plans, fully conscious, even though I'd deny it, that in the moment of truth my lucubrations would fall apart and I wouldn't know what to say or do. Shortly after midday, a ragged boy came to the house asking for me. He had a message: the foreign lady wanted to see me. I understood that I'd been hiding out of fear, not a fear of facing Max but a fear of facing María Coral. I got dressed, made sure I still had the pistol and that it was loaded, checked to see if I remembered how it worked, and set out for *Oncle* Virolet's house. The boy led the way, and the entire town followed, since by then they all knew something was up and were eagerly waiting for a bloody, spectacular finish.

Oncle Virolet's house was on a narrow, dark little street off a plaza where the church, the town hall, and the little barracks of the *Guardia Civil* were clustered. The curious stopped in the plaza, and I marched down the deserted street alone. I walked quickly, staying close to the wall, ducking down as I passed windows. Finally, I came to my destination, without even the slightest disturbance in the town's calm. I looked back at the last moment, tempted to ask for help or to run away. But it wasn't possible: this thing had to be resolved, and it was up to me to do it with the means at my disposal. Besides, the curious townsfolk did not seem eager to intervene actively: they'd taken up positions under the covered gallery in the plaza and were either rolling cigarettes or swigging from a huge bottle of wine.

The door to *Oncle* Virolet's house was ajar. I pushed it open and saw a long, dark hallway. I stepped aside and waited, holding my breath. Nothing happened. I poked my head in: the corridor just ran on straight ahead. At the end of it I could see a crack of light. I walked in and strode the distance that separated me from the light with extreme caution. Another door left ajar. I pushed this one open too. I stepped aside. Absolute silence. I looked and saw nothing more than an apparently empty room with a light in it.

"Is anyone here?"

"Javier, is that you?"

I recognized María Coral's voice.

"Yes, it's me. Is Max with you?"

"No, he went out and won't be back for a while. Don't be afraid to come in."

I did. The first thing I felt was the muzzle of a pistol against my head. Then a hand snatched my pistol away. María Coral was crying in a corner with her face hidden in her arms, which were resting on her knees.

"Poor Javier . . . oh, poor Javier," I heard her say, sobbing.

María Coral left us alone. Max sat down behind a table and asked me to sit in one of the chairs. I did what he ordered, and the gunman put his weapons in his belt, leaving my own pistol on the table, out of my reach. Then he took off his derby, loosened his tie, and asked permission to take off his jacket. *"Il fait chaud, n'est-ce-pas?"* I said it was hot, very hot. As he took off his jacket, I studied him carefully: his beardless face and his rosy skin showed no sign whatsoever of fatigue. He looked clean and fresh, as if he'd just taken a bath, complete with salts. He understood my look and smiled.

"Etes-vous fatigué, monsieur Miranda?"

I confessed I was; he smiled again and pointed to the mountains, bits of which could be seen through the windows.

"Qu'il fait du bien, le plein air!" he exclaimed.

Then there was a tense silence, and finally, he began to talk.

"You will have to forgive me, *monsieur* Miranda, for having used this unsportsmanlike trick to capture you. But my reasons for doing so are these: in the first place, you shouldn't reproach María Coral for her part in your shameful capture. She did it to avoid greater evils. As you can probably understand, I did not have to make use of this . . . this . . . *tricherie honteuse.* I could have killed you, had I wanted to do so, covertly or face to face at any time *à tout bout de champ.* I could have done it right after I was told, in Cervera, that you'd set out in our . . . *comme on dit? poursuite?* That's it, in our pursuit. Why didn't I do it? Now, you'll find out. Above all, I am not what you think I am. Notice, for instance, that my Spanish is correct, something which until now I have taken pains to dissimulate. I am not the classic *tueur à gages.* I've received some education, I think quite well on my own, and I am *au fond* a man of feeling. Circumstances beyond my control have led me to this sad profession, which I deplore, although I do recognize that I'm rather good at it. At no time, nevertheless, have I ever identified myself with the business of killing, and, as regards you yourself, *monsieur* Miranda, I never felt any dislike for you; I felt, rather, a certain sympathy. That, as far as I personally am concerned. With regard to María Coral, believe me, she is only an innocent victim you have not known how to treat justly. Excuse me if I interfere in your *affaires du coeur,* something I don't usually do and which I promise not to repeat during our conversation. Now, turning to the facts *en l'espèce,* I shall tell you that our escape is not the result of mere emotional causes, as you doubtless may have supposed, but comes of colder, but more comprehensible factors."

He interrupted himself, smoothed his straight blond hair, and closed his eyes, as if he were picking up the invisible thread of his thoughts.

"First of all, you must know that Lepprince did not tell you the truth. At least not the whole truth. And what he prudently hid from you, I will reveal now: Lepprince is . . . *en faillite,* how do you say that in Spanish? Bankrupt? Yes, that's the word: *bankrupt.* No, it's still not public knowledge, but it's known in financial circles. The factory is not producing, the merchandise is rusting in the warehouse, the creditors are attacking from all sides, and the banks have turned their backs on the business. Sooner or later, the situation will explode, and then Lepprince will be lost. Without money, without influence, and, to say it all, without me, his days are numbered. Those who have hated him *en silence* for years will now have the opportunity to devour his remains. And there are many on his trail, be sure of that. I won't say I admire them, but to a certain degree, I understand them. Lepprince liked to toy with the weak and did many bad things. It's only fair he pay now. But let's not digress."

He paused again. Outside, in the plaza, the church bells were ringing. A dog barked in the distance. The sky turned reddish, and the mountains now looked threatening.

"Under these circumstances, *monsieur,* it was logical that María Coral and I try to save ourselves, given that both of us were, and still are, the two persons connected most *étroitement* with Lepprince. Objectively considered, our attitude could be termed *déloyale,* but it isn't if we take into account the essential factor in our relationship, *c'est à dire,* money. With the money gone, it's logical that Lepprince would defend himself on his own (speaking for me) and that he would attempt *l'épanouissement* of his legitimate wife (I'm talking about María Coral). María Coral, and please don't take my remarks as a value judgment but rather as a statement of fact, cannot depend on you. Without Lepprince, with the company dissolved, you're left floating in midair; that's the way things are. So we decided to run away. If it hadn't been for the sudden *découverte de la grossesse* of María Coral, at this moment we'd be over the border, and you wouldn't have caught up to us. Now things have changed: she can't travel on horseback. Which is why we adopted the plan of luring you here and talking with you. Not so we could have a confrontation, which would only end in bloodshed, but in search of your help, since enmity, given the current situation, *n'a pas de sens.*"

He stopped talking; there was a long silence. I struggled to grasp the situation, analyzing the arguments presented by the gunman. What at the outset was a confused sentimental adventure was ending with a cold business transaction conducted at a table.

"What kind of help would you expect from me?"

"Your car."

"Wouldn't it be easier to take it away from me?"

"I suppose you'd offer resistance, and perhaps . . . the matter would have a disagreeable conclusion."

"Don't tell me you have scruples at this stage of the game."

"Oh no, don't misunderstand me. It's a matter of convenience. Rest assured I won't kill you. But be aware of the fact that Lepprince sent you to find us certain that I would kill you. But this is no time for explanations. Will you give us the car or not?"

"Why should I?"

"For her sake, *si vous l'aimez encore.*"

When the noise of the automobile faded in the distance, and silence once again possessed the village, I got up and left *Oncle* Virolet's house. It was almost night. In the plaza, there were only a few curiosity seekers left, boredom having dispersed most of them. As I passed, the tenacious ones, still waiting, enveloped in a bovine calm, evinced a mixture of reproach for the show they'd not been given and commiseration for the failure, which they guessed, of my adventure.

I went back to my room at Mrs. Clara's house and spent a long time stretched out on the sofa smoking and thinking about my existence and about all the twists and turns I'd taken just to get back to the beginning, older, with fewer illusions, and even less perspective. I remembered Cortabanyes's words: "Life is a merry-go-round that goes round and round until you get dizzy and then it stops at the same spot where you got on."

I was immersed in those meditations when I noticed a bit of an uproar in the streets of the town. Soon, the same ragged boy who'd brought me word from María Coral came. He was very upset, and the townspeople were all milling around behind him.

"Sir, sir, come quickly!"

"What's going on?"

"The *Guardia Civil,* bringing in your car! Come quickly"

I dashed out of the house. The entire town, carrying oil lamps, was gathered on the highway. A shadow of indistinct shape was approaching. When it reached the first lamps, I saw it was two *Guardia Civiles,* wearing their three-cornered hats, their capes, and with their carbines over their shoulder, pushing and braking Leprince's car according to the whims of the road. I approached the automobile: sitting at the wheel was Max, his face livid, his features haggard, his arms hanging, his shirt bloody; clearly dead.

"The *Guardia Civiles* killed the foreigner."

I accompanied the two *Guardia Civiles* to the little barracks. There, after a short wait, the corporal, a mature, lean man with curled mustaches, told me what happened.

"These officers were patrolling down in the hollow when they saw that car out there." He pointed toward the half-open door that faced the street, as dark at that hour as a wolf's mouth. "They signaled, and the car stopped. As they walked up to the car, they could see there were two passengers, the deceased here and a woman."

"What happened to the woman?" I interrupted.

"Let me finish. This is testimony. As I was saying, they asked the passengers for their identification, following the procedure as laid down in the Civil Code, and to their surprise the deceased (just to avoid confusion I'll call him that) started to pull out the gun he had in his belt with the intention of shooting at the two officers. Logically, they responded to the aggression with their carbines. They shot him dead."

He took off his three-cornered hat and wiped the sweat off his brow with a flowered handkerchief. A respectful subordinate appeared.

"The Penal Code you asked for."

The corporal left his hat on the desk and took some wire-rimmed glasses out of his pocket.

"Leave it here, Jiménez. This gentleman is the owner of the car. I'm going to take down his statement. I'll call for you later."

The subordinate saluted and did an about face. The corporal had his glasses on and was leafing through the code.

"Look, Mr. Miranda, it says it clearly here: 'Assault of an

Officer and Resisting Arrest.' You can see it as well as I can, right? I don't want problems."

"I see it. What I don't understand is how your agents escaped unharmed."

The corporal closed the code and used it as a prop for his little show.

"Look here. The foreigner had low-caliber pistols. He had to raise his arms up to fire *over* the car door." As he said this, he slid a finger over the code. "The agents, on the other hand, armed with their rifles, fired point-blank *through* the car. That allowed them to shoot faster and more accurately." He deposited the legal text next to his three-cornered hat and concluded, "That foreigner must have been a city gunman."

"And the woman who was with him?"

"That's the most shocking part of the story. Look, the highway has the mountain on one side and the ravine on the other, see?" Now the Penal Code became the highway. "Well, while the agents were reloading, the woman jumped over the seat and leapt into the ravine."

"Holy Christ!"

"Wait, here comes the good part. The agents looked over the side to see if she'd gone all the way down, but they found nothing. She'd vanished."

"Thank God," I exclaimed. And I added, to inform the corporal, "She's a circus acrobat."

"I see. She must have pelted down those rocks like a goat. But it was a useless trick. She'll be back soon, if she's still alive."

"Why do you say that?"

"She was lightly dressed because during the day it's hot. But at night it gets very cold. Besides, she took off her shoes when she jumped, because we found them on the rear seat. Look for yourself how much cooler it is now."

I looked through the barred window of the barracks. An icy wind was blowing, and I thought I heard wolves howling in the mountains.

"Are there wolves around here?"

"That's what the locals say. I never saw any," the corporal answered with indifference. "Now, if you don't mind, we'll take down your statement."

I was as evasive as possible. To tell the truth, I really didn't have to force things much to bewilder the corporal. I didn't know Max's last name, his age, where he was born, or any other personal information about the gunman. I lied about María Coral. I pretended not to know who she was so as not to give too many facts and make her easily identifiable. The corporal himself wasn't very incisive. The matter clearly bothered him. When we said goodbye, I took the opportunity to say, "If you find the woman, treat her gently. She's a minor."

The corporal patted me on the back.

"You Barcelona guys never miss a trick."

I spent the night waiting for María Coral sitting in front of the house. But morning came, and the gypsy still hadn't returned. Late that morning, I decided to call Barcelona and consult Lepprince. There were no telephones in the town, as I suspected, so I went to the power company offices, where I thought I could count on the influential help of the engineers.

Nevertheless, my plans were condemned to failure. On the path from the highway to the company building, I ran into a group of workers who blocked the way.

"Where do you think you're going?"

"To the office to make a telephone call."

"You can't. The office is closed."

"Closed? Today? Why?"

"We're on strike."

"But it's a matter of life or death."

"We're sorry, but a strike is a strike."

"At least let me try."

"All right, go on."

They let me by, but it was useless. Outside the iron gate there were groups of men armed with iron bars, tools, and other blunt instruments. Things, however, were calm. I waited, and no one took any notice of me. After a while, a dozen men left the building.

Two at least were carrying shotguns, and all of them wore red handkerchiefs around their necks. The men outside the gate opened it. Then the engineers' black car appeared. It was as crowded as a trolley car at rush hour. It passed the gate and disappeared, heading toward Barcelona. The workers then went into the building and locked the doors. I followed the car awhile, waving for them to stop. Naturally, they paid no attention to me.

I went back to town and tried the *Guardia Civil* barracks. The corporal was out. I asked if I could send a telegram.

"The telegraph doesn't work. The strikers have cut the wires."

"Hear anything about the lost girl?"

"No."

"There will be a search, I suppose?"

"Not a chance. We're going to have lots of broken heads with this strike. Now things look calm, but let's see what happens after a few hours. When this mess is over, then maybe we'll go out looking for her."

"And how long can this strike last?"

The officer shrugged his shoulders.

At midday we buried Max. Taking advantage of the distraction provided by the strike, I managed to have him buried with his weapons. I thought that wherever it is the dead go, Max would need his pistols. When they began to shovel in the dirt, several strikers appeared waving a red flag and an anarchist insignia, and paid homage to Max. I asked them why and they said they didn't know who he was but that the *Guardia Civil* had killed him and that was enough for them.

Chapter 9

FIVE DAYS HAD GONE BY since Max's death, and there was still no sign of María Coral. Made desperate by my attempts to get help from the *Guardia Civil* (they were completely absorbed in the social crisis of the moment), I hired a big-headed local boor, and together we searched the woods and mountains. In exchange for his services, he asked for "something made of gold," so I gave him my watch. To tell the truth, it was an exchange of frauds, because the watch was gold-plated tin, and the peasant, for his part, led me in circles around the town, taking advantage of my disorientation and never venturing into the wilder places of more difficult access. Meanwhile, the village blacksmith repaired the car. He made a terrible mess and charged me an arm and a leg, because "with this strike business, he could only work at night and by putting his life in serious danger." I paid him scab wages so he could totally destroy what was already broken.

The strike made itself felt in marginal details, since, aside from the company, there was no other industry in the town that could be paralyzed. Anarcho-syndicalist flags flew at the company office, and in the town square there were Lenin posters, which the kids promptly decorated with glasses, cigars, and obscenities.

The workers met daily and spent their time enjoying the sun at the tavern door, arguing, philosophizing, and circulating false rumors about revolutionary events in other places. At dusk, there were meetings in which the socialists and the anarchists mutually insulted each other. When the meetings were over, the orators and their audiences would congregate outside the church and taunt the priest, accusing him of being a loan-shark, a corruptor of minors, and an informer. The *Guardia Civil* never appeared at these events. As I confirmed later, they followed the progress of the strike from the window of their barracks house, taking note of the people, the statements made, and the tendencies of the speakers. They included everything in a voluminous testimonial the corporal dictated to his subordinates, who wrote it down with errors, scratched-out passages, and inkstains.

I would be given reports of the news, which kept the village in a high state of exaltation, at nightfall, when I'd come back from my treks through the hills, exhausted, frozen stiff, my clothes and skin torn apart by the brambles, and my throat parched from shouting María Coral's name in order, it seemed, to frighten rabbits. Finally, tired of looking for a needle in a haystack, and taking advantage of the fact that the blacksmith was bored with abusing the car, I decided to go back to Barcelona, fully intending to return to the village when things had returned to normalcy and a coherent, organized search could be carried out.

I left the village, intending to be home in less than forty-eight hours. It took me a week.

The first day, I drove several miles at a good speed, but as I came to the top of a hill, the car stopped, coughed, jumped, and began to give off purple flames. I had just enough time to jump out and hide behind a rock before the entire vehicle exploded. So I abandoned the charred remains of the *conduite-cabriolet* and continued on foot until I came to a place whose name I never bothered to find out.

The village in question seemed to be celebrating the festival of its patron saint. Actually it was the strike again. How those ancestral, isolated communities managed to synchronize their activities at the beginnings of the conflict is a mystery. Nevertheless, from what I read later in the newspapers and from what I myself witnessed in my travels, all Cataluña plunged into a general strike. Which did nothing but frustrate my plans, because all means of transportation—scarce to begin with—had stopped functioning. Nor could I use the telephone, the telegraph, or any other means of communication. When I got back to Barcelona, seventeen days had gone by, and during the entire period I was in total isolation.

But getting back to the story, I reached this small town during its festival and walked in without arousing anyone's curiosity. They no longer took notice of outsiders. Everyone had gathered in the town square, around the bandstand, to practice singing the *Internationale*. When the rehearsal was over, they dispersed. I went from group to group, asking how I could get to Barcelona. Most pointed to the highway and advised me to walk. Finally, a tiny little man who did not agree with the strike "because if he stopped working even for a single day he'd come down with tuberculosis" rented me a bicycle. I paid two weeks' rent in advance and signed a contract in which I swore "on my honor as a gentleman" that I would return the bicycle.

I hadn't ridden a bicycle since I was a boy, so I left the town swerving all over the road. Nevertheless, it soon came back to me. That raised my spirits, and I had some hope of ending my journey. But that was a mistake. The town where I rented the bicycle was on a plateau, so the first part of the trip consisted of gentle downward slopes. However, the road soon leveled out and then, after a few miles, began to go up a crag. Playtime was over; now the back-breaking part began. My legs just wouldn't pump; I was out of breath, sweating from every pore. I thought I'd die. Finally, seeing there was no hope for it, I decided to put the bike aside and continue on foot. I went on without stopping until I reached the top of the peak. From there I could see a blackish, desolate valley and beyond, other mountains and other valleys.

I rested until I thought I'd recovered, but the worst was yet to come. I couldn't move, my entire body ached, and just standing up was torture. I walked about a hundred yards and collapsed. I was afraid no one would ever pass by (the roads were practically empty because of the strike), and that I'd die of inanition and cold. It was getting dark, and menacing noises came from the forest. I curled up, resigned to the same fate María Coral had experienced.

I was feeling the first (perhaps imaginary) symptoms of paralysis when I heard the unmistakable growl of a motor. I jumped to my feet and stood right in the middle of the road, determined to stop the owner of the car even if it were the devil himself.

Although the hills and valleys kept me from seeing it, the vehicle was getting closer. I held my breath; I think my heart actually stopped. Finally I saw it come over the peak. It was an ancient jalopy that rattled along, emitting clouds of smoke and backfires. Its silhouette standing out against the setting sun seemed enormous, although it was nothing more than a light truck, the kind used in those days to transport small merchandise locally. It had two covered seats and a box behind it with vertical supports on which a tarpaulin could be strung to protect the cargo from the weather.

When the truck was close enough, I saw it had posters on both sides saying LONG LIVE FREE LOVE. In it were seven women, one very young, another elderly, and the other five scattered between twenty-five and thirty-five years of age. Except for the driver, the others had taken places in the box, where they were playing cards, eating, drinking, and smoking cheap cigars. They were not shy about showing their legs. They were heavily made up and perfumed and had red handkerchiefs on their heads, around their necks, or around their waists. I remember that the youngest's name was Estrella and the oldest's was Democracia.

They stopped and invited me into the box. I made myself as comfortable as I could, since there wasn't much room, and the truck resumed its labored course. I thanked the women for their hospitality, and the eldest answered me in the name of all of them that I did not have to thank them or humble myself before anyone because the hour of liberation had come, that everything belonged to everybody, and that all men were brothers, and that every man was a king.

"If you're hungry or thirsty, tell us and we'll try to satisfy you as best we can. And later, if you like, choose whichever of us you like best and satisfy your sexual needs."

In truth, I was a bit taken aback. I accepted a salami sandwich and a swallow of wine, but declined the second part of the offer, using the pretext that I'd reached the limits of my strength—which was the truth.

"Please don't be offended," I added, "but I should also add that I've just suffered the loss of a loved one."

They all took pity on me, and Democracia ventured to say that perhaps one of them might bring me a certain consolation. Seeing I was still firmly negative, she relented, and they left me in peace.

The truck, meanwhile, went on without respite through uncultivated fields and reddish heath. The night came on, and the card players put away their deck and began to sing. The oldest and the youngest (who couldn't have been more than fifteen, I guessed) told me all about their activities. Their explanation didn't give me a clear picture of their ideas, but I understood that they'd been on the road since the general strike began, with the intention of preaching free love in word and deed. They'd traveled the better part of the region and had made quite a few converts. They gave me a badly printed sheet on which there was a naked woman imitating the pose of a Greek statue. On the back it said:

The poor working man is oppressed by the rich man who does not work; but the poor man always has the undoubtedly sad option of taking revenge for the oppression he suffers by oppressing in his turn the woman fate has provided for him. This woman has no means to vent her rage and must resign herself to suffering hunger, cold, and the misery caused by bourgeois exploitation and, as if that were not enough, to suffer the bestial, inconsiderate, and offensive domination of males. And these are the happiest, the privileged ones, the favored daughters of Nature, because there exists some thirty or forty percent of these women who are much more unfortunate, since our social structure *even deprives them of the right to have sexual relations, to be women, or, which is the same, to show they are.*

Oh, Woman! You are the real victim of social infamy; you are the real object of the mission of the generous apostles.

"It's a beautiful, noble text by one of the masters of anarchism," the sweet Estrella told me, looking into my eyes with hers, which were deep and clear.

"We want to show men by our conduct that we are capable and worthy of understanding, equal in liberty," declaimed Democracia.

I didn't know what expression to put on my face. At first, I took them for common prostitutes who had decided to adapt their profession to the spirit of the times. Later I saw that they did not charge to exercise their apostolate, although they did accept food, wine, tobacco, and inexpensive gifts (a handkerchief, stockings, a bouquet of wildflowers, a picture of Bakunin). Over the course of the trip I catalogued them successively as lunatics, tricksters, nuts, and (in their way) saints.

The six-day trip to Barcelona had an air I think I could call bucolic. We traveled by day and at night slept in the stables of farmhouses, whose inhabitants took us in with fraternal hospitality. We snuggled up in the hay and covered ourselves with blankets the farmer would lend us. We tried to sleep, which wasn't easy because the farm boys, well aware of the moral precepts of their guests, would noisily pour into our common sleeping quarters. Once I was awakened by tremulous hands and had the following salutation shouted into my face: *"Collons, si és un home!"* (dialect for, "Shit, it's a man!")

For all that, the missionaries of free love were indefatigable. In the morning, after breakfasting on a splendid slice of ham or a sausage, fresh milk, and bread, we were on our way. Normally, I would drive, to pay them back in some way for all they'd done. After all, I shared their food and lodging without participating, as is logical, in their activities. If we happened on some other group of strikers carrying anarchist banners, they would order me to stop. Then they'd get out, talk, distribute their text about proletarian women, and disappear into the bushes, leaving me alone or in the company of the old men. In that way, I made lots of friends and received a good dose of philosophic indoctrination.

Contrary to all my early suspicions, their proselytizing among men (unmarried and married) was sincere, and the seven propagators of the dogma of free love were always treated with the greatest respect and deference.

In this way, we reached Barcelona. The impression it made on me was dramatic. What in the country had been liberation and joy became violence and fear in the city. The blackout plunged the entire urban area into a dark labyrinth where treachery was concealed and where all grudges could be settled without fear of punishment. If during the day, the streets were the kingdom of the preachers of equality and fraternity, at night they became the undisputed territory of thugs, thieves, and murderers. The closing of shops and the lack of foodstuffs ordinarily brought in from the countryside made the most essential products scarce, and the criminals took abusive control of the black market, where buying a loaf of bread took on the tragic aspects of a degrading act.

After seeing this pandemonium, I advised the preachers of free love to renounce their ministry and go back to the country.

"Our place is with the people."

"This is not the people," I replied, "this is the scum of the earth, and you have no idea what they're capable of."

After a vociferous argument, I convinced them to spend the night in my apartment. But when they reached the entrance and saw the seignorial air of the building, they became adamant and refused to stay in a bourgeois house. I begged them (knowing the gossip I'd be exposing myself to) to let me take charge of the youngest, Estrella, but nothing would convince them. They left me standing in the street and went into the black avenues with their truck, their posters, and their dreams. I never heard of them again.

I spent two days at home, eating whatever the neighbors could spare. Finally, on the third day after my arrival, the nineteenth of my trek home, electricity was restored, and the city went back to normal. There were still lampoons hanging on the walls which the first rains of early autumn washed away. The comic verses that went with the cartoons mixed in the gutters with the leaves of the plane trees, falling and revealing a closed sky of lightning and thunderstorms. Carriages glistened like patent leather under the rains; gaslights were reflected off the streets, windows were covered with thick curtains, chimneys smoked, and pedestrians wrapped up in raincoats accelerated the slow, tired pace of summer. Children returned from school in an ill-tempered silence. Maura was the head of the government and Cambó Minister of Finance.

I read about Lepprince's death in the newspapers.

A fire had totally destroyed the Savolta factory. Because of the strike, no workers were present, so there was no other casualty to grieve over except the Frenchman. After that, the versions printed in the different papers were all contradictory. One asserted that Lepprince was already in the factory when the disaster took place and that he couldn't escape; another said he'd tried to put out the fire with the help of a few volunteers and that he was crushed when a beam or wall fell on him; a third paper attributed his death to the explosion of the black powder stockpiled in the factory. The fact is that none of them went any further with its explanation, and they all sidestepped the questions that in my opinion had to be answered. What was Lepprince doing *alone* in the factory? Had he gone there on his own, or was this a crime *astutely* disguised as an accident? If that were the case, had Lepprince been brought by force to the factory and locked inside it? Or was he perhaps already dead when the fire broke out? *Why* was there no police investigation? Questions that were never answered.

On the other hand, the newspapers were unanimous when it came to emphasizing "the unique figure of the great financier." They forgot to mention that the business was in ruins and composed hyperbolic elegies to the memory of the deceased. "Cities are made by their inhabitants, and newcomers make them great" (*The Vanguard*); "He was French, but he lived and died like a Catalan" (*The Barcelonan*); "He was one of the creators of Catalan heavy industry, symbol of an era, beacon and compass of modern times" (*Graphic World*). In sum, mere stereotyped formulas. Only

The Voice of Justice dared to stir up old grudges and give a violent article this title: *The Dog Is Dead, But the Rabies Lives On.*

The afternoon of that same day I went to the Lepprince mansion. It was a sad autumn day, cold and rainy. The house was sunk in lethargy: the shutters were closed, the garden filled with puddles, the trees bent in the wind. I knocked and the door opened a few inches, a crack through which appeared the sharp face of an old serving woman.

"What do you wish?"

"Good afternoon. My name is Javier Miranda, and I'd like to speak to the lady of the house, if she's in."

"She's in, but she's not receiving."

"I'm an old friend of the family. I'm surprised I've never seen you before. Did you just join the staff?"

"No, sir. I've been serving Mrs. Savolta for more than thirty years, and was Miss María Rosa's nanny."

"I see," I said, in order to gain her sympathy. "You worked in Miss María Rosa's parents' house in Sarriá, isn't that the case?"

The old woman gave me an openly suspicious look.

"Are you a reporter?"

"No. I already told you who I am: a friend of the family. Would you tell the butler to come? He'll recognize me."

"The butler's gone. They all left when Mr. Paul-André died."

A gust of wind pelted our faces with rain. My feet were wet, and I wanted to end the argument once and for all.

"Tell Miss María Rosa that Javier Miranda is here, please."

She hesitated for a few seconds. Then she closed the door, and I heard her footsteps fade away until they were lost in the interior of the vestibule. I waited under the rain a short time that seemed long to me. Finally the muted footfalls of the old servant returned, and the door opened.

"Miss María Rosa says to come in."

The vestibule was in darkness, but I could still see that dust and disorder had taken possession of everything. Half feeling my way, I reached Lepprince's small private office. The shelves of the bookcase were empty, there was a chair turned over, and on the wall there was a whitish rectangle marking the place where the Monet Lepprince loved so much had once hung. When I lit a cigarette, I realized there were no more ashtrays. The little door that connected the office with the salon opened, and again the old servant appeared.

I walked into the salon where María Coral, María Rosa, Lepprince, and I had had coffee on so many evenings. The disorder was shocking. On the tables were stacks of coffee cups, some of which still contained the dregs of some gelatinous concoction. The floor was covered with cigarette butts, matches, and ashes. The air was thick. The shutters, as I'd seen from the outside, were closed, but now I could also see they'd been plastered from the inside, so only the weak, artificial light illuminated the room. María Rosa Savolta was lying on the sofa, covered with a blanket, while next to her swayed a cradle where a baby only a few days old slept. I noted that María Rosa Savolta had recovered her normal appearance, and concluded that the child was none other than Lepprince's son.

"I'm sorry to have bothered you, ma'am," I said, approaching the sofa.

"Don't apologize, Javier," answered María Rosa without looking at me. "Sit down and excuse this disorder. So many people came to the funeral."

I remember reading in the newspapers that the funeral had taken place over a week ago, but made no reference to that fact.

"Everyone came to the funeral, or so they told me," the widow went on. "I couldn't go because I was giving birth in my mother's house. They kept the news from me for fear that the shock might make me lose the child. I just found out two days ago about Paul-André. I'm sorry I couldn't be at the funeral. They say as many or even more people were there than at my father's. Were you there, Javier?"

She spoke mechanically, the way people under hypnosis talk.

"I was away from Barcelona and didn't hear the sad news because of the strike," I said, and then I added, without transition, just to get away from the funeral theme, "That maid of yours told me she's been in your service for more than thirty years."

"Serafina? Yes, she was serving in my parents' house when I was born. Mama lent her to me . . . our servants left without warning. I suppose they carried off all the valuables."

"Why didn't you stay on at your mother's?"

"I preferred to come here temporarily. I had no idea of the condition the house was in. We've put the Sarriá house up for sale, understand? Yes, we've had several offers, but that means a kind of turmoil I didn't feel ready to put up with: visits, squabbling over prices, you know what I mean. Now that people know we're in a bad way, everyone wants his slice and hopes to get everything we own for two cents. But no one comes here. The house has three mortgages on it, and until they come to an agreement and auction it off, they won't bother me. Cortabanyes says the business could take more than a year. There's nothing left to steal, did you see how they cleaned it out?"

There was no sadness in her voice. Instead, she seemed like some old globetrotter who recalls his anecdotes in pieces and who tells them with a kind of confused lack of differentiation that makes them all uniform.

"They say they came to the funeral, but it's a lie. Come, come, I know perfectly well why they came: to steal whatever they could. Ah, if only Papa had lived! He wouldn't have allowed it, that you can believe. Nor would they have dared, the jackals. But what can we do, two women alone? Cortabanyes tried to save something, or at least that's what he says, although he must have saved precious little, to judge by appearances."

She fell silent, immersed in her cataleptic state, her eyes fixed on the ceiling.

"After all is said and done, it's better Paul-André died. That way he was spared the spectacle of ingratitude. For God's sake, to pillage the house of a dead man . . . the house of a man to whom they owe the clothes on their backs. When Papa took over the business, most of them were nothing more than poor devils:

suppliers to repair shops and things like that. With Papa and Paul-André they made money hand over fist . . . and now they think they have the right to steal and to vilify the memory of the dead, because I know that now they go around whispering and saying bad things about my husband: that he was a bad administrator, that he didn't know how to change with the times, and who knows what else. I'd like to see what would have become of them if poor Paul-André hadn't lent them a hand so many times. They would come in a procession to this house and with tears in their eyes, almost on their knees, ask for a loan, for a favor, as they had before with Papa. And now it's the same people who want to buy up the Sarriá house for two cents. The two of them, Papa and Paul-André, were too good: they gave what they had with full hands. At times they even gave what they didn't have; they gave that too if they could help a friend, for the pleasure of helping, without demanding interest or guarantees, without pressure or documents, relying on a person's word of honor, the way gentlemen do business. And they would leave, walking backward, bending their backs, happy, servile. . . . But now, since there are no men around to defend us, look what they've done: they've stolen. That's the right word: *stolen*. Oh, God, how alone I am. If at least, at least Uncle Nicolás had lived or poor Pere Parells . . . They wouldn't have allowed it; they loved us, they were family. But they've all died, may they rest in peace."

For the first time, her eyes fixed on mine, and I perceived a tenuous shine, far from the hatred, the scorn, and the bitterness, a shine that shocked me, because I seemed to recognize in it a farewell to the world of sanity. I made another attempt to change the subject.

"And the boy, how is he? He seems good and strong."

"It isn't a boy. It's a girl. Not even in that did I have any luck. If it had been a boy, my life would have had an objective: to educate him and prepare him to vindicate the memory of his father and grandfather. But this unfortunate thing, what can she do but adapt and suffer what my mother and I have suffered?"

The baby began to howl, as if she'd heard her mother's words and understood the bitter meaning of the prophecy. Serafina came in and picked it up, cuddling it in her arms, rocking it softly, and humming a monotonous lullaby.

"I'm going to give her a bottle now because it's time, isn't that right, Miss María Rosa?"

"Very well, Serafina," answered María Rosa Savolta with an absolute lack of interest.

"Don't you want to eat something, miss? The doctor insisted you eat."

"I know, I know, Serafina, don't pester me."

"Sir, tell her she has to take care of herself," the old servant begged me.

"It's true," I said, without much faith in the efficacy of my urging.

"If not for yourself, miss, do it at least for this little angel of God, who needs you more than anyone else in the world."

"Enough, Serafina; go away and leave us in peace."

When Serafina had gone, María Rosa made an effort to get up, but finally fell back, exhausted.

"You're worn-out, don't move," I said.

"Would you do me a favor? On top of that sideboard over there is an embossed leather box. There are cigarettes inside. Take one and bring me one."

"I didn't think you smoked."

"I didn't, but now I do. You light it, do me that favor."

I found the box and lit a cigarette, which I recognized by its oval form and its multicolored paper as the kind Lepprince smoked and of which he had a good supply because they were so hard to get in ordinary tobacco stores.

"I don't think smoking can be good for you."

"Oh, leave me alone and let me do what I want. What good does it do to take care of yourself?" She inhaled the cigarette avidly, in an amateurish way, trying to look like a femme fatale in some melodramatic movie. "Go on, tell me what good it does to take care of yourself. Paul-André sang the same tune all day: take care of yourself, don't do this, don't do that. Look at him now, what good would it have done him if he hadn't smoked all his life? Oh, God, what misfortune."

The cigarette seemed to have a calming effect on her: her face relaxed, and big tears rolled down her cheeks. She coughed and tossed the cigarette onto the floor contemptuously.

"Leave me alone, Javier. I appreciate your visit, but now I'd prefer to rest if you don't mind."

"I understand perfectly well. If I can be of any assistance to you, all you have to do is call. You know where I live and what my telephone number is."

"Thank you. By the way, how is your wife? Now that I think of it, it's strange she didn't come with you."

"She's got a bit of a cold . . . she's at home . . . but she'll be better soon and come out to see you, rest assured."

She didn't seem to listen to what I was saying. She made a vague gesture of farewell, and I walked to the door, trying not to trip over the objects scattered in the way.

The old servant saw me to the vestibule, carrying the baby, who seemed to be sleeping. In the vestibule, I thought I heard a suspicious noise, like footsteps, upstairs. I asked the maid if there were anyone else in the house.

"No, sir. Miss María Rosa, the baby, me . . . and you, of course."

"It seemed to me someone was walking around upstairs."

"Jesus!" she exclaimed in a low voice.

We were both silent, and then we both heard the unmistakable sound of furtive footsteps over our heads. Serafina began to tremble and mumble prayers.

"I'm going to see what's going on."

"Don't go up, sir. It might be a thief, a thug, or a striker hiding out. Better call the police. There's a phone in the library."

Her suggestion was very sensible, but I harbored certain suspicions that impelled me to find out for myself who the mysterious visitor was. I was sure it was not a stranger or a common thief. Besides, risky situations had recently become part of my normal life.

"Don't move from this spot. If I haven't come down in ten minutes, call the police. Above all, say nothing to Miss María Rosa."

She promised to do as I said. I left her praying and tiptoed up the stairs. There was only darkness in the hall because the windows and balconies were sealed tight. I felt my way along. I didn't know the layout of the rooms or where the furniture might be, so I walked very carefully not to trip or make noise. At the end of the hall, I made out a weak light. I imagined it was a flashlight and walked toward it. The noises had stopped. As I reached the door of the room where I'd seen the light, I hesitated. I could just see a silhouette using a flashlight to go through the papers in a desk.

"What are you doing there?" I said to the man rifling the desk.

The silhouette turned and aimed his flashlight at me. Almost at the same time, a second person, whose presence I hadn't detected, jumped on me and began to punch me. I retreated, protecting myself with my arms and trying to repel my attacker. The man with the flashlight began to laugh and said, "Leave him alone, Sergeant, it's our old friend Miranda."

The punches stopped, and the one who'd laughed turned on a lamp.

"No use trying to be secretive, since he's found us out," he exclaimed, turning off his flashlight and putting it in his pocket.

This certainly was no stranger. It was Inspector Vázquez, whose presence in Barcelona surprised me.

"You thought it was someone else, didn't you?" he said, still laughing softly. "You can give up your hopes on that one, Miranda my friend. Lepprince is dead, good and dead."

After calming down the old servant, the three of us left: Vázquez, myself, and Sergeant Totorno, a squalid type, standoffish and boorish, who'd lost the use of an arm when he'd been shot in the attack Lucas, "the Blind Man," had perpetrated against Lepprince in a theater. Totorno excused his hasty behavior with grunts, saying, "It's better to have to say you're sorry than to get a knife in your throat." It was still raining, so Vázquez invited me to step into his car. We drove downtown, and on the way the inspector told me he'd been in Barcelona for over a month, back at his old job thanks to the recent ministerial changes, which had allowed him to appeal to Madrid and have his case reconsidered. As soon as he reached the city, and despite the fact that the Savolta affair had been closed, he'd dedicated himself to the investigation with his usual zeal. Searching Lepprince's house was part of the investigation.

"Naturally, I don't have and wouldn't have obtained a search warrant, so I decided to do it on my own, at my own risk. It is, of course, illegal, but I hope you won't turn me in," he said in a tone of comradeship.

I put his mind at rest, and he invited me to have a coffee with him.

"I know there was a time when you and I didn't get along," he added, "but that's history now. Accept my invitation, and let's let bygones be bygones."

I couldn't say no, and, besides, I knew the inspector was eager to tell me what he'd found out. So I accepted gratefully, and we parked outside a tea shop. Sergeant Totorno, who clearly did not like me—no doubt because he'd had to make excuses for something he thought perfectly normal—left us and went back to the station. The inspector and I went into the tea shop, ordered café au lait, and sat silently for a long time watching the rain through the window.

"Did you know, Miranda my friend," Inspector Vázquez began saying after a sip of coffee and a puff on his cigarette, "that for a long time you were my prime suspect? Don't get angry; I don't think so anymore. Actually, I don't even think you knew what was going on. But you'll have to forgive my suspicion: every trail led to you. That threw me off, but it also gave me the key to the mystery. Remember the night you found me in your house? You got mad, and that apparently trivial detail made me see things clearly. Your behavior didn't square with that of someone who knows he's guilty. I was looking for a confession or a cold denial, an alibi, which, had it been carefully prepared, would have confirmed my suspicions. But your attitude, your confidence bordering on foolhardiness, disarmed me. You didn't have an alibi because you were the alibi. Lepprince's alibi, you ask? Yes, of course. Who else's? Ah, I see you still know nothing. Well, I'll begin at the beginning, if you've got a few hours and give me some smokes. I ran out."

I had nothing to do, and, as might be imagined, I was dying to hear Vázquez's revelations. Which is just what I told him, and he fell naturally into his oratorical mode, which made me briefly remember those chats in Lepprince's house, when Lepprince and I would receive visits from the inspector and hear, half seriously, half jokingly, his long disquisitions on anarchism and the anarchists. But that was just a fleeting memory, because the inspector's words soon captured my attention totally.

"Did you ever hear of a guy named Nemesio Cabra Gómez? No, of course not. Nevertheless, he's got a leading role in what I'm going to tell you. Because, of all those who participated in this matter, except of course the main actors, he was the first and for a long time the only person to intuit the truth," here the inspector dedicated a slight smile to Nemesio Cabra Gómez's memory. "A clever man, poor Nemesio, I really think so. Although, thinking about it now, not even he totally realized what he knew. In any case, the events in the case happened like this."

The story Inspector Vázquez told me began thirty or so years ago, when the eccentric Dutch multimillionaire Hugo Van der Vich came to Spain, invited by some Catalan aristocrats to take part in some big game hunting in the Cadí mountains. One member of the group was a young lawyer named Cortabanyes who, over the course of a chat during a rest period—where, naturally, the subject discussed was brands and types of shotguns—convinced the Dutchman of the benefits of setting up a hunting rifle factory in Barcelona. Maybe the project included the manufacture of a more perfect weapon than those that existed then on the market; perhaps there were other considerations—of a financial nature perhaps—that impelled Van der Vich to put such a bizarre idea into practice. Anyway, the young Cortabanyes must have been especially persuasive. He was a brand-new lawyer, of humble origins, slim means, and few relations, who was fighting to make his way with no other weapons but his intelligence, his energy, and his ability to convince. It wasn't only a desire for money and prestige that moved him: the young Cortabanyes wanted to marry a pretty girl from a well-known Barcelona family whose parents opposed this quite improper match. In any case, Van der Vich let himself be seduced by the words of the ambitious lawyer, and the project became a fact. Then Cortabanyes began to put his plan into motion: from the bottom rungs of the stock market, he recruited a vulgar, stubborn, greedy broker named Enric Savolta and introduced him to the Dutchman as a skillful Catalan financier. Later he did the same with various individuals of obscure origins: Nicolás Claudedeu, Pere Parells, and others who are irrelevant to our story. Van der Vich believed in Cortabanyes and Savolta. It's likely he never even saw the fraud in which they'd involved him because he soon went back to his country, forgot the hunting arms factory, and went insane at the same time these upstarts were stealing his stock. So, when Van der Vich died in dramatic circumstances, Cortabanyes and Savolta had almost all the stock in their own pockets and were absolute owners of the business. They stopped producing elegant shotguns and began to produce military rifles. They made money, and the young lawyer could finally marry the beautiful society girl. Everything seemed to be going well when Cortabanyes suffered an unforeseeable disaster. His wife, after one year of marriage, died giving birth. It was a terrible blow for someone who felt safe, lucky, and in love. Cortabanyes sank into a depression, sold his stocks to Savolta, and opened a humble office, prepared to vegetate and forget his dreams of greatness.

"There's an obscure point in the story right here," said Vázquez, pausing to light a cigarette. "I have my own theory, but you are perfectly entitled to think it erroneous. I refer, of course, to Cortabanyes's son: what happened to him? Did he die at birth?

Did he live, only to be cast aside by his father, who would have blamed the death of his beloved wife on him? We know nothing, and Cortabanyes doesn't seem especially disposed to clear up this mystery. Anyway, if there was a son, he disappeared."

With Cortabanyes gone, the Savolta business continued its march upward. Thirty years passed with no changes. Savolta, Parells, and Claudedeu got old; the war broke out, and the company made an exclusive supply contract with the French government. It was at that time when a young dandy from Paris appeared in Barcelona. He'd fled Paris, so he said, to avoid the annoyance of the conflagration. His name, he said, was Paul-André Lepprince. He moved into the best hotel in the city and began to lead the ostentatious life of a man who has so much money he doesn't know what to do with it. Who was that mysterious personality in fact? The French police, with whom Inspector Vázquez was in contact, said they knew nothing about him, and, even stranger, the fortune the Frenchman showed off was nonexistent. Was he, then, just a confidence man, an international adventurer, a cardsharp, a man searching for a rich wife? Inspector Vázquez, as he said, had his own hypothesis. In any case, retracing the Frenchman's footsteps, he found out that Lepprince had been in touch with Cortabanyes ever since he'd reached Barcelona, and through the lawyer, with Savolta. Now, in the realm of conjecture: there could be no doubt that Cortabanyes was aware of the individual's fraudulent nature and that Cortabanyes used his old prestige and his old friendship to dissipate the fortune Savolta had doubtlessly saved up. Now, what could push the old, tired lawyer to shake up a thirty-year-old swamp and embark on an adventure that can only be called foolish? An enigma.

Lepprince was clever and, above all, skillful: soon he'd won over Savolta's confidence—at the same time that the old man's health had begun its rapid decline. It's possible that the magnate unconsciously let himself be taken in by the elegance, manners, and poise of the Frenchman in whom he saw, perhaps, an ideal successor for his commercial empire and for his lineage, since, as everyone knew, Savolta only had one daughter, and she of marriageable age. Thus it was that Lepprince became Savolta's right-hand man, obtaining an unlimited power over the business. If he'd been content to follow the flow of events, Lepprince would have married Savolta's daughter and inherited the business from his father-in-law. But Lepprince couldn't wait: his ambition was boundless, and time was his greatest enemy. He had to act quickly if he didn't want the hoax of his false identity discovered and his career cut short. The European war gave him the chance he was looking for. He made contact with a German spy named Victor Pratz and arranged for regular shipments of arms to the Germans, for which he, Lepprince, would be paid directly through Pratz. Neither Savolta nor any other officer in the company would find out about the business. The weapons would leave secretly by a clandestine, well-established route, through a chain of smugglers previously recruited. Lepprince's privileged position within the company allowed him to carry out the sequestering of materials with a minimum of risk. Certainly Lepprince was sure of amassing a small fortune in case his true personality and nature were discovered and his long-range plans were ruined.

The business was going full steam ahead, but problems arose, unfailingly and promptly. The workers were restive: they had to work under awful conditions a very high number of hours in order to produce the huge quantity of weapons Lepprince's secret arrangements required without a corresponding rise in salary. In sum: they either wanted to work less or earn more. There were attempts to organize strikes which, under ordinary circumstances, wouldn't have been serious, because Nicolás Claudedeu, who carried out his job as chief of personnel with an energy that had earned him the nickname of the Man with the Iron Hand, would know how to get around situations like that. But Lepprince could not let Claudedeu intervene because an investigation would have revealed his irregular activities. Advised by Cortabanyes and Victor Pratz, he decided to steal the march on the Man with the Iron Hand by hiring two killers who spread terror among the labor leaders.

"But an action of that kind is not exempt from risks, and

Lepprince was unwilling to run them," said Inspector Vázquez looking me straight in the eye. "A third man would have to be found, a man who could be trusted but who would be ignorant of Lepprince and Pratz's maneuvers, a man who could take the blame if things went wrong. A fall guy, understand? An intermediary."

"You mean me?" I asked, guessing the rest of the story.

"Exactly."

Lepprince, nevertheless, made a mistake that would cost him dearly: he fell in love with María Coral. A woman could only foul up his plans, but he was weak and succumbed to temptation. He had the gypsy abandon her comrades and installed her in the hotel on Princesa street where three years later she was to convalesce from her illness and from which I took her to be my wife.

The danger was allayed, but only provisionally. A definitive solution would have to be found, and chance provided it one night when Lepprince was walking home, absorbed in his machinations: a kid sold him a pamphlet. He bought it mechanically and read it out of boredom. It was *The Voice of Justice,* which contained Domingo Pajarito de Soto's article on the Savolta company. The ideas came out spontaneously, easily, convincingly. In less than an hour, everything was prepared and decided. Lepprince consulted Victor Pratz, and he judged the plan practicable. The only problem was that it had to be executed without errors.

The plan, in synthesis, was this: Pajarito de Soto was an innocent, incorruptible man, with no connection to any faction or party. Lacking support, he was therefore easily controllable. He was given facilities to investigate, which is what he did. All that had to be done was to follow his path and take advantage of his results as he obtained them. The investigations, conveniently directed, had a double objective: first, to subvert the workers' movement; second, to check on the irregularities committed by Lepprince. If Pajarito de Soto discovered something, he would include it in his report, the report would go directly to Lepprince, and he would then be able to correct the errors.

"Pajarito de Soto carried out the first part of his job wonderfully well. Following close behind him, Lepprince's men found the instigators and leaders of the subversion and took care of them. As regards the second aspect . . . well, Pajarito de Soto was less innocent than he seemed. He discovered the plot, but he was as quiet about it as a corpse. Perhaps he wanted to blackmail Lepprince in the future, perhaps he wanted to get revenge for having been used. A big mistake that would cost him and many others their lives," Inspector Vázquez sighed.

Made desperate by the failure of his mediating role in the social conflict and aware of having been used to help the company, the unfortunate journalist began to drink and to talk too much. One of Lepprince's agents—Lepprince had Pajarito closely watched—heard him refer to "a certain gentleman he could hurt if he wanted." Lepprince sentenced him to death, and Victor Pratz killed him one night in December as he was returning home.

But Lepprince wasn't the only one keeping an eye on Pajarito de Soto. Pere Parells had harbored suspicions about Lepprince ever since the Frenchman had made his spectacular entrance. Pere Parells was a sharp man, gifted with great common sense. He distrusted upstarts and was suspicious of easy success. Convinced that the unexpected intrusion of the Frenchman into matters of personnel was covering up other plots, he decided to follow Pajarito and worm the information out of him. To do it, he obtained the services of an obscure, picturesque police informer named Nemesio Cabra Gómez. Nemesio did the job, but he got there too late: he'd barely got to know Pajarito when Pratz killed him. However, before he died—he knew his time was up—Pajarito wrote a letter in which he gave an account of his discoveries in the heart of the Savolta business. Nemesio saw the letter but not the name of the person to whom it was sent. He told Pere Parells about it and, later, Inspector Vázquez. Perhaps because of some indiscretion of Nemesio's or from Pere Parells himself, or perhaps through one of his own agents, Lepprince also learned of the letter and went insane trying to get hold of it. Those were moments of anguish for the Frenchman; the days passed and the letter did not appear. Lepprince could see the sword of Damocles swinging over his head. Seeing that things were not going to be resolved either way, he decided to play his trump card and murder Savolta. If Savolta had the letter, the danger ceased to exist; if he didn't, Lepprince would take over the highest administrative position in the company—the marriage with María Rosa Savolta had already been carefully prepared—and he would be, relatively speaking, safe from accusations or at least well placed to stop the initial attack.

Pratz and his men killed Savolta on New Year's Eve, but the letter did not appear. Savolta's death was blamed on terrorists, and they were executed.

"Yes, I know that it was all my fault," said Inspector Vázquez, "but there's no reason to weep. Those men deserved execution for more than one reason."

The terrorists thought Nemesio Cabra Gómez had betrayed and sold out Pajarito de Soto. They demanded that Nemesio find out the truth in exchange for his life. Nemesio went to Vázquez, but the inspector paid no attention to him because at the time he hadn't noticed that the connections between the deaths of the journalist and the magnate were more complex than they seemed. Unable to bear the guilt for so many deaths—it was commonly thought he was responsible for the execution of the terrorists—Nemesio lost what little sanity he had and ended up in the insane asylum. The terrorists in turn assassinated Claudedeu. Without Claudedeu, Pere Parells found himself alone in opposition to an omnipotent Lepprince, so, out of fear or for other reasons, if he knew something, he said nothing. Confident of their position, Lepprince and Pratz came out of the darkness: Lepprince, by installing himself on Savolta's throne, and the German, using the pseudonym Max, pretending to be the Frenchman's bodyguard. With the failed attack of Lucas, "the Blind Man," against Lepprince, the first act of the tragedy came to an end.

"And to whom was the letter sent?" I asked.

Inspector Vázquez sighed. He'd been expecting my question and felt satisfied he could answer it. From the inside pocket of his jacket, he removed a wrinkled envelope and handed it to me. It was Pajarito de Soto's letter, addressed to me.

"He sent it to you, but not to your house. Look at the address, recognize it? It's Pajarito de Soto's own address. The unfortunate man wasn't as dumb as we all suspected. He wanted his compromising discoveries to get to you, but only in case he died. That night he must have sensed his end was near and wrote the letter. If he died, you would visit his house (he asked Nemesio to find you, which he did not do because he worked for Parells and Parells forbade it), and if he didn't die, he could recover the revealing letter and go on monopolizing his discoveries. Well thought out, no?"

Vázquez's smile became malicious.

"What Pajarito hadn't counted on was that you and Teresa were having an affair behind his back. Don't be surprised that I know it, Miranda my friend. Teresa herself told me everything. That's right, I found out where she lives now. No, I won't tell you where it is. She asked me not to, and, you must understand, I am a gentleman. From her I learned about your sentimental adventure and also about the letter. Read it: after all, it is addressed to you. I, of course, have read it. You'll have to forgive me once again. Professional things, you know . . ."

I opened the envelope and read the letter. It was very short, barely some hasty notes scribbled in a trembling hand:

Javier:

Lepprince is guilty of my death. He and a spy named Pratz are selling arms to the Germans behind Savolta's back. Take care of Teresa and don't trust Cortabanyes.

I folded the letter, put it back in the envelope, and returned it to Vázquez.

"Your remorse for having committed adultery made you and Teresa stop seeing each other. Teresa fled Barcelona with her son, and the letter went with them. And while the letter traveled around

Spain lost in a pile of diapers, men were killing each other here to possess it. Life certainly is complicated, my dear Miranda."

The second act of the tragedy began when Inspector Vázquez, dissatisfied by the turn events had taken, decided to dig up the case and begin to establish connections between isolated actions. He remembered Nemesio Cabra Gómez and decided to visit him in the sanatorium where he'd been held for a year and to interrogate him, providing his condition allowed it. Nemesio again mentioned the letter to Pajarito de Soto and mentioned my name. Vázquez thought he was seeing things clearly and came to my house, but my bad manners saved me from his suspicion. With me out of the way, only Lepprince was left. He, however, had the inspector under surveillance and lost no time. His position had won him influential friends, so he arranged the inspector's exile.

"Maybe he thought about killing me," bragged Vázquez, "but you don't kill a police inspector just like that."

Free of Vázquez, Lepprince could finally breathe easily. But an unforeseeable event twisted his life. María Coral, whom Lepprince still loved, came back to Barcelona. Pratz found her—the woman who owned the cabaret told me when I asked for the gypsy's address that another man had been there first with the same intention—and, without telling Lepprince, decided to kill her. It's almost certain he poisoned her. María Coral would have died if it hadn't been for my providential indiscretion. Lepprince and Pratz must have argued bitterly about her. The German insisted on getting rid of such a dangerous witness, but Lepprince dissuaded him. He married María Coral to me and then recommenced his amorous relationship with her.

"And now comes the moral to the story," said the inspector. Lepprince had killed, stolen, and betrayed in order to get control of the Savolta business, but once he had it, the company began to disintegrate.

The end of the war dashed the expectations of the arms factory. Lepprince was not a skillful businessman, as Parells and Savolta were, and did not know how to adapt himself to circumstances, open new markets, reduce expenses. . . . He began to sink in a swamp of credits, guarantees, mortgages, sureties, documents, and bonds. Cortabanyes advised him to get rid of his stock, and Lepprince made a few moves in that direction. Pere Parells found out about it, lost control of himself, and set off a scandal. Lepprince by then was trying to begin a political career that would protect him when the cataclysm struck. Parells's angry outburst couldn't have come at a worse moment and, at the same time, brought the old matter of Pajarito's letter back to life. Lepprince believed Parells had it, so he had his men kill Parells. It was a useless act: the old financier did not have the letter, and his death did not stop a process which by then was irreversible. The publicity about Lepprince's relationship with María Coral and her attempted suicide—which everyone blamed on the Frenchman—ended his political career. Lepprince was in ruins. Victor Pratz decided to flee and took María Coral with him. Without money, without friends, deserted by Pratz and his lover, Lepprince saw the earth opening under his feet, but he wasn't the kind of man who gives up without a fight, so he came to me and put me on the trail of the fugitives. He knew the route they would take, that is, the route used years before to ship arms across the border—Victor Pratz, sought by the French police, had no alternatives—and counted on my being able to catch up to them because I had my own vehicle. The Frenchman figured that I would be killed in the fight, which would free him of one witness, and would succeed in getting María Coral (whose affection for me he was aware of) to abandon the German. If, by an irony of destiny, I killed Pratz, Lepprince had no doubt I'd come back with María Coral. In any case, he never found out the results of his plot because he died.

"How did Lepprince die?"

Inspector Vázquez seemed elusive.

"I don't think we'll ever know. It might have been suicide, or it might have been an accident."

He paused, and seemed to struggle with a temptation to add something, and then, lowering his voice, he said quickly:

"Listen, Miranda, I've always thought Lepprince was someone else's pawn, someone . . . ," he pointed to the ceiling, "very high up, you understand what I mean. I think they killed him, but it's only a theory. Don't tell anyone I told you that."

He called the waiter and paid. His face had become somber, as if his words somehow constituted a prediction of his own death, which took place under mysterious circumstances a few days ago. When we left, the rain was letting up. We said an affectionate farewell, and never saw each other again.

The next morning I went to Cortabanyes's office, with the remote hope of dissipating a few doubts. It was raining, and the whole city was muddy. I couldn't find a coach and arrived soaking wet, in a bad mood. A young man I'd never seen before with a countrified look opened the door.

"What do you wish, sir?" he asked timidly.

"I want to see the lawyer, Mr. Cortabanyes."

"Your name, sir."

"Miranda, Javier Miranda."

"Please be seated for a moment."

He disappeared into the office and soon came out again, getting out of the way. Cortabanyes appeared, huffing and puffing, came to greet me, and gave me a warm, deferential hug. The boy stared at us in shock. Cortabanyes and I went into the office, and the lawyer shut the door behind him.

"What brings you here, Javier?"

"We have many things to talk over, Mr. Cortabanyes."

"Think so? None of them bad, I hope . . . If you've come to ask me for money . . ."

He didn't seem excessively affected by Lepprince's death. I thought Vázquez had let himself be carried away by his imagination when he made certain insinuations, although it might also have been that Cortabanyes was frightened and opted to dissimulate. I decided not to mention the matter directly.

"I seem to note the absence of Serramadriles."

"Yes, he left a couple of months ago, didn't you know? He's set up a small office on his own. I send him business . . . of little importance, things that take a lot of work and bring in very little. That way he'll develop a clientele for the future and take root in this slippery slope of a business. I think he's planning to get married soon, but he still hasn't introduced me to his fiancée. Better that way, don't you think? I'll save a wedding present, ha, ha, ha."

"And Doloretas?"

"Just the same, poor woman. I don't think she'll ever get better. See, in such a short period of time I've lost three collaborators. Now I've got this boy. He looks hardworking, but he's just arrived in Barcelona and is a little shocked by it all. But it's all right, he'll come around, I'm sure of it. Like all the others. And he'll do what he can, finally, to get me out of my chair so he can set his own ass on it. Like all the others, my boy, that's life for you."

He never stopped clucking like a hen, as if to underline each of his remarks. I thought the moment had come to bring up the Lepprince theme.

"Oh, my boy, I know nothing about it. Only what's in the newspapers, and even that I've had a hard time reading. My eyes get worse every day. Then, of course, there are rumors. Had to be. That he was bankrupt and all that. I personally think he was, that his things weren't going well. But penniless, absolutely penniless, I can't be certain of that. I know he was begging from bank to bank, and that they all slammed their doors in his face. It's logical. There will be no more wars, according to what they're saying now in Paris and Berlin and everywhere; this wonderful League of Nations will resolve conflicts, and we'll only need weapons for parades, museums, and hunting. I hope it's true, although I certainly doubt it. What? Oh yes, getting back to our subject, I don't think Lepprince would burn down his own factory just to stop the embargo and the auction. That kind of thing is simply no longer done. Yes, of course, it's possible, but I tell you I just don't believe it. No, I don't think there was any insurance, aside from the usual policies. You know: fire, theft, things like that. Of course the fire insurance will pay, but I don't think it'll cover even a tenth part of the debts. Of course no one's thinking of rebuilding the factory. No, the stock was taken off the market right after Savolta's death. In reality, when Lepprince took charge of the company it was already dead. I wanted to tell him, but there was no way to make him understand. Yes, he had fantastic ideas and wouldn't listen. That was his fatal error. Suicide? I don't even want to think about it, God forbid . . . Murder . . . it's possible. I don't see a motive, but to be frank with you, I don't see the motive for practically anything. Human actions surprise me . . . perhaps because I'm old."

When he was finished speaking, I got up, thanked him for everything, and got ready to leave. Cortabanyes held me back.

"What do you plan to do now?"

"I don't know. Look for work, first of all."

"You'll always have a job here, although the pay won't be splendid . . ."

"Thank you. I'd rather strike out in a new direction."

"I understand, I understand. Oh, I forgot! Holy Virgin! How can I be so forgetful? Lepprince came to see me two days before his death. He left something for you."

"For me?"

Cortabanyes misunderstood my exclamation, because he hastened to add:

"Don't delude yourself. It's an envelope with papers . . . manuscripts in it. I haven't opened it, word of honor. I looked at it through the light, that I did do; you'll have to excuse my curiosity. The old and the young enjoy certain privileges, isn't that so? To compensate for the disadvantages is what I say. The disadvantages . . ."

He rooted around in his desk drawers and pulled out an envelope of regular size. It was sealed, which explains why Cortabanyes hadn't dared to open it. I recognized Lepprince's handwriting. It was the second letter from beyond the grave that I'd received in less than twenty-four hours.

"If it says something interesting, tell me, eh?" begged Cortabanyes, struggling to hide his emotions.

He accompanied me to the door. The country boy stood up when he saw us pass.

Outside, it was still raining. I hailed a cab and went home. Once there, I proceeded to break the seal on the envelope. It contained a letter and a document. In the letter, Lepprince told me he'd learned of the deaths of Max and María Coral. "Now, dear Javier, I have only to await the end: I've lost everything." He knew about Inspector Vázquez's return and commented, "That old fox has sworn to get me and won't rest until he sees me dead." Was that a veiled accusation? Lepprince did not make much of that point. He asked me to forgive him and confessed his sincere affection for me. The letter, in sum, contained no revelations and ended in this way:

A few months ago, foreseeing the catastrophe that is now almost upon me, I took out an insurance policy with an American company. No one knew of its existence, and all the relevant documents are in the hands of the company of Hinder, Maladjusted & Mangle of New York, my lawyers. Keep it a secret and don't try to cash in the policy right away because my creditors would throw themselves on the money and not leave a cent. Wait a few years, however many you like, until the waters have returned to their course. Then get in touch with the lawyers in New York and cash in the policy. When you've done so, look up my wife and son, and give them the money. Hard times await them, and the money will help them when it's time for the boy to go to school. If you see them at that time, try by all means to keep the boy from knowing the truth about his father. If at all possible, steer him away from law. And now, Javier, good-bye. If you've reached the end of this letter, I'll know that in dying I had one friend.

Your most affectionate,
Paul-André Lepprince

Chapter 10

For two weeks I searched for work, but my well-known connection with Lepprince closed all doors to me. My slim savings were used up, and I began to sell off my belongings. I even thought of going back to Valladolid and looking up my father's old friends, although I knew that would be like burying myself alive. The truth is I lacked the courage to strike out in any direction, and I would have ended up a beggar if heaven hadn't taken pity on me and sent the only thing that could save me.

One night when I'd spent more than an hour deciding to go to bed without eating, someone knocked quietly at my door. I went to see who it could be without much hope but with considerable curiosity: I just didn't receive guests. On the landing, there was a small shape, covered with an old blanket. I thought I'd faint when I recognized it was María Coral. I asked her in, and she collapsed in my arms, totally worn-out. This, in sum, is what had happened to her: she'd survived the cold and the wolves out on the mountain and taken refuge in the house of some shepherds. She was very sick, and the hardships she'd been through had brought on a miscarriage. For many days, she hung between life and death. Finally, her strong nature won out and she slowly recovered. She lived with the shepherds (two old men and a boy), helping them with the domestic chores, until she felt strong enough to get to Barcelona. The journey was long and full of minor incidents. She had no money or food and could travel and survive only thanks to the more or less interested charity given her by people. She'd hesitated about coming to me, fearing she'd be received with scorn. She knew nothing about Lepprince's death or the events that followed it.

Her presence gave me new strength because I loved her and still love her today, as I write these lines. I made small sums of money pop out of nowhere to pay for her recovery. When the color returned to her cheeks and happiness to her spirit, we again thought about the future.

"Don't you remember our plans? We agreed we'd go to Hollywood, Javier; what are we waiting for?"

And so we left Barcelona, never to return. Cortabanyes, in an unexpected gesture of generosity—or perhaps to get rid of two people who knew so much about him—lent us the money for the passage.

We never got to Hollywood. We stayed in New York, where things did not go as María Coral had thought. We spent several years fighting poverty, the language, and the possibility of seeing the extension of our residence and work permits denied. I took on every conceivable form of manual labor and suffered every humiliation imaginable. María Coral worked as an extra in a filthy little Broadway theater. She never lost her illusions about triumphing in the movies and even managed to arrange an interview with Douglas Fairbanks—although Fairbanks, without bothering to make an excuse, never showed up. Only our love enabled us to survive the ordeal of those years.

As soon as I'd saved some money, I returned Cortabanyes's loan. He answered me in a handwritten letter in which he told me all the most important events that had taken place in Barcelona since I left. It all seemed strangely alien to me, except for the notice of Doloretas's death, which took place in the summer of 1920.

Finally, when I'd obtained United States citizenship, I entered the financial world of Wall Street—a mere salesman, but with a respectable salary—and retired María Coral from the world of the theater, I then decided to carry out the request Lepprince had made of me years before. The insurance company was surprised by my claim and refused to pay, but Lepprince's lawyers convinced me to go to court. These memories sprang from that trial and my statements to the judge.

I am alone at home. The trial is over, and all that remains is to wait until tomorrow to find out the result. The lawyers say our case is good, and that my statements have been skillful and prudent. María Coral has gone out. We have no children; María Coral was left sterile after losing Lepprince's child. We're getting older, but our love has become an attachment and a mutual understanding that illuminates and justifies our lives.

The mailman brought me an unexpected letter from María Rosa Savolta. I think it's the best way to end this story.

Dear Friend:

You cannot imagine how happy Paulina and I were at receiving the news that you were going to send us money from New York. Until the lawyers wrote us, we knew nothing about the policy that my husband (may he rest in peace) took out before dying. The lawyer explained the reasons for the delay in cashing in the policy. Believe me, we understand perfectly what impelled you to do things in this way, and we do not reproach you in the slightest.

These years have been very difficult for Paulina and me. Mother died quite a while ago, after a long and painful illness. At the beginning, we could survive on what Cortabanyes gave us. He behaved like a perfect gentleman, and, even more important, like a good Christian. After his death, we thought everything was lost. Fortunately, a young prestigious lawyer named Don Pedro Serramadriles took over his practice and has occasionally given me jobs which have kept us alive. Imagine how it was for me, a woman who had never worked in her life, to be a typist. Mr. Serramadriles has been at all times very considerate, friendly, and patient with me.

My only desire now has been to see to it that my little Paulina lacks for nothing. Unfortunately, I'm afraid her education is deficient. Since we've also had to sell off my jewels, the poor girl has grown up in a middle-class environment, so different from the one she should have enjoyed by birth. The girl, nevertheless, has not betrayed her origins, and you'd be surprised at her carriage and manners. Maternal pride aside, I can assure you she is extremely beautiful, and that she is incredibly like her poor father, whose memory she venerates.

The money you're going to send us could not come at a better time. I have all my hopes set on a good marriage for Paulina when she comes of age, something difficult to manage without the means. And, although I'm sure that many worthy men would have looked favorably on her, I don't think many would take the final step, for financial reasons. Now you can see how much we need that money you will soon be sending us.

You know that you always have us at your service here and that our gratitude for your generous help has no limits. Rest assured that it has contributed to brighten the black panorama of our lives and to rehabilitate the memory of the great man that Paul-André Lepprince was.

Yours affectionately,
María Rosa Savolta